FATED

―――――

SARAH READY

PRAISE FOR SARAH READY

PRAISE FOR FRENCH HOLIDAY

"Ready (The Fall in Love Checklist) whisks readers to the South of France for a saucy enemies-to-lovers romance...This is a winner."

— *PUBLISHERS WEEKLY* STARRED REVIEW ON *FRENCH HOLIDAY*

"Ready has written a tale that deliciously taps into its French trappings...A charming dramedy featuring a promising sleuthing duo."

— *KIRKUS REVIEWS*

PRAISE FOR JOSH AND GEMMA MAKE A BABY

"Romance author Ready gives Gemma rich and complex motivations for wanting a baby...An unusual and winning read about a little-discussed topic."

— *KIRKUS REVIEWS*

"A lively, entertaining, romantic comedy by an author and novelist with a genuine flair for originality, humor, and narrative driven storytelling..."

— *MIDWEST BOOK REVIEW*

PRAISE FOR JOSH AND GEMMA THE SECOND TIME AROUND

"In this sequel—which stands well enough on its own—the happily-ever-after moment is merely the starting point...Ready effectively leads readers to wonder if she isn't going to upend every single one of the genre's expectations. It's a testament to her exceptional writing skill that even the most romantic-minded readers won't be sure which outcome they prefer. A charming and disarmingly tough story of the many ways that love can adapt to crises."

— *KIRKUS REVIEWS*

PRAISE FOR THE SPACE BETWEEN

"...emotional roller-coaster, but in the end true love prevails. For hopeless romantics, this one's got the goods."

— *PUBLISHERS WEEKLY*

"A touching tale of adult reckonings and reunions with some heart-tugging reversals."

— KIRKUS REVIEWS

"...a compelling novel of longing, betrayal, friendship, as well as the undying belief that love and music can heal the world. An original and deftly crafted novel that will be of special interest to fans of contemporary romance laced with humor, "The Space Between" is especially and unreservedly recommended for community library Contemporary Romance collections."

— MIDWEST BOOK REVIEW

PRAISE FOR GHOSTED

"Ready's twisty plot keeps readers guessing how this couple could possibly reach a happy ending."

— PUBLISHERS WEEKLY

"Ready brings her trademark blend of lively tone, amusing details, heart-tugging romance, and adept plotting to this paranormal tale."

— KIRKUS REVIEWS

ALSO BY SARAH READY

Stand Alone Romances:

The Fall in Love Checklist

Hero Ever After

Once Upon an Island

French Holiday

The Space Between

The Ghosted Series:

Ghosted

Switched

Fated

Wished

Josh and Gemma:

Josh and Gemma Make a Baby

Josh and Gemma the Second Time Around

Soul Mates in Romeo Romance Series:

Chasing Romeo

Love Not at First Sight

Romance by the Book

Love, Artifacts, and You

Married by Sunday

My Better Life

Scrooging Christmas

Dear Christmas

Stand Alone Novella:

Love Letters

Find these books and more by Sarah Ready at:

www.sarahready.com/romance-books

SHE MEETS THE MAN OF HER DREAMS IN HER DREAMS...

Fiona Abry excels at keeping busy, running her family's Swiss watch company, and guarding her heart. She's so busy she doesn't have time for a vacation much less a love life.

But then she's given a family heirloom rumored to let you dream your greatest desire.

Suddenly, Fiona is spending her nights on a tiny tropical island in a completely different life.

She's married. She has two kids. She lives in a colorful cottage on the beach.

This dream life is so different from her hectic, busy life in the city that Fiona decides to live her dreams to the fullest.

Swimming in the turquoise sea. Picnics under palms. Star-gazing on the beach. It's a slow, seductive dream life that conveniently stays in her dreams.

But after kisses and confessions and long nights on the beach, Fiona starts to fall hard for her dream husband and her dream life.

But what happens when opening yourself to love means falling for a life that isn't real and a man who doesn't exist?

Because in the end, it's not fate, it's just a dream.

Fated

SARAH READY

W.W. CROWN BOOKS
An imprint of Swift & Lewis Publishing LLC
www.wwcrown.com

This book is a work of fiction. All the characters and situations in this book are fictitious. Any resemblance to situations or persons living or dead is purely coincidental. Any reference to historical events, real people, or real locations are used fictitiously.

Copyright © 2024 by Sarah Ready
Published by W.W. Crown Books an Imprint of Swift & Lewis Publishing, LLC, Lowell, MI USA
Cover Illustration & Design: Elizabeth Turner Stokes

All rights reserved.

No part of this book may be reproduced in any form or by any electronic or mechanical means, including information storage and retrieval systems, without written permission from the author, except for the use of brief quotations in a book review.

Library of Congress Control Number: 2024934398
ISBN: 978-1-954007-76-5 (eBook)
ISBN: 978-1-954007-77-2 (pbk)
ISBN: 978-1-954007-78-9 (large print)
ISBN: 978-1-954007-79-6 (hbk)
ISBN: 978-1-954007-80-2 (audiobook)

Fated

PROLOGUE

McCormick didn't change my life right away. I didn't fall in love with him at first sight.

Instead it was a gradual shedding of being, a chipping away of what was, until my life was something entirely new and unrecognizable. It was a gradual thing, like the flow of the gentle tide washing over a softly sanded golden beach.

At least that's what I tell myself when I'm lying. I often lie to myself when I'm awake and feeling generous.

But when I'm dreaming? Well, we don't lie in dreams, do we?

Everyone knows that dreams are where we tell ourselves the truth. All our hidden desires, all our yearnings, all our fears—they come out in dreams, don't they? In dreams we can fly, we can defeat dragons, we can go back in time, we can see our loved ones who are dead and gone, we can talk to a crowd while naked on a stage, and we can even fall in love.

In dreaming we do all the magical, wondrous things we are afraid to do in waking life.

Falling in love was always my fear. If you ask my therapist, she'll tell you it's because I have abandonment issues. If you ask me, it's because love isn't worth the hurt.

It's just like Lake Geneva in early summer, still freezing, turn-your-lips-blue cold. My brother Daniel always dives in, splashing frigid frothy water across the coarse sand, laughing at me, "Come on, Fi! You'll get used to it!" He teases that soon my fingers and toes will go numb and I'll stop feeling the pain of the cold and enjoy the swim.

Mila always joins him (since age two, in her Puddle Jumpers and hot-pink cozzie) because she adores her uncle and would follow him to the moon. They splash in the shallows, shivering and pink-cheeked, while I perch on the old tree swing beneath the great plane tree, digging my feet into the cool, shaded sand, watching over them. To me the pleasure of a swim isn't worth the blue lips, the numb fingers and toes, or the icy bite that nips into your blood and seeps into your bones. It's a bit like love. Not worth the pain.

I'd rather stay safe on the sandy shore than dive into the turbulent waters.

That's what I believed for a long, long time.

And then, I didn't.

Whether it happened in an instant or whether it was an ebb and flow that washed away everything I knew to be true?

Well, that's a matter of opinion.

My mum always claimed that someday all my dreams would come true. I always quipped, "I don't want my dreams to come true. I'd rather stay in real life, thank you very much."

But that was before I had dreams that were worth fighting for.

It was before Christmas Eve, before the gunshot, before Max proposed, before Buttercup gave me the watch, and before I dreamed.

Now I have one single prayer.

One prayer that crashes against the shore of my heart, beating out a single, desperate plea.

Dream.

Dream.

Dream.

Let me dream of him.

One more time.

1

GENEVA IS A DREAM AT CHRISTMASTIME. THE END OF November ushers in crisp blue skies, brisk alpine winds tinged with the hint of snow sweeping down the white-capped mountains, and the opening of the Christmas markets.

The old sophisticated city adopts an air of childlike glee. Glowing lights, evergreen wreaths, and garlands wind along the cobbled streets of Old Town, eclectic Carouge, and the Marché de Noël.

The Christmas markets sparkle through the city and on the shores of the lake. Little wooden stalls dot the markets, brimming with the tempting cinnamon-and-clove scent of vin chaud. The mulled wine mixes with smells of fresh gingerbread and roasting chestnuts. There's even skating in Parc des Bastions, where Mila and I grip mittened hands as we glide across the ice under the starry night sky.

On the weekend after the eleventh of December, Mila, Daniel, and I celebrate the fête de l'Escalade. In

1602 our Genevois ancestors defended the city and Mère Royaume threw her boiling cauldron of soup on the invaders.

So we join hands and chant, *"Ainsi périrent les ennemis de la République."* Thus perished the enemies of the Republic!

And then we lift our joined hands and smash a giant chocolate cauldron and cheer as marzipan vegetables and candies spill out. Daniel steals all the marzipan, chortling about younger brother rights, and Mila gobbles up the chocolate.

On a windless, moonlit night, Mila and I glide across the lake on a cruise, snug under wool blankets, warming ourselves with endless pots of bubbling cheesy fondue gathered on chewy squares of freshly baked bread.

At Christmastime there are lights, there are carols, and there is the most important tradition of all—the Abry Christmas Eve Gala.

This is the one hundred and fiftieth Christmas Eve Gala that my family has hosted, so of course, it's a big deal. In fact, Daniel has hounded the marketing team, the events team, and the public relations team for the past year to make sure this gala is one that will go down in history.

The chateau, which is drafty and imposing on the warmest summer day, is lit up like a Christmas tree. The soft glow of thousands of lights twirl around the stone towers and span the steepled roof, transforming the harsh stone into a welcoming Christmas wonderland.

The chateau lights reflect in the black waters of the lake and brighten the night sky. I glance out my second-story bedroom window at the long drive below, watching a line of chauffeur-driven Rolls and Benzes snake along the lantern-lit driveway.

The gala has begun.

"Can you help with my clasp?" I ask Mila.

I shove aside my thick hair, brushing it over my shoulder. It's auburn, tending toward mulled-wine red, and it's my most identifiable feature. My eyes are a forgettable hazel, my pale skin is typical of the easily burned, and I'm taller than average, thin.

Not because I exercise, but because I'm so busy I often forget to eat. I learned a few years back that if I want to eat I have to schedule a fifteen-minute block in my calendar. Otherwise my mealtimes are gobbled up by more urgent matters.

"I quite like this necklace," Mila says, sounding very grown-up for an eight-year-old. This isn't surprising though. I often think Mila was born grown-up.

"Do you?" I touch the cool gold links and the ruby and emerald stones. Max gave it to me as an early Christmas present and asked me to wear it to the gala.

A strange flutter kicks around my stomach as I think about the directness of Max's gaze when he asked me to wear his gift.

"Uh-huh. I helped Max pick it out. Of course I like it."

She manages to finally link the clasp, and the stones settle over my collarbone. They're cold and heavy.

"I didn't know that."

She nods, but she's already moved on from the thought of Max and necklaces. She skips across the bedroom, pirouetting around the gold satin ottoman, dancing past the walnut armoire, avoiding my pile of heels by the walk-in closet, and landing at the curtained window to peer at the arriving guests downstairs.

There are women in luxurious furs and long formal dresses, jewels glistening in the Christmas lights. Men in tuxes and top hats, their coattails blowing in the wind. Couples young and old. Dignified and not. Outrageous and staid. Old wealth and new. Politician and artist. Friend and foe. All gathered together to celebrate the season.

This is Mila's first gala. I went to my first gala at eight and now she will too. She's in an icicle-white dress flecked with strands of gold and silver. It poufs around her like the snowflake of a ballerina's skirt. My heart squeezes at the way she clutches the skirt in her hands and absently swings the fabric back and forth as she stares out the window.

I smile at her reflection in the glass and the little puckered line between her brows.

Her hair is bright, holly-berry red, and her cheeks are covered in freckles. I think she has freckles to remind her that life doesn't always have to be serious.

I imagine it's the same reason my mum named me Moonbeam Clover Fiona Abry. I must've been born serious too, and my mum, being my mum, decided to do something about it.

I have to admit, her strategy worked. You have to acknowledge that life can tend toward the absurd when you're handed a name like that.

At age eight I declared I would only answer to Fiona.

Moonbeam and Clover were no more.

As of now, Mila has yet to disown her much-bemoaned freckles. Maybe it's because Daniel has freckles too. Granted a lot less, but that's beside the point.

I lean into the mirror of my dressing table and apply a final coat of wintry red lipstick. It matches the deep burgundy of my floor-length velvet dress. From the front the dress is modest, tight but covering every inch of skin from my ankles to my breasts to my wrists. But then the back is wide-open from my shoulders to the base of my spine.

I wanted to look splendid. It's a one-hundred-and-fifty-year celebration after all.

And me and Daniel? We've managed to keep the company solvent, even thriving. When we inherited Abry Watch Co. Ltd, neither of us were certain the family business would even see the end of the year. I was quite terrified that after more than one hundred and eighty years of watchmaking in Geneva, Daniel and I were going to be the generation to lose it all.

We'd lose our legacy, our history, our home. We'd be known for generations to come as the siblings who failed the family.

Yet here we are.

With a whole lot of willpower, desperation, and sheer daring, we held onto Abry. Barely. But now we're thriving.

"Is Uncle Daniel coming to escort me downstairs?" Mila asks, turning from the window, her lips pinched with worry.

Daniel's late. Which isn't a concern—he's almost always late. He'll be chatting up an elegant woman in some corner or posing for the press, who are drawn to him like hungry tourists to chocolate shops.

"Of course he'll be here—" I begin, but there's a knock on the door.

Mila runs across the room, dodging my bed. She flings the door open. "Uncle Daniel!"

She hurtles at him, giving him a tight hug. Over their embrace Daniel grins at me, one eyebrow quirked high.

He's in a black tux, his dark blond hair smoothed back, his blue eyes filled with laughter.

He's tall and solid, and when in a tux he looks just like our dad. Except softer and kinder.

"Merry Christmas, ma choupinette," Daniel says, squeezing Mila.

I hide my smile, already aware that in less than two minutes we'll be walking down the grand staircase, entering the fray.

For me, this isn't a party. It's business.

Plus, Max will be downstairs, and I'm not quite sure what to expect from him.

Mila steps back, realizing she just displayed a vast amount of glee unsuitable for such a monumental and grown-up occasion. She smooths her hands over her frothy skirt then lifts her pointed chin, giving her uncle a firm stare. "You're late."

"Sorry, Mila. I was waylaid by the press on my way in."

She thinks about this, tilting her head. "Did you mention the new line we're launching? Did you kiss a beautiful lady and flash your watch for the camera?"

Daniel laughs, long and loud. His laughter echoes around the stone hall, merging with the violins and cellos drifting up from the ballroom. "You know me too well."

Mila nods solemnly then glances back at me. "Coming, Mummy?"

"Fi?" Daniel asks, holding out his arm.

I give in and smile at them both, my little brother and my baby girl. "Of course."

I lift a crystal bottle from my dressing table and spritz myself with a Christmas perfume—vanilla, sugar and spice, glowing stars, and snowy nights.

Then I take Daniel's offered arm and Mila's hand.

We're off to celebrate Christmas Eve.

2

The glitter of the night, the magic, falls over us as soon as we descend the staircase.

The ballroom remains empty most of the year, a hollow, cavernous room with high plastered ceilings, silk-paneled walls, and parquet floors. The room's sole purpose is to entertain, and it always seems like a lonely housebound woman who only comes to life when friends visit. When people arrive, the ballroom blossoms and the gloom and the empty, cavernous feeling fly away, swept aside for the glee of a party.

There are sixty Nordmann fir and spruce Christmas trees lining the walls, one for each country where we have an official presence—Italy, Cyprus, the United Kingdom, Japan, Germany, Singapore, Brazil, and more. They're decorated in the Christmas traditions of each country, including, of course, ceramic models of our timepieces. The heady scent of spruce and fir teases through the room, mixing with cinnamon and allspice and gingerbread.

In fact, against the windows, a life-size gingerbread house reigns supreme. Outside the frosting-glazed house, a giant working timepiece resides over the gala. It's crafted of silver spun sugar and shaped like the Chronomachen, our bestseller.

From the ceiling hang glittering snowflakes and boughs of mistletoe. Christmas lights twinkle from above like stars guiding wanderers home. A fairytale Christmas.

As we float down the steps I take it all in. I breathe in the evergreen and spice, feeling the heat of the room crackling from all the laughing, dancing guests, and take in the snapping excitement and the magic of it all.

"I never imagined it would be so beautiful," Mila whispers, and over her bright red hair Daniel grins at me. He's triumphant. A year of planning and prodding countless staff members and contractors and he has his niece's awe-filled approval.

"What does it matter if this gala goes down in history or not?" is what his gaze seems to say. What does it matter, as long as Mila likes it?

"I promised you a dance, didn't I?" he asks her as we descend the wide, curving stairs.

And then we're caught up in the clamor of the orchestra, the tinkling of champagne glasses, and the robust cheer of a hundred voices mingling.

Mila is right. Daniel outdid himself.

While I'm a quick study at estimated growth, foreign-market strategy, long-term planning, contracts with suppliers and distributors, and import/export negotiations, Daniel is the brains behind our brand, our marketing, our cachet. We're the best team because I'm most comfortable behind a desk, planning and combing through market projections, while Daniel shines out in the world, bringing our vision to life.

Of our sibling duo I'm the introvert, the thinker, while Daniel is the extrovert, the doer.

The day my mum dropped me on my dad's doorstep and I met two-year-old Daniel was one of the best days of my life. I had all my possessions in a scuffed baby-blue suitcase—two tie-dye dresses, a tumbled moonstone, a stuffed bichon more gray than white, a pack of peanuts I was saving for when I was really hungry—and my dad sent me up to the nursery where Daniel and his nanny were.

I crouched on the floor next to him and thunked my suitcase down. It rattled loudly in the cavernous, wood-floored nursery. The room was austere, clean, and Daniel had the chubby-cheeked glow of a well-fed, well-loved child. Downstairs I could hear my mum telling my dad she was leaving me, just for a short time, while she found herself in Bali. There was yelling. Quite a bit of yelling.

Daniel's blond fuzz of toddler hair glowed in the sunlight streaming through the window. His nanny, Brigitte, read a book about a mother rabbit always coming after her runaway son—never leaving him, always finding him, always loving him—and my lower lip wobbled.

That's all.

But my baby brother, who had been staring at me with wide blue eyes, caught the tremor. He reached up with his chubby baby hand and softly patted my cheek.

My mum left. She didn't find herself in Bali. Or in Kuala Lumpur. Or Jaipur. Or back home, on the Tor of Glastonbury. She never came back for me either.

But I didn't know all that then. I only knew the little brother I'd never met was patting me on my cheek.

Meeting him was one of my best days ever.

I didn't realize it at the time, of course, but we often don't realize our lives courses have changed until years after the fact.

So, Daniel dances with Mila while I watch from the edges of the parquet dance floor.

She dances twice with Daniel, and three times with Max. She twirls around the ballroom, her white tulle skirt puffing around her like the snowflakes spinning in the sky outside. Her cheeks are pink and her eyes bright. The orchestra conductor, sensing her glee, leads a rousing version of the "Dance of the Sugar Plum Fairy."

I weave between guests: Vincent from Swiss National Bank (shall our families plan a ski day this winter? Verbier?); Arne, the former mayor, and his wife, Mellisande (have you seen the new zoning proposal?); Phillipe, a competitor in the luxury watch market (sly comment about leather supplier superiority); Jean, a curator at The Musée d'Art et d'Histoire (angling for an invitation to view our private art collection).

And then, Mila finishes dancing and gorges herself on a plate of strawberry and pistachio macarons stacked like a Christmas tree and dabbed with flecks of edible gold. She drinks from a crystal goblet filled with spiced cider and pins a sprig of holly in her hair.

And finally, Annemarie, her nanny, leads her upstairs for a sleep filled with dreams of dancing, Christmas lights, and macarons.

And now it's nearing midnight and I'm wrapped in

Max's arms, spinning around the dance floor to the orchestra strumming out "I'll Be Home for Christmas."

Daniel left ten minutes ago, leading a gorgeous, lanky blond out a side door, his hand on the crook of her back. He's thirty, unattached, and cat nip for all women, age one week to one foot in the grave.

Sometimes I worry he won't find someone who appreciates him for who he is, especially when his face is always plastered all over the media, but he tells me not to big-sister him.

"You're thinking hard," Max says, smiling.

He's right. I give him an apologetic smile. "Mila loved the gala. Did you see her expression when the snowflakes fell from the ceiling?"

He studies me, taking in my dance-flushed cheeks. "The snow was beautiful. Almost as beautiful as you."

I glance quickly at Max. He shrugs and turns me around the dance floor.

The gala is quieting. At midnight everyone will filter out the door, into the cold night. Their breath will puff white in the darkness, and then they'll climb into their cars and wind back down the drive. Max will join them, back to being my old friend and not this stranger who seems intent on . . . something more.

As I swallow, wishing Christmas were here already, and then the New Year, Max's gaze shifts to the ruby and emerald necklace resting on my collarbone.

"Do you like it?"

I nod. "Of course I do. Mila said she helped you pick it out."

He smiles. He softens when he smiles. Usually his hard-planed face is austere with a wry light tinting his brown eyes. His expression is often hawkish and determined, reminiscent of his Roman ancestors crossing the Rubicon. But with his smile the hawk turns into a dove. Gentle and offering a peaceful retreat.

"I admit, I may have asked her for a bit of advice." He smiles so openly that I don't even object when he pulls me closer.

His black tux is well-fitted, custom-tailored, and winter-sleek. The gloss matches the high shine of his black hair. Like me, his family has been here forever. But unlike mine, his was first in gold and then in diamonds and then in jewelry. The Barones have been here as long as the Abrys. Which is one of the reasons why Max and I get along so well.

We've been friends since my dad's funeral, when he made a joke about all six of my dad's ex-wives weeping in front of the chateau, saying in French, "They're like Henry the Eighth's wives, except they all survived. A bit morbid, isn't it? How many of them lived again? I can never remember English history."

"Divorced, beheaded, and died. Divorced, beheaded, survived," I said, eyeing my mum sobbing over a handful of rose quartz.

"Wow. Very nice. Who was he to you? Not anyone important, I imagine. Half the people here are just clamoring for a handout in the will."

"Really? What would you want? If you got a handout."

He thought about this for a moment, staring up at the gray stone walls of the chateau hunched under the heavy gray sky. "I'd ask for that brass umbrella stand in the entry. It's hideous, and I could hide all sorts of important items in it. Diamonds, documents, my passport. No thief would ever suspect it on account of its ugliness."

I scoffed. That ugly umbrella stand was a wedding gift from my mum. "Don't you have a safe?"

He shrugged. "What's the fun in that? I bet old Abry kept the family jewels in that stand. What would you angle for if you were in the will?"

I thought about it for a moment. I already knew what I was getting. The family business, near bankruptcy. I was also eight weeks pregnant and in over my head.

But what would I want if I were just clamoring for a handout?

"There's a watch that went missing years ago. It was the first timepiece Adolphus Abry ever made. I'd ask for that."

Adolphus Abry is my renowned ancestor and founder of the family business.

Max whistled. "Big ask. Not for mere hangers-on and acquaintances like us. Who was old Abry to you anyway? Family friend? Business associate? Are you seeking charity for a just cause? It makes a difference in what you'll get. He was a cantankerous old goat."

I lifted my eyebrows.

Apparently, Max didn't hold with not speaking ill of the dead.

"I'm the cantankerous old goat's beloved daughter."

Max stared at me, mortified. He was twenty-six at the time, the same age as me, and he'd take over his family's worldwide jewelry conglomerate the very next year.

"I'm sorry. Forget we met. Forget I said anything.

Oh, one of those wailing banshees is your mother? Is that right? Now I'm truly sorry."

I couldn't tell if he was saying sorry that he'd insulted my mum or sorry that Buttercup *was* my mum.

At that I laughed. It was the first time I'd laughed since Daniel called to say Dad had died of a heart attack.

The next week I couriered Max the umbrella stand with a red ribbon and a card that said, "For your family jewels, from the old goat."

Two months later, with a small baby bump, I ran into Max at a charity concert. He looked at my bump, looked at the expression on my face, and then said, "Are you on your own?"

I lifted my chin. "No. I have my brother."

"You can have me too."

At my look, he said, "As a friend."

And so we've remained friends for almost nine years.

But as he reaches up and carefully sweeps a loose tendril of hair behind my ear, I know Max doesn't want to be friends anymore.

"Max. I can't—"

"Don't," he says, shaking his head and pulling me closer.

His brown eyes flash with worry and I can feel the vulnerability in him. It's rare that he shows that, so I relax into the steps of the dance and the soft sigh of the music.

I'm comfortable in his arms. I always am. He's not quite six feet tall, lanky. He always wears a gold ring studded with a large ruby on his right ring finger, with the family's crest imprinted on the gold. He twists it when he's nervous. Long ago his ancestor was beheaded during the French Revolution. The daughter of the beheadee escaped la Terreur, met up with a Barone, and married him. The Barone business adopted the crest as their own.

Like Daniel, Max is always showing off his wares to the world. He always has a new pair of cufflinks at his wrists, gold or platinum or silver, a diamond-studded tie pin, or a sapphire and diamond wristwatch. But unlike Daniel, Max isn't my brother, and apparently, he doesn't want to be just friends.

Across the ballroom, the spun sugar timepiece reads 11:48 p.m. The Christmas Eve Gala is near its end.

"You don't have to say yes or no," Max says, looking out over the gala. Looking everywhere but at me. "But I wanted you to know, sometime in the past year, or maybe the past nine years, I've developed—"

"Max, please. I know what you're going to say and I don't want you to say it."

He looks back at me then, his mouth pressed into a firm line. He carefully watches my expression.

"I love you," I tell him. "As a friend. I've always loved you as a friend. Please don't ask anything more of me. You know I can't—"

"Can you say that absolutely? Without a doubt?" He leans close, and I'm reminded of the days we've sailed on the lake together, of him helping Mila learn to ride her bike, of the nights we sat side by side and worked late into the evening with a carton of takeout between us, without talking, just being.

He sees my hesitation and presses, "Fiona." He whispers my name. "What if we try? What if I take you to dinner? What if I bring you flowers? Can you say absolutely that I can never make you happy? Can you know for certain that someday I can't be the one?"

I grip the warm sleeves of his tuxedo jacket, the fabric slick against my fingers. I'm so close to Max that I can see the quick beat of his pulse in his neck. His nervous swallow.

I don't want to hurt him.

But I don't want to hurt myself either.

I take a breath, his cologne, an earthy, sanded wood smell, mixing with my Christmas vanilla-and-spice. There's a stinging at the backs of my eyes.

Max has always been my friend. He's always been just a friend. As reliable as the changing seasons.

I shake my head. Try to focus on the steps of the dance and the music weaving around us.

There are still dozens of people here. Large clusters of groups portioning off, couples dancing, business deals brewing over champagne and cranberry tarts.

Max's expression turns hawkish again, his austere coating back in place. "This wasn't the right time. I'm sorry."

No.

"Max. I—"

I'm cut off by a sharp, high-pitched scream.

The scream breaks through the noise and slices through the ballroom.

Then there's the shattering crash of a dozen champagne glasses smashing to the floor.

The orchestra fumbles, cellos slide to silence, and violins screech to a halt. A cymbal ricochets and quiets.

I yank out of Max's arms, searching for the woman who screamed.

Max tugs at me. "Fi. Stay behind—"

He's seen something I haven't.

He's trying to push me behind him.

But truly, there isn't enough time. It happens in an instant. Like the champagne glasses sliding from the silver tray and smashing against the wood floor. Once the fall has begun there's no way to stop it.

You can't rewind time.

I blink as Mellisande and Arne dive to the side.

My skin runs cold as Phillipe stumbles and slams to the floor.

I falter and feel a thick, halting heartbeat knock against my ribs as Jean's glass of champagne slips from his fingers and shatters.

Max grabs my hand. "For god's sake, someone stop—"

It's too late.

There's a small woman. She's wearing a bulky black winter coat, the hood is pulled tight. Fur lines her face and obscures her features.

The only thing recognizable is the gun.

It's compact. Black. Aimed at me.

"It's Christmas Eve. Remember, it's Christmas Eve. *Tell them it's Christmas Eve.*" She says this and she sounds as if she's trying to impress the fact on me. As if she's speaking to me, and only me.

And then the boom of the gun.

Max dives in front of me and I slam to the ground, buried beneath him.

There's a crack. A crash.

The intense jolting pain of a thousand Christmas bulbs shattering in my chest and piercing my lungs.

I drag in a gasping breath.

Max rolls off me, his face white, eyes wild. His hands roam me, checking to see if I'm hurt.

"Fi? Are you all right?"

There's a roaring. A strange whining noise in my ears. It drowns out the shouts and cries of the people running toward us.

I stare up at the snowflakes floating above. They really do look real. Daniel did a wonderful job. I remember the look on Mila's face when she first saw them, and I smile.

Then I look down at myself. At Max's hands running over my velvet crimson dress.

"You're all right. You're all right," he murmurs.

But then the blood that was seeping into my dress spills to the floor. And he realizes at the same time as I do that my dress and my blood are the exact same color.

"Don't be scared," he says, yelling behind him for Dr. Gaertner, a surgeon—is he still here? "Don't be scared," Max says again, clutching my hand.

His grip is tight, as if he's the one who's afraid.

"I'm not scared," I say, my mouth horribly dry. There's an ache building in my head and a numbness racing down my limbs. It feels like it does when you slide into Lake Geneva on an early spring day. Too cold.

"I'm not scared," I say again. I look down at my dress and frown. "It's only, I really liked this dress. It was one of a kind."

Max's face clears of emotion.

And then I slide into oblivion.

I don't dream.

3

IF THE CASE OF A WATCH IS ITS BODY, THEN THE DIAL is its face. We humans gaze into the luminous hand-enameled surface, mesmerized by the fragile metal disk that translates the secrets of the hundreds of mechanisms beneath it into a simple message: 11 a.m. or 3 p.m. or Monday or the twelfth of June.

When the universe of wheels, pinions, levers, and springs inside is in working order, then the dial translates the watch's secrets into a language we can all learn to read.

Even a complicated timepiece, requiring three times more parts than the simple self-winding caliber, can be read by a child.

When a watch hand points to a baguette diamond applique number, you know, for example, that it's three o'clock. A watch in working order doesn't lie.

Perhaps that's why for months after Christmas Eve my brother, Max, the employees at Abry, even Mila, watched my face as if they could read me as easily as a watch.

Daniel's gaze roamed over me, continuously on edge, searching for signs of fatigue or pain. Max watched me with a hawklike intensity, as if he was afraid I'd disappear on him. Even Mila would startle and turn to me quickly, as if she had to check on me every few minutes to make certain I was okay.

Their concern was worse than being shot.

So I gave them all a face as brightly polished and luminous as a cream-buffed dial, hand-enameled in opal and pink, hand-set with diamonds and eighteen-karat rose gold.

There's a technique we use at Abry called guilloché. Lathes engrave grooves that are three hundredths of a millimeter deep, forming a patina of geometric patterns that catches the sunlight and reflects it back in brilliant rays. I imagine my smile in guilloché, reflecting all the light back into the world.

And when I smile at them they all relax, as if like a watch my smile accurately reflects the heart of me.

A dial at Abry can take up to two hundred intricate operations to create, from blanking the dial to milling and guilloché to electroplating and varnishing. I only required two operations, which I think shows great restraint on my part.

The gunshot hit my spleen and, being a pseudo-vestigial organ, it had no apparent purpose other than to cushion the rest of me from a bullet.

I was up and walking within a week and back at my desk after two weeks. I learned years ago that the best way to deal with things you don't want to think about is to keep so busy you don't have time to think at all.

So I crammed my schedule, filling it daily from 5 a.m. until midnight. So even if I wanted to ponder being shot in the middle of my Christmas Eve Gala, I didn't have time—unless I penciled it in.

Days look like this:

5 a.m.–6 a.m. Cardio.

6 a.m.–6:30 a.m. Shower, dress.

6:30 a.m.–7 a.m. Mila up, dressed, breakfast.

7 a.m. Mila to school.

7:33 a.m. Arrive at Abry HQ.

It goes on from there, broken into fifteen-minute segments, including meetings with the casemaking production team for cases and bracelets, initiatives with post-production managers, a search for a new industrial facility for components production, meetings with the quality control team, updates on new technologies/tools/productions in our sphere, data on reserves and revenue, focus on clean air technologies for the white rooms, etcetera, etcetera. Until:

6 p.m. Home, dinner with Mila, homework help, soccer practice.

8 p.m. Mila to bed.

8:30 p.m. Back to work until I collapse into bed at midnight.

Some days Max or Daniel come by for dinner or a night out. The point is that I stay so busy I don't have time to think, and at night I'm so tired I don't dream.

Unfortunately, this strategy doesn't always work, and my dreams are haunted by a woman with a blurred face urgently repeating, "Christmas Eve. Christmas Eve."

I always waking up gasping and clutching my chest. It feels as if I've been plunged under a giant violent ocean wave and I can't break through the surface to find air.

Luckily, though, no one knows I dream about the woman or that I dread the mention of Christmas.

The woman was never found. No one even knows who she was. She disappeared in the chaos after she shot me. If I didn't have the nightmares and the raised sunburst scar on my abdomen, I'd almost believe she never existed.

The police determined it was a random act of violence. A mentally unstable woman who stumbled upon the glow of the chateau.

Daniel accepted the explanation. So did Max.

I'm not so sure.

It felt . . . It felt as if she was telling me . . . something.

Mila asks every now and then, her voice quavering, "What if she comes back?"

I don't have an answer. But I always say, "She won't. There's no reason for her to come back."

Then I turn Mila's attention to something else.

Keeping busy.

Always keeping busy.

It's how I've lived life since I was six years old and didn't know what to do with myself.

". . . about Christmas Eve?"

I jerk my head, squinting at Hugo Lebrun, director of casemaking at our production facility. "What did you say?"

My voice comes out more harsh than normal. It's four o'clock and the bright summer sun is glaring through the tall glass window in the conference room.

My eyes are gritty and I'm craving an espresso. I didn't sleep well last night—nightmares.

Daniel frowns at me from across the long mahogany table and I lift a shoulder in a Gaelic shrug. He reaches for the silver carafe of coffee and pours the steaming liquid into a small white mug. Then, with a wink, he pushes it across the table to me.

Hugo's repeating what I missed and his two team members, both new associates, are scratching notes and nodding. He gestures to the TV on the far wall tuned to the news. It's the usual. A scrollbar reads that a politician in Canton Vaud has been charged with accepting perks, the Swiss National Bank has a new director, there are road closures downtown. On the screen a reporter looks dispassionately at footage of some natural disaster in a far-off place.

"The leather supplier in Brazil," Hugo says. "They were affected by the earthquake too. Their manufacturing and tanning facilities were destroyed. I think we were better served in the end, when we shifted to Austria. But . . ." He shrugs. "I was informed they still have not recovered."

"Fi sent aid," Daniel says. "We sent clean water, food, medical supplies, temporary shelter."

I sigh and turn away from the TV, now showing the rubbled remains of a small fishing village. I don't want to see the rubble of someone else's life—not while mine is still a mess.

I barely remember the earthquake or sending aid. I think perhaps I've been keeping myself *too* busy if I can't remember events that happened little more than a year ago.

I take a sip of the coffee Daniel poured me, and the bitter cocoa flavor bites on the way down.

"We're all set?" I ask Hugo.

He gives me a startled glance and I smile to soften my tone.

Gosh, I'm tired.

I rub at my abdomen. There's an ache where the bullet hit. It's been throbbing all day.

Hugo nods, then he and his associates gather up their laptops and notes and file out of the conference room. Daniel and I are left alone, the wooden door swinging shut with a humming whoosh.

I look down at my watch. It's a 1956 Liebspielen, a perpetual calendar Abry with an art deco bracelet in pearls and diamonds. It was the first watch made under my dad's leadership and the first watch he gave me. I've had it since I turned sixteen.

It's six minutes after four—I'm late for my next meeting. My stomach growls. I forgot to schedule lunch.

"You're running yourself ragged," Daniel says, cutting into the silence.

He's switched to English. Usually, we speak French at work and in the city, but when it's just family, or when we're with Max, we always speak English.

It comes from the fact my first language is English, and for years after my mum left me I refused to speak a word of French. I was convinced she'd return for me, and I felt that somehow, if I gave in and learned French, she never would. Stubbornly, I didn't speak a word of French until age twelve.

It was six years after she left that I finally accepted the fact she wasn't coming back for me. So, unlike

Daniel—who can juggle a half-dozen languages in his head at the same time—I have the slightly accented French of a native English speaker and a lifelong loyalty to my mother tongue.

I take in a long breath. The air in the office is cool and dry. Outside the wall of windows, the blue mountains climb over green fields. On the other side of the building the outskirts of Geneva sprawl toward the city center.

"I didn't think you'd notice."

"I noticed."

I smile at Daniel, stretching back in the leather chair.

Our headquarters is modern, a design we purposely selected to mimic our forward-thinking philosophy. We moved our headquarters five years ago, after we realized we needed new space for our growing in-house production—casemaking, components production, finishing, post-production—as well as all our support staff. There wasn't room in Geneva's city center, and the building Abry was always housed in was an old five-story building on the bank of the Rhône with manufacturing partitioned around the city.

When my dad and grandad ran Abry, everyone was headquartered in those old stone buildings. There were large windows with light that shone over work desks, tinkling bells heralding the tea-service cart, and gifts of ham to every employee at Christmas. It was a different time.

Now we have sleek leather chairs, cream marble floors, a six-story lobby with a giant glass entrance, and bronze wheels and springs and pinions decorating the white walls next to a ten-foot replica of the Chronomachen.

It's not quite as cozy as the old stone building that housed our family for more than a century. But we've stayed in business and we're still moving forward.

"I'm keeping busy," I tell Daniel, swallowing the last of the coffee. I can already feel a buzz flowing through my veins.

He considers me, and I hate to admit it, but for the first time in six months I think he sees right through me.

"Maybe we shouldn't keep so busy all the time," he says, shoving his fingers tiredly through his collar-length hair.

I feel a pinch in my chest. I have a memory of my dad making the same exact gesture in his office chair when he told me one day, if I worked hard enough, I'd be a watchmaker too.

"And why not? Life is great. I have Abry, I have you, Mila, Max. Me being busy is a reflection of how happy I am."

Daniel narrows his eyes and drops his elbows to the table, cradling his chin in his hand. "You're a terrible liar."

"I am not."

He flashes a smile. "I was thinking, you used to worry about me . . . finding someone who appreciates all my charm."

"I don't worry anymore. I gave that up. You're hopeless. If I see another reality-show star on the yacht with you, I'm going to—"

"What? At least I go out. The last time you went out, it was to pick out a hedge trimmer with Max."

"That counts."

"It doesn't, and you know it."

I don't argue. There's no use. "What's your point? I have another meeting."

"My point is, Fi, this can't keep on. Ever since Christmas Eve"—he can't bring himself to say, "since you were shot"—"you've been running yourself to the ground. You need to take a break. You need to, maybe . . ."—he narrows his eyes—"open yourself up."

He holds up his hands at my protest.

"I'm only saying," he says, "I think . . . you want me to find someone to appreciate me. I want the same for you."

I press my hands to the cold shellacked surface of the wood table. Outside the conference room someone knocks on the door. When they open it, Daniel shakes his head and gestures them away.

"Why are you such a meddler?" I ask him.

"Fi."

"You know it isn't the same for me. You know why. I can't do it."

Daniel doesn't say anything—he only watches me with eyes as calm as the ocean on a windless day.

Then he says the exact thing he said to me that day nearly a decade ago. "Then we'll do it together."

My heart squeezes at the memory of those words. I can almost hear the crash of the ocean that went along with them.

So I say the exact same thing I said then too. "All right. Together."

4

A cool breeze drifts off the water, gentling the summer heat. My car windows are open, letting in the rich loamy air and leafy sunshine smells of the countryside.

I wind down the narrow road that edges the lake, the rippling blue water on one side and the cool, shaded forest on the other. I skate the middle, staying out of both.

A grey heron sails past, veering toward the lake. Her choice is easy. She's a water bird—she'll go to the water. Human choices aren't so easily made.

Wouldn't it be nice if we had the instinct of a heron? Then when we made a choice, for someone or against someone, for something or against something, we'd never have to doubt it.

We'd always know what we were meant to do.

I turn on the radio—classical—to tune out the piping bird calls and the roll of the waves. Then I let the sun stroke my face as the light feathers through the leaves, falling across the road.

Daniel and I made a deal. A bet. An agreement.

We'll both open up. We'll open ourselves to the possibility of finding someone. We'll stop being so busy and so consumed by Abry and we'll be open to finding a partner. Maybe even love.

I think he only agreed to do this because he's worried about me. But I only agreed to it because I'm worried about him.

That's the way with family though. Worry is the ticking second hand while love is the watch case holding everything together.

Anyway, whoever finds love first wins, and whoever doesn't will have to do something they hate. For Daniel, that's posing shirtless for an Abry billboard ad. For me, it's taking a two-week no internet, no phone vacation at the beach.

I take a long sip of coffee—my third cup of the day. It tastes like cherries and roasted almonds and richly roasted beans. I swallow more from the steaming cup. I'm running on fumes and I have to help Mila with her spelling words for her test tomorrow.

The chateau is ahead, framed in the bright blue daylight. It's nearly 6 p.m., but today is the summer solstice, which means the sun will stay high above for hours more. Sunlight slants down over the chateau's dove-gray stone and spills over the two towers with their curved windows and high pointing roofs. Usually, when I round the bend and see the home my family has lived in for generations, I feel a ping of happiness.

But today that ping is popped when I see the cars lining the circular drive.

There's Daniel's BMW.

Fine.

Max's AC Cobra—the red one he brings out on nice days.

Also fine.

And then there's another car. A 1985 Vauxhall Cavalier. Bluish Gray. Rusted undercarriage. A cracked headlight. A bumper sticker that reads "Powered by Good Vibes."

Not fine.

My mum's back for the first time in years.

5

When I open my front door, the wheezing sound of a kazoo fills the air and a handful of glitter confetti rains over me.

"Happy birthday!"

I blink and stare dumbly at my mum. She's in a silver birthday-party hat and a yellow tie-dye party dress, and she's tossing handfuls of multicolored glittery confetti into the air.

"Happy birthday, Moonbeam!"

The chateau smells like a birthday party. There's the vanilla-and-sugar of chiffon, the tart lemony scent of curd, the mellow sweetness of clotted cream. There's the sweet scent of chocolate melted into milk, simmering on the stove. And layering over it all, my mum's favorite birthday surprise; orange-and-almond Victoria sponge.

I remember my fourth birthday, my fifth birthday, and my sixth birthday, and each of them smelled exactly like this.

Because my mum has been trying to find herself since before I was born, she's never stayed still long enough to have a home. Instead we used to sleep on couches at her friends' houses, floors of acquaintances' flats, and makeshift tents in the fields outside Glastonbury Festival.

When I was very small and she said, "Moonbeam, I'm on a journey to find myself," I believed she had literally lost a part of herself, like an arm or a finger or a toe. I'd scan her worriedly, wondering where her missing part could possibly be and how she could have misplaced it.

I'd even lie awake at night staring at the leaking flaps of the rug tent she'd built, listening to the music of the festival and the crackling fires outside, where grown-ups debated self-actualization, and I'd wonder, did finding yourself always mean there wasn't enough to eat?

But then my birthday would come and my mum would find us a friend's flat or a rambly cottage to stay in for a week or two, and she'd stir hot chocolate on the stove and bake me lemon chiffon and orange-and-almond Victoria sponge.

There'd be a bowl of forbidden party nibbles—forbidden on account of them being consumeristic. Chocolate Smarties, Cadbury Buttons, Kinder Eggs.

The little toy inside the egg was my birthday present. Twice it was a two-pence-size yellow plastic animal of indeterminate species, with a smashed face and malformed knees. Once it was a car whose wheels didn't spin.

There's a bowl full of Kinder Eggs now on the sitting-room coffee table, right next to a three-tiered lemon chiffon cake, pink birthday candles ready to be lit.

The chateau, being hundreds of years old and the home of generations of Abrys, is part-comfy house, part-museum, and part-entertainment showpiece. The sitting room leans toward shabby comfy and is our favorite place to lounge. There are two lumpy avocado-green and orange-striped couches from Grandpa's fifties fever and a boxy walnut coffee table.

Mila convinced me to buy a pair of pink beanbag chairs and a massive projection screen for movie night. The screen hangs on the wall opposite the stone fireplace.

There are a few wooden chairs with cross-stitched padding from the early 1900s—evidence that one of our great-great-aunts loved stitching spaniels and chubby babies in cloth nappies. There are shelves lining the walls with old clothbound books, and random artifacts from around the world (an Abry from the 1880s went on a world tour and brought back art for inspiration). A few portraits hang on the walls, mostly men with pocket watches who look a lot like Daniel in old-fashioned clothing.

It's a hodgepodge shabbily comfy room, a dichotomy to the curated splendor of the public rooms. My mum lived here for three months with my dad before their divorce, so of course she'd know this is the place to throw a party. She's draped the walls in multicolored bunting and filled every spare space with wild clover blossoms, giving the room a festive feel.

My mum flings the rest of the confetti over me and a few pieces stick to my lips.

I blow them away.

Behind my mum Daniel throws me a look that says, "I have no idea what's happening and I'm as shocked as you are."

Max has a sort of "I've just been run over by a lorry" look.

Mila can't seem to decide between excitement over cake or confusion over her grandma's sudden appearance and subsequent party.

Annemarie, Mila's nanny, peers around the hall door, wide-eyed and curious, and then she pops back around the corner when she sees the confetti blizzard raining over me.

"Oh, happy birthday, Moonbeam!" My mum gives me a radiant smile.

I take a moment, gauging her smile, wondering if she's serious. You can never tell.

"Mum, it's not my birthday."

My birthday isn't for another four months.

She widens her hazel eyes, a mirror of mine. "But it *could* be. Why are you attached to a specific day? Attachment is the root of pain. Let's have cake."

I step forward and hug my mum. "It's nice to see you."

She pats my back. "I know."

My mum pulls away, gripping my arms and studying me. All the while, sweet, sugary scents flow around us. She frowns at whatever she finds in my expression.

"I had a feeling," she says finally, "and I was right. You need to find yourself, Moonbeam."

I try to hide my flinch, but since my mum's holding my arms, she notices it right away. She shakes her head and then steps back.

Mum has red hair, lighter than Mila's, and it's faded through the years. Her skin has a translucent quality that makes her look younger than she is. She also has a unique air—one that's hard to put your finger on.

Back when I was in primary school I learned about the alpine swift. It's a small bird that can stay aloft for up to two hundred days at a time. When I read about that bird I realized that was the feeling my mum gave off. She doesn't stay and she doesn't land.

"I'm glad I came." Mum gives me her brilliant smile again. "You are in dire need of a birthday."

At that she sweeps her party dress behind her and turns toward the kitchen—and presumably the Victoria sponge.

She stops at Daniel's disapproving stare. His arms are folded over his chest, his mouth tilted down at the corners.

Daniel's mom was our dad's second wife, a glamorous and gorgeous American heiress from New York. She remarried a Texas oil tycoon and left Daniel with Dad shortly after Daniel's second birthday.

For some reason my mum never liked Daniel, not even when he was a little kid. And Daniel, for his part, never much liked my mum. He told me once that it's because she hurt me. He couldn't care less what she thinks of him. He only cares how she's treated me.

"Daniel." My mum tilts her chin in the air, taking on a haughty look that doesn't match her silver party hat and tie-dye dress.

"Buttercup," Daniel says, curtly nodding his head.

She glowers at him, her lips pursing. "Still chasing the capitalist's dream? Materialism and consumerism your rotten bedfellows?"

My brother gives her a feral grin. "Still chasing your shadow around the world? Selfishness and blindness your faithful companions?"

Max coughs into his hand. He's only met Buttercup once, and that was at my dad's funeral when he patted her shoulder and offered her his handkerchief. "Shall I get some plates for the cake?"

My mum breaks her stalemate staring contest with Daniel. "Who are you again? I didn't invite you."

Judging by the look she casts Daniel, she didn't invite him to my fake birthday party either.

Max gives my mum a hawkish smile, his glossy black hair shining under the light. "Max, remember? I introduced myself at the door. Maximillian Barone, a friend of your daughter's."

"No." She waves his statement away. "That's not what I meant. Aren't you the man who sold me that miniature hoover with the selenite insert that could dust up negative energy? From the curiosity shop in Bern."

"Excuse me?"

"Yes, that was you. I know that supercilious look. You owe me fifty-five pounds, the hoover didn't work. You're a purveyor of rubbish."

Max gives her an affronted look. "I can assure you that wasn't me."

Daniel grins and rocks back on his heels, enjoying Max's reddening face.

Mila is tiptoeing toward the coffee table, her eyes on the glossy vanilla icing layered over the three-tiered lemon cake.

"Oh no, I know it was you. I can smell the guilt all over you. As thick as the smoke in a hookah bar."

"That's not guilt. It's commercialism. It coats him like smog," Daniel says, grinning.

The look on Max's face almost makes me laugh.

Mila's reached the cake. She darts her gaze around, checking to see no one's watching. Then she swipes her finger through the frosting near the base of the cake, pulling up a bright, sugary, glistening layer.

She pops her finger into her mouth and then smiles, her eyes widening.

I can just imagine the flavor. My mum always could bake a delicious cake.

"Mr. Barone, I expect a refund. Furthermore, you may not pursue my daughter. Clearly, if you can't be trusted to sell a functional hoover, you can't be trusted to perform in other ways."

With that my mum grandly sweeps away to the kitchen.

This time Daniel's coughing into his hand, covering a laugh.

Max stares after my mum then mumbles, "My hoover functions just fine."

I hide a smile and dust the brightly colored confetti from my dress.

Max turns to me, his hands up. "Fi, I came to drop off your jacket. You forgot it last week. I don't mean to intrude." He looks in the direction of the front door. "I should go."

"You should stay," Daniel says, clapping Max's arm.

"You should stay," I agree, wanting Max here. "After all, we're having a birthday party."

At that Mila lets out a desperate squeak. The chiffon cake, which she'd been swiping frosting from, tilts. It wobbles. And then it tumbles off the platter and onto the floor.

It hits with a whoomph, a squelch, and then settles into a pile of frosted, cakey goop.

"Oh no," Mila whispers, her lips covered in cake crumbs.

"You might clean that up," Daniel says to Max. "Show Buttercup your hoovering abilities."

"Sorry, Mummy." Mila stares at the cake. Her lips wobble. The lemony chiffon looks for all the world like a crushed sandcastle.

I tug her to me and hug her close. "Don't worry. There's still the Victoria sponge. It's orange and almond."

Mila looks at me with hopeful eyes. "Two cakes! Do you think even though it isn't your birthday that you'll still get presents? I'll sing you 'Happy Birthday' if you do."

I smile and ruffle her hair. "Knowing your Grandma Buttercup, I'm certain I'll get presents."

At least, I'll get a few Kinder Eggs.

Or maybe, judging by the look on my mum's face, something more.

6

Max and Daniel are gone, Annemarie has left for the night, and Mila's in bed. I lean back into the lumpy green-and-orange couch and twirl my glass of wine. watching the ruby-red color catch sparks of light.

My mum sits cross-legged on the couch next to me, her yellow dress flowing around her.

The ruined lemon chiffon was cleaned away, and the coffee table holds the remains of the Victoria sponge and our empty mugs of hot chocolate. Orange-and-white foil Kinder wrappers are crumpled and littered around the table. Plastic Kinder toys, as misshapen as ever, clump around the near empty cake platter.

I swipe my finger across my plate and gather up the rich double cream, the almond sponge crumbs, and a bit of raspberry jam. Then I pop my finger in my mouth. The sweetness and the tartness blend perfectly.

I sigh and smile at my mum.

"I'll leave tomorrow morning," she says, reaching for her cup of tea.

I nod. I didn't expect her to even stay the night.

I curl my legs under me. My dress stretches over my knees, the light summer wool scratching my skin. It feels a bit like the emotions dragging over me. My mum always brings up a stewpot of emotions. Happiness, the desire of a little girl wanting her to stay, annoyance, discomfort at her unpredictability, fear that she'll leave again, and then relief when she does.

"Where will you go?" I ask.

"Mmm. Chamonix, for a minute. I love the Alps in summer. Then I think I'll drive down to Greece for a bit. I've been meaning to visit the Temple of Delphi."

I think about her driving her old car through multiple countries and my stomach dips. "Do you need money for a new car?"

My mum sets down her teacup with a hard snick. Then she turns her censorious gaze on me. "You know how I feel about money. About material possessions. When old Henriette finally passes on to the great car afterlife, the universe will provide me another mode of transportation."

"Yes, but the universe could provide you a new car right now. Through me."

My mum ignores my suggestion. She's always been this way. It's why she refused alimony when she divorced my dad. Why she didn't accept any child support. It's why out of all of Dad's ex-wives she was the only one who didn't contest the miserly sum handed out to the exes in his will.

"You've done well with Mila. She's a good girl. Very bright."

I let my mum change the topic. "Thank you. I think so too."

She catches the love in my tone and the smile on my face. "My spiritual advisor in Laos said you're still angry with me for leaving you."

My lungs pinch, and for a moment I'm robbed of breath. I sit still. Take a breath. Then, carefully, I set my wineglass on the table.

I turn to my mum. She is who she is—I accepted that a long time ago.

"Perhaps," I say.

She takes another sip from her cup. "I do wish you'd buy proper tea for my visits."

"Right."

"Fiona."

I wrap my arms around my middle and nod. This must be important since she's using my name.

"I had to leave you."

"I know." My throat is dry and achy. I stare at the ruby-red color of my wine.

"I wasn't good for you. I wasn't. You needed a home. You're not like me. Even at six you wanted to stay put and settle in. Every time we moved to a new place you cried. It broke my heart. But I couldn't give you what you needed. Not me. But your dad could. He could give you a home. A brother. School. Stability."

"I know, Mum. I understand."

"It's only . . ." She reaches for me, touches my hand. "You were the one thing I've always regretted leaving behind. I wish . . ."

Mum stops, pulling her hand from mine.

"It's fine, Mum. You were right. I love it here. I loved Dad. And Daniel. I have Abry now. My life. My daughter. I wouldn't have all that if not for you. You made the right choice."

"Did I?"

I lift a shoulder.

"Seeing you, I'm not sure I did."

"Mum. I'm happy."

"What about your dreams? You used to dream as a little girl."

I look away from her. I remember those dreams. A decade ago I thought I'd found them. I hadn't, so I let them die the death they should have done a long time ago.

"I can tell, you know. I can tell you don't have dreams anymore. I worry I'm the reason you don't."

I shake my head. "Don't be conceited. I'm the reason I don't."

She smiles at that.

Then she pulls a small gift wrapped in brown paper from the pocket of her dress. "I brought you a birthday gift."

"It's not my birthday."

"Summer solstice gift then."

I let out a huff of air. My mum presses the rectangular box into my hands. The wrapping is thick butcher paper and the box is tied with twine. The paper is torn and stained and looks as if it's been shoved under the front seat of her Vauxhall for a few years.

I smile. "Thank you."

The rough twine slips through my fingers and the paper crumples free, revealing a long wooden box. I'm intrigued.

I look back at my mum. The wood is warm in my

hands and heavy. "What is it?"

She flashes a bright smile. "Open it."

I fold up the little gold latch and lift the lid of the box. The scent of musty velvet and dry wood fans toward me. Light catches on the object inside and I suck in a shocked breath.

"Where did you get this?"

"Do you like it?"

"Where did you get it?"

It's the watch.

The watch.

The watch that I joked with Max about after he asked what I'd want to inherit. The first watch Adolphus Abry ever made.

It's been missing for nearly eighty years. Stolen, misplaced—no one ever knew exactly what happened to it. I've only ever seen black-and-white photos and drawings.

But it's easy to recognize.

It's a work of art.

In old Geneva there were many goldsmiths. When the protestant revolution arrived, wearing adornments and jewelry was made illegal. What were hardworking goldsmiths to do? They turned to watchmaking.

The goldsmiths, the Huguenots fleeing France—all of this melded to make Geneva the pinnacle of the world's watchmaking empire. In 1838 Adolphus Abry was an apprentice watchmaker. Family legend says the first watch he crafted on his own held all his dreams. He poured his dreams into the gold, into the enamel powder, into the perfectly ticking second hand.

He wanted to create beautiful art. To build a business that rivaled the best. To earn enough so he could marry the girl he'd been in love with all his life. That watch made his dreams come true. With it he received enough commissions to build Abry.

The pocket watch is nestled in black velvet.

The light catches the watch's gold case. It glistens under the lamplight as if it were just polished this morning. The buttery yellow gold gleams, and the gold chain circles the round case. There aren't any gems, no hand-cut sapphires or diamonds. There's only the smooth, rounded yellow gold and the lustrous, gleaming enamel the color of vibrant lapis lazuli gently flowing into the soft, creamy white of sea-foam.

I can see now why everyone who's ever seen this watch says it holds Adolphus Abry's dreams. Staring into the deep blue of the dial is like staring into an ocean of dreams. You can almost see them set there in the watch face, mirrored back to you on the surface.

I hesitate, then I reach forward and touch the edge of the watch case. The gold is warm, not cold, as if it's recently been held in someone's hands.

There's a spark there, a feeling like the one you get when you sit at the top of the Tor in Glastonbury or when you walk into the seven-hundred-year-old Salisbury Cathedral and all the stained-glass windows are lit and glowing from the sunrise.

"Magical, isn't it?"

I smooth my finger over the edge of the gold and nod. "How did you find it?"

The watch is still, the gold hands unmoving. It's manually wound mechanical movement. The last I heard, it still keeps time perfectly.

I wonder what will happen when I wind it.

"Six months ago, after you were shot—"

I flinch, though my mum continues unaware.

"—I decided to visit Carl, the goat herder. Great hands. Remember him?"

"No." I wonder if my mum finds it odd that after her daughter was shot she decided to visit a goat herder rather than her only child laid up in hospital.

"You know, Carl. Harry's brother. From Wiltshire. Marjorie's son."

I have no idea who any of these people are.

"Anyway, on my way to see Carl—he's in Croatia now—I was thinking about the woman shooting you on Christmas Eve and I remembered your father's great-uncle Leopold."

I raise my eyebrows in question.

"It was the strangest thing. Every time I thought about you being shot, I thought, 'Buttercup, you *must* visit Leopold.' He came to the wedding and gave your father and me a silver tea service. Everyone at the wedding refused to acknowledge him. But I liked his shoes. They were shaped like crocodiles."

"Sorry, what?" Uncle Leopold? I narrow my eyes and concentrate on remembering the many branches of our family tree. "I don't remember an Uncle Leopold."

Some people might think it's terrible that after I was shot my mum could only think about visiting a goat herder and an elderly relative she hadn't seen in years, but I'm inured to this sort of thing.

"You wouldn't," she says, "He must be ninety-eight years old—no, ninety-nine. He fell out with the Abrys on account that he despised time."

"And he gave you the watch?"

"Oh no." My mum beams at me. "I stole it from him."

I blink. "You stole Adolphus Abry's watch from a centenarian?"

My mum laughs. "It was easy. He served me weak tea in his library and told me a story about how this watch can make your dreams come true. He said if you wind it then fall asleep with it in your hand, it will show you your heart's desire. And then once you've dreamed it, you can grasp it. I took it for you so that you can dream again. This watch will make it happen."

I shake my head. "That's just a story."

She tsks at my denial. "He claimed it's what made him leave Switzerland. He said in the summer of 1940 he left Abry and went to Poland to find his lady love. All because of this watch."

I pause. "Did he find her?"

"No. She died during the invasion. It's why he hates time. He was too late." My mum waves this away.

"Then I think maybe this watch doesn't work like he said."

"No. It does. He was very clear that it lets you live your dreams."

I study the face of the pocket watch, catching sight of myself in the dark, glistening surface.

"It's why I stole it. The watch was practically begging me to bring it back to you. I could feel it asking me to take it. That was, hmmm, right after last Christmas. I remember he served plum pudding from a tin."

I glance quickly at my mum and she shrugs.

"You shouldn't have stolen it—"

"He stole it first. I'm merely returning it to the Abry Watch Company."

"Hmm."

She reaches over and clutches my hand. Her fingers are cold on mine.

"Fiona. Tell me. Tell me you're living the life you've always dreamed of. Tell me you're happy, and I'll admit I was wrong and throw this watch in the lake—"

"Don't do that. This is a historic piece of horology and my family history—"

"See. I knew you'd like it."

I pause. My eyes are drawn again to the gleaming gold and the smooth lapis face.

Lately I've been run-down. Tired. The nightmares keep me awake.

I might not want my dreams to come true, but I'd like the nightmares to stop.

"It could show you your heart's desire."

"I have Mila. I have Daniel. I have Abry. I already have my heart's desire."

My mum gives me a flat stare. For a woman who only raised me until age six, she knows me quite well.

"But if you could ask for one more thing? Just one dream that you never let your waking mind linger on. What would it be? Wouldn't you want it?"

I don't answer.

Instead I close the wooden box, shutting the gleaming watch away in the dark.

The sound of the box closing is loud between us.

"I think"—my mum tilts her head and stares at the last slice of the Victoria sponge sitting alone on the platter—"I'll slip out before you and Mila wake. I don't care for goodbyes."

I scoot across the couch and give my mum a tight hug. "Thank you for the watch."

She pats my back. "You're welcome. Sleep well."

7

My bedroom is dark and cool. Moonlight filters through the wavy glass, casting a soft glow over my bed. It's nearing midnight and the longest day of the year is coming to a close.

Outside the winds kick through the trees, rattling the branches. They answer to the rumble of thunder, a far-off growl echoing down the mountains and across the lake.

I'm in bed. The cool sheets rub against my bare legs and the crumple of the light gold duvet catches the moonlight. Except for the wind and the far-off thunder my bedroom is silent.

Usually, the old stone tower room has a sleepy, walled-off-from-the-world feel. But tonight there's a breath-held expectancy riding through the dark. It mirrors the air outside, where the trees and the grass and even the wind wait for the coming rain.

I shift, leaning back against my pillows, and the scent of lavender flows to me. Next to me, on my nightstand, the watch sits unopened in its wooden case.

I stare at the ceiling, the darkness pressing down on me. I'm wide-awake. An electricity curls through me, keeping me from sleep.

I tap my fingers against the bed.

I stretch my legs across the cool sheets.

I roll over.

I punch my pillow.

Thunder rumbles, grumbling over the lake.

I kick my blankets loose.

I roll onto my side.

The gold latch on the box catches the moonlight and winks at me.

Oh, for goodness' sake.

It's just a watch.

I mean, it's *the* watch. A historic piece of great significance. But all the same, it's just a watch.

It isn't as if it can make dreams come true.

Per se.

But what if it could?

I roll onto my back and let out a long sigh. Rumbling thunder responds.

If it could . . .

What exactly would I dream?

There's a whisper in my heart, almost too quiet to hear.

I think about my mum, telling me she knows I don't dream anymore. Telling me I need to find myself.

I think about Daniel, pushing me to open up.

I think about Mila, how above all things I want her to always know love.

And then I think about the day I let my dreams die.

The whisper in my heart grows louder, then thunder hits, cracking like a gunshot.

I flinch, the noise ricocheting through me.

"Enough," I tell myself, consciously relaxing the tension clenching my muscles.

It's enough.

It's just a pocket watch.

I'll either dream or I won't.

It's not as if dreams are reality. It's not as if dreams come true.

But...

What could it hurt to try?

Nothing will happen. Except maybe I'll have a nice dream. A pleasant, peaceful, restful sleep full of lovely dreams instead of the recurrent cycling of nightmares.

Decision made, I reach over to the wooden box and lift the lid. The velvet is as dark as the night sky and the gold glows in the moonlight. The glinting metal seems to vibrate under the light. I reach forward and scoop the watch free.

It's heavy, solid, and warm in my hands. The deep blue watch face soaks up the moonlight and the second and hour hands stand still.

Slowly, breath held, I wind the watch. The metal twists between my fingers, and then, surprisingly, the watch begins to tick.

I let out a whoosh of air. It works.

I set the date and time. The twenty-first of June. 11:48 p.m.

Outside the rain begins. It falls across the window in a slow, tapping patter.

I lie back and pull my blanket to my chin, letting

the scent of lavender and the weight of the blankets comfort me.

The drumming rain, the wind, and the rumbling thunder roll over me. I sink into my mattress and close my eyes.

In my hand I clutch the warm round pocket watch. Its ticking is a heartbeat keeping time.

In the quiet of my mind I whisper, *Dream.*

I fall asleep to the music of rain.

8

THE SUN IS BRIGHT LIKE THE FLASH OF A POLAROID, startling me out of sleep.

I moan and bury my head under my pillow, not ready to face the world. It feels as if I just closed my eyes. In one blink I was drifting off to the sound of rain, and the next the sun is flashing insistently over my eyelids.

I suppose one mystery is solved. I didn't dream. Not at all.

The time between falling asleep and waking up was a millisecond.

I'm sure Mila will run in soon, jump on my bed, beg for waffles and chocolate sauce and a trip to the beach with her uncle. It's a Saturday after all.

Outside the querulous call of a gull cuts through the morning quiet.

If Mila hears that we'll definitely be headed to the beach.

I frown into my pillow. Usually, the thick stone walls

of the chateau dampen any birdcall. Even more, there's the sound of waves, crashing, rolling. A muffled roar that recedes with a foamy hiss.

That's not the sound of Geneva's placid lake.

That's the sound of an ocean rushing and receding.

My skin prickles, goose bumps rising.

I drag in a breath. The scent of lavender is missing, replaced by a salty, damp-air smell, mixed with . . . man?

Definitely man.

My bed always smells like clean laundered sheets, crisp fresh air and lavender. This pillow? This bed? It smells like hot nights, sweat, and naked, salty skin.

My bed is soft, deeply cushioned, with a feather mattress topper. This bed is firm, with worn sheets that feel like an old T-shirt washed too many times.

Outside the gull calls again, joined by the shrill whistling sounds of birds flying over.

And that's when the hair on the back of my neck rises, my heart kicks around my chest, and I decide I'm not in my bed.

And I'm not in Geneva.

Slowly, I open my eyes and lift the pillow.

Sunlight floods over me, partially blinding me with its brightness. I've not seen sun this bright since I was sailing the Greek isles with my dad years ago. It's the sort of bright, direct light that's only found reflecting off jewellike seas and white sand beaches.

Sunspots dance in my vision and then clear away, unveiling a bedroom I've never seen.

It's tiny. Barely large enough to fit the bed. There's perhaps a half-meter of space between the wall and the bed, and I'm fairly certain the door hits the mattress when opened.

The walls are white and scuffed. They reflect the bright light from the room's window—a three-foot-wide, single-paned window lined by unfinished wood. Its view is a bright cerulean blue sky, no clouds, no trees, nothing to tell me where I am.

There's a plastic clothesline hanging from the wall at the foot of the bed. Dresses, T-shirts, shorts. It's loaded with women's clothing that's worn and faded. The dresses are beachy, flowy, and remind me of something my mum might wear if she were staying at a beach commune.

On the other half of the plastic clotheslines, there are men's clothes. Light colored T-shirts, jeans, cargo shorts, a few wrinkled button-down shirts worn at the seams, a pair of khakis.

There isn't much else in the bedroom. A single bulb with a pull chain hanging from the ceiling. A box fan in the window, spinning slowly, emitting a low hum. A driftwood-framed wedding photograph hanging on the far wall.

It's of a woman in a mermaid-style wedding dress, short, strawberry-blonde hair, pale skin, pale blue eyes. She grins triumphantly at the camera—a bride at the pinnacle of happiness. She's standing next to a young man.

He's in a gray suit, tall and solid, with the type of muscled build that would lead people to assume he's a star footballer. He's black-haired, brown-eyed, bronze-skinned, square-jawed, and classically handsome in a carefree "I'll be your summer fling and you'll never forget me" sort of way.

They're standing on a long stretch of beach, the white sand glistening, the surf running over the train of the woman's wedding dress. I'd be surprised if either of them was older than twenty.

The wedding . . . it must have taken place at least a decade ago.

Because the man?

That wide-shouldered, square-jawed, dark brown-eyed man?

He's in bed next to me.

Except he's not twenty, he's my age. Early thirties. His face has squared off even more. His jaw is hard, dark morning stubble lining his sun-weathered face. His messy hair dips over his forehead and he regards me with a sleepy smile.

The sun glides over his skin, carving lines across the hard plane of his shoulders and down his chest. There's a dusting of hair. Tattoos covering his biceps and pectoral muscles, wrapping around his abdomen. What are they of? I don't know. I don't look.

Because he's naked.

As naked as the day he was born, and he's smiling at me.

I drop into that smile. I tumble headfirst into it. My stomach drops as if I'm falling and then lifts as if I've caught an updraft and I'm soaring free.

He's smiling at me like he knows me. Like we've spent thousands of nights together and he wants to spend a thousand more with me. He's smiling at me like he knows me inside and out—that I love coffee before breakfast, that beautifully painted enamel on a watch dial can make me cry, that I love roasted chestnuts at Christmas and giving gifts more than receiving them. Like he knows I'm scared of being left behind and I'm terrified of giving my heart away again—he knows all this and he loves me for all of it.

That smile tells me that if I fall into his open arms he'll hold me, and I'll be safe with him.

My breath is short, my lungs tight. The gulls screech outside and the hum of the fan moans over the sound of crashing waves.

I struggle to draw in the humid, salt-tinted air.

"Who...? What...?"

He leans forward. The mattress tilts, rolling me closer to him. He brushes his fingers over my cheek, his touch whisper-soft.

"Morning," he says.

His voice is rich, mellow, sleep-filled. It rolls over me like a wave licking over bare skin. There's the hint of a musical, rolling accent, subtle and warm.

He smiles. "You must've been worn out from last night. I was wondering when you'd wake up."

9

The man leans forward, his eyes morning-warm, focused on my mouth.

He's going to kiss me.

The salt air crackles with electricity, and unbelievably, I *want* him to kiss me. I *need* him to kiss me.

I'm even leaning forward in anticipation of his mouth pressing against mine. I can practically feel the scape of his fingers over my breasts, tugging me close.

Which is what decides it for me.

I don't know this man.

I have no idea who he is.

I've never seen him before.

Not in my entire life.

There's only one explanation. He kidnapped me. He drugged me, hauled me to some shoddy, dilapidated ocean cottage, and he's holding me for ransom.

Or...

"We have a few minutes," he says, his voice making it perfectly clear how he'd like to make use of that time. There'd be hands and tongue and very fast, very hot orgasms. Guaranteed.

At that I grab my pillow and smack him over the head.

He flinches, throwing up his arms, and I hit him across the face. The pillow makes a soft whap noise as it slaps him.

He scrambles up in bed, the sheet dropping and displaying a large, naked man ready for loving.

I hit him again and then leap off the bed. I back against the door, feeling for the handle while holding the pillow between us.

Looking down, I'm only in a pair of unfamiliar pink heart underwear and a matching push-up bra. This creep undressed me and put me in cotton underwear. I haven't worn cotton underwear since puberty.

I hold the pillow like a shield in front of me. "Don't come near me."

The man holds up his hand. "If this is about the party, we don't have to..."

He stands as he talks, making his way around the bed, inching past the clothesline. With every word he comes closer. Every naked inch of him.

The tiny room is even tinier with him moving through it. Standing. Coming closer.

"I said don't come near me." I shake the pillow at him.

I wonder, is he talking about the birthday party my mum threw? Is that the party he means?

"Do you know my mum?"

Without looking he grabs a pair of shorts from the

clothesline and shoves his legs through them. "What kind of question is that? You feeling all right?"

He takes another step forward. Only the smallest space separates us. He reaches out, as if he's going to feel my head for a fever.

I fling the pillow at him. "Stay back!"

He snaps the pillow from the air, catching it before it can hit him, and then casually drops it to the floor.

"Maybe you should come back to bed," he says, his expression one of concern.

Yeah. Right.

I'll get back into bed with him when hell freezes over.

Hopefully, he hasn't locked the bedroom door.

"I don't know what you want, but whatever it is, you aren't going to get it."

He frowns.

"And, you have a wife." I point at the wedding picture. "What kind of immoral psychopath are you? What would she say?"

He gives me a funny look. "I imagine she'd say we should go back to bed. She'd probably ask for coffee. You want some?"

Oh my word.

He's out of his mind.

"I'm going to leave, and if you try to stop me, you will regret it for the rest of your life."

His forehead wrinkles and his mouth falls slightly open as if he has no clue what I'm talking about.

I take advantage of his momentary confusion. I dart forward and kick him in the shin. When he bends over in surprise I shove him, pushing him back. He stumbles and trips backward over the bed. He grabs at the air, his arms pinwheeling. His arm catches on the clothesline and the clothes fall on top of him.

While he's buried in a pile of worn-out beach-bum wear, I grab the dress on top and fling open the bedroom door.

Thank goodness it wasn't locked.

I clutch the dress and run into the hall.

I look in both directions. I have maybe five seconds before the man climbs out of the clothing avalanche and is on my heels.

To the right there's a closed door with a handwritten "Keep Out" sign on it and a tiny bathroom with a gray tile floor and a shower drain, a rusty toilet, a soup-bowl-sized chipped sink, and a rusty shower head over the toilet.

To the left, down the short hallway, there's a small kitchen with a pint-size refrigerator, a two-burner stove, and a three-foot-long wooden counter with a bowl of fruit on top, a bag of bread, and a drying rack full of baby bottles. There's also a round four-seater kitchen table and a small living room where a rattan loveseat with a tropical leaf print and two rattan chairs surround a glass coffee table.

The living room is piled with baby toys—colorful alphabet blocks, a toy telephone, an army of yellow and red dump trucks and garbage trucks, a stuffed whale.

I sprint toward the living room and to the door I assume leads outside.

Behind me, from the hallway, I hear the piercing wail of a baby crying. Then I hear a loud thump as if the man's fallen. Then a low swear. So yes. He must've tripped again.

I run through the living room, jumping over an alphabet-block tower and dodging a red dump truck.

As I pass the couch I startle. There's a gangly teenage girl there, dressed in a black bikini top and cutoff jean shorts. She has short, curly brown hair and cheeks that still haven't lost their baby fat. She's all arms and legs and big eyes. She's lying upside down, her legs propped on the back of the couch, reading a book.

When I step on a baby doll and it cries, "Mama, mama," the girl looks up from her book.

"Finally. I'm starving. Can you make banana pancakes?"

I stop at the front door, my hand on the cool metal doorknob.

This teenager knew I was here?

She expects me to cook for her?

"Why are you in your underwear? Where are you going?"

Oh gosh. She's in on it. The teenager is a delinquent, following in her criminal father's footsteps.

But then again, maybe not. Maybe she doesn't know the truth. Maybe she'll help me.

"Your father has kidnapped me," I say, my voice urgent and low. I dart a look back at the hall to make sure he isn't coming yet. "If you call the police and turn him in, things will go easier for you."

"Dad!" the girl shouts, sitting up and dropping her book. "Mom's acting crazy!"

There's another bang and the crying of the baby grows more insistent.

Mom?

Mom?

"Becca, can you get Sean?" the man yells, his voice echoing down the hall.

He's coming.

He's coming for me.

I can hear his footsteps on the wood floor. He's getting closer.

And that's when I decide I'm not sticking around any longer.

I fling open the door and sprint into the bright light of the day.

10

The heat hits like the door of an oven yanked open. It blasts me with broiling temps.

The sun presses down and the heat singes my lungs as I draw in a quick breath. I've not felt heat like this before. Geneva in the summer has a gentle sun that strokes your skin and warms your blood, the wind brushing coolly over your cheeks. It's a gentle warmth, like the cooing of a mother to the baby in her arms.

This?

This heat is a marauding army of sun and heat and humidity. It presses over me, cloaking me in a sweltering sauna. There's no cool breeze. No dry air. No soft, gentle sun. No.

There's only the loamy, salty, wet-aired humidity of . . .

This place.

My word. Where *am* I?

I blink in the blazing sunlight, my eyes tearing at the bright light.

And then I run across the wooden front porch, jump down the three rickety steps, and land in the spiky, short grass growing in hot sand.

The grass tickles, the sun-hot sand burns, and little gnat-like bugs rise from the grass to swarm my bare legs.

Less than thirty feet away, down a short bluff, the sparse grass loses its battle to thrive and gives way to a long stretch of flat white sand. The salt-and-sea smell? The crashing hiss of waves?

Well, I'm not in Geneva. I'm not even in Switzerland. I'm definitely not in Europe. In fact, I'm not sure I'm in the Northern Hemisphere.

The sea stretches before me. Which sea? I don't know.

The water rolls over the beach, rushing forward in frothy white waves that kick up tiny pink-and-white seashells, tinkling with a musical sound, and then pull back into the shallows. A gull swoops down, its white wings stark against the brilliant blue sky. The water is a stain of every shade of blue I've ever seen, all bleeding into one another, forming an endless tapestry of indigo, cerulean, turquoise, and sky-blue. As far as I can see it's only water.

Water and nothing more.

No boats.

No ocean freighters.

No land in the distance.

The heat, the bright sun, and the roar of the waves crashes over me.

Behind me, back in the tiny ocean cottage weathered by wind and salt, there's a muffled call—"Becca!"—drowned out by the waves.

In front of me is the endless ocean expanse.

The sun prickles my skin like hot needles poking at my bare flesh. My ankles are starting to itch, the little gnat bugs feasting on my bare legs.

I can't go back. Not to that house and that man.

I can't jump in the ocean and swim away—there's nowhere to swim.

A few seconds have passed since I burst from the house. The realization I'm in trouble wraps around me like a tight fist, making my breath short and desperate.

"Well! She's naked, isn't she? I told you she had her breasts done. I told you, Maranda."

"Be quiet, Essie!"

I swing to my left at the outraged voice of the older woman.

Fifteen feet away, under the dappled shade of a squat tree—one of those thick, succulent-leaved, twisted, grizzled bark trees that thrive on salt air—sit three old women at a folding table. They have a pile of dried palm leaves that they're twisting and weaving and making into . . . fans? Rope? Baskets? I don't know.

They're all staring at me as if I'm a rat they found swimming the backstroke in a bowl of sugar.

It's hard to tell them apart. They're all shriveled and dry like prunes left out too long in the sun.

The one who spoke, Essie, has thick, swollen knuckles—the kind that come with arthritis and age. Liver spots coat her hands and face. But she's working hard, the dried palm flashing between her fingers as she stares at me.

"Put that dress on!" the one called Maranda snaps. She's small, a tiny woman with short white hair, long ears, and dark, nearly black eyes.

"You shoulda raised her better," says the woman whose name I don't know. She has salt-and-pepper hair, but I think she's the oldest of them all, maybe mid-nineties. She has a voice as creaky as a squeaky rocking chair.

"That boy shoulda taught her better," says Essie. "Seems he can't control her, don't it? Running round naked. I never seen breasts that stand up like that."

I inch toward them, taking slow, small steps while darting nervous glances back at the cottage where the man and his daughter are.

It seems I'm in a small beach community. Past these three women are a half-dozen more cottages. They're small, square, probably no more than one or two bedrooms each. They're painted bright colors—seashell pink, coral orange, turquoise blue. The sun and the salt air has weathered the wood, so peeling paint and gray wood peeks through on all of them. Even the glass windows have salt and sand coating them, so they don't quite glisten in the sun.

There are tall palm trees spaced about, green coconuts hanging in clusters from some. A line of bushes weaves around the cottages. Bright fuchsia, pink, and salmon-orange flowers bloom in profusion. It's a sunbaked postcard of a tropical paradise.

Slowly, so I don't scare the women, I approach. I drop the dress over my head, the white cotton whispering over my skin. When the shade of the tree falls over me, the sand between my toes turns cool and the temperature folds from scalding to bearable.

"Excuse me," I say, turning to Maranda. She seems to be the one in charge. At least the other two seem to take their cue from her, and she has a presence I recognize from business as that of a leader.

    I glance back at the house again. The doorway is still empty.

    I lean close, sweat prickling my brow. "I'm here against my will. The man in that house brought me here without my knowledge. I need help. Can I use your phone to dial the police?"

    As I speak, a change drifts across the women like a stiff breeze. First confusion, then astonishment, and finally, laughter.

    Essie snorts into her swollen hands, eyeing me like I just said the funniest thing she's heard all year. The woman with salt-and-pepper hair cackles with a creaky laugh and slaps her thigh.

    Maranda stiffens, her back straightening and her hair nearly standing on end from a sudden gust of wind from the sea. "You what?"

    "My name is Fiona Abry. I'm a British and Swiss citizen. Please, if you let me use your phone, I will pay you."

    The laughter stops.

    "A phone?" the woman with salt-and-pepper hair asks, her forehead wrinkling and creasing in confusion.

    "Who's Fiona Avery?" Essie asks.

    "Me." I point to my chest. "Fiona Abry. I need to contact the police."

    "Would you like a cup of tea?" Maranda asks, standing suddenly.

    I was right, she's only about four foot eleven and her shoulders are stooped, and her light green housedress nearly swallows her, but, she's definitely the one in charge.

"No, I'd like a phone. I'll pay you. A thousand dollars for a phone."

"A thousand dollars!"

"What kind of dollars?"

"Shh." Maranda cuts her hand across the chatter. "Dee, you know she doesn't have a thousand dollars."

Behind me the noise of a door slamming rattles. I swing around, goose bumps rising on my neck.

It's the man. He's standing on the front porch. He raises his hand to shield his eyes from the sun and then focuses on me under the shade of the tree. When his gaze lands on me, a hot shiver rolls over my skin and a drop of sweat falls down my chest and glides over my breasts.

I feel pinned in place by his gaze, like he's holding me down beneath him, trapping my wrists in his hands and pressing his thighs over mine.

My mouth goes dry, my skin prickles, and a hot flush races through me, pooling finally in my abdomen.

"He's grouchy this morning," Essie says. "Didn't you make breakfast? He's always cranky if he doesn't get breakfast."

He steps forward, his eyes on mine. He's coming this way. My heart beats out a painful tattoo.

"A phone," I choke. "Get me inside and to a phone and I'll give you ten thousand dollars."

Dee lets out a wheezy laugh. "What did you do? He mad at you?"

"Probably he doesn't like her running outside naked. It's those new breasts. I told you, Maranda. Maybe I should get them. I'm tired of tucking mine into my trousers. Hanging too low. Next time I fly to Miami I'm getting some."

He's striding across the lawn now. He moves with purpose, his shoulders straight, arms loose, as if he's used to walking on a wildly rolling boat and he could balance on anything. He has that gliding grace you sometimes see in athletes or men who love to sail.

He took the time to dress. He's in shorts, a faded gray T-shirt, and running shoes. His hair is combed, no longer sleep-mussed. He still has stubble, though, and a sleepy morning look.

But I'm not fooled. There's focus in his eyes and in his gait. He's coming for me.

"A phone," I say again. Then, desperately, "Fifty thousand dollars."

"What are you on about?" Maranda says, looking between me and the man. "You know there aren't any phones on island."

I jerk my gaze back to her. A shock jolts through me.

"What?"

I'm on an island. And there aren't any phones.

"That's not true," Essie says. "Jordi has that sat phone at the shop."

"Where's the shop?" I ask, clenching my hands and digging my feet into the cool, shaded sand.

Dee gives me a funny look, shaking her salt-and-pepper hair. Then she points past the houses, past the flowering bushes, to a small, bumpy gray road half-sand, half-paved gravel.

The man is only ten feet away.

"Stall him. Don't let him follow me."

I can feel his nearness. I can feel him like the sun beating down on me and the sound of the waves crashing over me. I can feel him in me and over me.

I take off at a sprint.

11

THE GRAVEL AND THE BROKEN CONCRETE BITE INTO MY feet as I sprint down the road.

My white dress flaps behind me like the wings of a seagull. Sweat beads over my forehead and runs down my face.

The air, fresher near the ocean, grows even more thick and soupy as I sprint down the road, further inland, toward the green, jewellike mangrove forest and teeming wetlands.

Dozens of snow-white egrets perch on long, spindly legs in the shallow blue-brown waters lapping over the dense forest of tube-like red mangroves. The egrets turn their long necks, their feathers ruffling as I sprint past them.

The mangroves rise out of the water like gnarled old men standing on stilts, their branches and leaves threading together so that one tree becomes another.

As my shadow flicks over a mangrove's tube, a fist-sized crab scuttles down the wood and dives into the water with a quiet plunk. Just as quickly, the egret nearby spears the water lightning-quick, snatches the crab, and tosses it down its long yellow bill.

I keep running. The heady, spice-like, musty scent of the mangroves stings my eyes, similar to a mosquito buzzing in my ear. In the distance the shrill whistling noise I heard in the cottage sounds again, and a V formation of brown ducks flies overhead.

I'm a quarter-mile inland, past the small cluster of rainbow-colored beach cottages. Two hundred meters ahead the mangroves open up and lead to another beachy clearing.

There's a white gazebo on the beach, three picnic tables, and a concrete shower stand with an outdoor shower and a toilet. Under a tree there's a tree swing. I almost stumble on the road, now mostly gravel and sand, because that tree swing looks almost identical to the one I swing on over Lake Geneva.

I can almost hear Mila's laugh and Daniel calling me to come for a swim.

My chest clenches. I hope they aren't too scared. I pray they're okay. As soon as Daniel knows I'm missing he'll come for Mila. He'll take care of her.

Ahead there's a man standing in the road.

He's tall, spindly like the egrets, with skin dark from the sun. He's in a fluorescent orange vest and is wearing crisp black cotton trousers, a white button-down short-sleeve shirt, and a black hat with a short brim.

When he sees me approaching he leans down, picks up the large octagonal sign next to the metal folding chair he's positioned under the shade of a tall palm, and moves quickly to the middle of the road.

I slow, and then the man holds up the sign, turning it to face me.

It's a stop sign.

Up close he has a broad forehead, thick eyebrows, a bushy black mustache, and sweat running down his face in branching rivulets. He also has the firm-jawed, tight-backed look of an officer.

"Wait. You know the rules." His voice has that same rolling lilt the man had, and the old women under the tree. They're speaking English, but I can't place the accent.

"Are you a police officer?"

He ignores me, instead scanning the road behind me, then the road behind him. We're at a junction where the road opens up, becoming almost wide enough to let two lorries pass each other without squeezing.

As the road opens there's a sort of settlement across from the beach. The buildings here aren't wood, instead they're single-story concrete boxes, painted bright orange or goldenrod yellow. There are about a dozen of them, and on the farthest building—a marigold-orange one with a bead-curtain entry—there's a painted sign that reads "Shop."

I try to move around the man—a crossing guard, I think—but he steps in my path and holds out the stop sign.

"Excuse me. I need to get to the shop."

"It's the rules, isn't it?"

"But I need to use the phone. It's an emergency."

"Emergencies don't mean you break the rules. If we broke rules in emergencies, then the rules weren't necessary to begin with."

"Excuse me, but are you an officer?"

The tall man finally looks properly at me. He stiffens, standing even taller, and his shadow stretches across the gravel, giving me a tiny bit of shade. "What's wrong with you?"

"I don't belong here. A man back there took me. I need the police."

"There isn't no man back there but Aaron."

Aaron.

Is that his name?

"Tall. Muscles. Tattoos. Black hair, brown eyes—"

"I know what he looks like." The man's getting impatient. "Seems to me you're the one who took him."

"I didn't!"

The man snorts.

"Are you the police or not?"

"You know there aren't any police on island. They're all on the big island."

There aren't any police? There aren't any phones but one?

"If you're not the police, what are you?"

"Crossing guard."

"There aren't any cars. Let me pass."

"I'm not looking for cars."

This place. It's insane. None of these people make any sense.

"What are you looking for then?"

I check behind me to make sure the man—Aaron?—isn't following me. He's not in sight.

The man makes a disgusted noise. "Planes."

"Excuse me?"

He jabs his finger at the widened road behind him. The concrete and gravel tapers off, leaving only hard-packed sand. "Planes. On the runway. You can't just run onto the airport landing strip. You have to wait. Just like you wait every time you want to go to the shop."

I stare at the man. At his broad, sweat-soaked forehead and his bright orange vest.

"That's a runway?"

The sandy road that runs along the ocean is a runway? But where's the airport? More importantly, where are the planes?

He sighs.

"You have planes here?" My heart trembles out a hopeful beat. If there are planes I could hire someone to fly me out of here. Home. Or at least to . . . the big island?

He frowns at me. "Not now."

My hope deflates a bit.

"Are any coming today?"

"No."

"Tomorrow?"

"No."

"Then why are you making me wait here?"

He lets out a loud humph. "Because it's the rules."

"But if there aren't any planes and there aren't any cars, then—"

I cut myself off at his indignant expression. Even the sweat on his face quivers in indignation.

"When is the next plane coming?" I ask while he scans the sky.

There aren't any clouds, just an expanse of sun-bleached blue as desolate and barren as the ocean crashing on the sand.

Overhead one giant brown seabird soars, caught on

a current, holding still on the air. Its shadow falls over us and remains while it hovers above.

The man watches the seabird for a moment, then he answers, "Sunday."

"Tomorrow?"

"No. Next month Sunday. With the groceries and the mail."

Next month Sunday is three weeks away. That's unacceptable.

If I can call the police, someone will be here today. Even if I can't reach the police, Daniel can have a jet here in hours. I just need a phone.

"Can I pass?"

The man looks at his watch—a Cassio with an unraveling black fabric band—and watches the second hand tick for exactly eleven seconds. Then he looks at me, drops the red stop sign to his side, and says, "All clear. You may proceed."

"Thanks."

Then I'm running past him, down the sun-hot sand that stings my feet, past the beach gazebo, past the flat concrete houses surrounded by sand and palms, past a wooden sign that reads "Clint's Backyard Rum Bar," past a garage with two scooters parked out front next to two lime-green kayaks, past a large building about three times the size of the houses with spicy pepper and smoky paprika smells drifting out, and then finally to the orange building that reads "Shop."

I burst through the wooden beads at the front door. They clatter and clank, and the concrete of the floor is blessedly cool on my feet.

The shop is small. Ten feet by fifteen feet at most. The walls are lined with unpainted plywood shelves, stocked with cans of food—corn, green beans, beets, olives, tomato sauce, chicken soup, spam—boxes of food—pasta, cereal, shelf-stable milk, cookies, crackers—and glass jars of food—olives, onions, marinara, oil.

There's a tall freezer stocked with vacuum-sealed frozen beef, frozen chicken, frozen shredded cheese in plastic bags, and a few cartons of rum raisin ice cream that are covered in freezer burn and look like they were produced in 1982.

The shop is dim and smells like plywood, cardboard dust, and ocean. There's a rotating floor fan near the door with green streamers attached to it. It moans anemically and kicks a weak draft of humid air around the room.

Opposite the door there's a plywood counter loaded with packs of spearmint gum and candy jellies. I'm guessing there's no chocolate, because it would melt and weep from the heat in two seconds flat. There's a large metal tackle box that says "cash" in permanent marker and a large black stereo from the 90s with a tape deck playing a tinny-sounding "Kokomo" by the Beach Boys.

Behind the counter there's a man—Jordi, I assume—and a woman in their late twenties in a heated argument. They haven't noticed me. Instead they're facing off.

The woman is about five foot three. She has bright red hair and sunburned cheeks. She's pregnant, maybe four or five months, and has the look of someone who hasn't slept well in weeks. She looks hot, miserable, and like she wants to take the tackle box and drop it on the man's head.

He has long, sun-bleached hair, ocean-weathered

skin, and the earnest puppy-dog expression of a man who knows he's in trouble and doesn't know how to get out of it.

"You told me you ordered the crib—"

"I did!"

"Yesterday! It'll take six months to get here. The freight forwarding, the shipping container, customs on the big island, then the boat here—it won't get here in time—"

"Baby . . . " He holds out his hands and she smacks them.

"Don't 'baby' me! You had one job! One job! A crib. I wanted a crib for my baby and you—"

"Come on, baby, don't be mad. It might get here before—"

"I'm not a dolphin! It's not like I gestate for a year! Is that what you think?"

"No—"

"I never ask anything of you. All I asked for was a crib—"

The man turns then, ducking his head, and when he does he sees me.

"Babe."

"No."

"Babe."

"No!"

"Hi," I say, and the red-haired woman stops.

"Oh!"

I wave my hand. "I need to use the phone. You have a sat phone, right? I can pay whatever fee you need. I just need to use it. Quickly. Right now."

The man and the woman stare at me as if I'm speaking another language.

Maybe I am.

"The phone. Please."

"Is this about the party?" the woman asks, rubbing her belly. The pink in her cheeks is fading, but she still looks miserably hot and uncomfortable.

Wait.

Do they know about the party too?

Does everyone on this island know that Aaron (maybe) brought me here? Maybe with the help of my mum after my fake birthday party, and maybe not.

"That party," Jordi says. "So much trouble."

"No," I say quickly. "Please. Let me use the phone."

The man, Jordi, pushes his hair back from his face and gives me a long, confused look. "The phone?"

"Yes." I nod emphatically and take a step forward. "The phone. I need to use it."

"Really?"

I nod again, my chest tightening.

The woman rubs her belly in a slow circle and frowns at me. Then she asks, "Did you get the ice cream I sent over? With Amy."

I glance at her. "Excuse me?"

She raises her eyebrows. "And they say *I* have placenta brain."

Jordi has ducked beneath the plywood counter. There's rustling, the sound of metal knocking together, a creaking, and then he pops back up, a gray hard plastic case a little smaller than a briefcase in his hand.

"Got it."

He drops the case on the counter. It's scratched and covered in dust. My eyes widen as he flips the latches and opens it up.

Inside there's gray plastic with vents holding a

bricklike black phone. It's a long rectangle with a tiny plastic screen, large white buttons, and a black phone cord like landlines had in the nineties. There are cords and plugs and instructions on the plastic in Japanese. The hard plastic on the phone is cracked and the edges have melted and warped.

"The phone," Jordi says as if he's flourishing a national treasure.

I lean forward. There's an old musty smell rising from the case. I lift out the black plastic phone. It's heavy. Bricklike in both weight and looks. And broken. Clearly broken. One of the cords is frayed, the metal connector is bent, and the phone looks like someone left it in an oven for fifty minutes while a cake baked.

But just to be sure, I ask, "Does it work?"

Jordi frowns. "It hasn't worked since 2002."

Since 2002? It hasn't worked in decades?

I clutch the cold, sticky plastic phone in my hand. "This is the only phone on the island?"

Both of them nod, watching me like I'm the one who's lost my mind.

"But how do you contact anyone?"

My fingers start to ache from how tightly I'm clutching the defunct phone.

"We do it when the mail plane comes," the woman says, giving me a funny look, "just like always. Do you need some water? Or Coca-Cola? I saved a bottle from our last batch in case I craved it, but you can have it. I think you need it. You don't look very good, Becca."

For a moment I'm too focused on the fact the only contact these people have with the outside world is through a mail plane. Then I register the last thing she said.

"What did you call me?"

The woman and Jordi exchange a look.

"Becca?"

I shake my head. "No. That's not my name."

"I'll get that Coke," the woman says, then she turns and takes quick steps through another bead curtain, back into what must be the storage room.

Jordi scratches the stubble on his chin, then he leans his elbows on the plywood countertop. "You don't want to be called Becca anymore?"

"I've never been called Becca."

His eyes scrunch down and he has that helpless look again—the one he wore when the woman was yelling at him about the crib.

Wait, that's it. "The crib. How did you order it?"

"Um. Through Kyle. On the mail plane?"

Why is that a question?

"Is there any other way to get word to the outside world? Any way at all?"

"No." He extends his "no" as if he's not sure why I'm asking. He looks back at the beads behind him. "Find it, baby?"

"It's down on the bottom shelf," she calls, out of breath. "I can't bend down to reach it! My belly keeps getting in the way!"

Jordi gives me a quick glance, seeming relieved to have an excuse to end our conversation. "Right back."

I nod.

He hurries into the back.

I wait for a moment. Then I drop the phone back in its case and run out the front door, the beads knocking aside.

The full sun, the heat, and the sound of the ocean hit me again.

It's hard to breathe in the heat. You can see the waves of it rising from the road and the sand, making squiggly lines in the air.

My chest is tight. My heart flings itself around my chest like a grasshopper stuck in a glass jar desperately trying to find its way out. I'm dizzy.

I think I'm going to pass out.

So instead of giving in to the hand-swiping black lines in front of my eyes and pushing myself toward oblivion, I sprint to the beach. My feet hit the wet sand, sinking into the cool, foam-soaked, powdery surface.

I drag in quick, frantic breaths, and then the cool waves snap around my feet. The shells and coral rocks picked up by the waves knock against my legs.

I plunge further into the water, letting the waves yank me deeper. I stand then in the sinking sand, the waves up to my knees, the white dress floating on top of the water like a cloud.

I let the cool water flow over me, tugging the panic out of me. As I stand in the crashing waves, unsteady in the shifting sand and swirling water, my chest opens. My breath comes easier. I drop my fingers in the water, drag my hands through the current, and stare out at the unending blue.

Where am I?

Why did they call me Becca?

Why did the old women think they knew me?

Why did the girl call me Mom?

And the man, Aaron, he shouted Becca too.

I stand there, my mind whirling as fast as the eddies swirling around me.

I hold still and quiet, not turning, when the man comes, wades into the water, and stands next to me. The water laps at the bottom of his shorts.

He stands less than a foot away. He's taller this close, his shoulders broader, the magnetic feel of him so strong he's impossible to ignore.

He stands quietly next to me, not speaking. His isn't a gentle quiet though—it's more like the sound of the waves on the beach, restful or tempestuous depending on your perspective.

He holds a glass bottle in his hand, a Coca-Cola. Condensation drips down the lip and coalesces in round beads on the gleaming glass. He stares at the horizon, at where the world seems to drop off into nothing.

"Junie said you needed this," he says finally, holding the bottle toward me. "You all right?"

I reach over and take the bottle, my fingers brushing over his as I do.

My heart clamors, and for some reason I feel like for the first time in my life I've finally dove straight into the turbulent waters.

"Aaron?" I ask, unsure if that's actually his name.

The ice-cold of the bottle seeps into my hand and the condensation runs over my fingers.

He looks over at me then, his hair glinting black in the sun, the light reflecting off the hard planes of his face. A wave crashes against us, swelling over my thighs, plastering the white dress against my legs. The wave drops and the sand below swirls over my feet, sinking me lower into the mire.

He smiles then, a flicker across his face, as fast as the waves rolling past. "You never call me that."

I don't call him anything. I don't know him.

"What do I call you then?"

He laughs, reaches over, and settles his hand around my back, tucking me close. "You're all riled up today."

"Who are you?" I ask again.

He lifts his eyebrows at that, his arm stiffening at my back. "Becca?"

"Tell me," I say insistently. A cresting wave hits me, the foam spraying up, and I knock against Aaron. He steadies me, his hand brushing against my back.

"I didn't realize our fifteen-year anniversary would rile you so much. I thought a party was a nice idea."

I turn to him, staring at the line of his jaw, his deep-set dark eyes, the apology in his expression.

Above a gull cries out and an icy line traces down my spine.

Fifteen-year anniversary?

There's something wrong here. Something very, very wrong.

Everyone on this island is acting as if they know me.

As if they've known me forever.

And this man . . . he thinks he's my . . .

"You're my husband."

He lets out a small huff of air, a stunned laugh. "Ye-es."

I stumble out of his arms, the sand pulling at my feet. A wave crashes against my thighs, nearly knocking me under. A bit of the cola spills out of the bottle over my fingers. The liquid is sticky and cold on my hand.

"Becca, you all right? Should we cancel the party?"

The water grabs at my dress, pulling it down as I scramble up the sandy shelf, out of the water. I back away from him, the tide tugging at me, wanting to force me back to him.

I stumble again as another wave crashes into me. I drop the bottle, and it spills fizzing black liquid across the white sand. A second later a wave sweeps over it, wiping it free.

Aaron snatches the bottle, rescuing it from the water.

When he looks at me, smiling with the bottle in his hand, I'm struck again by how he watches me with such familiarity. It has my stomach clenching and rolling and my heart picking up speed.

"Come on," he says. "We'll go home, get some breakfast. Amy said she wants banana pancakes and I can't make them like you. After we eat we'll talk. We can cancel the party. It's fine. I know you weren't keen on it. I didn't realize how much."

He's guiding me up the bluff, back toward the runway/road, and I'm letting him.

Not because I trust him or like him or think he's sane, but because I'm desperately trying to figure out what's going on.

I don't think he's dangerous. I don't think any of these people are. But I do think they're all suffering from a mass delusion.

As we pass the shop Jordi hurries out, a platter in his hands with a cake on top. "Junie wanted you to take this. She said it's the last chocolate box cake on island. Just for you."

Aaron takes his arm from me and reaches out for the cake. "Thank you. We owe you one."

"Forget it," Jordi says, already hurrying out of the sun, back to the shade of the shop.

The white icing has already started to melt, streaking along the sides of the brown/black cake. However, it's not the sweating icing or the pink frosting flowers leaking over the sides that I'm interested in.

No.

It's the words written on top of the cake in blue frosting.

"Happy Fifteen Years," it says.

And below that there are two names.

Becca.

And McCormick.

12

THE PARTY, AS ALL PARTIES, MUST GO ON. AND SO, unsurprisingly, when McCormick and I round the sandy bend to the circle of colorful cottages, a group of four men are setting up a white marquee tent, metal folding tables, and folding chairs.

One of them—a hugely muscled bald man with a face like a bulldog—stands on a ladder at our front porch. He's tacking up a long fabric sign that has the hand-painted words, "Congrats, Becca and McCormick."

"Becca!" he shouts when he sees me. "How's it look?"

Under the shade tree, the three old women glance up from the game of cards they've moved on to. The largest rooster I've ever seen, rusty red and iridescent black, and two reddish-brown hens scratch in the sand at their feet.

The other three men stop, folding tables and chairs

in their arms. All eyes are on me, waiting for my judgment.

How does it look? It's a white sheet with hand-painted red letters. Some of the paint has dripped down from the letters and splattered over the fabric. There's a splotch of red in the corner looking grotesquely like blood. So. How does it look?

It looks like a ransom note from a horror film.

"Good," I say, giving the bulky bald man a thumbs-up.

At that McCormick gives a stifled laugh. The rest of the men move back to setting up for the party.

The rooster under the tree decides he's tired of scratching in the dirt and jumps on the fluffier hen. He mounts her and she squawks, flapping her wings while he goes at it for about 1.5 seconds flat. The outraged clucking drowns out the noise of the setup. Then, once the rooster has jumped off the hen, Essie kicks at him. "Buy her a drink next time, you! Quick on, quick off. Reminds me of Gilbert, god rest his soul."

McCormick grins down at me, the chocolate cake in his arms. The heat has melted the frosting, so the pink flowers run in waterfalls down the side and the scripted words have morphed into "Horp 15 leals Becco & Moomick."

"I better get this in the fridge," McCormick says, raising an eyebrow at the writing.

I don't care about the cake.

I've got my head wrapped around the situation, and I think I know what's going on.

"I need to talk to you."

He nods then gestures toward the cottage. "While

we make breakfast. Amy's hungry, Sean's up. This crew's going to want food."

My chest grows tight again, so as he turns toward the little house I say, "What do I look like?"

He stops mid-step. "What?"

"What do I look like?"

McCormick looks around the yard, at the chickens, at the men, at the ocean, as if he's asking for help. "Beautiful," he finally says, "As beautiful as the day we married."

Oh, gosh. "No. I mean, what color do you think my hair is? What color are my eyes?"

"She wants a compliment!" Dee shouts as she slaps an ace on the table and grunts, "Ha!"

McCormick nods as if my question suddenly makes sense. "Your eyes are blue."

"Blue?"

My eyes are hazel. An unremarkable hazel.

"Mmm." He shifts, looking down at the cake. "Blue like tumbled glass washed up onshore with the sun shining through it."

I squint at McCormick. The sun's behind him, coating him in a golden hue.

"And my hair?"

"Yellow."

"I have *yellow* hair?"

"Blonde," he corrects himself.

"You're failing, man." A short, thin man with a bushy black mustache, cutoff jean shorts, and flip-flops punches McCormick on the arm.

McCormick lets out a long exhale. I feel almost bad for him. Except I don't have blue eyes. I don't have blonde hair. Yet all these people seem to think I do.

Which means...

This isn't a mass delusion.

This isn't some man who dragged me to an island where the entire population is playing along with his twisted marriage plot.

This is... a dream?

Could it be a dream?

I've never had a dream this real. I've never lived a dream where I've felt so much. But, I don't usually remember my dreams. The only ones I remember are the nightmares about Christmas Eve.

But when I fell asleep I was holding onto Adolphus Abry's watch. My mum said Uncle Leopold claimed it would let your dreams come true.

What if he meant that your dreams would *feel* true?

Because all this feels true, but it isn't.

My mum asked what I wanted. This watch supposedly made dreams come true.

Secret dreams.

Dreams of longing.

So, all my life, have I been longing for an isolated tropical island? Have I wanted a husband of fifteen years? Two kids? No Abry, no loneliness, no loss. Is that what I wanted?

If I could, would I take Mila to an island outside the rush of the world and forget about all my responsibilities? Would I want to find a man who's stayed with me and loved me for fifteen years?

I study McCormick's profile. He's watching two of the men struggle to unfold a long table.

If this is a dream, then I have to admit—at least in the privacy of my own mind—that he's exactly the kind of man I would want to dream about.

He's easygoing, calm, and soothing like a smooth day sailing on the lake. His presence is like a soft balm rubbed over tired muscles. Every time I look at him I'd like to stretch out next to him in the sand and rest my head in the crook of his arm while he kisses me with leisurely patience.

I'd like to taste the salt of the ocean on his lips and the sun on his skin.

I'd like that very much.

That is a dream I can get behind.

I'm afraid to fall in love in real life, but in a dream, where I'm not me and the people don't actually exist? I could open my heart then.

It's funny, when Daniel and I made the agreement we'd open up, I made the forfeit a two-week vacation at the beach with no internet and no phone. Maybe this dream is my subconscious giving me what I thought I didn't want, but what I really, really need.

I suppose there's only one way to find out.

"I'll be right back," I say, waving at McCormick.

"Where—?"

I run toward the wet sand, sprinting through the grass, then across the beach toward the blue waves and the salty mist hanging in the air.

I keep running, not looking back as my feet sink into the sand, pools of water filling my tracks. The waves crash over the coral pebbles, carrying them forward. A clump of seaweed with crabs trapped in the fronds twists at my feet. The scent of sand, salt, and the spice of wet tropical foliage twists around me.

I dash into the water, the waves tugging at me, the cool salt water enveloping me.

"Wake up," I say. "Wake up, wake up, wake up."

I pinch my arm. Hard enough to bruise.

"Wake up!"

And then I dive under the cool water, blowing the air from my lungs in streaming bubbles as I kick deeper, deeper.

I keep my eyes open, the salt stinging. The water is clear. Hundreds of tiny silver fish flash past, moving in formation, and a long needle-nosed fish speeds after them. Fist-sized flat fish with bright yellow and black stripes dart past, and plum-size blue fish glowing like neon signs dart to the sea floor where a cluster of coral camouflages them.

I kick and swim down, down. My lungs burn. My eyes sting. I'm desperate for air.

Wake up, I chant in my mind.

My lungs scream.

Wake up.

Wake up.

I kick deeper. The water pulls at me. I lose sight of the fish, of the coral.

Wake up.

Black seeps across my vision.

Breathe.

I need a breath.

I can't—

Wake up.

Wake—

13

I gasp, dragging cold, dry air into my seizing lungs. I clutch at my chest, drawing in breath after breath. My heart hammers painfully in my chest and a metallic taste coats my tongue.

My vision is black. I can't see a thing.

But then, one shuddering breath after another, I realize that isn't true. The moon sends a silver sliver of light through my window to spear my bed. It illuminates the room enough for me to see.

I'm in my bedroom. In Geneva.

The cold air, stone cool and still, coats the room in silence. There's only the sound of my quick, tight breath.

"It was a dream," I whisper, my voice tight and ragged, as if I truly did hold my breath until my lungs were screaming.

"Mummy?"

I glance to the door as it squeaks open and Mila

tiptoes in. She's in yellow-striped pajamas, her hair bed-messy and poofed around her head in a little halo.

"Hey, you." I hold out my hand to her.

She edges through the room, around the ottoman and the armoire, past my vanity, her footsteps soft on the thick carpet. When she reaches my bed she climbs up onto the high four-poster, rustling the comforter as she does.

"I heard you shout," she whispers once she's snuggled down into the blankets and has buried herself against my side.

"I'm sorry. It was a dream."

"A bad dream?" She looks at me, her head resting next to mine on the pillow.

She smells like bubble bath and the baby shampoo she still insists on using. I drop a kiss to her forehead, desperately happy she's here and I'm here, and that it was truly just a dream.

Anywhere without Mila is a place I wouldn't want to be. Not in real life.

"Not a bad dream. Just a dream."

"A good one then?" she asks, then she lets out a big, jaw-cracking yawn.

"Go to sleep," I whisper, stroking her downy-soft hair back from her head.

"Can we go to the beach in the morning? With Uncle Daniel?"

I smile. Her eyes are already fluttering closed. She lets out a soft exhale, and then her chest rises and falls in a steady rhythm.

I settle back into the soft mattress and sink into the silence. I relax into the comfort of knowing my daughter is near, that I have a phone and internet, and that I'm Fiona Abry here.

Then I clasp my left hand, where I'm still holding the gold pocket watch. I haven't let it go.

I hold it up and let the moonlight catch the dial and the steadily ticking hands. It's only 2:12 in the morning.

There are still hours left to dream.

The question is, do I want to?

Do I want to go back to that place, to that man, where I'm not Fiona but someone else, in another life?

I could be someone else there. I could do all the things I'm scared to do in this life. I could discover what it is that the whisper in my heart has been trying to tell me.

My entire life I've felt as if there's something missing. I've felt as if I woke up suddenly in this life and I left something behind. Something forgotten in dreams or memories.

Maybe these dreams will help me find that.

And knowing they're only dreams? I'll live them. I'll live them without fear, because no matter what happens I can always wake up, and real life will go on.

All right.

Here goes.

I close my eyes, clutch the watch tightly in my hand, and will myself back to the island. Back to Aaron McCormick.

14

I'm jerked through the swirling water, a hand clutched tightly around my wrist yanking me to the surface.

I break through the grasping, choppy water and drag in a painful, coughing breath. The air burns my lungs, and my throat spasms and seizes as I cough on salty ocean water.

A wave rolls over me, dunking me again. I come up gasping.

The sun berates my eyes, a bright orange ball in the sky. I blink into the tropical light, my eyes stinging from the salt water. I'm assaulted by color—turquoise sea, cobalt sky, pearl-white sand streaked with gold—and heat—pressing over me, sizzling with surf and sea salt and loamy palms and mangroves.

I'm back.

I'm back in this dreamland.

A man swears viciously. He yanks me toward him,

another wave swelling over us. I swallow some of the water and come up coughing again.

"Dammit, Becca."

I kick my legs, chopping through the water, and Aaron—it's Aaron—yanks me to him. My hair, blonde and long, is plastered over my head, dripping water into my eyes. My dress tangles around my legs and drags through the current.

"What the hell were you thinking?"

He's shouting at me. I don't hear half of what he says. My ears are full of water and the world has a dizzy, dreamlike quality.

He kicks back, his legs cutting through the water, and tugs me to lie against him so we float with the waves, our heads bobbing above the water.

I'm plastered against his chest. His T-shirt is coarse and wet, lifting with the current and flashing the flat, hot plane of his abdomen. I press against the heat of him. He wraps his arms around me then, holding me between the planes of his chest and the firm strength of his biceps.

He kicks in powerful bursts, propelling us back to shore. He's still shouting at me—something like ". . . foolish. . . can't swim, . . . riptide. . . die. . ."—and the whole while I stare up at him, bobbing in the clear blue ocean with canary-yellow and neon-blue fish darting between our legs and bumping our toes.

Aaron's dark face has bleached of color. His full mouth is a thin white line and he's dragging in short, sharp breaths. I press my hand to his chest and feel the heavy, startled beating of his heart.

". . . can't swim worth a damn and—"

"I can swim," I interrupt.

He blinks, pulled from his soliloquy. "No. You can't."

"I can. I just don't like to."

And then, because he looks so scared and so confused, I reach up and press my hand to his cheek. I scrape my fingers over his stubble. He's warm, wet, and I drag my hand over his jaw. A wave crests and we ride it, pushed toward the shallows.

He draws in a shaky breath, and so I press my thumb to his lip, smoothing out the tight line of his mouth. He closes his eyes and waterdrops fall from the dark lines of his eyelashes.

"Thank you," I say, floating closer to him. Then, because I want to, and because this is a dream and he's the man who tried to rescue me, I take my thumb from his mouth and replace it with my lips.

He tastes like salt and sea, almost like tears caught at the edge of your lips, salty and sorrowful on your tongue. His mouth is hard, but as I brush my hands over his checks and tangle my fingers through his smooth, wet hair, a wave presses me closer to him and his mouth opens to mine.

He makes a low, broken noise, and then he grabs my hips and pulls me closer. I wrap my legs around his middle, grip his face, and dive into his kiss as if I'm diving into the sea.

He stumbles as his feet hit the sand, the water shallow enough for him to touch, and then his hands are on my back, reaching down to my thighs. His fingers dig into my legs and tug me to him, pressing me against him.

A sharp jolt jumps through me as I settle against the hard length of him. Then I kiss him, lick his lips, touch the tip of my tongue to his, and delight in the heat that arches between us and lights my insides as bright as the noonday sun.

His hands scrape over my thighs, and his fingers and the current drag my dress higher. The buoyancy of the water presses me closer, and all around us there's salt and ocean and heat.

Aaron kisses me as if he's never kissed me before, as if he's drowning and the only way to survive is to press his mouth to mine and devour me. He kisses like a man given a second chance at life.

He doesn't kiss like a man married fifteen years. He kisses as if this is our first time and he's been aching for me for years.

His hands draw over me, as soft as the salty sea. His mouth is firm, slanting over mine, breathing me in. He tugs me into him, pressing every wet inch of us together, as the waves rock us closer.

And then, as suddenly as he dove in, he yanks his mouth from mine. The shock of his sudden absence has me blinking, stunned, into the bright light.

I'm panting, blinking at the blinding sunlight glinting in crystal sparks off the sea. Aaron takes a heaving breath, and his chest shudders as he slowly exhales. Finally, looking away from me, he carefully takes his hands from my thighs, setting me back from him to float free.

Even though I'm the one who—in this dream—almost drowned, he's the one who looks shaken and pale.

On the beach, the three old women under the tree stare in our direction, their hands shielding their eyes from the sun. The four men, working to set up the party, are all turned our way. Not worriedly, but more curious. Except for one of them—a long-limbed, taller one with copper-colored hair, who is jerking the chairs open and punching them down into the grass with a force that borders on angry.

On the porch of Aaron's house, the teenage girl dressed in her bikini and shorts peers our way. There's a toddler in her arms, waving a yellow plastic beach shovel in the air.

"Why did you do that?" Aaron asks. His shirt is plastered to his chest, now see-through and showing the outline of his abs and the lines of his tattoos.

"Kiss you?"

He turns to the side, his jaw hard. I'm not sure why, but I get the impression he's angry about the kiss. Although that doesn't make sense considering earlier he wanted to take me back to bed and make long, sweet love.

Hmm.

"Why did you run into the water when you know there's riptides and you know you can't swim? And you know what happened and how it—"

He cuts himself off, his mouth closing again into that tight, rigid line.

What happened?

"What?"

His eyes darken, the brown tinging to velvety black. "I know you haven't been happy. Not for a long time. But . . . don't . . ."

I scared him, this dream man.

"I'm sorry." I smile. "I'm happy. Why wouldn't I be?"

His eyebrows rise, and I get the feeling I said something he didn't expect.

"What?" I ask.

"You're happy?" He doesn't seem to believe me.

I look around. Feel the soft, air-like salt water cradling me. Take in the colorful island cottages on the beach. Feel the sun stroking over me in hot-tongued heat. Smell the sea and the loamy tropical scents bursting with spice and floral perfumes.

This place is uncomplicated. It's far from life, and I don't have to worry about missing anything, because when I wake up I'll be back in Geneva.

I can be happy here.

"I am," I say, smiling at him.

He still looks skeptical. His brow is furrowed and water runs down the side of his face and down his neck, back to the sea.

I wonder...

"Aren't you?" I ask, wondering about this morning and the rescue and the kiss.

His gaze moves to my lips and then just as quickly flickers back to my eyes. Then he forces a smile that doesn't quite reach his eyes. "Come on. Let's get cleaned up and make banana pancakes. We have a busy day."

He takes my hand and pulls me from the water. The sea flows off us in rivulets as we climb from the sandy shelf onto pink seashells and rounded sea stones. The shells poke my bare feet and the cool, frothy surf pools around my toes, trying to tempt me back into the water.

Aaron's grip is firm, his hand slick and hot as his fingers twine tightly through mine. He tugs me up the beach and my feet sink into the soft, wet, powdery sand. The breeze has kicked up and my wet dress, sticking to my skin, flops in the wind. The wind prickles as the salt and water wicks away.

At the edge of the sand and the grass, Essie calls

out, "What's in your head, girl? Aaron dropped the cake to go after you, and now look! No chocolate box cake!"

Aaron's grip tightens on mine, and I take a step closer to him as I turn to look where Essie's pointing. In the spiky grass and the sand the chocolate cake is smashed and goopy. All three chickens parade through the mess, pecking and gobbling, white, blue, and pink frosting painting their beaks in icing lipstick.

It reminds me of the cake Mila tipped over last night, only a wilder version. I wonder if my subconscious pulled that scene into this moment. It's like when I have a stressful day at work and one of my VPs shows up in my dream juggling flaming clocks or cracking open chocolate cauldrons.

"Sorry, I'll get another." I stare as the rooster makes a dash at one of the hens and they slide around the frosting.

"There isn't any more box cake on the island. Junie said this is the last." Essie gives me a disgusted look and then stares pointedly at my wet white dress.

That's when I realize I'm wearing white, it's wet, and now see-through. Everyone can see my lovely pink heart cotton underwear and bra. It's like those dreams when you're naked in front of people—oh wait, it *is* a dream where I'm practically naked in front of people.

Thankfully, the men aren't staring—they're all politely turned away, arranging the tables and chairs—and all the women except Essie have their attention on the cake remains.

Aaron steps closer, shielding me from the men's view. "We'll figure something out," he says to Essie, then he squeezes my hand.

I look up at him and he stares down at me, his eyes

clear of the hunger and need that was there when we were kissing.

"Mom, can we eat yet?" the girl calls from the porch.

I startle and pull my hand from Aaron's grip.

The toddler lets out a babble and a shout that sounds a lot like, "Bana pan bana pan!"

I frown. This could be trouble. I'm a terrible cook—this is why Annemarie cooks for us, and even Daniel, and sometimes Max. Not me. My cooking repertoire consists of cheese toasties, beans on toast, and eggs on toast. Even porridge is beyond me—it always ends up tasting like half-dried glue with the consistency of pebbly cement.

But you know what? It doesn't matter. It's a dream.

I can swim. I can kiss. I can love. And I can cook.

15

Okay, I can't cook.

Not even in dreams.

The pancakes are flat, gelatinous, wriggly frisbees that have the consistency of squid and the taste of wet socks. You'd think the bananas would've rescued the breakfast, but apparently I was supposed to cook them and not just peel them. So I mashed them up and put them in a pan, and I don't know how it happened, but suddenly they were black and burned and bitter.

I chew a bit of the banana, and a crispy chunk of charcoaled fruit crunches between my teeth. It's bitter and burnt, but sadly it tastes better than the pancake.

The acrid scent of burned banana curls through the air and the only sound at the little table is the slow scrape of forks across ceramic plates. Aaron hasn't looked up from his plate. He's hunched over it like a soldier wading through a battle he's not sure he'll win.

The teenager is stabbing at the pancake, cutting it

into smaller and smaller bits, then scraping them around her plate like she's creating abstract art.

Even the toddler is quiet. He's currently staring at a clump of pancake he's squeezing like Play-Doh between his fingers. He gums at it and then wrinkles his nose in disgust and drops the ball of goop to the wood floor.

The toddler is maybe eighteen months. He has wispy copper-penny hair, blue eyes, and a chubby baby belly, chubby cheeks, and even chubby fingers. He has the habit of smashing food in his fist and then watching it squirt out between his fingers. If it makes a squishy noise he chortles with glee.

When he first saw me he lifted his arms and said, "Mamamamama."

There were tears at the corners of his eyes and his little button nose was red. I pulled him into my arms and he dropped his head to my chest and sighed as if to say, "Where have you been?"

I kept him close as I dried off and changed, letting him toddle around me dressed only in a nappy, dragging a raggedy-eared bunny over the wood floor behind him.

I set down my fork and lean back in the old wooden chair, its joints swollen in the humidity. It creaks and moans as I do. The only delicious part of the meal is the coffee. I make good coffee.

I take a sip of it now, cradling the chipped orange mug in my hands. The heat of it spreads through me and a drop of sweat drips down my back. I set the mug back on the table.

"It's so gross. I can't eat it—"

"Amy," McCormick says, shaking his head.

"It is! Even Sean won't eat it, and he chews on flip-flops if you don't stop him." She smacks her fork to the table and Sean squeals at the noise.

"Mom isn't feeling great—"

"Neither am I! Mom." She focuses on me, leaning across the table. "I want to go to New York this Christmas, and I want—"

"You're not going to New York." McCormick glances at me—a look that tells me this isn't the first time he's had this conversation with his daughter.

"But why not? I've never left the island. Never. I feel like I'm in a prison. I'm fourteen years old and I've never been *anywhere*. I'm stranded at sea like Robinson Crusoe, except he eventually gets to *leave*."

"Maybe next year—"

"You say that every year! Yet here I am, stuck on four square miles of rock in the middle of the ocean. Forever. I hate it here. I want to go to New York. I want to meet people. I want to explore. I want to live!"

I'm caught up in her passionate plea. Her dark hair is wildly curly and bounces around her cheeks with every word. She's so animated. Her hands flash through the air, darting like the silver fish that swam below us in the ocean. She flings herself forward and back in time with her argument. She's red-cheeked and impassioned, extolling all the reasons she should be allowed to break through the bars of her prison and fly to New York City for Christmas.

Watching her, I wonder, was I ever that passionate? Did I ever want something so badly that I nearly vibrated from the desire?

Once, maybe.

But then that potion turned out to be poison, so I haven't trusted that impassioned feeling since.

"Amy—"

"Dad! You don't understand." She picks up the paperback book on the table next to her plate. It's a tattered, yellow-paged copy of "Robinson Crusoe." "The fictional people in this book are more alive than I am. They've lived more in three hundred pages than I've lived in my entire life! Sometimes I feel as if I'm going to die here, never having left, and no one is going to notice and no one is going to care. How can I live if I'm not allowed to leave this island? Am I even alive if I'm not living? What's the point?"

Well.

I've never had a dream where the people in it are having an existential crisis. It's actually somewhat disconcerting. She's so earnest, so vehement in her desire, that I reach over and press my hand to her arm.

She isn't alive. Not at all. She doesn't exist in the world, but she seems alive, so I tell her exactly what I'd tell Mila. "The point of living isn't where you go or what you do. You can live in a small place, you can live a small life, and it has as much value as any other. The point of living is loving, and you can do that anywhere."

Amy stares at me, her eyes unblinking. "Oh my gosh. Mom. You literally just got back from New York. You and Robert were there for two weeks. You lived in Miami for a year, and Dad, he's been all over the world. And so not letting me go is like, like—"

Who's Robert?

I glance over at McCormick as Amy searches for a metaphor to end her plea.

He winks at me and the wink settles over me,

prickly warm and happy. I flash a surprised grin and he hides a smile, burying it in his coffee mug.

I notice he made a valiant effort to eat the charred banana and gelatinous pancake.

"Hypocritical!" Amy shouts, slamming her hands to the table, ecstatic at finding a word to fit her situation.

McCormick stands then and says, "You can go to New York when you're eighteen."

Amy deflates, sighs like a balloon losing its air, and slumps back in her chair. "Four more years trapped on the rock. Super. Thanks, Dad."

He gives his daughter a salute and then grabs the plates from the table.

"I think," he says, nodding at the stack of pancakes in the center of the wooden table, "we'll not share with the others. I liked these so much I'll eat them later."

Amy snorts.

Sean, who was content to watch his sister's woes, finally decides to throw the squishy banana leaking from his fingers. He flings it, and the banana arcs toward me and then smacks me in the cheek. It sticks for a moment, then it plops to the table. There's a cool, goopy mess on my face.

Sean squeals with delight and claps his hands, little chunks of banana spraying in the air.

I wipe at the banana, smearing the goo from my cheek. It's sweet-smelling with a tint of smoke. I pop my finger in my mouth and the baby laughs. It's not too bad. It tastes like a campfire-charred banana marshmallow.

"Gross, Mom," Amy says as Sean squeals and claps his squishy hands.

I smile. Then there's a knock on the front door and

the copper-haired man who was helping with the setup steps inside. Light floats in, spearing the room, as he stands in the entry.

He's tall, built like a long-distance bicyclist, with hair cropped close to his head and high cheekbones. He's in dark jeans and a flax-colored linen shirt buttoned to the collar. He stands out compared to the other men on the island, all in shorts and T-shirts.

He holds himself in a way that's earnest, with an intelligence that seems to be purposely mixed with naivety. He's the type of man I would never trust in business negotiations because he'd say one thing to your face and behind his back he'd be moving a dozen machinations against you. I've met his type before and successfully left them bleeding (metaphorically) from the encounter.

This is why Daniel always lets me lead negotiations.

"Hey, Becca. We need advice on the music list for the party. You got a minute?"

Gosh, he's so puppylike. There's definitely a wolf underneath.

I glance back at McCormick. He's at the sink, the plates forgotten in his hands.

"Okay?" I ask.

He blinks at me as if he's surprised I'm asking.

There's a tension here. A strange tension curling through the room like smoke from a fire, burning, raging, its flames unseen.

"Robert," Amy says from where she's perched upside-down on the couch, her book in her hands. "Please tell my dad it's necessary for my mental health that I go to New York for Christmas."

Oh.

So *he's* Robert.

The man I supposedly went with to New York for two weeks.

He chuckles then, a deep, scraping sound, and runs a hand through his short hair. "No can do, kid. Your dad knows best."

"But you're his best friend. You can change his mind. You go to New York. Mom goes to New York."

I watch the muscles in McCormick's jaw tense.

So does Robert. His gaze flicks to him and then away.

Robert doesn't seem to note the tension, because he gestures to the door, an innocent, puppylike smile on his face. "The music?"

"Sure," I say, glancing at McCormick. He's moved on to scraping the pancake bits from Amy's plate into a plastic tub. "Be right back."

He nods without looking up.

Robert smiles at me then, a warm light in his eyes.

I follow him out the front door into the afternoon sun, the humidity closing around us. The perfume of the sea and the scent of fat tropical leaves broiling in the sun blankets me.

The yard is filled with six long tables and about fifty folding chairs, a white marquee tent providing a sliver of shade. There are four three-foot-tall black speakers on the porch and the bloody "Congrats" sign hangs from the eaves.

The three chickens peck drunkenly at the remains of the cake splotched over the grass. It's nearly gone, and soon I think they'll have gorged themselves into a sugar coma.

The old women have migrated from the shade of the tree and moved to the shade of a porch at a sunset-pink cottage two doors down. The three men sit on the porch steps, drinking from tall, ice-filled glasses. A porch fan spins lazily over their heads.

"Over here," Robert says, his voice low.

He strides around the cottage, his movements deceptively casual. I frown, glancing back at the closed front door of the house.

Then I shrug and hurry down the steps, sticking to the cooler shade of the eaves, and make my way through the grass. It prickles against my bare feet.

The rooster, seeing me, raises his chest and lets out a long, cake-filled, "Ah uh ah uh oooo."

I laugh at the glutton as I round the corner of the cottage.

Then Robert grabs my wrist and swings me around into the deep shade of the roof and the tall, wide hedge filled with fuchsia flowers. Their scent is floral and cloying and heavy.

I spin around, stumbling as Robert pulls me further into the deep shade, the grass cool and prickly under my feet.

"Finally," Robert growls.

Then he thrusts me against the wood of the cottage. My back knocks against the slats and they dig into my spine. The breath whooshes from my lungs as he presses against me, capturing me between him and the cool, sea-weathered wood of the cottage.

"What the hell," he says, as he bends his head down, eyes hungry on my mouth, "were you doing kissing him?"

Then, before I can respond, before I can shove him away, his mouth crashes to mine in a hot, claiming, possessive kiss.

16

I gasp and swing my arms, shoving and hitting—
Air.
Bedsheets.
I blink, opening my eyes.
"What ... what ...?"
I blink again and my bedroom sharpens, the furniture and the soft morning light coming into focus. My vision blurs and I scrub at my eyes, trying to adjust to the softer, gentler light of Geneva as compared to the bright, scalding light of my dream.
As I do I take inventory. I dropped the watch when I took a swing at Robert. It glints in the sunlight and winks at me from where it rests in the duvet. It's 6:30 a.m.— or at least, it was 6:30 when the watch stopped ticking. I glance at the clock on my nightstand. Yes, 6:30 a.m.
So when I wake up the watch stops?
Hmm.
I glance at Mila. Her eyes are squeezed tight, and

she's stretching and burrowing her face in the pillow. She's always been a slow riser. She'll need to stretch, squint, and yawn herself awake. It'll take a few minutes, but then once she's up she attacks the day with zeal.

I pinch my cheeks, shaking myself out of the dream and trying to shift back into reality. It's strange. I've never had a dream that felt so real. It feels just as real as real life. In fact, I swear I can still taste the robust coffee I was sipping and the smoky sweetness of the banana. My skin feels tight from the salt and the sun, but when I rub my hand across my legs and arms there's no residue of sand or sea.

There wouldn't be though. It only feels real. It isn't actually real.

I'd doubt that fact if I hadn't woken up. That's how real it feels. But I did wake up.

I study the watch as Mila lets out a long, noisy yawn.

I think a lot of people would be freaking out right now, wondering how or why this is possible, trying to understand the mystery. Or they'd be so freaked out that they'd shut the watch back in its box and bury it in a deep, deep hole.

But I spent the first six years of my life with Buttercup traveling from henges to sacred burial grounds, to crystal shops to drum circles, to past-life regression camps to—well, to a vagabond existence where my mum was on a trip to find herself and I was swept along for the ride. I learned before I could walk or talk that some things just are.

I thought Uncle Leopold was just telling a story.

Well, he was, but the story was real.

The watch lets you dream your desires.

There's this thing called lucid dreaming. One of my mum's friends, Roger, used to regale us with stories about it while he smoked a pipe and blew fantastic smoke rings. I remember him because in dreams he'd always make himself fly and eat mountains of sweets and visit the Egyptian pyramids at sunset. He said if you train yourself you always know when you're dreaming, and you can control the dreams and do anything you want. You're completely aware that you're in a dream world.

I think this watch must let you lucid dream.

The watch dial, that deep ocean-blue enamel face, winks at me, shining lustrous in the sunlight.

I scoop up the watch then, and before Mila opens her eyes I close it back into its velvet-lined box and tuck it into my nightstand.

I stretch then, rubbing the back of my neck and the raised flesh there, trying to get rid of the sudden chill.

Robert kissed me.

I didn't want him to, but he did.

In fact, he asked why the hell I was kissing my own husband.

Is it my desire to have an affair? Is it my dream to cheat?

Or is this my subconscious finally dragging up from the darkness the pain I chained up, locked tight, and threw down into the deepest cave of my soul? I thought I'd locked it away; lost it in a labyrinth with no center and no way out.

But here it is, rising up, peeking at me, like a monster with yellow glowing eyes peering in my bedroom window at night.

I'll have to face it, won't I?

That is, if I want to keep dreaming, I will.

Years ago, my therapist told me what's buried won't stay buried forever. Hidden things have a way of crawling into the light.

She was right.

Mila yawns again and then slowly opens her eyes, blinking up at me. Her red hair tangles around her face. She brushes it from her eyes and then smiles brightly.

"It's the weekend."

I nod. "Mm-hmm. Morning, sweetheart."

She darts a quick glance to the window. The sky is summer-blue, light, and clear. Already the green leaves are glistening and twisting in the breeze, and beyond that the lake ripples with cheery good-morning waves.

She bolts up, bouncing on the bed and rustling the blankets. "Let's go to Montmartre and have waffles with chocolate sauce!"

Montmartre is Mila's favorite breakfast place, where wicker café tables are cobbled together under tilting dandelion-yellow umbrellas and tuxedoed waiters flourish plates stacked with waffles as thick as a brick and as fluffy as a cloud, dripping with melted chocolate.

"Yes."

"And orange juice! I want orange juice."

"All right."

"And let's go to the beach with Uncle Daniel! I want to swim!"

She bounces up and down and the bed rocks and sways under her exuberance. Her flame-red hair flies in the air and her nightgown lifts like a balloon with each delighted jump.

I laugh and grab her arm, tugging her down to me and squeezing her in a tight hug. "Are you certain you want to go to the beach?"

Her eyes light up, excited at the prospect of a morning, and possibly an afternoon, spent together. "As certain as pudding after dinner."

"Then I suppose I'd better call Daniel."

We'll go to the beach.

The golden-sanded, cold Alpine-watered, mountainous Swiss beach.

17

I SWING IN THE SHADE OF THE GREAT PLANE TREE, rocking back and forth with the cool, coarse sand dragging across my bare feet.

The sunshine flickers through the lush leaves, splashing green gems of light across my eyelids. The flicking of the leaves makes a soft, mellow hum that rolls soothingly through the late-morning air.

The wooden tree swing is cool beneath my bare legs. I grip the worn hemp rope as it gently swings from the swaying tree limb, my shadow skittering across the leaf-dappled sand.

The little beach with its shade trees, cool yellow sand, and cold blue water is nearly empty this early in the morning. In June the lake still has a chill that bites your toes and jolts you awake.

Daniel and Mila splash in the shallows. I smile as he lifts Mila in the air, water dripping from her bright pink cozzie. He launches her through the air and into the water.

She shrieks with delight as she flies and then hits it with a splash. She bursts to the surface a second later and shouts, "Again! Again!" darting back to Daniel. He turns toward me, a lopsided smile on his face, and I wave at them both.

The wind kicks up and I notice the loss of salt and seaweed and spicy tropical flowers. Here it's fresh water, cool grass, cement, and city mixing with clean mountain air. It's the scent I know. That tropical scent? The heat and the turquoise ocean?

I look to Daniel. He raises his hand, waving back.

I haven't been back to an island with a turquoise sea in nine years.

Daniel, Dad, and I were sailing the Greek isles. Sailing was one of Dad's favorite things, and every year we all went for a family sailing trip that ended at Santorini. I didn't know it at the time, but this was the last trip we'd all take together. My dad would be dead in a few weeks.

But the last night we were on the island, I left the villa and walked along the pebbled beach with its rust-red volcanic formations and towering cliffs. The waves crashed and beat at the pebbles and stormed up on the shore.

I stood there in the moonless night contemplating walking into the sea and not coming back out. The water wrapped around my ankles and tugged me toward the black depths, and I thought, for a moment, that the cool depths would be better than staying alive in the dark and the cold.

The pebbles shifted and I heard footsteps before I saw Daniel. He'd been at university—I hadn't seen him since Christmas. Somehow my little brother had grown up in the past few months and I hadn't been there to see it happen.

He stood next to me, a foot between us, and faced the ocean crashing toward us. The roar of it nearly drowned out his words when he asked, "What is it?"

I hadn't told anyone. Not my friends, not my mum, not anyone. But this was Daniel. And my whole life, whenever I told him something, he always knew exactly what I was talking about without me having to explain. He always understood.

So without looking at him I said, "I'm pregnant."

He looked at me quickly, but I didn't turn toward him.

"Does Joel know?"

"Yes."

And in that one word, in the rawness, in the way it scraped and tore my throat when I said it, he understood.

Joel was my fiancé, if that's what you'd call it. We'd been dating for two years. He was ten years older. He wore custom suits, drove a red Ferrari, and traveled between Singapore and Geneva for his consulting business. He was the type of person who made you feel wildly sophisticated, who made you feel as if you were someone when you were with him—as if you mattered. I loved him with the desperation of a man dying of thirst in the desert begging for a drop of cool water.

He was that drop, and he would give it or withhold it at will.

"He told me to get rid of it."

My voice came out monotone and quiet, as if I was speaking from a great distance.

Daniel studied my face. "Is that what you want?"

Yes. No. *No.*

"He's married," I said instead.

"What?"

"For ten years. He has three kids, a wife. They live in Singapore."

"Hell. Fi, what—?" He cut himself off with a vicious swear, but then, seeing my expression, he stopped, lifted his hand, and then let it drop.

"How?" he asked, and I don't know if he meant how did I find out, how could Joel have done something like this, or how could I have been so trustingly stupid to fall for it.

In that moment I hated Joel and I hated myself, and even for a millisecond, I hated my pregnancy, because if it hadn't happened then I'd still be blind and happy and loved.

I dropped my head, shame making me shake. "I told him we'd have to get married earlier than we planned. I didn't want to be showing at the wedding, and he . . . he told me to get rid of it, and when I said I didn't want to, he . . . he said I was . . ." I stopped at the rigid line and the restrained rage on Daniel's face. "It doesn't matter. In the end he told me he has a family already, our engagement was a sham, and I wasn't ever meant to be anything but the other woman."

"Fi," he said, and I could hear the helpless rage in his voice, cresting over the crashing waves.

"I don't know what to do. It hurts and I don't know what to do." I wrapped my arms around my middle, conscious there was someone there, a baby growing inside me.

I was bewildered, full of stunned disbelief, that someone I had loved so well and for so long could drop me, discard me, so easily, so quickly. It was as if I'd plunged from the sheer red cliffs behind me and smacked to the rocks, cracking open. It hurt so much I could barely breathe, and the pain wasn't fading.

I thought maybe if I did get rid of the pregnancy, if I did wipe it all away, then this pain would be easier to forget. Maybe I could forget I'd been discarded, not once but twice, in my life by the people I loved most.

But then I knew that wasn't the answer. Deep inside, I knew this baby, she or he, would be someone I'd love. I'd love them very much, and even if it hurt, it wouldn't always hurt. Not this much.

And when I looked at them I wouldn't see my pain or my shame or how dirty I felt for being used, but instead I'd see...

I pictured the cool waters of the lake, the calm, mirrorlike surface with silver mist rising in the morning. Not these turbulent waves, but a restful, peaceful lake.

...I'd see someone I loved.

"I want her," I whispered then, my hand clenched and my voice raw. "Or him. I do. But I don't...I don't know how. I don't know if I can do it. I'm scared. I don't think I can do it on my own."

I was filled with so much bewildered pain and overwhelming grief, and yes, even rage. And fear. I didn't know if I could manage it on my own.

"I don't think I can raise a baby on my own."

Daniel looked at me then, and I saw him as that chubby toddler the first day we met. Then he reached over, took my hand, and said, "Then we'll do it together."

"All right. Together."

And then I wept. And Daniel held me.

I think of all the brothers in the world, I was given the best.

I look out now, over Lake Geneva, to Daniel tossing Mila in the air, with her shrieking happily on her way down to the water.

God, I love them so much.

Daniel sees me watching and waves his hand. "Come on, Fi! The water's great!" He grins. "You'll get used to it!"

I wouldn't dive in. Not usually.

But I think maybe that island dream has helped me. Because for the first time in years I want to jump in. I want to join them in the cold water.

I stand and pull off my cotton beach dress, revealing a black bikini to the gentle summer sun and the cool lake breeze dragging across my skin.

"Mummy!" Mila shouts, her voice filled with delight as I stick a toe in the icy water.

Is the island exorcising my demons? Is Robert helping me finally banish the specter of Joel? Or was it that kiss with McCormick in the soft, salty sea that has me wanting to dive into the cool, fresh water?

I don't know.

"Come on!" Mila calls, splashing cold water in a rainbow arch.

So I do.

I jump in and join my family in the bright, cold water.

18

It's night. The sheets are cool on my legs, my bedroom is dark, and the wind whispers against the old windowpanes and the smooth stone of the chateau. I clutch the gold watch in my palm, its warm metal a heavy weight in my hand.

"Am I really doing this again?"

Yes, the watch winks at me.

"Maybe it was coincidence. Maybe tonight I won't dream."

I stare at the blue enamel, so much like the frothy waves of the sea coursing over the white-sand shore. The watch doesn't answer.

I take in a deep breath, one filled with lavender and wood and hundreds-year-old stone walls.

"There's only one way to find out."

I wind the watch, twisting it back to life. The hands spring into motion, ticking down the seconds. I lie back, close my eyes, and—

Robert's kissing me.

My back digs into the cool wooden slats of the cottage. The hot tropical air assaults me. The heady, spiced scent of fuchsia flowers, salty sea, and loamy forest grips me.

I'm pinned between the hard thrust of Robert and the cottage. The slats are scratchy from peeling paint and warped from the humid sea air. I spin dizzily, trying to land back in this moment. The leap from Geneva to here has me spinning.

Robert's kiss is punishing. Hard and fervent. He grips my waist, drags my hips to his, his fingers biting into my flesh. Then, with a harsh exclamation, he lifts my dress, and that's when I finally land in the moment.

"I need you now." Robert swears against my mouth. "Seeing him touch you—"

I rip my mouth from his and shove. Hard.

He doesn't move.

Instead he grabs my chin. "What?"

"I'm married," I say, jerking my chin from his fingers.

"Yes," Robert says, his eyes flicking with impatience. "I'm aware."

I stare at him, my chest heaving, my head still spinning.

I landed right back in the moment I left. It feels just as real as it did before. The prickle of sweat running down my back, the taste of coffee on my lips, the press of Robert's thighs against mine. From around the corner the rooster lets out a scratchy, triumphant crow and a man and woman laugh.

Robert looks toward the noise, waits, and, when there's no more sound, turns back to me.

"Becca," he says, his thumb running a circle over

my hip, "by Christmas we'll have enough money to leave. But until then you know I hate it. I can't stand it when . . ." He pauses, taking in my expression. "It's so hard to love you. It hurts when I want to touch you, knowing that I can't."

My word.

He loves me.

This dream man, who I don't—absolutely don't—love.

In fact, I find him horrible. Like the awful taste of orange juice after black coffee.

I take his hand, the one stroking my hip, and pull it from me.

"I'm married," I say again. "And even if this is a dream, what you're doing, it's not okay." I gesture between the two of us. "Whatever this is, it isn't okay."

Robert leans close and looks into my eyes as if he's checking if I'm serious.

"Becca." He mimics my gesture, motioning between us, "*This* has been going on for three years."

Three years!

"Does he know?"

Robert scoffs, a bitter sound. "The great Aaron McCormick? You know as well as I do that his ego would never allow him to suspect that his wife and best friend don't love him as much as the rest of the world. You know he doesn't know." His eyelids twitch then and he focuses on me. "Unless, he said something?"

Unbelievable.

My demons, they've reared up to the surface, and here they are, ready for me to slay. "What happens when we leave?"

Robert's shoulders relax and he leans over me, the

muggy heat swarming us. "We move to New York. Start over, just you and me."

"The kids?"

"Don't tell me you're having second thoughts. They're better here. Aaron will take care of them."

"That's reprehensible."

His mouth tightens. "It was your idea. It's what you want."

My breath catches, because leaving them behind would be just like what my mum did to me.

"I want to leave my own kids? To live in New York with you?"

"Yes," he says, his voice urgent, eyes on my mouth.

"I love you?"

"Desperately."

"And not my husband?"

"Not for years. Not ever."

"And not my kids?"

"You don't want them."

"I'm an asshole."

"You're an angel."

"You're an asshole."

"You love me that way."

I duck under Robert's arm and move closer to the light puncturing the deep shadow of the eaves and the tropical leaves. I straighten my dress and wipe my mouth with the back of my hand, wiping Robert away. "I'm going to say this once, and only once."

Robert tilts his head and I notice that air of naivety is gone, replaced by simmering intelligence and drive.

"I don't do this. We aren't doing this. I don't leave my kids. I don't leave my husband. I don't have affairs."

Affairs are like clinging white-knuckled to a

wrecking ball as you smash into skyscrapers, shattering windows and destroying lives. There may be a thrill in swinging through the air on that giant ball, but you can't stop the pendulum's swing once it's begun, and the destruction goes on long after you want it to stop. And the ruins left behind leave a scar that rips far into the future.

I wouldn't do this to my worst enemy. Not ever. Not again. It was unknowing the first time, and it sure as hell won't happen a second time with my knowledge. Not even in a dream.

"You don't have a marriage," Robert says. "You don't even have half a marriage. I'm more yours than he's ever been. What the hell is wrong with you? Is it the party? This stupid anniversary party? His last-ditch effort to try to blow a spark into a cold, guttered flame? Come on, Becca. Remember how much fun we had in New York? That's our future." He cuts his hand across the air, flinging it toward the sea. "Not this dying island."

Something more needs to be said. Something to end it all. "My marriage isn't guttered. Last night McCormick and I made love all night long."

At that Robert's eyebrows lift, and then, instead of shock or anger, he lets out a deep laugh.

"Last night," he says, laughter in his voice, "we all cooked for the party until 5 a.m. and then you and I made love behind the cottage while I held my hand over your mouth to keep you from screaming as you came all over me. You and McCormick, you haven't been intimate in two-and-a-half years."

Two-and-a-half years?

I do the math. Blink. Do the math again.

Does that mean—?

I think of Sean's copper-penny hair. It's not like McCormick's thick black hair. It's not like my (Becca's) blonde hair.

"Sean—"

"I don't want to know," Robert says, shutting down my question. "We promised it was better if we didn't know."

I take another step back, moving toward the light and back to the front of the cottage.

If this dream is about fixing my life, if it's about facing my demons, then there's something I need to do.

"I don't love you," I say to Robert. "I don't like you. I don't want you to come near me again. I'm married. I'm staying married. I love my kids. You and me? We're done."

He doesn't protest. In fact, he's studying me as if he's never seen me before. Not in his whole entire life.

I back out of the rippling shade and into the light. The sun hits me and I blink into the brightness. Robert stands still in the shadow, staring after me.

I hurry around the cottage, and then, with the grass prickling under my feet and the ocean roaring in waves over the beach, I run onto the cool wood of the porch and back into the house.

19

I think about what Robert said for the rest of the afternoon. That the great Aaron McCormick's ego won't let him even consider his wife and best friend could betray him.

I'm not so sure.

There was that tension riding through the cottage like the scent of smoke curling in the air, warning of an unseen fire.

When Amy mentioned New York he kept his head down, meticulously scraping the fork along the breakfast plate, refusing to look my way.

I've replayed that scene dozens of times and I've come to one conclusion.

This is *my* dream.

And according to Uncle Leopold, Adolphus Abry, and my mum, this dream shows me my greatest desires. My secret wishes. My dreams.

Apparently, ever since Joel, it's been my dream to

put a cheater in his place. To right a wrong I took part in without my consent.

And maybe it's also been my dream to have fifteen years of marriage where a man has stayed with me. By my side.

And since this is my dream, I'm going to take a taste of love.

Safely.

I'm going to glut myself on love. I'm going to swipe my finger through its rich vanilla icing, devour its velvety-crumb cake, and lick the chocolate ganache from my lips. I'm going to relish every bit of loving, because there's nothing to be afraid of.

McCormick can't leave me—he isn't real.

He can't hurt me—he isn't real.

I can feast on love again without any of the pain that accompanies it.

I can explore all the flavors of our kiss. I can dive in and relish every taste, every feeling.

I like how McCormick looks at me.

I like how he kisses me.

I like how I feel when I'm near him.

And then, when I've had enough, I can leave this dream world. I can close it up, not having lost, only having loved. I can shut the box tight and never look back.

My mum was right. This watch is showing me my dream. I want to be able to love without ever having to fear loss.

McCormick isn't real. He only feels real.

Maybe it's a bit like training wheels. I can learn to ride a bike again, learn to love again. And when I'm confident, I can discard the training wheels and ride on my own.

I smile, thinking of Mila learning to ride her bike. She was wobbly and scared. Her pink handlebar streamers flew behind her as she pedaled hard. She kept her training wheels on longer than she needed them, but then one day she woke up and decided it was time to set them aside.

Perhaps that's how this will be.

One day I'll decide that I can set the watch and McCormick and this island aside.

But until then I'm going to ride.

I smile. The evening breeze is cooler now that the sun is down, and gray-blue clouds skitter across the star-studded sky. There's a night perfume in the air, a soft floral scent that mixes with the barbecue chicken and grilled fish and the potatoes roasting in the hot coals of the beach fire.

The constellations are different here than in Geneva. The stars are brighter, flashing white and blue and red. That's Mars and Venus and even Jupiter. The sky isn't like this in Switzerland, and not in Greece or New York or Beijing. I'm not sure I've ever seen a night sky like this.

There aren't any city lights to smother the stars. There are only the cottages winking sleepily and the fire, sparking and glowing blue and orange in the sand, sending up little fireflies that wink out before they reach the sky.

It's a beautiful night and a beautiful party. There are sixty-five people here—the entire population of the island. And they're all drinking and laughing and dancing and congratulating me on fifteen years of marriage.

Junie is entertaining Sean, playing peek-a-boo with a palm leaf. A group of five kids, ages four to eleven, runs past, waving fizzing white sparklers in the air. Amy sits cross-legged on the beach reading a book by the fire, ignoring everyone. The three old women dole out huge slices of coconut rum cake—a last-minute, much bemoaned substitute to the chocolate box cake.

Across the yard, at the outdoor grills, McCormick catches my grin and his mouth spreads into an answering smile. He says something to the man next to him, his eyes on me. Then he hands the man the metal spatula he was holding and strides across the grass.

I drag in a breath of salt-smoked air and my heart taps out a quick beat.

The speakers blast music, drowning out the waves and the chickens and muting the laughter and conversations.

I watch McCormick cut through the dark, his gaze on my smile.

I wonder what happens when I leave here. I wonder what happens to him. I suppose he ceases to exist.

McCormick passes a group of men drinking beer under the marquee. They all shout at him, lifting their beers. He waves back. Robert's with them. I've ignored him all night, only catching bits of conversation—fishing, hurricane season, off-island trips—and he's ignored me too.

Hopefully it stays that way.

Finally McCormick reaches me.

There's a tautness between us, a rubber band

stretched tight, waiting to snap. The closer he comes the stronger the feeling is.

I'm at the edge of the light, past the marquee, between the grass and the sand, halfway between the ocean and the party.

McCormick draws close and looks down at me. There's his smile and a questioning light in his eyes. And now I know to look, there's also a wariness, almost as if he's scared he's about to be hurt—that he's expecting it.

"You're not joining everyone?"

I lift a shoulder. "I like watching. I always have. I'm more an on-the-edges than an in-the-middle kind of woman."

His eyebrows draw down. "Since when? You're always the life of the party. You and Robert, you always—"

He stops then. Looks away from me. The silence stretches, and that tautness between us stretches too, vibrating with tension.

"McCormick?"

He looks down at me. Swallows. The bobbing of his Adam's apple looks painful.

"Yeah?"

I glance up at him. He's bulky. He takes up a lot of space, both physically and with that something else, that leashed power. The darkness likes him, it brings out the highlights in his coal-black hair, like the blue gleaming of the fire. His eyes swallow the light and the brown-black of them wink with starlight.

His face is more rugged in the dark, and maybe because he thinks I can't see him as well it's less guarded. I could trace the lines of hope and fear from his jaw to his mouth. I know them well because I see them every time I look in the mirror.

I wonder why he loves me. Why he's stayed with me, in this dream life where I'm not good for him.

"Why do I call you McCormick?"

He turns back to me, a single eyebrow rising. He shrugs. "You always have."

"But why? Your name's Aaron. Shouldn't I call you that?"

He looks at me then, really studying me, as if he's searching for something. The roar of the ocean becomes a soft mumble as I step closer. I'm only a foot away now, and I can smell the smoke on him, the charcoal and the heat.

His gaze flicks to a drop of sweat rolling down my neck, sliding along my collarbone and dipping to disappear at the collar of my white cotton dress. Then his mouth presses tight and he says, "You said you like calling me McCormick because it reminds you of who I really am."

"Who's that?"

He lifts a shoulder. "An almost. A never was. A dream that didn't happen."

Well.

"I'd rather call you Aaron then."

He lets out a huff then, an almost laugh. The firelight flickers bright and the tattoos on his arms gleam in the light. His biceps are covered in them, and they trail up and over his chest and abdomen. I can't see them under his T-shirt, but I know they're there.

"I don't mind McCormick. It's true what you said, and it'll be true no matter what you call me."

"Do you like being married to me?"

He glances at me then, turning his gaze from the fire. He thinks about my question. This is something I like about him. He contemplates things. He doesn't answer without thinking—he takes his time.

"I want you to be happy," he finally says, watching me. "I want the kids to be happy."

That wasn't an answer.

Down the beach a firecracker is set off. It whines and then pops in the sky, bursting like a bright white flower, raining sparks down on the ocean. There are yells and cheers and shouts for more. The bulky bald man from the setup bends over to light another, and the crossing guard stands behind him, keeping the kids at bay.

The music has shifted to a slow song. One made for dancing in the sand.

"You wouldn't ever leave me, would you?" I ask, considering the solid line of him, his patience with Amy, the way he scooped up Sean this morning and rubbed his cheeks free of banana before dropping a kiss on his nose.

"I won't leave the island," he says. "I'll live and die here. So as long as you stay, then..."

That's the answer. This island is my dream and he isn't leaving it. As long as I'm here, he'll be here too.

"I'll stay," I tell him, whispering over the waves and the cresting music. "I think I like you." I step closer, bridging the gap between us. The heat of him swirls around me. I ride on the current of it, the taut vibration tugging me closer. "I'll stay so I can learn more about you."

"You already know everything about me." His eyes are fathomless and unreadable.

"Not true. I don't know anything about you."

"Do you want to dance?" he asks, and I realize we're already moving toward each other and my hands are already searching for his.

When I clasp him and settle against the hard line of his abdomen, the tension rolls out of me. I fold into him and rest my head against his shoulder. He lets out a shuddering breath, and it shifts my hair and caresses my neck.

I wonder what it would be like to lie down in the sand with him, to have the scratch of the sand abrade my back and legs as his mouth treads softly over my skin. I think I would glow as hot as the fire nearby.

I wonder. I wonder what he thinks about. I wonder what he does. I wonder who he is. I wonder if people in dreams also dream.

"There's something different about you today," he says, and when I look up at him he seems shocked he said that out loud.

Maybe he is. It wasn't thought-out, only felt.

"Are you real? Do you feel alive?" I ask.

He smiles then glances across the beach at Amy, hunched over her book. "I feel alive some days more than others. I used to chase the gold to feel alive. Then ... you know. Now I'm here."

"What's the gold?"

He laughs and pulls me tighter against him. A glow flows over me like sunlight spreading over the Alps in the morning, brushing them in molten light.

"How about you? Do you feel alive?"

I consider his question.

Have I been living my life, or have I been living a half-life?

I think my mum would say I've only been half-alive. If you don't let yourself experience passion and love, joy and sorrow, then it's a half-life, isn't it?

If you're always caught at the edge of the water or caught in the shadow between the light and the dark, never fully committing to one or the other, then . . . you're not living. You're only watching life pass you by.

I love Mila. I love my brother. I love Max as a friend. But I never let myself venture beyond those safe color-inside-the-lines forms of love. So do I feel alive?

It's uncanny that this dream, this moment, feels rich with life.

Rich with possibility.

Another firework explodes over the ocean, and then another, and another, the loud pops echoing over the music. The sky lights and white sparks stream over us.

Finally, I tilt my chin and look into McCormick's eyes.

"I'd like to feel alive," I admit, and then, "I think I can. With you."

At that we stop dancing, held still in the pregnant heat of the night. He stares down at me as if he's been caught off-guard by my statement, as if he doesn't quite believe me but wants very badly to let go of his doubt and say yes. Yes to whatever, to anything. To this moment.

"Kiss me?" I pull my bottom lip between my teeth and McCormick follows the dragging motion. The breeze stirs between us, bringing up smoke and sea.

"Please," I say.

And then, after a breath-held moment full of tension and struggle, McCormick tilts his head and raggedly says, "You're certain?"

"Yes. *Yes.*"

So he leans down, the warm breeze rustling his hair, blowing sand over my bare feet, catching the sound of music floating in the air and the scent of fireworks and bonfire, and he clutches my hand tightly —clutches it so hard that I feel the weight of him—the heavy, solid weight in the palm of my hand—and then Mila says, "Mummy, I really want to go to the Jardin Anglais to see the flower clock," and I say,

"Not now."

"But I really want to go to the Jardin Anglais. Max said he'd take us this weekend. I heard him on Friday. He said he would."

I blink at McCormick. He's staring down at me, a frown on his face.

I look around. What's Mila doing here?

"Mum, wake up."

McCormick clutches my hand and his grip is smooth, heavy, metal-cool.

"I want to kiss you," I tell him.

And he smiles that smile that reaches deep into my chest and grips my heart.

"Wake up, wake up! The flower clock is waiting! Mum!"

Another firework explodes and a flash of bright white light, as bright as daylight, hits, and I gasp, open my eyes wide, and—

Wake up.

20

The Flower Clock, or L'Horloge Fleurie, is on the west side of the Jardin Anglais. The clock is five meters wide and is made entirely of blooming flowers and plants. It was first created in 1955 to celebrate the one-hundred-year anniversary of the park. The celebration mixed horticulture with horology, and the clock keeps time precisely.

"But *how* does it keep time precisely?" Mila asks, squeezing my fingers as she jumps up and down to see the sloping clock and the giant ticking second hand.

The metal hand is two-and-a-half meters long—the longest second hand in the world.

"It's controlled by satellite," I answer, smiling at her enthusiasm.

"I thought it was controlled by flower power," Max says, winking at Mila.

She laughs and then lets go of my hand and runs down the wide paved path, unable to resist the lure of six thousand flowers bunched together, blooming in a giant ticking clock.

I understand the appeal. My dad used to bring Daniel and me here on Saturday mornings after he'd checked in at the office. On blue-sky summer days, rainy and leaf-soaked autumn days, even days when the smell of snow tinted the air, my dad would sit on one of the green wooden benches lining the path, read the newspaper, and smoke a cigar. The sweet cigar scent would float over the grass and tickle my nose. Daniel and I would run exuberant circles around the small hill and time our races to the ticking of the flowers.

Four times a year the gardeners would change the clock flowers with the season, and my dad would be sure to bring us to see each new clock face. I can count the years, see the seasons through the changing of the flowers on this clock—ice-green succulents, sunny yellow chrysanthemums, plum-purple geraniums, snow-white phlox.

Max smiles over at me and then steps closer, falling in step beside me as we follow Mila.

I woke him when I called at seven, but being Max, he didn't mind. He arrived forty-five minutes later, unshaven, bleary-eyed, and wearing jeans and a leather jacket. It's Max, incognito.

"I'd hate you if I didn't love you," he'd said, mumbling into his phone.

I'd laughed and told him to come pick us up for a morning at the flower clock with coffee and pastries. And then Mila said, loud enough for him to hear, "You promised!"

Max's hand brushes against mine, but instead of

pulling back, he leaves the back of his hand resting on mine.

"How was the party?" he asks, his voice careful.

I glance at him quickly, stunned and confused. How does he know about the anniversary party? How does he know about the island and McCormick—

"After I left. How was it? Is your mom still here?"

"My mum?"

He nods. "Yes. Your mom. The not-birthday party."

Oh. Ohhh.

That party.

I take a moment for my heart to settle back to its normal steady beat. Around us the Jardin Anglais brims with summer-morning life. The sun is a soft yellow ball rising above the leafy trees. The air is soft summer-warm, and the old plane trees spread wide branches over the curving paths. The shade cools the grass and draws brindled light before us. The grass bends from the morning dew and smells sweet. It's a morning smell—the kind that rises with the sun.

Already there are tourists taking photographs in front of the clock. There are families roller-skating, following the long, straight promenade along the lake. Joggers run past, their brightly colored clothes flashing as they speed by. A family with three kids hurries past, the children's shrieks and laughter blending with the birdsong.

It's busy here in the Jardin Anglais. Behind us is the bustling road, the whoosh of cars quiet. Ahead is the lake, deep golden and blue in the morning. The Jet d'Eau sprays its fountain of water hundreds of feet into the air and little white boats bob along the wooden dock.

Mila has already begun her circuit of the clock, running in a joyous loop around the thousands of blooming orange and yellow marigolds and the cherry-red geraniums.

"Do you know," I say, turning to Max, "I think it went rather well."

He raises his eyebrows.

I bump his shoulder. "I know. Surprising. But it was good. My mum's left."

"Ahh," he says, searching my face, trying to decipher whether I'm happy about this or not. Max knows about my mum leaving me when I was young. He knows about Joel. He knows me better than anyone except Daniel.

He's my closest friend, and I'm his.

It's been six months since Christmas Eve, when he pressed his hand against my bleeding abdomen and fought to keep my life inside me. That was the night he asked if I could see us being more. I wasn't ready then. I didn't think I'd ever be ready.

But I wonder.

"There's something different about you today," he finally says, carefully studying my expression.

I let out a surprised huff of air. "Do you know, you're not the first person to tell me that lately."

At that he stops walking, pulling me to the side of the path, under the shade of a leafy tree. Mila sprints past, checking the second hand and then waving as she takes off again for another dash around the path.

I wave back and Max lifts his hand. We watch until she rounds the flowering bend.

"I've been thinking—"

"Not too hard, I hope." I smile but take a nervous

swallow. My throat is suddenly tight and dry.

Max lifts one shoulder in a small shrug. "I try to leave thinking to minds better equipped for such pursuits. You know me. I prefer a life of stupor and stupefaction."

I snort. Max has one of the sharpest minds of anyone I've ever met. The only reason he'd roll into a stupor is because he's seconds from death.

Or, I suppose, after making love. He might relax then.

I glance over at him and he gives me a half-smile. It's the one he uses to disarm people when he's about to pounce. He'll lull them into a sense of ease and then, boom, he'll take over their business or eviscerate them politically. He once used this exact same smile when an underhanded diamond dealer tried to sell him illegally obtained stones. The aftermath was something to behold. And it was all preceded by this smile.

It's his lulling, "don't mind me, I'm just a sweet, lazy lion lying in the shade" smile.

I laugh, the tightness in my throat loosening and my nervousness evaporating.

This is Max. My best friend. There's no reason for me to be nervous around him.

But then, at my laugh, his eyes catch on my mouth and I know exactly what he's thinking.

It reminds me of the moment when McCormick kissed me in the sea. How his eyes darkened and he caught my mouth as if it was the only chance he'd ever have to kiss me.

"Max," I say, my voice raw from the remembered kiss.

He blinks.

"Mummy! Watch me!" Mila shouts, skipping past. I yank my eyes from Max and turn to her, waving. She cartwheels in front of the clock, three, four times, then five. I clap and cheer as Mila dizzily bows. Then she's off again, running another flower-clock circuit.

I can feel Max's attention on me. It's like the breeze running over my bare skin, soft yet insistent. He put aside this conversation last Christmas and never brought it up again.

But it's time.

"You still feel the same?" I ask Max, watching for Mila as the breeze drags over me and tugs at my hair. "As you did at Christmas?"

Max lets out a long breath, his exhale unsteady. "Are you asking if I still love you?"

I turn to him then. My heart echoes around my chest like the beating of a hollow drum. His expression is grave, his gaze steady.

It's funny. Max looks nothing like McCormick. But in this moment, Max reminds me of him.

McCormick is tall and solid, a large, muscled, athletic man. Max is thinner, more like a rapier than a claymore.

McCormick has tattoos roping around his arms and abdomen. Max wears rings and diamonds but leaves his skin ink-free.

McCormick wears work-worn clothing and has an air of physicality and self-sufficiency suffused with an innate sense of decency.

Max wears tuxedos, suits, and on weekends jeans and his leather jacket, all brushed together with his wry sense of humor and steadfastness.

Yet while McCormick and Max look vastly different,

they have something in common. It's the feeling I get when I'm around them. That with them I'm safe. With them I'll never be let down.

With Max I know it's true. With McCormick? I sense it is.

Still, McCormick isn't real.

Max is.

He's real and he's right here.

Max watches me now with the expectation of his ancestors looking upon Rome after a long, arduous campaign. He nervously twists the ring on his finger. His family crest spins, catching the rising sunlight.

He's waiting for my answer.

"Yes," I say softly. "That's what I'm asking."

He exhales then, as if he was holding his breath. He drops his hands to his sides and looks out over the Jardin Anglais, toward the second hand ticking over the sea of red geraniums.

Mila flashes past, her pace slowing. Soon she'll make her way back to us, ready for pastries and a cold drink.

Finally, Max looks back to me and my chest tightens painfully. I see something in his eyes that he usually keeps hidden behind friendliness and laughter. It's a deeper feeling, a yearning. It's the difference between seeing a picture of the ocean and standing in front of it, feeling the cold surf on your feet, your insides vibrating from the roar of the waves.

"If you're asking whether what I feel has faded? No. If you're asking if it's grown stronger? Yes. If you're not asking any of that, we can walk with Mila to La

Potinière, sit at a café table, have a coffee and a pastry, and pretend this conversation never happened. It's up to you."

I stand arrested between the shadows and the light of the leaves overhead, half-in, half-out, frightened of what taking this path would mean.

Walking to the café behind the flower clock, sitting at the outdoor tables beneath the umbrellas, laughing and joking and pretending this never happened—it's tempting. So tempting.

I have to ask, "How do you know it isn't only deep, abiding friendship? How do you know it's love?"

Max tilts his chin and scans the sky. Above us cirrus clouds, feather and paintbrush-light, trail across the blue. His black hair is tugged by the breeze and he pushes it off his forehead.

"How do you know there's wind?" he asks, looking back at me. "No one has ever seen the wind. You only feel it. You know it exists because you feel it. You see the effect of it on the world. You feel it. It's real."

At the flower clock Mila perches on the metal railing, leaning over the side to peer at the blossoms. I watch her for a moment, making sure she's safe.

Then I say quietly, voicing my fear, "I'm terrified to lose your friendship. I don't feel what you do. I don't know that I can. I don't want to start this if it will only hurt you."

Max smiles, a closed-lip, self-aware look. "Let me worry about my hurts."

"Max."

"What's life without risk? It isn't life. It isn't living."

"But if I lose you—"

"Fi." He presses a hand to my arm, solid and sure. "No matter what, I will always be your friend."

I give him a dry look. "That's what I'm afraid of."

He laughs then, grinning at me. "You can't get rid of me. I'm sorry. That boat has sailed."

We smile at each other, living in the memory of a Saturday night eight years ago. His family had been gone for six months. His dad, his mom, his older brother, dead in an avalanche while on a ski holiday. Max was raging his way through Geneva, wrecking his life, his reputation, and his family's business.

I barged into his house to find him surrounded by half-empty bottles of liquor—brandy and cognac—a mountain of cheap, half-smoked cigars, two weeks' worth of beard growth, dirty-clothed, and hollow eyed. It lit an ember of rage in me to see him that way.

I grabbed the closest bottle of cognac and the stainless steel lighter lying near the cigars. And then I marched to his back garden. He followed. I dumped the wine into an ostentatious marble birdbath. Then I flicked the lighter and set the whole thing on fire.

It burned like a torch, raging and twisting.

"That was my dad's favorite cognac," he said, hollow-voiced.

"I don't give a shit," I said viciously.

He blinked. "The brandy was my mom's favorite."

I nodded, stormed back into the house, grabbed all the cognac and brandy I could find, and then brought them clanking in my arms to the garden.

"Do it."

Max studied me for a moment, life slowly edging its way back into his eyes. Then he grabbed two bottles.

The flame in the birdbath had already died, the alcohol burned away. He poured the contents of the bottles into the marble bath, the ruby and amber liquid catching in the dull gray half-light of dusk.

Then he set it on fire.

And I brought him bottle after bottle, and he fed the flames and let the spirits burn.

When he was done, a pile of bottles lay like bones picked clean in the grass. The air smelled sweet like smoke and incense. The veins of the white marble birdbath were blackened. A low blue flame still burned. The sky was dark.

Max turned to me, his cheeks red, eyes alight. A spark of life was back inside him.

He stared at me for a moment, then, "They're gone."

"I know."

"I hate them." His voice cracked and the night closed in while the flame in the birdbath burned low.

"Do you hate them a little less now?"

"They were a terrible family. I never would've chosen them. Sometimes, when I was young, I'd lie awake wishing—"

He cut himself off, unable to say it.

"I know."

His dad was a vicious man, known for his rages. Max's brother was just the same. His mom was hard and unhappy. Max's childhood had a terrible beginning and a terrible ending. Because he stayed and he never escaped them.

"They're gone," he repeated, "and I'm full of guilt. I hate them for leaving. I hate them for leaving me this."

He gestured to the expansive back garden, to the

mansion outside Geneva full of ghosts, and even to the rest of the world.

"You could burn it all. Wreck it. You've been doing a good job. I'd say in a year, eighteen months, you'll lose it all."

He nodded.

"Or you can burn what you need to burn. I'll help you. And the rest of it, you can rebuild it. Make it your own."

"What would you do?"

"I'd rebuild it. I'd make it something great."

"Do you know, I think you would. If I try, will you watch me?"

"I won't just watch. I'll cheer you on. I'll be your friend."

"Aren't we already friends?"

"Not like this." I nodded at the pile of bottles. In the dark they were the bones of a whale's carcass washed ashore and picked dry. A great behemoth, dead and gone. The flamelight danced over the bottles, macabre in its dying. Finally, the flame guttered and Max nodded, decided.

"All right," he said.

"All right?"

Then he smiled and stood tall. For the first time that night he looked at me as if he really saw me. His eyes burned bright. "In the morning I'll take you and the baby for coffee. I could use coffee. I could use your help strategizing how to raze and rebuild."

"Mila."

"What?"

"Her name's Mila. Babies have names, you know."

He nodded. "I know. But I like calling her the baby. It's cute."

I laughed and punched his arm.

And that was the moment when Max decided we'd be friends for life. He told me the very next morning. I'd decided we'd be lifelong friends when he knew I was expecting and offered his friendship and support. The both of us reached the same conclusion at different times. Friends.

But now Max has reached another conclusion. One I haven't arrived at. Not yet. Maybe not ever.

He smiles at me as we stand under the leafy green of summer with the morning breeze blowing past. Nine years of friendship between us. Nine years of trust.

"If you don't want—"

"Yes," I say, putting my hand over his. "I'll go to dinner with you and let you bring me flowers, share a kiss, see where it might lead."

He smiles at that, surprise flickering in his brown eyes.

Perhaps, just like my dream let me dive into the lake with Mila and Daniel, perhaps it's letting me open up in this too. Perhaps allowing myself to love McCormick in my dreams will let me open up to loving Max as more than a friend.

Perhaps that's what my dream is telling me.

I don't know. Right now I'm not sure of anything.

"You're truly certain?" I ask him. "Even if this doesn't lead to more. You'll stay my friend?"

"Don't worry," Max says, brushing his finger across my cheek. "I'm not going anywhere."

I nod and rest my cheek in the palm of his hand.

And then Mila runs to us, skipping between us and

grabbing our hands. She pulls us into the light, her red hair flashing in the sun, and then we're walking hand in hand down the path, off to have pastries and coffee.

We'll spend the morning together, me, Max, and Mila. It's the same as a hundred mornings before. Yet looking over Mila's bouncing head to Max, I acknowledge it's also very, very different.

21

I fall asleep thinking of Max, worrying at the way he squeezed my hand when he said goodbye. I worry that the only place I'm capable of loving is in the safety of my dreams. Although I don't even know if I'm capable of loving there.

The warm weight of the gold pocket watch settles in my hand, the ticking vibrating through me like a heartbeat.

I wake up to neon-bright sunlight shining over my eyes. The light hits like an ice pick and I flinch, fluttering my eyelashes open. I'm on the lumpy rattan couch in the living room of the cottage. The worn canvas fabric scrapes against my bare skin, and my thin cotton dress tangles around my legs.

The warm, humid air thick with old wood and salty sea drags over me. There's the bracing scent of brewing coffee mixed with the lingering smell of bonfire stuck in the fabric of my dress. My legs are tucked tightly into my stomach, and when I look around, the room tilts like a sailboat tossing about on a rough sea.

I moan, dizzy, and the noise ricochets, hammering through my head.

My mouth is cotton-wool dry. It tastes as though I ate a bucketful of sand.

"What happened?" I ask, and my voice comes out like the croak of a dying frog.

"You got drunk."

I blink and even the fluttering of my eyelashes is painful.

Amy sits cross-legged on the floor in a pair of blue pajama shorts and a tank top. Her hair is a mass of messy curls, some of them sticking straight up in the air. She has on a pair of round glasses and she's holding a three-inch-thick novel—Dostoyevsky.

"It's too early for Dostoyevsky," I tell her, burying my head in the scratchy couch cushion. The rubber nipple of an empty baby bottle pokes me in the cheek. I shove the bottle deeper in the cushion and open an eye to peer at the capricious light of the living room.

Amy isn't impressed.

Sean squats nearby on the wooden floor, gripping a wooden hammer. It's one of those toys where babies hit colorful pegs, nailing them into a wooden block. He whacks a peg.

Bam!

I moan.

Bam!

Oh no.

Bam!

Apparently, these toys were made to punish parents for drinking.

Except I didn't drink. "How *much* did I drink?"

Amy shrugs, sticking a finger in her book to keep her page. "Oh, I'd say about . . . hmm . . . there was the rum shots, the daiquiri, the piña colada. It was enough to make you stand on top of the dessert table and sing 'Kokomo.'"

"What?"

"And then there was the tequila, which is when you decided to dance with Robert on the same table."

"My word. Why? I would never do that."

Why would my dream-self keep sabotaging me by making terrible decisions when I'm not around?

"Mom, please." Amy flips the pages of her book, the noise a quick fluttering, and then she slams her finger to the page. "'Above all, don't lie to yourself.'" She looks up, a bit of pride in her smile. "See? It's never too early for Dostoevsky."

Oh gosh. I press a hand to my skull. The hammering there beats in time with Sean whacking his toy hammer on his wooden board.

"I always lie to myself though," I mutter. "If you lie to yourself enough you forget the truth, and then the lie becomes your reality."

Amy drops her book and it thunks to the wooden floor. "That's deep."

The pages of her book flap open in the yellow smudge of daylight.

I shrug. "You can't lie in dreams though."

I slowly raise myself on an elbow and then push myself upright. My stomach rolls a bit, still fighting a battle on a rocky sea.

"Mamamamamama," Sean shouts, gurgling gleefully. His copper hair glimmers in the morning light and his chubby cheeks are rosy-red. He's dressed in a blue-striped onesie and there's a bit of dried milk flaking off his cheek. He waves the hammer at me and I smile even though the motion pinches the backs of my eyes painfully.

"Good morning," I tell him.

"Mamamama!"

"I think he should be speaking more," Amy says, pushing a red wooden car toward him. "At two I was quoting poetry. He's eighteen months already. Sean, repeat after me, 'All alone beside the streams and up the mountain-sides of dreams.'"

I press a hand to my stomach.

"Dadadada," Sean says, waving his hammer.

And then McCormick is there, kneeling in front of me, a cup of coffee in one hand and a glass with a yellow-and-red concoction in his other.

"Morning," he says, his voice scratchy and low. The single word rubs over me like a calloused hand stroking across my bare thigh.

My stomach flips. This time not from hangover, but from McCormick's nearness. It's a pleasant up-and-down sliding, the gentle fall into someone's arms.

I lean toward him, my wrinkled cotton dress whispering over my legs. He smells like soap and fresh sea air. He's clean-shaven and clear-eyed. It's clear he didn't engage in the same nighttime revelry.

A slow heat steals across me, as hot as the outside air. The last time we were this close I asked him to kiss me. I was in his arms, the cool sand was soft under my feet, and he was looking at me as if he wanted to pull me down the night-dark beach, lay me down under a palm, and taste me.

I give him a hesitant smile.

Did we kiss?

Did something more happen?

I study his features. And as I do, the fluttering of my pulse slows and the heat on my skin cools. We didn't. We couldn't have. Because that closeness I felt yesterday is gone. He's holding himself stiffly and his expression is distant and guarded. There's a wariness there, telegraphed as loudly as Sean banging his hammer on the floor.

McCormick clears his throat, glancing away from me, breaking eye contact. "Two eggs from the hens," he says briskly, "olive oil, tomato juice, Worcestershire sauce, salt and pepper. Bottoms up." He holds the glass out to me.

I stare at the concoction, my stomach revolting. "I'd rather the coffee."

I point to the steam curling from the chipped yellow mug in his hand. The black coffee smells so inviting and lovely.

His mouth twitches and he shakes his head. He tips the glass, and the two round yellow yolks slide across the bottom, slipping through the cloudy egg white. The sauce and splash of pulpy red tomato juice congeal in little red plasma-like balls in the olive oil. Salt and pepper sit like fleas on top of the raw eggs. I've never seen anything so revolting in my life.

"No."

This is a dream, isn't it? I'll just magic myself better.

I close my eyes and think, *Cured, cured, cured.*

"What are you doing?" McCormick asks, a hint of amusement curling through his voice.

"Imagining I'm better."

"Drink this and you will be."

Ha.

I open an eye and squint at him. There's a slight smile on his face, the wariness receding.

"Mamamama," Sean says, banging his hammer on the floor. McCormick sends a grin his way and Sean switches to, "Dadadadada."

"This is exactly how I feel about staying on island for another four years," Amy says, pointing out my revulsion for the slimy drink. I get the impression she never misses an opportunity to drive home a point.

"Well said," I tell her, and she smiles.

Then, because my positive thinking didn't cure the dizziness or the rolling in my stomach, I grab the glass, plug my nose, and then tilt my head back and chug the nasty glass of doom.

It's awful.

It's horrible.

It's like two fat slugs sliding down my throat, with an aftertaste of peppery tomato.

I cough, hit my chest, and my eyes water.

"Mama?" Sean says, concern tinting his baby voice.

McCormick watches me with a carefully neutral expression.

"I'm okay," I say, coughing again and then wiping my mouth. The pepper and tomato bite my tongue and the olive oil coats my mouth. It's horrible.

Amy shakes her head and then grabs her book. "I'm going to read on the hammock."

She leaves then, the door banging after her. A gust of wind, hinting of morning blooming flowers and sand, blows through, lifting the ends of my hair.

McCormick takes the glass from my hand then and

replaces it with the mug of coffee. The ceramic is hot, the steam rising. I take a hesitant sip.

It's good. Thank goodness.

McCormick gives a tight smile as my shoulders relax and the coffee chases away the taste of the eggs and oil.

"Thank you."

He nods then and starts to stand. He's turning away, and I can tell there's a lot that isn't being said. A lot that happened between our almost kiss and now.

I reach out and press a hand to his arm, arresting him mid-rise. "Wait."

He stops, crouched before me.

My heart clatters at his guarded look.

"What happened?" I ask.

He shakes his head. "What do you mean?"

"What happened last night after we kissed?"

He jerks back then as if I knocked him off-balance. It takes him a moment to steady himself. Finally, he looks me directly in the eyes.

"We didn't."

"We didn't what?"

"Kiss."

I can't fathom that. There isn't anything I wanted more. In fact, the concoction is already starting to clear my head, and after a shower and brushing my teeth I might like to resume kissing again.

"Why not?" I ask, taking in the hard line of McCormick's jaw and the furrowing of his brow.

"Because you pushed me away."

I shake my head.

"And then went and had rum with the guys."

Oh no.

"And danced with Robert?"

"Right."

What the heck is wrong with me?

"I'm sorry," I tell him, searching his expression for a hint of what he's feeling.

"It was a party." He shrugs. "You're meant to have rum and cake."

I shake my head. "You can be angry if you like. I think you're taking this stoic thing too far. I'd be angry if I were you."

He raises his eyebrows. "You want me to be angry?"

I shake my head. I think about what Robert said. "Was that kiss in the water you trying to breathe life back into a guttered flame?"

McCormick stands then, his shadow falling over the wood floor. Behind him Sean toddles over to a set of blocks stacked in a pyramid. He knocks them over with a quick shove. They clatter to the floor and Sean laughs, shouting, "Uh-oh!"

"No," McCormick says, glancing at Sean and then back to me. "I kissed you," he says in a low voice, "because—"

"Because?" I clutch the cotton of my dress in my hand. A sharp heat snaps between us.

"Because for the first time in my life it felt like if I didn't kiss you, I'd . . ." He looks away, his jaw tightening. When he looks back he almost seems angry. "It felt like if I didn't kiss you I'd regret it for the rest of my life."

The warm air is heavy as I draw in a breath. The taut tension between us expands, pulling back, ready to snap. Carefully I set the hot mug of coffee on the side table. Then I stand and close the distance between us.

My breath is short in my lungs. McCormick watches me stepping closer, his gaze cautious, but he doesn't move back when I press into him and fold my arms around him.

He's warm, solid, and his heart beats solidly under my cheek. I breathe in the clean scent of him. He holds himself still, not moving his arms around me, but not pulling away either.

Once that kiss began, "I felt the same."

He lifts his hand then, stroking it gently down my hair. The softness of his T-shirt rubs against my cheek. I settle closer.

"I wonder," I say, my lips next to his heart, "if you'd like to spend the day with me. I want to get to know you."

"I don't understand," he says, running his hand through my hair. "Since yesterday it's like you're two different people. And I don't know who I'm going to get from one minute to the next."

Yes. The dream me and then the me who wreaks havoc when I'm not around.

"Maybe you need to get to know me better too," I say. "You don't know me at all."

His hand pauses then and he looks down at me, studying my expression. "I don't?"

I shake my head. "No."

"You want to go on a date?"

"It's the weekend, right?"

He nods.

"And we don't work on the weekends?"

"No."

"Maybe today you can pretend we've never met, and I've never been here, and you're giving me a tour of the island. We can take the day and see where it leads us."

He takes a long moment to consider. The only noise is the clack of the blocks as Sean stacks them one by one.

Finally, McCormick lets out a long breath and his muscles relax under me. "All right."

I smile up at him and he gives a hesitant smile back.

22

The breeze sluices over me, running warm hands through my hair and tugging my shirt behind me. I speed down the hill, my bike tires hissing through the sand.

Overhead the elegant casuarinas bend in the breeze, casting shadows across our path. McCormick and I slice through the shadows, and the light and dark flicker over us as fast as the turning spokes of my bike wheels.

I grin over at McCormick as we sail down the hill. The wind whistles nimbly, my stomach rises at my speed, and I feel just like I did as a little girl on a playground swing, kicking my feet in the air, suspended over the earth, my pigtails flying behind me. This is that moment, the exuberance of free fall, where you let yourself go and trust that when you hit bottom you'll spring back up to the sky.

A laugh is pulled from me. I haven't felt so free in years.

We're at the highest point on the island, a seventy-foot rise on the eastern edge. Laid out before us is the entirety of the island. It's a green pearl rimmed by lustrous white sand, set in a flat turquoise sea. Four square miles—tiny—with a long, thin strip of sand off the northwestern edge.

McCormick claims the thin strip of land connected to the circular island made explorers name this place Frying Pan Island.

Far off, toward the southwest, there's a coral reef off the shore. The waves hit and then crest in white froth. The water is indigo-blue until it reaches the reef, and then, with the calm, it settles into a gentle translucent green-blue. I think I'd like to create a watch dial enameled that exact shade.

Past the reef-calm beach, on a half-moon of sand, the cottages line the sea. I can pick out the white and turquoise of our cottage and the salmon-pink, sea-blue, and coral-orange of the others. They sit under waving palms, their porches facing the sea.

Then, through a stretch of green, along a snaking yellow-sand road, the little beach runway and the congregation of marigold-orange and goldenrod-yellow concrete buildings glimmer in the sun. That's the town, and it's just as small from above as it is down below.

Beyond that there's only green. Vibrant, jewellike, lush, leafy green. It's the dark green of the mangroves, filled with life and deeply shadowed mysteries. It's the lime green of the palms, their narrow leaves flipping in the breeze like the fluttering of a hummingbird's wings. It's the rosemary green of the casuarinas, coolly elegant and noble, sending hints of evergreen and Christmas pine through the air.

I take a deep breath of it now, pulling in the subtle pine scent. The speed of my bike slows as the slope evens out then crests into another rise. I pedal, pushing to climb the small rise. Needles from the casuarina trees—the whistling pines—crackle under my bike tires. The path narrows here and my bike bumps over the shallow root system of the pines.

A drip of sweat trails down my neck, then down my chest, pooling under my breasts. My cheeks are hot—pink, I'm sure—and a line of sweat beads my forehead. My heart pumps from the effort of the climb, and I drag in another pine-rich breath.

At the top of the hill, beneath the dappled shade of a tall, wide-limbed casuarina, McCormick pulls to a stop.

His skin gleams with sweat and his black hair is messy from riding through the wind. His sun-dark cheeks are pink from the sun and the heat, and there's a happy "just sped downhill with the wind whipping around me" contentment radiating from him.

I wheel beside him, setting a foot in the sand to prop my bike upright beneath me.

We stand quietly for a moment, our breath loud, the wind whistling through the needles overhead.

A dove-gray bird with a white-striped tail perches in the boughs overhead. It lets out a melodic song and then launches from the limbs, its wings flapping loudly, seeking another spot to shelter.

My heart rate has slowed and the shaded breeze sends a cool hand over my prickly-hot skin.

After I showered and ate a quick bowl of porridge for breakfast—made by McCormick—we kissed Sean goodbye and thanked Amy for babysitting. She promised to enthrall her baby brother with poetry and then visit their Great-Grandma Essie for lunch.

McCormick pulled two bikes out from behind the cottage. They were old beach bikes with dented frames and sun-bleached seats. But the tires were thick for pedaling in the sand, and when I rode the hills it flew, and when I braked it screeched to a stop.

When I first saw the bikes I laughed and asked where the car was, and McCormick gave me a funny look and said, "There aren't cars on island," so I said, "Remember, we're pretending I've never been here. You have to tell me everything."

So while we biked along the sandy gravel road that circles the island, McCormick pointed out the large rectangular metal generators that power houses and businesses (they don't always run—often the islanders go without power), the large circular cisterns that collect rainwater, the vegetable gardens growing glossy peppers, sweet potatoes, clusters of dangling green bananas, fat mangos, and papayas. The names of trees —ironwood, casuarina, silver palm—and the names of the beaches—Moon Beach, Bloody Bay, Turtle Grass Beach—as well as the name of the town—Charlestown —and the names of the people—Junie and Jordi, Essie, Maranda and Dee, Robert, Frank, Erol, Aldon, and more—and it all whirled around me like the wind kicking up behind us.

And while McCormick pedaled next to me, his low voice rising and falling with the wind, I fell a little bit in love with this island. He had a story for every tree, every bend in the road, and every person who sat in the shade of their porch and waved as we pedaled past.

It would be so easy to fall wholeheartedly,

completely in love with this place. Not just a little bit, but totally in love.

I watch McCormick as he sets his bike against the trunk of the casuarina. He turns to me then, the shade splashing over him. He runs his fingers through his hair and gives me a soft smile.

He has quite a few different smiles. I haven't been able to catalog them all. Not yet. But already, I've learned a few.

There's his hesitant smile, where his lips barely turn up at the corners. He gives me that smile most often. Then there's his wary smile, where his mouth is flat and his eyes hold his emotions back. There's his laughing smile—the one he gives Amy when she pokes at him with perfectly timed sarcasm. There's the eye-crinkling, dimpled smile he gives Sean when he picks him up for a cuddle. There's the soft smile he's giving me now—the one that reminds me of cool water running over hot skin. And then there's his teasing grin, the flash of levity, where he's laughing with me. And finally, there's the soft parting of his lips, the relaxing of his mouth into a soft curve, right before he bends down to catch my lips with his.

I like that smile best.

But the soft smile, the one he's giving me now—I'll take that over wary or hesitant.

I roll my bike through the sand and prop it next to his. Then I turn to look through the swaying pine needles at the island below.

"It's beautiful." I look at him and find he isn't looking out at the green and the sea but at me.

"You never much liked it before." He studies me, curious but not judging. He's waiting for me to explain.

I can't.

I run my fingers over the cracked blue vinyl of the handlebar. My pointer finger bumps over the hot vinyl and then hits the metal.

"I think," I finally say, "it's easy to dislike something you don't understand. Sometimes you have to see something through the eyes of someone who loves it. And then you can love it too. Or at least you can see how someone else would love it. Then it's very hard to dislike it. You can't anymore. I think you loving the island made me love it too."

He stares at me, arrested by the light and shadow flicking over my face. "You're different."

"You've said that."

"I mean it. I don't know what to trust. My head telling me this isn't real or my heart telling me it is."

It's funny. I've wondered the same thing. He's a dream. He isn't real. My head knows this. My mind tells me this. But my heart has something completely different to say.

"When I'm different than I am now, what am I like?"

McCormick studies me for a moment as if he's trying to decide if this is a trick question. The breeze tugs at his hair, brushing it over his forehead. He pushes it aside and then says, "You're Becca. You're the same Becca you've always been."

"Yes, but what does that mean?"

He frowns, considering my question. Then he smiles. "When you were seven you organized all us kids and made us build you a castle from driftwood and dried seaweed so you could be the sea queen. The whole summer you ruled over us, making everyone bring you shells and sea glass.

And we did it, because you've always been able to make people want to make you happy. When you were fourteen and said you were going to live in Miami and become famous we believed you, because you were you."

McCormick's brow furrows and he looks at me to see how I'm taking this.

"And?"

He shakes his head. "And that's it. You've always known what you want. You wanted to live in Miami or New York. You wanted more than this life. You were always too big for this island, and you were always determined to do whatever it took to leave it."

"But not anymore?"

I think about Robert then, him pressing me against the cool wood of the cottage, kissing me and promising that soon we'd leave the island, the kids, my husband, and make our life in New York.

"I don't know," McCormick admits, looking out over the island. Then at the melodic call of the dove-gray bird, lonely in the breeze. He looks back at me. "You haven't said. Do you want to leave?"

I shake my head. "No."

He smiles at that. His soft smile, hinting toward wary. But then he turns away from me and scoops the pack off the back of his bike. He packed the canvas bag with a blue-and-white-striped cotton blanket, two bottles of lemonade, a large red-and-green-fleshed mango, homemade tortilla chips with black bean and mango salsa, and for dessert thick slices of homemade banana bread.

He spreads the blanket then, next to the trunk of the giant casuarina tree. The blanket billows out in the breeze, a parachute ballooning to the shaded, pine-needle-covered sand.

"Hungry?" he asks, and when I nod he pulls the lemonade and the food from the pack, setting the dishes in a small circle in the center of the blanket.

His head is down and he concentrates on his task. His movements are quiet and efficient. I've noticed he doesn't waste movement. Everything he does is purposeful. It makes me wonder again what he does, who he is, what he wants.

I sit on the edge of the soft cotton blanket and fold my legs under me. Closer to the ground, the scent of crushed pine needles floats up.

When McCormick finishes setting out the food he leans back against the craggy trunk and gives me a smile.

I take that as my cue and pull open the lid of the black bean and mango salsa. When I do, a bright, tart lime-and-mango scent greets me. I glance up at McCormick. "Who made this?"

He flashes his grin. "You did. Friday."

I nod. "I thought maybe you did."

"You've never shared your secret recipe."

And I'm not about to start now, seeing as I don't know the recipe.

I take a chip and scoop up the salsa, catching black beans, cubed mango, the bright confetti of red and green peppers, and sprigs of cilantro. When I bite into the crisp tortilla chip I close my eyes at the burst of flavor. There's the brightness of lime, the subtle sweetness of sun-ripened mango, the umami of black beans, the astringent tartness of cilantro, all dashed with sea salt, and finally, a warm heat from the peppers that grows and grows until your mouth, your whole body, is glowing with it.

I open my eyes to find McCormick watching me with a hungry look on his face.

"It's delicious," I say, pushing the container toward him. "Have some."

"You're enjoying it."

I nod. "I don't get to enjoy food often. Meals are rushed or skipped. And when I do sit down, it's usually fondue, because Mila—"

I cut myself off at McCormick's confused expression.

"I mean, I don't often take the time to just enjoy."

Because McCormick's still looking at me strangely I grab another chip and scoop up more of the salsa. I close my eyes and enjoy the experience. After a moment I hear him shift, take a chip, and then join me in feasting.

It doesn't take long for us to finish the salsa and chips. The crumbly sweetness of the banana bread follows, and then the fresh mango.

McCormick pulls a knife from his pack. He holds the mango and slowly scores the fruit, slicing the orange flesh into perfect cubes waiting to be plucked free. Juice runs over his fingers. The heat has lulled me, the gentle breeze has soothed me, and I have that floaty feeling that arises when you're full and content.

McCormick holds a mango half out to me, and our fingers tangle as I take the slick fruit. Then, smiling at him, I bring it to my mouth and pull a square free. The juice coats my tongue. It's warm and sweet and tastes just like a lazy afternoon under the hot sun, ocean waves cresting at your feet.

I look at McCormick to see if he's enjoying the fruit as much as I am. His lips are glossy and he takes a final bite. Then, without knowing I'm watching, he licks his fingers, taking up the last of the juice.

My heart crashes in my ears like the roar you hear when listening to a conch shell. The world is ultraviolet bright, all the colors more saturated than real life. My skin tingles and prickles, and all I want to do is crawl across the blanket and taste his lips.

He looks up then, alerted maybe by the shuddering sound of my exhale.

"Becca?" When he sees the expression on my face he stiffens and leans forward. "What?"

It's the "Becca" that does it. A cold splash hits me and I tumble down from the high. I want to kiss him. Desperately. But then what happens when I stop dreaming? Will I hurt him again? It's not fair to pull him in one direction and then push him in another.

So instead of running my fingers across the dark stubble lining his jaw, I scoot across the blanket and ask, "Can I lean against you?"

He considers me, and then he leans back against the tree and opens his arms.

I settle against him, cradled between his legs. Then I drop my head to his chest and listen to the steady beat of his heart. After a moment he drops his arms around me and begins to stroke my back.

"Tell me about you," I say, listening to the drone of a dragonfly flitting overhead.

"What do you want to hear?"

His deep voice rumbles over me and I tuck myself closer.

"Start with when you were born and end with today."

"That's a long story." There's humor in his voice. "And you know it already. You lived it with me."

"Pretend we just met. Remember?"

His fingers drift through the ends of my hair and kiss over the back of my neck. My hair curls there, damp with sweat from the heat. He rubs the silk of my hair between his fingers. All the while his other hand strokes slowly over my back.

I float in a haze and my eyelids flutter, pulling me into a dream sleep, where he begins in a lulling voice, "We moved back to the island when I was seven. It was because of me my family left, and it was because of me we returned."

23

The soft, dreamlike scent of lavender oil drifts up from the round mortar. I lean closer as Luis Forscham, our enamel expert, mixes another drop of oil into the enamel powder. He carefully turns the pestle, a scraping hum sounding over the hum of the air conditioning.

We're at Luis's work station, on the third floor of Production, opposite the Abry Headquarters. His wide work table is lit with the natural light that spills from the tall windows and bounces off the clean white walls. He's a careful, slow-moving man in his early seventies, with a long white mustache and stooped shoulders. He perches on his tall wooden stool and hunches over his work, taking slow, infinitesimal movements.

I'm so excited that I press my lips together to keep from urging, "Hurry, hurry, I want to see it!"

Some people think age has made Luis slow-moving, but I've known him since my dad introduced us twenty-five years ago, and he was slow-moving then too. Every motion he makes is deliberate and his hands are unbelievably steady. It's key for the precise work he does, sometimes with a paint brush that is one single hair.

Luis makes another twist of the pestle, grinding the fine, sand-like powder with expert patience.

His work area is quiet except for the scrape of his movements and the ticking of the clock on the wall. Behind me Daniel shifts, waiting for my judgment.

I rushed into his office this morning, waving my notebook at him, talking so fast he couldn't understand a word I said. After he thrust a cup of coffee my way I sat down and showed him my sketch.

When I fell asleep in McCormick's arms, I woke up back in my own bed. I felt rested, at peace, with a warm sense of contentment I haven't felt in years. And in my mind I saw a watch. A beautiful watch.

"Is that it?" Daniel whispers, tilting his head to see over Luis's shoulder. Just like me, he knows that you whisper when Luis is at work.

I smile.

I'm captured by the sea-green and iridescent blue powders coalescing in the lavender oil, flowing like the sea rolling over the beach. The color pulls at me. It's as if I'm back on the island, in McCormick's arms, looking out over the water.

"That's it," I whisper, excitement pinching my chest. "That's the exact color I envisioned."

"Hmm," Luis says, taking a pencil and scratching notations on his notepad.

When he sets his pencil down he slowly turns on his stool, holding the mortar for me to see. As he shifts it the colors swirl and dance in the sunlight, just like the waves of the sea.

"You can replicate this? You can create a dial with these colors and make it look like the sea falling over a white sand beach?"

Luis looks at me as if I just insulted his ancestors and all his unborn great-grandchildren. His white mustache quivers, and slowly he sets the mortar on his table. "You doubt me?"

"No," Daniel says.

I smile. "Thank you, Luis."

He nods and then, without saying goodbye, he turns back to his station to tinker and take more notes.

Daniel and I let ourselves out and head down the long hall toward the elevators. It's early evening and I'm late in getting home. Everyone except Luis has already left for the day. It's quiet and our footsteps echo as we walk down the hallway.

Daniel glances at me out of the corner of his eye. "I haven't seen you this excited about a prototype in years."

He's tired today. Or maybe he's tired every day and I haven't noticed because I've been tired too. And busy. I suppose when you keep yourself busy you fail to notice the small things. Like how your brother has purple smudges under his eyes and his hair is messy, as if he's been running his hand through it in frustration.

His shoulders are tight and there's a firmness around his mouth that wasn't there a few years ago. Maybe I'm only noticing it now because of how relaxed I feel. How invigorated.

I hope our agreement to open up will help him find

someone. He deserves good things. He deserves to be happy.

At the elevator, Daniel presses the button then loosens his tie. He's in a suit as usual. He grins over at me.

"It's going to be a gorgeous watch, Fi."

I nod, thinking about the swirl of the enamel. "Thank you for getting carried away with me. I know you could have told me to slow down or asked for market forecasts, been the voice of reason, or—"

"It looks like the first watch Dad had made." He lifts a shoulder. "The pearl bracelet, the yellow gold. It's similar. I like it. It's almost an homage. You know me. I'm a sucker for pointless displays of sentimentality."

I let out a huff of air and smile at him. He's right. It's a bit like the watch Dad gave me for my sixteenth birthday. But it's also unique.

There are three rows of opalescent pearls interspersed with bright green emeralds for the bracelet. The round case is reminiscent of the island. A ring of yellow gold, with the textures of waves rippling over sand brushed into the metal. The gold case surrounds the sea-green and wave-blue dial. Hand-set diamonds set the time, with yellow gold marking the seconds and the hour. The components will be our best, the timekeeping precise, and we'll sell it as a limited edition.

The elevator dings and the metal doors sweep open.

I step on and Daniel follows, the door shutting after us. As the elevator descends I'm buoyant, happier than I can remember being in a long time.

"What are you going to call it?" Daniel asks, nodding at my notebook and my sketch of the watch.

"McCormick," I say, smiling.

"Odd name for a watch."

"Isn't it?"

Daniel lets out a laugh as the doors slide open.

Outside the lobby the sun hangs in the sky, descending toward the blue-green mountains. A field of yellow flax, just beyond the parking lot, ripples in the wind.

It's a beautiful day. A perfect day to relax.

"Come have dinner with us tonight," I say, turning to Daniel.

He sends a hand through his hair and lets out a sigh. "Can't. I've got a date tonight."

"Really?" I raise my eyebrows as we make our way to the glass doors. I lift a hand to the guard stationed at the tall, semicircle desk. "Good night, Frederic."

"Madame. Monsieur." Frederic nods as we cross the lobby and push free of the production facility.

The early-evening air hits us, scented with freshly cut grass and the hot pavement of the parking lot. I pause on the sidewalk and Daniel stops with me.

I'm in a long-sleeve navy dress and a blazer. There's a white silk scarf around my neck. Even so, with the sun setting, the air is shading toward cool.

"Is it hard to believe I have a date?" Daniel asks, putting his hands in his pockets and giving me a wry look.

"No. You have plenty of dates. I was only thinking, are you trying to open up? Like we said we would?"

His eyes crinkle at the edges. "Not tonight."

I laugh and shove at him. "Then what's the point?"

He glances at the Chronomachen, our bestseller, on his wrist. "The point is, my date was just in a

Hollywood Blockbuster, and we're going to the theater, where we'll be photographed. And, of course, I'll be conspicuously checking my watch every time a camera flashes. She'll get a publicity boost and so will we."

He drops his hand then and his jacket sleeve falls over his wrist. I frown at him, worried at the tightness around his mouth.

"You know, you don't have to do that anymore."

He lifts his eyebrows. "I didn't have to do it in the first place. I did it because I wanted to save us."

I clench my hand. We both did a lot of things in the first years to make sure our heritage wouldn't die with us. But I never thought my brother would suffer because of it. I think he has, though, even if he won't admit it.

"I'm sorry I ever asked you to do it."

It was me who told him to pose for the paparazzi every chance he got. Weeks after Dad died, I saw a newspaper article featuring Daniel and his friends on a yacht. The picture was from before Dad's funeral. It was a piece decrying the sorry state of spoiled youth. The column took up an entire page, and Daniel was standing on the yacht in a pair of shorts and a collared shirt, his watch glinting in the sun. He was credited, "Daniel Abry, of Abry Watch Co." I thrust the paper at him and said, "This. This is how we save Abry."

From there on out he made himself the center of attention—premieres, galas, races. Every photograph-worthy event, Daniel was there. The cameras love him, and he loves giving the cameras a view of our watches.

But then Italy happened, and Daniel hasn't been the same since.

"Don't be sorry, Fi," he says, taking in my

expression. "I may be your little brother, but I'm an adult. I made my choice."

"At what cost?"

He smiles then and tugs me close under his arm. "Come on. I like sailing. I like diving in submarines and sending rockets up to space. I like dating beautiful women. It's no hardship."

I shrug out from under his arm and round on him. "Don't you charm me, Daniel Abry. I want you to be happy too. Someone asked me recently, are you even alive if you're not living—"

"Hey. I'm alive. I'm living."

"But you won't always be," I say, thinking about McCormick, Amy, and the rest of the people in my dreams. Someday Daniel and I will be just a dream too. We'll leave behind the people we loved and they'll only have the memories of us.

"But that's a long time away," he says, his voice light.

I wrap my arms around my middle and stare out over the parking lot toward the sloping hills and the mountains shrouded in dusk. The bright yellow field of flax has dimmed to a shadowed bronze.

"Fi?"

I nod. "You're right. I guess I'm just worried about you."

"Worry about yourself. I predict that in six months' time you're going to be marooned on a tropical island with no phone and no internet. I'll have won our bet, and you'll be stuck reading a paperback on the beach. Your worst nightmare."

I smile at him, wondering how after only a few days my worst nightmare has become my fondest dream. "Right. Well. I'd better get home then. Mila asked for pasta, and Annemarie has prawns and white sauce on the stove."

"Mmm . . ." Daniel's eyes lose focus as he contemplates Annemarie's famous pasta. "Maybe I will cancel my date."

I shove him with a laugh. "Go on. You never know, maybe she's the one."

He salutes me then and steps into the parking lot, heading toward the BMW at the north entrance. Before he's out of earshot, he tosses over his shoulder, "Stop laughing, Fi! You'll be on that tropical island in no time! And then who'll be laughing?"

I grin after him.

Who indeed?

24

I FALL ASLEEP EXPECTING TO WAKE IN MCCORMICK'S arms, snuggled under the piney boughs of the casuarina tree. I imagine the warmth of his chest, his solid heartbeat, and the golden afternoon light filtering through the pine needles as he tells me his story.

Instead I stumble as I land back on the island, tripping over myself on a dark, cold-sanded beach. I catch myself and shake off the disorientation.

My skin is cold and clammy, the air is humid and tropical-wet, and a heavy, thundering weight presses down on me. The beach is pitch-dark. Indigo-black clouds sweep across the sky and hide the crescent moon. Down the sand, the battery-powered light of a half-dozen torches slices the sky. The thin streams of light slice up then down, then out across the black water. Dark figures scan the beach, searching for something—or someone.

They're shouting—a name—but the roar of the waves drowns their voices. The ocean is choppy and agitated and a wave smacks the sand and then rolls over my calves, slapping me with salty water. I stumble again and someone reaches out and steadies me.

"Are you all right?"

"Ye—"

I stop.

It's Robert. He grips my forearm, keeping me upright as the wave is yanked back toward the ocean. The salty sea air punches at me as I peer up at him. His fingers are tight and he wraps his arm around my waist, pulling me out of the surf.

Behind us, past the dark smudge of forest and the dark sky, the beach cottages stand dark and empty. A single light burns on a porch. It's the yellow glow of a hurricane lamp. Essie stands in the light, Sean in her arms. She's looking this way.

"There he is," Robert says, his voice tight. He's shrouded in the night, his expression indiscernible. His copper-colored hair is almost inky black in the darkness.

I follow the line of his gaze and squint out over the black sea. The torches bounce off the water and the matte black of the waves sucks in the light. Even so, I catch a glimmer of something. There's movement in the water. About fifty meters out there's the flash of metal glinting in the light of a torch. It's a watch. Someone is out there, swimming in the dark.

"What...?"

"He's gone after her," Robert says.

When I stiffen Robert spreads his hand over my back. He pulls me against him. "Don't worry. He'll find her. If she's there, he'll bring her out."

And that's when the entire scene that I've landed in

snaps together. I can hear the people shouting now—"Amy! Amy!"—and I can see they're searching the waves.

Now I see there's a boat on the water too. A twenty-foot outboard motor fishing boat. It's bobbing on the waves, moving slowly with a pale light shining over the depths.

They're searching... for Amy?

"No," I say, stepping into the sinking sand and the dark, cool water. It grips at me and my feet slide in the murky sand. My bare feet nick on the sharp broken shells. I make it to my thighs, the water foaming around me, before Robert yanks me back.

"What the hell are you doing?" He shakes my arm. "You can't swim. What are you going to do? Make it so McCormick has to save you both?"

"Let go of me." I yank my arm, freeing myself from his grip.

"Becca!" Robert tugs me up the sand, away from the roaring water.

I search the waves, trying to catch another glimpse of McCormick. I remember his fear from the other day, the white lines on his face, the urgency in his voice when he pulled me out of the depths and shouted, "You know there are riptides."

And now he's out there again, in the dark, searching for his daughter.

If people die in dreams, do they come back? If Amy dies tonight, will she be here the next time I dream? If McCormick drowns, will I come back tomorrow and find myself in his arms?

I catch a glimmer of him again, a flash of muted moonlight glinting off his skin. He slices through the water, moving through the waves with powerful strokes.

I see what he's doing now. He's combing the water, searching in a grid. Ten feet forward, turn, ten feet back. Again. He's meticulous. Solid. Yet the threat of the riptide and of Amy, lost, makes a battery-acid fear rise in me.

It reminds me of the day I took Mila to the Parc des Bastions at the center of Geneva. It was spring, the sun was finally shining warmly, the grass was green, and flowers were stretching drowsy heads toward the blue sky.

Mila was four. She wanted to run, to play chess in the park, to see the monuments. I looked down for one moment. I was searching for a bottle of water in my purse, and when I looked up Mila was gone.

The terror of that moment, of frantically scanning the trees, the empty benches, the families in the grass, and not finding my daughter? It strangled me in a tight, mindless grip. For five desperate minutes I lived in the terror of losing my daughter.

And then she skipped out from behind the wide trunk of a tall chestnut tree. She was smiling widely. There was a caterpillar in her dirt-coated hands. "Mummy, isn't it pretty?" The swelling of relief was immediate and immense. I can still taste both the terror and the relief.

Right now I see that same desperation in McCormick's relentless search of the night-black waves. There's a desperate fear in the driven way he pushes through the water.

"What happened?"

Robert glances over at me and then back to

McCormick. "Why'd he go in? Essie told us Amy said she was going for a swim. That was an hour ago. You know Aaron. If Amy drowns it'll kill him."

I stare at Robert then. The way he said that—it wasn't the way someone would state a fact. It was more ... bitter. Surprising in its bitterness.

Robert grabs for my hand. I jerk my fingers away. "What do you mean? What are you talking about?"

He glances at me. His mouth twists in the dark and the light of a torch slices over us. There. Gone. For a moment I can see his eyes. He's watching McCormick with a strange mix of emotion—admiration, bitterness, love, hate.

The hair raises on my arms and I shake my head. "I'm going in to help—"

I start to lift my dress over my head. I'm not an expert, but I *can* swim. And I can't be hurt. I know if I drown here I'll just wake up in my soft, cozy bed.

Amy though?

McCormick?

I don't know what happens if they don't survive.

Robert grabs my wrist and spins me back around. "Becca. No. You aren't thinking."

"He needs help!"

"He needs you to stay on the beach. Safe. He needs all of us to stay on the beach. Safe. You know this better than most."

I shake my head and try to pull free of his grip. His hand shackles my wrist.

"I want to help him."

"Aldon has the boat out. We're searching the beach—"

"But what if he gets caught in the riptide too? What if—?"

Robert lets out an incredulous laugh, and it echoes over the hiss and roar of the waves. I stop fighting his grip and watch the shadows play over his face.

He shakes his head then and drops my wrist. "You know as well as I do, others may die, but not McCormick."

"I don't know what you're talking about."

"He killed his best friends, didn't he? And now he might have killed your daughter."

Lightning-quick, without thinking, I reach out and slap Robert. The crack of my hand is like a gunshot.

Robert blinks at me then sets his hand to his cheek. When he touches the bright red imprint of my hand he winces. "You know it's true."

"You hate him." I'm incredulous at the realization.

He shakes his head. "He's my best friend. I love him like a brother."

"You have a terrible way of showing it."

He holds out his hands as if to say, "We're in this together, you and me."

"I need a torch," I say.

Robert sighs then takes me to a cottage with a line of flashlights on the steps. I grab one, flick it on, and then start my search of the beach.

For two hours I pace the wet sand, running the light through the churning surf beating against the shore. At times I think I see a person rolling in the waves, but it turns into driftwood or seaweed or the glimmer of the moon on the water.

I pass others searching, Jordi and Junie, the crossing guard, Maranda and Dee. As the minutes pass and hope seeps away like water evaporating in the sand, I avoid the worried looks of every person I pass.

Instead I call out, "Amy! Amy!" until my voice is raw and my throat aching. The misty salt stings my eyes, and my feet are raw from the sharp coral rocks and the broken shells.

The night cools in increments, until at midnight I begin to shiver.

It's been two hours.

For one hundred and twenty minutes I've searched for Amy. Every few seconds I've been tugged to turn my eyes to the water. To find McCormick and make certain he's still swimming. I'll catch him—a flash of his watch, the light of his arm—a movement that lets me know he's okay.

He hasn't stopped searching, swimming. And so I keep my eyes on the water, and I keep my eyes on him.

But finally, at midnight, with the moon buried behind a black cloud, McCormick turns toward shore. The boat veers our way too, its light aimed toward the beach.

We all gather in a semicircle, two dozen people waiting to see if McCormick's found her or if he's giving up.

I can't imagine him giving up.

Which means...

I hold my breath, my lungs burning as he stands in the shallows. He's a dark shadow rising from the ocean. The water sluices off him, catching the dull moonlight.

He's in Speedos, his muscles bunching, his shoulders tight as he climbs from the ocean. He's wide, powerful, the tattoos covering him blending into the night. I search his face. His jaw is tight, his expression devoid of any emotion.

He doesn't have Amy.

It's just him climbing from the water.

I'm filled with relief, but also fear.

"I couldn't find her," he says, looking me in the eye but speaking to everyone. There's an apology in his voice. Frustration. Self-castigation.

I take a step forward and he shakes his head.

"I need two minutes, then I'm going back out." He looks through the group, then stops at a short, gray-haired man. "Erol, are you up for a night dive?"

When he asks that the collective mood shifts. Like a cold winter wind shifting through a barren forest, it grasps the last autumn leaf and tugs it free from the branch.

"If you think . . ." Erol trails off, looking down at the sand.

"Just in case," McCormick says. He clenches his hands and looks away, burying his expression in shadow.

He means just in case Amy has drowned and she'll be found underwater, by the diver.

"All right," Erol says. "I'll go out with Aldon on the boat."

"Thank you."

Across the group Robert watches me, a look of sympathy clouding his features. I shake my head at him, refusing to believe Amy's gone, and when I do, McCormick catches our exchange.

I turn to him, stepping forward and putting my hand to his arm. His skin is cool, wet, and his muscles are tight.

I want to tell him it will be okay, that he'll find her, but the words won't come.

So he looks down at me and catches my expression as if he knows what I want to say without me having to say it at all.

Finally, I find my voice. "It will be all right."

A cloud passes through his eyes as if he's seen this before and it wasn't all right. As if he already knows how this ends.

"I need a minute," he says, "then I'm going back in."

My chest clenches. How long can he swim without endangering himself?

But at the determined look on his face, I can only nod and take my hand from his arm.

I fold my fingers into my palm, wishing I could hold him for a moment. Hug him. Give him a bolt of energy to keep him swimming for as long as he needs.

Instead I can only stand there and watch, impotent, as he turns toward the cottages.

And then—

"Dad?"

His head jerks up. His shoulders rise.

A swell of relief rides over me. She's here. She's alive.

"Why's everyone at the beach?" Amy asks, blinking sleepily at her dad.

"Amy!" Maranda cries.

"Thank goodness," Junie says, clasping a protective hand across her belly.

Amy's in jean shorts and a bikini top, her hair messy, a book in her hand. She stands there blinking in confusion at the gathering of islanders.

McCormick makes a raw noise and then he's in front of her, crushing her in a tight hug.

"What?" she protests. "Eww. Why are you so wet? Were you swimming? Why?"

He merely holds her, his arms wrapped tightly around her, his shoulders shaking.

After a moment Amy realizes this wasn't a nighttime swim party—it was something more.

"I thought I lost you," McCormick whispers, his voice ragged. "I thought I lost you." He drops his head to rest on hers. Then he takes her shoulders, and says, "Dammit, you know not to swim by yourself! You know not to swim on this beach! Where were you?"

Amy stares up at her dad, stunned at the emotions. "I was . . . I didn't swim. I changed my mind. I fell asleep reading in the hammock."

McCormick lets out a half-laugh, half-sob, and then he's hugging his daughter again. "You'll be the death of me," he says, "You'll kill me some day. I swear."

"Dad." She shoves at him. "I'm okay. It's okay." And then, when he doesn't let her go, she hugs him back. "I'm okay, Dad."

His shoulders relax then and he takes a step back, his gaze sweeping over her. I understand. He just spent adrenaline-fueled hours chopping through the waves searching for his daughter. He didn't know if she was alive or dead. It's hard to adjust to the reality that she's been fine all along.

I imagine his heart is pounding, his ears are ringing, and the world feels a bit unreal to him right now.

Amy holds up her book. "I'm sorry, Dad. If you want to blame someone, blame it on Descartes."

"What?" McCormick says, shaking his head. Water drips down his neck, trailing over his back.

"Descartes. 'Let whoever can do so deceive me, he will never bring it about that I am nothing, so long as I continue to think I am something.'" Amy points to her book.

McCormick stares at her blankly. So she lifts the thick book and tries again.

"'If you would be a real seeker after truth, it is necessary that at least once in your life you doubt, as far as possible, all things.'"

The fear has flown out of me and I'm left with a strange, giddy sensation. I want to laugh, and it bubbles inside me and catches in my throat.

I step forward then, crossing the cold sand, and pull Amy into a quick hug. "You're very loved."

At that, everyone on the beach gathers to give Amy a hug or a pat or a teasing scold for scaring the ever-loving daylights out of them all. After fifteen minutes, everyone has drifted back to their homes.

Thirty minutes later we've collected Sean from Essie and put him to bed. Amy's asleep with her book tucked under her pillow.

And I'm alone with McCormick.

25

THE CLOUDS HAVE FLOWN TO THE NORTH, LEAVING A clear, inky sky studded with winking stars. The heavy, humid, thundering air has blown away, replaced by a salty night-flower breeze. The frogs that hide in the mangroves have come alive, singing their song to the crescent moon, now bathing the black water with silver cobwebs of light.

I find McCormick on the beach, where the spiky grass meets the sand. He's a lone figure, tall and dark, outlined by the glow of the moon. My feet whisper over the grass and my clothing, a silky white cotton nightdress, rustles in the breeze.

McCormick's shoulders stiffen when he hears my footsteps. He doesn't turn when I stop and stand next to him. Instead he continues to watch the waves cascade across the sand.

There's a hypnotic rhythm to the thunderous waves. The foam glistens in the moonlight and the coral and shells tinkle musically as the waves tug them back into the sea.

McCormick is quiet. The deep quiet that you find in a sunlit glade in the middle of an alpine forest, or the quiet my mum loves, when you sit cross-legged at the Tor and bathe in the solemnity of centuries passing by.

After a short time dreaming of him I know a bit about McCormick. I know he loves his family. I know he thinks before he speaks. I know he's careful, cautious. I know he's given his trust to the wrong people. I know he's patient and kind. I know he feels the pull between us, the ebb and tide of the sea, as strongly as I do. I know there's a reason I'm dreaming of him.

But I don't know what he's thinking. I don't know his story. I don't know what he does when I'm not dreaming him, or even if he exists at all when I'm not here.

It makes me think of the quote Amy just gave, "Let whoever can do so deceive me, he will never bring it about that I am nothing, so long as I continue to think I am something."

If McCormick believes he *is*, does that make him as real as me? Does that make all of this real?

I look to him then, glancing up at the line of his jaw and the rough stubble growing in. His hair is still damp, and it curls in black loops at the nape of his neck. My fingers itch to reach up and brush his hair back from his forehead. I'd like to hold his face in my hands, rub my fingers over his stubble, and press my lips to his. A gentle kiss that tells him it's all okay.

He looks down at me, his brown eyes nearly black in the night.

A bird flutters in the sea grape bushes behind us. There's a quick flapping of wings and then a white egret bursts free and sails high, a flash of white against the night. It veers toward the wetlands.

I press a hand to my chest, my heart pounding.

The right side of McCormick's mouth lifts and I reach over and loop my hand in his.

My feet sink into the cool sand and I relax into the warmth of his fingers. I want to fold into him, hold myself to him, but I let the tangle of our fingers be enough.

McCormick stares at our locked hands for a moment and then lets out a long breath.

"I thought we'd lost her," he says, and his voice still has the remnants of that broken anguish.

I squeeze his hand, clinging to him. "I wouldn't have let that happen."

I decide then that I truly wouldn't have. I would have dreamed something else. I would have dreamed her back to life.

He smiles then. The smile that crinkles at the corners of his eyes, a surprised flash of laughter at the edge of his mouth. "You sound like you believe you can change the world with willpower."

I glance up at the stars overhead. Venus is out, the brightest light in the sky, only dimmed by the moon. "Maybe I can. In dreams you can do anything."

"Hmm." He nods, looking out over the sea. "Except this isn't a dream."

I lean into him then, and he wraps his arms around me and pulls me into his warmth. I watch the slow slide of the ocean over the beach. I listen to the night frogs sing. I breathe in the salt and ocean scent of McCormick.

A dozen feet behind us, at the cottage, Sean's bedroom window is open. We'll hear him if he cries. But for now, perhaps for the rest of the night, he's asleep.

I watch the sea.

I wait to wake up.

And when I don't, I say, "You never finished telling me your story."

"You fell asleep."

"And then what?"

He tilts his head, studying me. "And then you woke up, hopped on your bike, and rode back home without a word. You didn't speak to me again until we found Amy."

"Why not?"

"You were with Robert." He says this without inflection.

Robert claims McCormick doesn't know he's planning to run off to New York with me. I'm not so sure.

"Do you think you trust too easily?"

He watches me for a moment, taking in the moonlight falling over my face.

"I don't trust easily," he finally says, and when I lower my eyebrows he explains. "I learned a long time ago that if you don't trust, then you'll live a lonely life. You have to choose. You can trust or you can die alone. I chose trust."

I swallow, my throat still raw from the search for Amy. It hurts thinking about what he said. Because while he chose trust, I chose to be alone. After Joel I made the choice to smother the chance of any relationships because I felt incapable of giving my trust.

I couldn't. Not even to my best friend.

"And if you're betrayed by the people you trust?" I ask, contemplating my worst fear. Loving and then losing.

"Then I'll move on. I'll survive."

"It's not so easy."

He glances at me, waiting for an explanation.

"It hurts. You'll want to rage. Maybe you will. You'll be so angry you shake. You'll be so sick with grief that you can barely stand. It won't be so easy to trust again. It's not so easy to move on—"

"Becca."

I turn to him. His expression is resolute.

"What?"

"If I'm betrayed by someone I love—"

"Yes?"

"I might rage. I might be so angry I shake. I might be consumed by grief. But most of all—even if it's the hardest thing I've done—I'd hold my anger. I'd hold my grief. So I wouldn't say or do something I'd regret. God knows the tears of regret hurt more than the tears of sorrow."

I stare at him, stunned. "You sound like Amy. Are you a philosopher too?"

He gives me his dimpled, eyes-crinkled smile. "I only mean I can handle grief. I can handle anger. But regret? It's a weight I wouldn't wish on anyone. So if I'm betrayed, then I'll do my best to keep loving that person. If I gave them my trust, then I imagine they're worth it."

He reaches out then, taking a strand of my hair that's fallen free of my braid and tucking it behind my ear. I sway toward him, caught up in the quiet gentleness of the moment.

"You would stay in a situation that hurts you?"

"No," he says. "I'd stay in a situation to help someone else. And then I'd go."

Now I wonder if we aren't talking about Becca and Robert. Maybe we're actually talking about us. Fiona and McCormick.

He's here. I'm here. I'm opening up, allowing myself the possibility of love.

But when that's done, when I've felt all the heady-night, starlit love I can, I'm going to leave him.

He's helping me even if he doesn't know it. Is that a betrayal of him? And if it is, will he be the one to go first?

A stinging ache presses at the backs of my eyes and my throat feels swollen and achy. I can't imagine it. He couldn't be the one to go first. Dreams don't work that way.

"I want you to tell me your story," I whisper.

The crescent moon has risen high, spilling over the water. It's the middle of the night, the perfect time for sharing secrets.

"Even though you already know it?"

"Pretend I don't."

I pull him down to the sand to sit in the cool, fine grains. He comes softly, settling behind me. When he opens his arms I rest against him.

His heart thuds against my ear and I wait for him to begin. The humid, perfumed air blankets us, the waves and the frogs play our soundtrack, and the breeze drags sand across our bare legs.

McCormick's hand plays a slow circle over my back.

"You came back to the island when you were seven," I remind him.

I feel the curve of his lips as he presses his mouth to my temple. And then he begins.

"My parents left because of me, and they came back because of me. I was born here, in Essie's cottage."

"Really!"

He laughs, a deep rumble. "You already knew that. You were born down the street."

I was born in Glastonbury.

"A week later, my parents decided they didn't want to raise their son on an island with so few opportunities. They wanted a big life for me."

"Most parents do."

He nods. "So they packed two suitcases and flew to New York. My dad found work as a porter at a seedy hotel near Times Square. My mom found part-time work at a wash-and-fold laundry and more night work at a garment factory. We were the kind of poor where you know the balance of your bank account down to the last cent and you know you're not going to have enough money to make it to the end of the week, much less the end of the month. We didn't buy clothes. I was on the end of a neighborhood hand-me-down chain. All my clothes had been worn by at least five or six kids before I got them. They were frayed and stained, and my shoes had holes and the rubber soles were peeling off. Kids at the playgrounds would point, call me nasty names. My mom always lifted her head when she heard them and said, 'Don't you listen to them. You're a good boy, Aaron. You're my boy.'"

He looks out over the water, a faraway look in his eyes. I grip the fabric of his T-shirt in my hands. I can picture him, a little dark-haired boy, pale and brown-eyed, standing in ragged clothes while kids pointed and called him names. The kind of poor he's talking about, I know it too. I can still feel the hunger of a gnawing empty stomach, sleeping on someone else's floor.

You wouldn't know it now. No one would, looking at me or reading about my pedigree.

But we're all a thousand layers making up a single life.

"Your mom loves you," I tell him, glad she was there to stand up for him.

"She did." His voice is warm, happy with the memory. Then he shakes his head. "When I was seven I was already smoking joints and drinking liquor. When my mom came home early from work one day—she was sick—she found me and the neighbor kids sharing a forty-ounce." He laughs then. "I was on a bad road. Fighting, skipping school. Only seven and already cursing, drinking, smoking. Our two suitcases were packed that night. And me, my mom, and my dad were back on the island the very next day."

I'm stunned. "You were a deviant at age seven."

He strokes my back. "You liked me. You followed me around for weeks until I finally decided to talk to you."

I would have liked to have seen that. I imagine he would have fascinated me, a hard seven-year-old from the city, transported to this tiny island. He was a legend, I'm sure.

"And then you decided to stay here forever. Your

own tropical paradise." I lean into him, breathing in the salt and the sand.

He laughs. "Right. Or the opposite."

"The opposite? Like Amy?"

"Like you," he says, smiling down at me. "You wanted to live in the big world, and so did I. This island always felt like a prison. One that was impossible to escape." He tilts his head to the sky. "Whenever I looked up at the stars, all I saw were bars. I wanted to leave in the worst way."

I think I know exactly how he feels. Because right now I'd like him to leave the island too. I'd like him to step out of this dream and into Geneva. I'd like to see what might happen if he were real.

But he's right, this island is a prison. The bars are the confines of my dreams.

"I started swimming," McCormick says. "I took to the water like I'd been born swimming. You couldn't get me out of it. I'd spend hours in the sea. So much so that Essie's banana bread was the only thing that could tempt me out."

I think about the honey taste and the crumbly texture of the banana bread we ate on the hilltop and I wonder if Essie made that. If so, I can see why it pulled him from the water.

"Then, when I was eleven, I terrified my parents and everyone else. One day while swimming I decided I was going to swim around the whole island in one go. So I took off without telling anyone. It's an eight-mile circumference. When I climbed back on the beach I was grinning from ear to ear, so proud of myself. I got a different reception than I thought I would."

"I bet they were frantic," I say, thinking of the scene on the beach tonight.

McCormick sobers. "I know exactly how they felt."

"Did you stop?"

"No." He shakes his head and his eyes glint in the moonlight. "I couldn't stop. I was addicted to the thrill of it. My parents decided to stop fighting it. I started training for long-distance marathon swims. At fourteen I swam South Eleuthera to Nassau, Bahamas. It took more than forty hours of straight swimming. At fifteen I crossed the English Channel four times in a row, swimming unassisted for more than fifty hours. Any record, any long-distance swim, I wanted to be the one to do it. I swam from Ibiza to Mallorca. I circumnavigated Barbados. Current neutral ocean swims were where I was at my best. I wanted to swim the world. I wanted to beat all the records."

"My word," I say, staring at this man who raced around the world. Does it make it less impressive if it isn't real?

Yes. I suppose so.

But in this dream world it's real.

Which is why no one was concerned when he spent two hours in the swells and the strong currents searching for his daughter. If he'd spent fifty hours cutting through the ocean, what was two?

"You don't have to pretend you don't know this," he says, and there isn't pride in his eyes but a quiet sadness. A carefully hidden grief that pinches my chest.

"I want to hear it in your words," I say quietly.

He takes in a deep breath, his chest rising beneath me.

Something happened. Otherwise he wouldn't be on

this island. He'd be out in the world. Breaking records. Living the life he was made for.

He nods then and tugs me close. My nightdress is damp from the sea mist and the humidity in the air, and it sticks to my skin. When I move against him the fabric drags a damp heat across me.

I smell a hint of lavender, and when I do, my heart quickens. Don't wake up. Don't wake up. Not yet.

"What about us?" I ask, urging him to hurry, to tell me everything before I wake and my dream-self leaves him again.

"You were in Miami. Waitressing at a beach bar, the . . ." He furrows his brow and looks down at me.

I shake my head. I don't know the name of this fictional bar.

"The Sand Bar," he says, nodding. "I was in Miami for a swim. You called me, an old friend saying hello. We met up. We drank. We had sex."

The way he says, "We had sex," low and rumbly, like sand scraping over my bare legs, makes a warmth pool inside me. A hot sensation steals over me and I resist the urge to turn my face up to the moonlight and take McCormick's mouth in mine.

"A month later we married. Two months later I had my Gulf Stream swim and . . ." His voice trails off, and then he says, "And then we came back to the island."

"To stay?"

"To stay."

"You didn't swim again?"

He hesitates. Stares down at me, his brow wrinkled. "No."

Something happened there. Between Miami and

his last swim. "You married me because I was pregnant."

"I married you because I was in love."

Thinking back on that wedding picture hanging on the bedroom wall, I think he was.

"Did I love you?"

He smiles. "You married me because you were pregnant."

"And?"

He shakes his head. "And you knew I'd keep you off the island. I was your ticket."

"Is that what I said?"

"Not before the wedding. But after. After the swim . . ." He shakes his head. "Look. We both have things we regret. It was a hard time."

I think about what Robert said. How he claimed Amy drowning would destroy McCormick because he'd already killed his two best friends.

"Because of your best friends?" I ask, and McCormick's chest stiffens beneath me.

Behind us, at the edge of the grass, the wind rustles through the palm leaves, rattling and hissing. I shiver at the sudden cold gust. At my shiver, McCormick's tension eases and he pulls me close.

"Every marathon swimmer has a crew," he says, his voice faraway, as if he's holding himself away from the pain of what he's revealing. "They're in kayaks, with you the entire way. They're your support, and you rely on them for sustenance, hydration, navigation, record-keeping, first aid, life support. Everything. You have a crew on the land checking weather, currents, and you have your crew in the water. I always, from the first, worked with Scott and Jay."

"Scott and Jay," I repeat.

McCormick nods and blows out a breath. The breeze, still sending a cool wind, tugs at my hair and sends it over McCormick's hands.

I shift in the sand. The fine powder, once comfortable, is now cold and hard.

"Twins. Dee's grandsons. Me, Robert, Scott, and Jay were inseparable. Every swim, they were there with me. Scott and Jay in the kayaks, Robert on land. I had this idea. It'd been eating at me for years. I wanted to set the record for the longest current positive swim in history. I'd leave from the eastern coast of Florida, catch the Gulf Stream, and fly through the water. If you ride that current you can swim faster than humanly possible. A hundred kilometers in just over ten hours. I wanted to swim three hundred kilometers. It'd take a little over thirty hours. I was high on the idea. Robert wasn't sure. It wasn't what I did. It wasn't what I was known for. The Atlantic Ocean had large swells, rouge waves, storm bursts could crop up. We hadn't trained. Scott and Jay thought we were ready. I did too."

"So you swam."

"I swam. We hired a boat with a twelve-person crew. A captain, deckhands, paramedics. Scott and Jay switched off every few hours with crew on the boat. Everything was going well."

An itch crawls over my skin like an ant tracking over my bare arms. I shiver and McCormick rubs my arms.

"Go on."

He drags in a breath. "A storm burst when we were a hundred kilometers out. Robert was on the radio, screaming at us that it was coming. He called in the coast guard. The boat crew was as surprised as we were. No one saw this coming. A thirty-foot swell came out of nowhere. It was this giant fist that reached into the sky and then crashed into us. I went so far into the depths I didn't know up from down. I picked a direction and swam and kept swimming until I thought I'd die under the water. I was down for two minutes. I kept count in my mind, knowing my limit was two forty. When I got to the surface the rain was slamming so hard I couldn't see. Waves hit from every side. I caught flashes of the kayaks. The emergency beacons. I fought to reach them, but when I did—"

He cuts himself off. His hand, resting in the sand, curls into a fist.

"They were gone?"

But McCormick doesn't take it as a question. He takes it as a statement of fact.

"Scott was gone. I couldn't find him. He was nowhere. Just swallowed by the ocean as if he never existed. If he'd been taken down as far as I had there was no way he would've made it back up. Jay, he was still in his kayak. The crewed boat was at least five hundred meters off. It was cresting on the waves and slamming down. I could barely see anything through the rain. I thought if I could only get to Jay we'd make it."

A wave hits the sand, crashing loudly against the beach, and I flinch at the noise.

"I made it to Jay, grabbed his kayak. He clutched my hand, shouted over the rain, 'Scott?' I shook my head. 'I can't find him.' Then another wave rose above us. Jay looked up and"—his voice cracks—"he looked so afraid. I gripped his hand, 'Don't let go,' and then the wave hit. He didn't let go. I did. I couldn't keep ahold of him. He was ripped from me. And . . ."

"It's okay," I say, resting my hand to his chest. "It's okay."

McCormick stares out over the water, his dark eyes glinting in the moonlight. "I treaded water for three hours before the storm died. I treaded for three hours knowing my best friends were gone and it was my fault. For three hours I barely kept my head above water."

He looks down at me then, lines bracketing his mouth. "You know all this though."

I shake my head.

He grips my hand. "I think sometimes I never actually made it out of the water. I've been treading ever since. Just barely keeping my head above the waves."

I nod. Take my arms and fold them around him. Run my fingers through the curled ends of his hair. "Why'd we come back to the island?"

He wraps his arms around me. "Because I didn't want the thrill or the fame anymore. I wanted to give back to Dee what I'd taken. I wanted to give back to the island that had raised me. I wanted my daughter to be safe. I figured I did life my way and I only had regrets. I was going to try life another way."

"I wasn't angry about coming back here?"

"You were furious," he says, his hand stilling on my back. "It's when you started calling me McCormick."

I remember now. McCormick. An almost. A never was. A dream that didn't happen.

"What would you say if I called you Aaron?"

I feel his smile then in the way he curves around me. "I'd say you aren't yourself."

I nod. That's true. I'm not the me he knows.

"How about, if you ever want to know if I'm myself—the me of right now—just say 'Fi'? And if I say yes, then that means I'm me and I want you to kiss me."

"Fi?"

I nod, tilting my chin up to look at him. "Yes."

His eyes light and the crash of the waves swells, sweeping over the shore. A gull flies overhead, a lone figure in the night sky.

"You want me to kiss you?" he asks, his eyes catching on my mouth.

My lips tingle as his gaze softens and strokes over my lips. "Yes," I whisper.

He reaches up then, drawing his fingers over my cheek, his touch featherlight. I lean into his hand, turning my mouth to set a kiss over his fingertips.

"It will be okay," I whisper as he reaches out and brushes his fingers across my lips. "I'm here. You're here. It'll be okay."

The night is pregnant with desire, and the floral scent tangles between us. The air takes on a wavy, dreamlike feel. I'm floating, lost in the sensation of his fingers slowly tracing my lips.

I grab his wrist then and pull his hand free. He smiles and says, "This feels like a dream."

"I know."

And then I remember what he said before—how he told me he felt that if he didn't kiss me he'd regret it for the rest of his life. He's a man who has lived with regrets. It's not something he would say lightly.

He has the same look in his eyes now. And so I lean forward, rocking in the cool sand, and grip his shoulders.

I kiss him. I taste the salt on his lips. I taste the tears he didn't shed. I taste his regret. I taste his love.

He exhales a sharp, pained breath. And then he flips me beneath him, pressing me into the sand. He covers me. His clothing scrapes over me, and he captures my wrists with his hands and presses them into the sand.

His heat lines me, and the weight of him settling over me sends a liquid heat through my veins. He takes my mouth and kisses me. Gently. Softly. Like the breeze over a calm sea. Like he's memorizing me and savoring me and thanking me.

But I don't want him to thank me. I don't want his softness.

I want to touch him, hold him. I want more.

I strain at his hands shackling my wrists. And then I rock my hips into him, the thin cotton of my nightdress scraping against the length of him, hard beneath his canvas shorts. He makes a surprised hum in his throat and releases my wrists. I reach out, sending my hands under his shirt to the heat of his skin.

The breath whooshes out of me as he rocks against me, hitting me perfectly, so that a bright light sparks through me. I gasp against his mouth and he catches it. He sends his tongue across my lips and then rocks into me again. The fabric between us scrapes and abrades. There's an insistent growing ache pulsing where he's rolling over me. The motion of his mouth matches the motion of his hips. He crests with the waves—a steady, luxurious rhythm that sends a warmth glowing over me.

I cling to him, sending my hands over him. Tasting him and touching him. And then, as I curl my fingers into his shoulders and wrap my legs around his hips, he raggedly whispers against my mouth, "Fi."

The light sparks, and I crash against him as he takes my cries in his mouth.

"Yes. Yes."

I come.

I come on the beach, under the silver-mooned sky, with the waves crashing over the sand and Aaron McCormick kissing me into senselessness.

I come from a kiss.

And then, when I collapse, breathless, he pulls me onto his chest and we lie in the sand, staring up at the stars until they fade from the sky and the pink blush of sunrise steals over us.

I wake up alone.

26

The bookshop is on the road to Carouge. The shop is all glossy antiqued wood and arched windows that let in ribbons of golden light. Dust motes float like dandelion seeds in the musty, paper-scented air, and breathing in, you're automatically assured this is a place where books are sold.

    Old books. New books. Rare books. Used books.

    All the books.

    When Mila and I push through the tinkling glass door, a quiet hush envelops us. She stops in the entry, her eyes wide and darting wildly across the antique wooden bookshelves holding a veritable forest of stories.

    At the sound of a book page turning, the whisper of paper over paper, Mila grips my hand and whispers, "Mummy, do you think they have poems here?"

    I smile down at her, avoiding the curious gaze of a fat gray cat perched on the cushioned window seat near the entry.

"I think they have hundreds of poems." I point to a sign over a shelf near the back of the cozy shop, the word "Poetry" written in decorative calligraphy. "Go and see."

With that bit of permission, Mila releases my hand and half-skips, half-walks to the back, darting around comfy wingback chairs, baskets full of books, and overstuffed shelves.

Mila has an assignment for her summer art camp. She must find a poem she loves and bring it to camp tomorrow. She'll make a visual-art representation of the poem using watercolors or pastels or clay, or whatever she desires. But first she must find a poem.

We could search online, but sometimes feeling the smooth crease of a book under your hand, tracing the cool paper and following the smudges of ink as the words fall down a page—that is what you need to fall in love with a poem.

So here we are.

At the back of the shop, Mila stands on her tiptoes and pulls a hardcover book from the shelf. The large book dwarfs her as she clutches it in her hands, and then, looking around, she drops to the thick rug and opens the pages.

I smile, wave to the bookseller behind the counter—a short man with a tuft of feathery gray hair and a kind smile—and meander toward Mila. The bookshop is nearly empty. There are three other customers browsing shelves, and, of course, the fat gray cat.

The cozy shop has a soft, dreamy feel— the sort of place where you can easily imagine the pages of books are windows to other worlds. It reminds me of Amy. I think she would love it here.

I picture her piling books into her arms until her load is so high it reaches to her nose. She'd hurry from shelf to shelf and drag all the books down—classics, philosophy, poetry.

The image of Amy here, sharing a line of poetry with Mila, Sean chasing the cat through the rows, is so vivid that I have to blink to clear it away. Before I know it I'll be imagining McCormick here too—no, Aaron. He's Aaron now. If I don't stop I'll picture him taking Amy's load of books with his laughing smile so that she can collect another dozen to read.

Aaron isn't here though. Amy isn't here. Not Sean either.

They stay in my dreams.

Maybe it should worry me that I'm bringing them into my life, creating watches based on afternoons with Aaron, thinking of Amy's delight at a bookshop, but I push the thought aside.

Mila glances up from the book as I kneel down next to her.

"I like this one," she says, pointing to the illustrated poem on the page. It's an ink drawing of a little black-haired boy in a sun hat holding a bucket by the sea. "It reminds me of when we go the beach. I'll do a painting of the lake with me and you and Uncle Daniel."

I read the poem. It's a rhyming verse about a little boy at the seaside, digging holes for the sea to fill up.

"I like it."

Mila nods, her red hair curling around her face. She's in a bright pink dress and her cheeks are red from our stroll down the sun-soaked sidewalks.

"Well done, you. Who's the poet?"

Mila flips the book closed, displaying the cover. My

chest squeezes at the gold-scripted name. Robert Louis Stevenson. The book is "A Child's Garden of Verses."

"May I see it?" I ask, and Mila nods and hands me the cool, glossy-paged book.

There's something niggling at me. Amy was reading "Treasure Island" by Robert Louis Stevenson, but she also quoted a poem to Sean, asking him to repeat after her.

I flip through the pages, their smooth vellum flicking across my fingers. Until—there—I hit my finger to the page, pressing sharply into the cool paper.

All alone beside the streams
And up the mountain-sides of dreams.

She was quoting a poem from this book. She was quoting "The Land of Nod."

Goose bumps rise along my arms and I close the book.

"Mummy?"

"Grandma read this same book to me as a little girl," I tell her, thinking of the tattered copy my mum kept for nighttime stories. "I was remembering a poem."

"Can I have my own book?" she asks, her small nose wrinkling. "I'll bring it to camp, and if you like, I'll paint a picture of your poem too."

"Yes, of course you can have your own copy." I reach over and tug on a strand of her hair, then I hand the book back to her.

"Before we leave, may I pet the cat?"

Mila loves animals. Dogs, cats, fish, insects—really any living thing. It's why I'm never surprised if she holds out her open palms and there's an angler worm or a ladybug in her hand.

"We'll ask the man," I say, nodding toward the counter.

A moment later, he confirms Gilbert is the type of cat who loves to be pet, especially under his chin and behind his ears.

As we turn toward the window seat where Gilbert stretches lazily in a circle of sun, there's a chirping ring, muffled by my purse.

It's Max's ringtone.

Mila glances between me and the cat, then toward me again.

"If you'd like to pet Gilbert, I'll just say hello to Max."

She's off in a flash, her pink dress spinning with her. I smile and pull my phone free.

"Hello, Max."

"Fiona," he says, his voice rolling over my name with a laughing lilt.

I have a flash of Aaron raggedly whispering, "Fi." My gut clenches, and then I squash the memory. It's not for this place or this time.

I turn my attention to Max. "You're in a good mood." I can tell by the lightness in his voice.

I smile as I drag my hand across the colorful spines of a dozen paperbacks, my fingers thumping over the glossy binding.

Close by, Mila perches on the edge of the window seat, carefully inching toward Gilbert. The cat watches her with yellow-eyed, lazy indifference.

"Am I?" Max asks, the sound of traffic and wind rushing through the connection. "I hadn't noticed. It's strange. People have been ducking around corners and hiding behind ugly potted trees all day, every time they see me coming. I thought it was the fact I look like I could chew up a bicycle and spit it out. But perhaps they're running from my charm."

"A bicycle?"

"Hmm?"

"Did something happen?"

"No. The ducking and hiding is a normal day. I've been told I'm unapproachable."

I cover a snort. "I'm sorry." My smile widens. "What did you want? Mila and I are doing very important things."

I can almost hear the gears turning in his mind. Outside the golden light of sunset has spilled down the red-tiled roofs and fallen into a dusky evening gray.

A car horn sounds and then Max asks, "How important?"

"Supremely."

"I've been told I'm excellent at disrupting supremely important plans. It's one of my best qualities."

"Is this flirting?" I ask, wondering at the wry note in his voice.

"Fiona, if you can't tell, then it is definitely not flirting."

I laugh. The cat twitches his ears toward me and Mila looks up, smiling as she scoots another inch closer to Gilbert.

I think she's being cautious and slow so he doesn't run away at her approach.

Perhaps that's what Max is doing. Or it's what he's been doing since Christmas Eve.

My stomach dips at the thought of Max flirting with me. It's not anything we've done before. It's beyond the bounds of our friendship, like the high-tide mark, never to be crossed.

But now, soon, we'll be crossing it.

I've known Max for so long I know him as well as I know myself. He makes me smile. He makes me laugh. But he doesn't make me glow.

But what am I learning from my dreams? From the dreams that supposedly show me my greatest desire.

It's that I want to be loved. To love.

That I have to trust. Or risk living the rest of my life alone.

I have to trust.

I press the phone against my ear. "As we've never flirted before I wasn't sure."

"For the love of— Fi, you'll be sure. When I flirt, you'll be sure." Max sounds grumpy now, and the rumble of rush-hour traffic accentuates his tone.

I smile even though he can't see me. "Well then, what do you want? I have cats to pet, books to buy, and . . ." I think for a moment and then decide. "Ice cream to devour."

We passed a patisserie on the way to the bookshop with a small freezer of ice cream displayed in the window. There was strawberry with ruby-red chunks streaked through the pink. Strawberry with chocolate sauce is Mila's favorite. It reminds her of the small, tartly flavored mountain strawberries that are only found in markets in the first few weeks of June. We always buy containers full and dip them in melted chocolate. We come away sticky and buzzing, with strawberry juice dripping down our cheeks and melted chocolate drizzling down our fingers.

"What kind of ice cream?"

Of course he would focus on ice cream. Max has a sweet tooth that knows no bounds.

"Strawberry. I saw hazelnut in the window as well."

Hazelnut is Max's favorite. Mentioning it is practically an invitation.

He knows it. "I'll be there. Where are you?"

"At the antique bookshop in Carouge."

"I know the one. I'll be there in five."

"Is this a date?"

"No. I have to fly to Paris in the morning until Friday. I wanted to see you before I left."

I smile softly. Mila has finally scooted next to Gilbert. She strokes her hand gently over the gray fur on his head. He closes his eyes and tilts his chin, offering her the smooth fur underneath.

"You wanted to see me?"

"I always see you and Mila before business trips."

That's true. But this time it feels different.

Mila glances at me, triumphant as Gilbert begins a slow, rapturous purr. Her patience paid off.

"I'm here." I look up as the bells on the door jingle and Max strides inside the hushed atmosphere of the bookshop. When he sees me, his brown eyes spark and he gives me a happy smile.

He's in a light gray summer suit, his black hair wind-blown and messy. Clearly, he came here directly from work.

He takes in the scene—the paper-musty scent, the muffled quiet, Mila on the bench petting a boneless cat

—and then he walks directly to my side and says in a soft voice, "You look beautiful."

Mila turns to him, puts a pointer finger to her lips, and then nods at Gilbert. He's rolled on his back and is kneading his paws against Mila's legs.

Max nods and pretends to zip his lips.

I glance at him from the side and whisper, "Was that flirting?"

He gives me a flat look that causes a laugh to bubble in my chest. I keep it contained for fear of disturbing Gilbert's ecstasy.

"Apparently not," Max says, the grumpy tone back.

I grin at him, and his flat look vanishes into a smile of shared history and friendship.

Max turns his attention to Mila and kneels down to carefully stroke Gilbert behind the ears.

The bookseller walks next to me and says in a quiet voice, "We close in five minutes."

I nod, ready to check out.

But then I have a thought.

Or... I wonder.

Looking at the hundreds of books lining the shelves, the worlds waiting to be explored, I wonder, where does Amy get her books? Are they all tattered copies, read dozens of times, like the worn ones I've seen her holding? Do they come from neighbors? Or the yellow concrete one-room schoolhouse in Charlestown? She doesn't have internet. She doesn't have a bookstore. She doesn't have any way of getting new books in the dream world she lives in.

I scan the bookshop, my eyes lingering on the sign that reads "Poetry."

I can't take a book to her. But what if I memorized a poem for her? And then another? One poem at a time.

"I have a question," I ask the bookseller as he rings up Mila's book. "If you wanted to buy a book for a fourteen-year-old girl who loves poetry, what would you get?"

He thinks for a moment, rubbing the tuft of gray hair on his head. "French, German, English?"

"English."

He nods. "Emily Dickinson." He stoops down to reach below the counter. When he stands he has a small leather-bound book in his hand. "This just came in."

"She'll like it?"

I've never read Emily Dickinson.

The man gives me his kind smile and flips quickly through the ivory pages, the words flying across them like birds, until he lands on the page he wants. He turns the book to me.

"Here. Read."

I press my hand to the cool paper, keeping the pages beneath me.

"Hope" is the thing with feathers—
That perches in the soul—

My eyes fly to the man's and he nods. "She'll like it."

"Yes. She will."

I smile then and buy a book for a girl who doesn't exist.

On the walk to the ice-cream shop Mila runs ahead,

hopping over the cracks, skipping through the swathes of lamplight flickering on now that dusk is here.

In the cool summer breeze, and the gray dusk scented with old stone roads warmed in the setting sun, Max reaches over and gently takes my hand.

My heart taps out a cautious, worrying beat.

He glances down at me, dark and austere in the shadows, until he steps under a streetlight, and then he's smiling again.

"Can I take you to dinner Friday, when I'm home from Paris?" He runs his thumb over the back of my hand carefully, slowly, like Mila petting Gilbert.

The light in his eyes—

It reminds me of the poem.

Hope is a feathered thing.

I choose to trust. I choose to give it wings.

"Yes."

27

I tumble into my dream. My mum would laugh to hear me say it's like sliding down a moonbeam.

My namesake, given life.

Yet there's a sliding, falling sensation and wind rushing in my ears. My stomach rises and falls, shooting down, down, until—

I open my eyes.

The wind rushing in my ears is the noise of morning waves, slate-gray and crashing over the sandy shore. White gulls sweep overhead, calling out a harsh, querulous morning alarm. I blink into the dawn light. The sky is half-dark, half-pink, and gold and orange as the sun slips along the water's edge. The gold light reflects in the wavy surface.

I stretch, my muscles sore and my neck pinchy. Cold, shaded sand shifts under me and sticks to my bare legs.

I'm thirsty. I have to pee. Yet I don't want to get up, because I'm lying on the beach, my head on Aaron's chest, his arms wrapped around me. I have one leg thrown over his. He's warm and his chest moves in a lulling rhythm as steady as the rolling waves.

"Do you think we should get up?" he asks, his voice sleep-roughened. "Or should we sneak inside and try to sleep for another fifteen?"

His hand drifts over my back, tracing a slow circle at the base of my spine. A tingle rides over my skin. I lift my head then and peer down at him.

He gives me a sleepy smile and I'm reminded of the day I first woke to find him. He smiled at me then too. Although, now that I know him better, I think I misread the situation.

"Last Saturday..."

His hand pauses on my spine. "Yeah?"

"When I woke up and you told me we still had a few minutes... what did you mean?"

Aaron's eyebrows rise. "That we had a few minutes."

"To?"

"Sleep."

"Sleep?" I repeat.

His eyes soften with a dreamy expression. "It's been years since I've slept past five thirty. Wouldn't it be nice?"

Oh. Okay. Yes. I completely misread the situation. He didn't want me to get back in bed for a long, orgasm-filled morning. He wanted to sleep.

I don't know why this makes me cranky. It's not as if I wanted to have sex with him on Saturday, but I tense and move to roll off him.

"Fi?" he whispers, the word barely heard above the sound of the waves.

I still. My eyes fly to his and I sink back into his

warmth, my muscles loosening. A soft hum steals over me, running over my skin.

"Yes?"

He smiles then, his eyes warming. "Just wondering," he says, then he cups my face in his hands, his thumbs rubbing over my cheeks, and pulls me down for a kiss.

His lips brush across mine, whisper-soft. And I exhale, the breath forced from me at the feel of him. His fingers stroke my skin and an ache builds in my chest as he runs his mouth over mine. I breathe in the salt of the sea, the perfumed flowers opening and tilting their heads toward the sunrise. My blood thrums in time with the sea.

He pulls back then, the heat of his mouth still on mine. His heart thunders beneath me. When I shift over him he makes a small, deep noise in the back of his throat.

"Morning."

I smile. "Good morning."

His fingers curl on my cheeks. "You're still here."

"I am."

"I thought you'd go in to bed. What does Fi mean?"

I stare at him, unsure how to answer. Do I tell him it's my name? With that, though, I'd have to convince him I'm not Becca and that he doesn't actually exist outside my dream world.

"It's a code word."

He lets out an amused huff of air and then takes his hands from my face. "Why?"

I shrug. "It's so you know I'm me."

Me, and not the other dream Becca. The one who loves Robert and wants to leave the island.

He looks as if he's going to argue, but then he must decide against it.

"We should go," he says, looking across the water at the rising sun. "We have to get Amy and Sean up, head to work."

Wait.

Work?

As in, work, work?

I *work* in my dreams?

In Geneva I work twelve-hour days. Before Mila I often spent eighteen hours at the office. I'm not averse to work. In fact, I love what I do. However, I didn't think I'd take that passion with me into my dreams.

"It's Monday?" I ask.

Aaron nods, his black hair blowing in the wind.

I wait for him to say more, to tell me where exactly I work and what exactly I do, but he doesn't. Instead he sits up in the sand, taking me with him.

I squeak and wrap my legs around his waist as he stands.

I grab his shoulders and hang on as he holds my hips. Sand rains from my skin and my nightdress falls around my bare legs. The ocean air wraps around us, and at the grass line, crickets begin to sing a morning melody.

The air is morning-cool, not yet tinged with humidity and heat. The cottages are still dark and sleepy, and it's just Aaron, me, and the rising sun.

He tugs me close and I keep my arms and legs wrapped around him. He rests his forehead to mine, looking into my eyes.

"Thank you," he says, his voice low.

"For what?" My heart thuds in the space between us.

"For last night. Thank you for listening. Thank you for . . . coming into the water after me."

He doesn't mean literally. I know that. I think he means that for maybe the first time he doesn't feel as if he's treading water alone, trying to keep his head above the waves.

"Anytime," I tell him. "I'll come into the water after you anytime you need."

With that, I swear he's going to kiss me again. My lips tingle and warm.

But then he only smiles and carries me across the sand, through the shaded, dew-covered grass, onto the wide porch, and into our home.

28

I STARE RESOLUTELY AT THE GLASSY ORANGE EYE OF THE snapper, its black pupil perfectly round and accusing. There's a case of them—the snapper—all flashy red and silver scales and pink cheeks. The smell of freshly caught fish, salty and sea-rich, spices the air.

It's 8 a.m. and the sun hangs like a bright nectarine in the sky, ripe with heat. A trickle of sweat drips down my back and not even the scant shade of the gazebo or the breeze off the sea can chase away the rising humidity.

Overhead a flurry of gulls circles, certain they'll be feeding on entrails soon. In the shallows, at the water's edge, dark dorsal fins—they look like sharks, but Maranda said they're tarpon—churn the water impatiently.

I'm at the beach gazebo/makeshift fish market/my job.

Down the sandy road (and sometime runway) the

crossing guard—I learned his name is Odie—lounges in the shade of the tall, glossy leaved tree, playing solitaire in the sand. He interrupted his Queen-Jack-Ten layout to hold up his stop sign and then finally give the all clear.

Across the road the shop is open. Junie waved when she dragged a heavy display of mangos and bananas onto the street in front of the store. She huffed and puffed, her pregnant belly getting in the way of the bins, until finally she managed to tug it to a spot in the shade. Jordi came out then, pushed the large bins a few inches to the right, and declared the job satisfactory. Junie shoved him back into the shop.

Charlestown is awake. Amy's at summer-school classes for gifted students—this includes her, a six-year old named Reija with encyclopedic knowledge of all the country flags in the world, and an eleven-year old boy named Olly who wants to be a marine biologist. Amy claimed it isn't truly for gifted students, it's just for kids who want to learn even during the summer.

"If this island is a prison, I may as well expand my mind beyond the gates," she said this morning as she spooned porridge into her mouth and shoved her books into a scuffed backpack.

And then she was gone, rushing out the door. And Aaron hurried from the shower to the bedroom to the kitchen, strapping Sean into his high chair and giving him porridge and mashed bananas. Then he kissed me, one last feathered touch of our lips, and he was gone.

So when Maranda knocked on my door and said, "You aren't ready!" I let her stomp in, grab baggy jeans, a long-sleeve cotton shirt, a sun hat, and yellow rubber wellies, and thrust them at me. "Get dressed!"

She was so brisk, her white hair sticking on end, her dark brown eyes sharp and demanding in her sun-wrinkled face, that I tugged on the clothes in a hurry.

After I did she dropped Sean's baby bag in my arms and pulled him, banana-smothered and happy, from his high chair.

"We're late," she said.

For what, I didn't know. Until we arrived at the little beach across from the "airport."

Aldon and his tall, wiry son, Chris, were hopping off their fishing boat, dragging crates of gasping or post-gasping fish onto the beach.

Aldon and Chris are in the water now, repairing gear and scrubbing barnacles from the hull. Chris mentioned casually he didn't get any sleep. Up till midnight searching for Amy, then out at three for the morning catch. He seemed proud of himself, though, with the confident, easy grin of a twenty-year-old.

"Glad she's all right," he said. "She's a funny one. Told me I should read 'The Old Man and the Sea.' I told her, 'Not until I'm an old man—then it'll be a biography.'" He shook his head and laughed then dropped his final crate of flopping fish onto the concrete floor of the gazebo.

For me.

To clean.

And sell.

And then deliver to the people who have scheduled orders, and also to the restaurant. I'm amazed there *is* a restaurant on this island.

In the shade of the gazebo, next to the low slatted wooden bench, Sean pats the sand with a yellow plastic shovel. He has a line of small toy cars, and every time he finishes digging a hole, he shoves a car in and shouts, "Uh-oh!"

Standing around the plywood table with glistening snapper lining the surface, Maranda, Essie, and Dee all stare at me.

"What's wrong with you?" Essie asks, the liver spots on her face dark and her knuckles swollen from arthritis. She grips a knife in her hand and forcefully chops the tail from the fish in front of her. It makes a crunching noise, like scissors cutting through corrugated cardboard.

She picks up the tail fin and tosses it into a lined ten-gallon plastic bucket. It hits with a thunk, and overhead a gull swoops toward us with a throaty, insistent call.

I flinch at the noise, and then at her sawing through the dorsal fin at the top of the chunky fish.

I wish I didn't have that mango porridge. It was the exact color of the snapper's orange flesh.

Not that I'm against eating fish. This is just ... gross.

I could handle this, except for the noise of the knife ripping through the fins. *Kwwwwkkkk. Kwwwwk.*

I take a deep breath of fish-tinged air as Essie reaches a swollen knuckle into the side of her snapper and hooks her finger to tug out the gills. They release with a sharp pop.

"You get paid by how many you clean," Dee says, not looking up from the pile of fish in front of her. She has a dozen fish in her bucket. Essie has fifteen. Maranda has eight.

Me? I have zero.

"This is my job?" I ask again, just to be sure. "This is how I make money?"

Why in the world would I dream this?

"No," says Maranda, shooting me a look. "This is what we do Monday mornings. And Thursday mornings. The rest of the time you work at Grinders."

Grinders?

"Are you still pretending you're Swedish?" Dee asks, pulling slimy entrails from her fish's stomach.

"Swiss." I pick up my knife. How hard can this be? I get five cents per cleaned and prepared fish. Which begs the question, why am I doing this for five cents a fish?

Maranda's pulled another snapper from the crate and slapped it onto the table. I watch her out of the corner of my eye, determined to do everything she does.

Across the table, Dee tugs a giant, bulbous gray fish with a fat, blobby head onto the table. It hits with a squishy thud.

"Grouper," she calls, cackling happily. I've never in my life seen a tiny, ninety-plus-year-old woman lift such an ugly, fat-lipped, freakishly large fish (it must weigh seventy pounds) with so much excitement.

I concentrate on watching Maranda without her knowing I'm watching. I grip the cold handle of the knife and slice through the fins on the sides of the fish. They cut with a jagged, zipper-tearing noise. I flip the cold, scaled fish and cut through the other fin.

Maranda's moving quickly. I hurry, trying to keep up with her slicing through the tail, then the dorsal fin.

"You never told us," Essie says, tossing entrails into her bucket. "What did you do in New York?"

"Me?" I ask, blinking at her.

"Yes, you. None of us have been to New York," Essie

says, a spark of something in her pale blue eyes. It's then I remember she's Aaron's grandmother, my grandma-in-law.

She doesn't look like Aaron. She's wrinkled, sun-browned, covered in liver spots. She's small and hasn't been exactly warm, but I remember how Aaron said her banana bread was the only thing that could bring him out of the water. He loves her. And Sean does too. He gave her a raspberry kiss when he saw her this morning.

"You and Robert," Essie says, prying at the fleshy cheek of the snapper under her knife. "What did you do?"

"She had an appointment with her parents' lawyer. For their will. You know that," Maranda says, scowling at Essie. She pulls the gills free and I follow suit, tugging my snapper's gills loose with a pop.

I highly doubt I had an appointment. From what Robert said, the only appointment I had was with him.

"But why was Robert there?" Essie asks, still digging at the snapper's mouth.

Exactly.

"He was visiting friends," Maranda says. "Becca and Robert didn't *see* each other. They merely took the same plane."

"They were in the same city at the same time. Of course they *saw* each other."

"It's a big place," Maranda says, chopping at her fish.

"Not that big."

"Millions of people isn't big? How would you know, Esmerelda McCormick? You've never left this island! You couldn't imagine it if you tried."

"Well!"

"Well, don't talk about things you don't know about. That's what I say."

I imagine Essie's about to say something like, "It's fishy," but Dee says quietly, "Robert brought back some of the boys' things."

Essie and Maranda turn toward her, their argument forgotten. The sound of old grief was in Dee's voice, like dried flowers left in the pages of a book too long. One touch and they'll crumble.

"That's what he was doing in New York. Jay lived there for a few months, remember? His landlord found a box when clearing out the storage unit. It wasn't much. Jeans, T-shirts, a jar of change, that little good-luck seashell he carried with him everywhere. Robert promised he'd bring it back to me."

Everyone is quiet. Even the gulls have ceased their shouts for scraps.

"That was good of him," Maranda says, peering out over the sea. "Jay did love that seashell."

It's clear, if Essie has it now, he wasn't carrying it with him the day of the Gulf Stream swim.

"I was thinking about giving it to Amy," Dee says, looking out over the slate-gray waves. "Since she wants so badly to leave. She can take a bit of the island with her."

I don't know what to say, so I don't say anything. Neither does anyone else.

Essie reaches over and squeezes Dee's arm.

Dee's shoulders lift with a sigh and then fall. "Well," she says briskly, staring down at the bulbous-headed fish in front of her, "I do love grouper."

Essie hums an agreement.

"You can never get tired of eating grouper," Maranda agrees.

Then she slices open the belly of her snapper and hooks her finger inside, dragging out the guts. I follow her motions, slicing deep and then pulling free the insides of my snapper.

My stomach churns at the slimy, gushy feel. I drop the guts into the scrap bucket. Then I lay the fish in my bucket.

I wipe my wet hands on my apron in satisfaction.

"Well done," Maranda says, a joking light in her eyes. "You've done one. Five cents. That'll get you a banana."

Dee cackles and Essie hides a smile behind her hand.

I squint across the street at the placard above the fruit bin. Bananas are fifteen cents each.

So, in reality, I can't get a banana.

The price is high considering there's a banana grove in the cottage's back garden, dozens of yellow bananas dripping in great clumps down the pearl-necklace-like chains.

Another drop of sweat trails down my back and the smell of fish guts drifts up on the humid breeze. Sean lets out another "Uh-oh!" while Maranda and Essie begin a heated debate about the best way to cook grouper.

Dee sends me a gentle smile, the soft lines of her face folding, her salt-and-pepper hair sticking up in the ocean breeze. She's wearing a rubbery apron. We all are, but hers dwarfs her she's so small.

"Not feeling like yourself?" she asks quietly, the sound of her knife thunking on the plywood table.

"I guess," I say, considering the fish in the crates waiting to be cleaned and gutted. "I'm trying to figure out why, exactly, it's my dream to gut fish."

She laughs then—her high, amused cackle. "You do it to keep us honest," she says, her eyes dancing with laughter. "Essie always tries to cheat us out of five cents. It adds up."

"Really?"

"Or . . ." She thinks for a moment. "You do it because you love your Maranda. She loves the fish market, being useful, seeing her neighbors, but she's not strong enough anymore to carry the crates or do the deliveries. You do that for her now."

I give Dee a startled glance and then look over at Maranda, my dream grandma. She's still arguing with Essie about the merits of coal fires on the beach versus cooking in a smoker. Both of them are slicing at their fish, cleaning with efficient, practiced hands.

According to Dee I'm here, on the hot, humid beach gutting fish, because I love my grandma and I want her to feel useful.

I let that knowledge settle inside me. I don't have a grandma in real life—both of them died before I was born. Neither of my parents ever talked about them.

I didn't realize there was a hole in my heart the shape of a grandmother with quick hands, no-nonsense eyes, and a ready smile. I didn't realize I had that longing. But then Maranda looks over at me, catches me staring, and winks.

She slides into my heart right then and there. In that empty space.

A grandma.

One who loves me.

At my stunned look, Maranda pats my hand and I grip hers. Her skin is papery thin and wrinkled, her warm hands fine-boned and calloused.

"Done," Essie says, wiping her hands on her apron.

Sean hits the sand with his shovel and says, "Bana bana bana."

Essie gives him a quick nod. "Yes, time for banana bread. You smart, smart boy. He takes after my side of the family."

Maranda snorts and releases my hand. "Hardly. He clearly takes after Becca, who takes after me."

And they're off again.

The next two hours are spent selling fish to anyone who stops by. The remaining fish are packaged in heavy coolers, and I'm pushed by Maranda down the road with a pointed finger to the Saunders' house, to the restaurant called—from what I can see—EAT, to Junie's shop, to the community center where a group of kids are playing in a yard with free-roaming chickens, a slide, and a merry-go-round, to the house with the green kayaks out front.

Maranda chats with everyone we see while I carry heavy loads of fish and Sean devours fistfuls of banana bread with Essie and Dee in the shade.

At ten the sun is a bright slice of light lacing through the palm trees, baking the sand. I'm ready for a cold iced drink. The lukewarm water in Sean's baby bag is not quenching my thirst.

It's then, after Aldon hands me five cents with a twinkle in his eye, and while I'm cleaning off the plywood table, I see Aaron.

He's down the sandy road, past Odie the crossing guard, near the edge of town. He's at a small, square yellow house, kneeling next to the wooden porch, swinging a hammer.

Okay.

I'm not the type of person who gets excited about men with hammers. This is not a fantasy I've ever had.

Ever.

I wouldn't choose to dream about it. Not consciously. And I wouldn't look forward to watching it.

But Aaron's leaning forward, and his white T-shirt stretches tightly across his shoulders. The muscles of his back are highlighted by the sun falling through the gables of the porch. As he swings, the muscles in his arms tighten and strain.

If I thought I was thirsty before, now I'm dying of thirst.

Even though he's fifty meters away, I swear I can see a drop of sweat trickling down his neck. I want to put my mouth over him. I want to know the salt and sweat of him.

He repositions the board he's working on, places a nail, and swings again.

I catch my breath. It's sticky-hot and I'm sweaty, covered in fish guts, and dying of thirst, and all I want to do is cross the sun-hot sand, push Aaron onto the shaded grass, and ask him to whisper my name.

"What is he doing?" I ask, my voice scratchy and parched.

"I asked him to fix my porch step," Dee says, looking in the direction of my gaze.

"Is that his job?"

Is he a carpenter? A handyman? Is that what he does now?

"Job? No."

I watch him insert another nail. It glints in the sun, and then he strikes it, nailing the board in place.

I'm overheated. The air is suddenly heavy with salt and sand and the memory of lying beneath him as he kissed me senseless. I'm glowing with the memory of his mouth on mine.

"What does he do then?" I ask, watching him work.

Dee glances at me. "What he's always done. Whatever anyone asks of him."

I look at her then, tearing my eyes from Aaron. "What does that mean?"

She frowns at me, her wrinkles wrinkling. "You know. He fixes. He helps." She holds up her hand and ticks off on her fingers. "Repairs—carpentry, plumbing, electric, roofs—whatever you need, he'll do. Hurricane prep—trimming trees, taking down coconuts—and cleanup in the aftermath—downed trees, flooding, home repairs. He's our only certified paramedic besides Nurse Nancy—he saved Errol's life, remember that. He's island council, organizes beach cleanups, community service. He does import/export paperwork and orders and distributes supplies. He's president of the council, he goes out with Aldon and Chris if they're expecting a big catch, he . . ." She narrows her eyes. "Do you need me to go on?"

I stare at her, the waves roaring onto the beach, echoing the strange sensation inside me. "There's more?"

"Hmm. Swim lessons, swim safety, CPR. Boat repairs. Generator repairs. You have that back garden—he's out there a lot. He teaches the ocean science class at the school. He's taken to walking Whiskers every morning since Ayla broke her leg. What else?"

"He's a dad," I say, a curious sensation rushing over me.

Dee smiles and pats my arm, studying my expression. "Becca, you look like you're falling in love with your husband."

I send her a startled glance and she laughs.

"Do I?"

Am I?

Have I already?

I said I would. I said I'd take all this dream had to offer—the happiness, the love, the everything.

I look back at Aaron, the line of his shoulders, the black flash of his hair, the solidity of him. My heart beats wildly, wings fluttering in my chest.

Would it be so dangerous to love him? Would it be so wrong to fall irrevocably in love with a dream?

I didn't think so before.

"You do," Dee says, a satisfied smile on her face.

My chest pinches as I remember Aaron thanking me for coming into the water after him. *Anytime,* I promised. *I'll come after you anytime.*

He stands then, and when he turns his gaze immediately lands on me, as if he knew I was here the entire time. As if he could feel my eyes on him.

And from fifty meters away I feel the heat of him. His dark eyes, the tilt of his head—they make my stomach flutter and my heart race.

For five seconds, ten, we stand separated by a sunlit street, looking into each other's eyes.

And I decide, yes, I'm falling. It feels like sliding, tumbling, into a dream. As Aaron lifts his hand, holding it up to me, I know that when I fall into this dream, he'll be here to catch me.

I'll come into the water after him. And he'll always come for me.

29

Grinders is a coffee shop owned by Robert, which shouldn't surprise me, but it does. It isn't like the coffee shops of Geneva, serious about espresso and cream and flaky pastries. Nor is it like the coffee shops of England, the uniformly eclectic chains of Costa or Nero.

Instead Grinders is on the first floor of a bright, butterscotch-yellow concrete house facing the sea. It's across from the fish market gazebo, down from the "airport" and Junie's shop. It's probably the most lovely coffee shop I've been in in my entire life.

Outside there's a line of blooming bougainvillea bushes, vibrant with coral and fuchsia flowers. The bushes shelter the deep wooden porch with its wide planks and lazily spinning ceiling fans. A band of sunlight crosses the worn planks and leads to the double front doors. They're swung wide to let in the sea breeze and the salty, sandy smell of the water. In the back I have another door open so that the breeze rushes through, tugging at my hair and cooling my sweat-dappled skin.

The coffee shop is small—there are only four tables and a wooden counter with tall metal benches lining the windows overlooking the water. But the smallness is perfect. The tables and counter are made of sea-gray driftwood. The wooden floors are old, rubbed-down and smooth from years of sand-coated feet treading over them. The walls are painted a pale gray-blue, the exact color of the foam that caps the waves as they break against the reef.

There's music, a collection of old jazz CDs playing on salt-battered speakers, currently tuned to the lyrics, "*Never gonna die, baby, you know we're gonna live forever.*"

Behind the counter, at the espresso machine, with the perfume of Jamaican Blue Mountain beans rising around me and the crash of the waves filtering through the open doors, I can almost believe the lyrics.

Maybe the people here, in this world, do go on forever.

Robert leans his elbows on the counter, dropping his chin into his hands. The sun glints on his copper hair. He's wearing his "I'm innocent and naïve" expression—one that must've fooled a large number of people for him to keep using it.

He watches me with a quizzical smile, waiting, I think, for something. Although I'm not sure what.

I washed up after the fish market and changed into a yellow cotton dress. Junie came by the cottage ready to gather Sean. This is apparently a long-established pattern—she chatted about doing warm-up runs for when her baby's born while she gathered a baby bag and filled it with crackers, purees, sippy cups, and nappies.

Then Maranda walked me to the coffee shop, telling me again that I was "late."

Robert was inside waiting for me. Maranda left right away. I wish she hadn't.

"Would you like a coffee?" I ask, ignoring the question in his eyes.

He sighs then and straightens to his full height. He's tall, long-distance-cyclist-thin. He's handsome. Whether he's my taste or not, it's empirically true. He has a perfectly symmetrical face with high cheekbones and a sharp nose. He walks with a loose stride, that earnest easiness. The only thing that gives away his true nature is his close-cropped hair, his clothing—linen dress shirts, crisp pants—and the flicker of shadow that sometimes breaks through his smooth gaze.

"Your coffee?" he asks, the edge of his mouth twitching. "Are you trying to punish me?"

I turn on the espresso maker and send a stream of steaming water through, cleaning and sanitizing.

Apparently, just like people here think I can't swim, they also think I can't make coffee.

"How about a latte?" I ask, tamping down the espresso and then placing two shot glasses beneath the machine.

He smiles at that, tight lines forming around his mouth. "If that's what I have to do. I'll drink a thousand terrible lattes to get back in your good graces."

"If my coffee is so bad, why did you hire me?"

As soon as I ask the question I know the answer. An energy crackles off Robert—the same one that shot from him when he spun me behind the cottage, caged me against the wood siding, and cursed, "It hurts when I want to touch you, knowing that I can't."

I break the hold of his gaze and send the steaming water through the grind. And instead of looking at Robert, I set the metal pitcher under the spout and steam the milk.

The noise is loud. The hissing of the steam and the grinding of the machine interject into the heavy silence.

The bitter scent of the espresso and the warmed milk climbs up as I swirl the milk and froth into a mug.

Robert clears his throat, glancing behind him at the open doors. The sun is high overhead, white and hot. It's nearly noon and the shadows have run away with the heat.

I push the mug toward him. It's chipped. A generic white ceramic mug with gray scratches in the glaze. Robert ignores it.

Instead he stares at the curling of my blond hair around my ears and the perspiration lining my forehead. "I'm sorry about last night."

I cross my arms over my chest. "I don't know what you mean."

His mouth tightens. "Becca."

"Apology accepted."

He frowns, a hint of frustration in his eyes. "Can I see you tonight?"

"No."

"Tomorrow morning?"

"No. Not ever."

"You said that before. Then you came. Is this a game? Is that what this is?"

I clutch the edge of the counter. "I don't play games."

"You play plenty of games."

I shake my head. "You should go."

His jaw tightens and he scrubs a hand down his face. When he looks at me again, his eyes are tired and his expression worn. "I don't know what you're playing at. But you're not doing McCormick any favors. It's because he's my friend I'm telling you this. Stop making him believe you care. Stop giving him hope. It's cruel—"

"I don't know what you're talking about."

"I saw the way he looked at you. Fifteen years he's been your husband. He's been your friend. Don't make him think it's more. Because when we leave it'll destroy him. If you make him love you and then we leave— That's not what I signed up for."

"He already loved me. He loved me when we married."

"Not like this. Not like what I saw this morning."

"What exactly are you saying?"

"I'm saying"—Robert leans forward, his expression earnest, anguished—"leave him be. He doesn't need the hurt you're aiming to pile on top of him."

I stare at Robert, stunned at the vehemence in his voice. Suddenly I wonder if he's a part of my subconscious warning me about Max.

Is this what I'm doing to him?

I chose to give him hope. To see if love can grow.

But I've been worried that in the end it will only hurt him. Is Robert telling me my fears are founded?

"You're hurting him too," I say, my voice a whisper above the waves.

Robert's shoulders slump and he looks down at the counter, a bitter twist to his mouth. "I know. I wonder, am I doing it to punish him or myself? Or is this truly just love? I tell myself he'll thank me someday."

The door bangs then. It slams against the plaster wall. I jump at the sharp, cracking noise, and Robert half-turns, looking toward the sunlit entry.

No one is there.

When he looks back at me his expression is earnest and innocently blank again, the heavy emotions blown away on the sharp gust of wind.

But I have something to say. "I told you before. I'm not leaving with you. I'm married. Whatever you feel, it has to end."

Robert shakes his head as if he's disappointed in me. He taps a long finger against the counter and then straightens, looking back at the door. "I'm working with McCormick this afternoon. We're trimming trees. Essie says she feels a storm coming. Her hands are aching."

"A storm?"

Suddenly he grins at me. A crackling, hollow-eyed smile. "Yes. A storm."

And then he turns and strides toward the open doors.

"You forgot your coffee."

He raises a hand—leave it.

I sigh and lean against the counter. I stare at the swirl of the foam and the rich caramel color of the espresso. After a moment of contemplation I lift the mug and take a sip.

The milk is light, creamy. The espresso is nutty and sweet, hinting at toffee and sugar. The coffee coats my tongue and I smile.

If nothing else, I can still make a fantastic cup of coffee.

I'm still smiling when Amy strides in, a bulky backpack slung over one shoulder. She looks around at the empty shop, slides onto a bench at the counter, and says, "Dad wanted me to give you a message."

30

The jazz music has shifted into piano-banging, trumpet-roaring swing. It matches the shift in the wind from stiff breeze to white-capped gust. Outside gulls hug the shoreline, surfing on the wind.

"About the storm?" I ask, my heart kicking up speed either from the burst of caffeine or from Amy's mention of Aaron.

It's funny, the sensations here. The feel of my rushed pulse, the salt-heavy air wicking against my damp skin, even the dip in my stomach when I picture the way Aaron last looked at me. Every sensation, the cool sand on my skin, the texture of Aaron's callouses as he dragged his fingers over my cheeks, the heat that curls through me at the thought of him. Even the creamy, rich foam of the latte that coats my mouth and the buoyant laughter that bubbles in me when I look at Amy perched on the bench—it all feels so real.

As real as real life.

I've already accepted that this dream life feels real. But that doesn't stop me from being surprised when my heart races or my skin prickles from the hot sun.

Amy slouches on the bench, dropping her heavy backpack to the floor. It hits with a loud thud—evidence she stuffed about twenty books inside.

"What storm?" She glances out the door, checking the growing waves and the gathering gulls against the clear, unclouded blue of the sky. She blows out a breath and the dark curls around her face fly up and out. "Maybe tomorrow. Or the next day, I guess."

Then she eyes my half-finished latte on the counter. "Whatcha drinking?"

"A latte. Do you want one?"

She gives me a horrified look that's just like Robert's, only tuned up a thousand notches. "I'll have some water."

"I can make it decaf since you're still a kid," I say, knowing the "just a kid" line will tempt her. Then I pick up my mug and take a sip, closing my eyes and moaning in pleasure.

"Oh my gosh. No. Mom. Your coffee is gross. Not even Dad'll drink it. Stop faking."

I open my eyes and put down my mug with a thud. "What message did you have?"

"From Dad?"

I nod then pull a tall glass from the shelf below the counter and fill it with water. I set it on the counter in front of Amy and start scooping out espresso. I'm going to make her a latte. One rich with cream and milk and sugar. She's going to love it.

I can picture her in Geneva, at one of the bookstore

coffee shops where you can browse for hours, snug among rows and rows of books, a perfectly made coffee warm in your hands. She would love it.

Amy takes a long drink of the water and then wipes the back of her hand across her mouth. She has the gangly arms and legs of a teenager not fully grown into herself yet. She's sharp-lined and narrow-boned, and even when she's still you can see her mind moving a thousand miles a minute. She drops the cup to the counter and then runs her finger through a drop of condensation falling down the glass.

"He asked me to ask you if you wanted to go to dinner with him, because if you do, Junie said she'll babysit Sean. Also, then he'll have to let Sue know so that she can keep the restaurant open." Amy looks up from the trail of condensation on her glass. "Well?"

"A date," I say, thinking of Robert's warning, thinking of Max.

"I don't know. Do married people go on dates? I think Dad just wants some of Sue's fried snapper."

Or . . .

I tamp the espresso grinds down and start the machine. It groans and hisses, and then frothy caramel-brown espresso falls in a thin stream into the shot glass.

I keep busy, tilting the metal pitcher of milk, letting it froth and steam until a soft foam rises. In the cup I add a shot of simple syrup made from raw sugar. It's golden amber, its flavor sweet like wildflower honey. I add espresso and the steamed milk and make a foam clover on top. My mum would be proud.

I push the mug toward Amy. "Try it."

She looks at the latte as if it's a dead snapper, glassy-eyed, cold, and ready to be gutted.

"Go on." I wave my hand.

Gingerly she lifts the cup and takes a cautious sip. When she does her eyes light up and she smiles. "What happened? How did you do that?"

I brush my hands together and say, "I know a few tricks."

She snorts and then takes another drink. "I wonder," she says, "if this is what coffee tastes like in New York."

I shake my head. "No. This is what coffee tastes like in Geneva, Switzerland."

She tilts her head. "How would you know? You've never been there. I bet this is New York coffee. I'm going to picture it." She closes her eyes. "Me in Manhattan, drinking this coffee on the steps of the New York Public Library. Can you see it? The lion statues are on the stairs next to me. There are taxis rushing by. It's fall. No, winter. I've never seen the snow. It's falling, and some of the snowflakes fall on the pages of my book. I'm reading—mmmm, it's. . ."—her eyelashes flutter—"a book of poetry. A new one I've never read. One we don't have here. And—" Her eyes open then, and she shrugs. "I don't know its name. But I'll know it when I see it."

She smiles and takes another sip of the latte. She peeks at me from above the rim of the mug, her eyes happy.

"I have a poem for you," I tell her, leaning against the counter. Another gust of wind rushes through and the door rattles against the wall.

"You do?"

I nod. "I memorized one for you."

Her eyes light up. "When?"

"When I was at a bookshop. I asked the bookseller what sort of poems you'd like."

"Do you have the book?" She sits straight, her eyes hungry.

I shake my head and she deflates, her shoulders slumping.

"But I memorized it. I'll tell you a poem every day until there aren't any more."

She thinks about this, her eyes flashing, her mind whirring. "How about I write them down?"

"All right."

She tugs her backpack onto the bench next to her and unzips the bag. She pulls a notebook free, a pen, and then flips to an empty page. "Ready."

I pull the poem to me. Hold it in my mind. Picture the words and the way they fly across the page.

I think about the words, the meaning that calls to me and makes me want to do things I've never dared do before.

I think about the way Aaron held me as the sun rose over the slate-gray water. I think about how Dee said that I looked as if I was falling in love with my husband. How Robert told me Aaron looked at me as if he was falling—hard.

He wants to take me to dinner.

"Tell your dad yes," I say to Amy, "when you go. Tell him yes. That I want to go to dinner."

She nods, chewing on her pen's cap. "Aren't you going to tell me the poem?"

I smile. "Of course. Write it down. Then if I'm not here you won't forget it."

Then I begin.

And Amy bows her head and writes in quick, breathless letters—

"*Hope*"

31

I sit on the smooth wooden steps of the front porch in the mellow light of the early-evening sun. The shadows are long and the shade is deep and cool. After a day of humidity, the smell of wet soil and thick foliage tinges the air.

I curl the hem of my dress in my hands. I was home a half hour ago. Sean's with Junie. Amy's having dinner with Essie. I faced an empty cottage and a plastic clothesline full of dresses I'd never worn. I thumbed through them, running my hands over the cotton, the linen, the faded colors, and the worn edges. Finally, I found a coral-pink dress with little navy flowers and a ruffled neckline. It looked . . . hopeful.

It matched my appearance here. Shorter, blonde, and round-cheeked, with soft, sepia photo kind of looks. Nothing like me in real-life. I'm taller, sharper, auburn-haired, and more classically elegant than this floaty, dreamy look.

I put on the dress with a pair of sandals, braided my

hair, and then put on a soft pink lipstick I found on the nightstand.

And I was ready.

For our date.

So when I see Aaron walking down the sandy road, his shadow long in the setting sun, I stand.

At my movement he looks toward me. When he sees me he stops walking for a moment, as if he's stunned by my appearance, and then he starts toward me again, his gait faster.

In a tree nearby with wide limbs, fat green leaves, and burgundy flowers shaped like trumpets, a group of blackbirds chatters noisily. They drown out the sound of my thumping heart.

There's something different between us. It started on the beach last night, continued this morning, and then coalesced on the road when we stood far apart, not speaking, not meeting, just . . . acknowledging.

That something had happened.

Something was there.

Aaron climbs the wooden steps and pauses in front of me. He's sweat-covered, his black hair damp, a line of perspiration glistening on his forehead. His T-shirt and jeans are covered in grass stains and dirt. He's been cutting limbs, trimming and cutting back overgrown branches, for hours. There's a small cut on his face—one that wasn't there this morning.

He's watching me take him in, his hesitant smile in place.

I reach up then, touching the red mark on his cheek.

He sucks in a breath. Not in pain, but from the feel of me.

"The way you look at me," he says, his voice low, "it makes me want to do things."

I stare at him, arrested in the moment, sunlight streaking over us. My finger presses into his cheek and I drag in a slow, thick-aired breath.

"Fi?" he whispers, searching my expression.

I smile. A warm glow unfurls and spreads through me until I'm languid in the feel of it. "Yes."

His smile grows soft and he steps closer. He lifts his hand to cup my cheek but then thinks better of it and instead presses his mouth to mine in a gentle caress. He nibbles at my lips, pressing kisses to their corners, taking them in his mouth. I tilt my chin up and let him love my mouth.

I lift my hands to his shoulders and open to him.

He makes a frustrated noise, his breathing sharp.

He takes his mouth from mine and glances at the tree with the chattering blackbirds. "It's . . . six thirty. Sue'll be expecting us."

I give him a bemused smile, dizzy and glowy-warm. "Did you just look at that tree to tell the time?"

"Sure." He looks back at me. "It's a clock tree."

I snort, and then, when he lifts an eyebrow, I grab his grass-stained shirt and pull him against me. I kiss his jaw, tasting the salt and the leaves and the sea. "You can't tell time from a tree. Trust me, I know a little bit about time. A flower clock, yes. A tree clock, no."

Aaron's breath quickens as I trace my mouth over his jaw. He turns his face to mine and catches my mouth. "You know as well as I do," he says, "that's a clock tree. The world's best teller of time. The flowers open at sunrise and then they close with the setting sun. You can tell the time by how shut tight they are."

I stare into his open, warm gaze. "Really?"

A clock tree.

"Yes. It's why you never wear a watch. You always said you don't need one."

I would *never* say something like that.

I think about Aaron's wristwatch, a Tag diver's watch, the one he was wearing last night. I'm surprised it's not an Abry. You'd think my subconscious would know better, but still.

"You wear a watch."

He nods. "I like watches. I have a few."

He *likes* watches. He has a *few*.

I grin at him—a full, face-splitting smile.

At my smile a bright red flush spreads across his cheeks and the bridge of his nose. He runs a hand through his hair. "I'll get cleaned up."

And before he can take my mouth and carry me back into the cottage and drop me into our bed—which I know he wants to do—he ducks into the cottage.

I fan myself and wonder if I'll be able to make it through dinner without kissing him.

Or waking up.

32

Sue's, the only restaurant on island, is not called EAT. It's actually called Sue's Home-Cooked Delicacies Made-to-Order for You to Eat. It's a mouthful, which I think is why Sue decided to paint the word "EAT" on the chipboard sign tacked above the front door and leave it at that.

I clasp the handwritten menu and the grease-stained paper crinkles in my hand. There are three options for the main: fried catch of the day, baked catch of the day, and grilled catch of the day. Two appetizers: mango salad or crab mango salad. And three desserts: banana cake, coconut rum cake, or chocolate cake. However, the chocolate cake is scratched out with pencil.

I remember from the anniversary party that we had the last chocolate cake on the island.

Or the chickens had the last chocolate cake on the island.

I smile across the little wooden café table at Aaron.

We're outside, in the back garden behind Sue's. Her generator isn't running. Instead of lights, we're surrounded by the yellow flames of a dozen pillar candles. They're set in buckets of sand, and the soft glow bounces off the garden, highlighting the white pom-pom flowers blooming in the bushes. They let off a soft jasmine scent, mixing with the crickets that started singing at the first hint of dusk.

Aaron hasn't looked at the menu. Maybe he knows something I don't. Instead he's been watching the leaves flip and turn in the cooling breeze and the ribbons of sunlight that prismed through the garden as the sun dipped to the ocean.

He was quiet on the walk over, deep in thought. He was even quiet when Sue, a gregarious woman in her fifties with gray hair and a warm, motherly air, pulled him in for a quick peck on the cheek and thanked him profusely for fixing her fryer.

He's quiet. Not looking at me.

But just like Amy, I can see the thoughts swirling through him, his mind moving a million miles a minute. And even though he hasn't looked at me except to give quick smiles, I can feel his attention.

He's focused on me completely.

It's as if his hands are stroking over my bare skin, his fingers whispering over my breasts and my thighs, his mouth whispering over my pulse. It's all there in the thick, humid air perfumed with jasmine and flickering with candlelight.

Robert said Aaron had never looked at me this way before. That he'd never felt this way before.

But the truth is, I've never felt this way either.

Before, with Joel, when I thought it was love, I was

in a desert and he was the only drop of water. That single drop was a mirage.

But this?

This feeling?

Aaron looks at me then and the feeling expands, a warm wave rolling through me, washing over me like the turquoise sea gently sweeping over golden sand. My body grows heavy as a languid heat engulfs me, heady and dizzying.

The heat, the flowers, the seclusion of this back garden are doing funny things to my heart.

Aaron's lips tug upward and his dark brown eyes shine in the candlelight. He sets his hand on the table between us, resting it palm-up. When I reach forward and lay my fingers in his, his smile widens and his eyes warm.

I run my fingers through his, tangling our hands together. The whisper of my skin over his sends sparks shivering through me. They lodge deep in my middle, a glow brighter than all the candles combined.

In the tree nearby the blackbirds end their evening song.

Aaron runs his thumb over the sensitive part of my palm. "I can never decide," he says into the sudden quiet, "what I like better. The blackbirds singing or the moment right after."

I think about it. There's the chatter, the song, the piping notes, and then there's the silence when the music is still echoing but you know it's gone.

"While they're singing," I say.

"After," he decides at the same time.

His eyes crinkle and he leans forward, coming closer so I catch the fresh scent of the soap he used in the shower. We're in a little bubble, a private fairy-tale garden.

"Why?" he asks.

"I like being in the moment," I say, gesturing to the garden and the candlelight. "I like the moment, not the memory."

He nods, considering my words. Then he says, "I think, for me, the fact that it ends is what makes it . . ." He shrugs.

"Ah. You only appreciate something when it's gone."

"No. Not exactly. I've known too many things that have ended not to appreciate something while it's here. It's more . . ."

"Like the moment right after we kissed?"

His eyes fly to mine. A buzzy, heady heat arches between us. He rubs his fingers over my palm, tracing the delicate skin of the underside of my wrist. His thumb rests on the galloping of my pulse.

"Right," he says, his voice low.

Suddenly I know just what he means. It's the moment when you're in your love's arms, limp and falling, right after an earth-shattering orgasm. When you're mindless and euphoric. Held close and loved.

Above us the sky has turned to a deep plum, speckled with the first golden stars.

"Thank you for the date," I say, scooting forward in my chair, trying to get as close to him as possible. "I know you worked all day preparing for the storm."

"Is it wrong to say I wanted to spend an evening alone with you?"

I shake my head. "I'd be disappointed if you didn't. I'm here to . . ." I look at his shadowed jaw, the glow of his eyes, and consider how much to tell him. How much can a person in a dream understand? "Love," I finally say. "I want to love." And then, in case he doesn't understand, I add in a quiet voice. "I want to love you."

He reaches up, dragging his fingers across my cheek. "I'd ask why now," he says, "but I can't. I feel it too. It feels different. It feels like a rip current pulling me along—I couldn't escape even if I wanted to. I used to want you to be happy. Now I want to be happy with you."

I swallow down the fluttering in my throat, the fear mixed with longing. I close my eyes, turn my mouth into his palm, and press a kiss to his warm skin.

He lets out a harsh exhale. "I'm afraid this isn't real."

It's not, I want to tell him. *It's not real.*

But I can't. Because it feels real.

"I keep thinking I'll wake up and you won't be you anymore, you'll be . . ." He shrugs. "Becca. You'll be the Becca I've always known."

"We could live in the moment," I say. "And if it ends, we can savor the ending."

He smiles at me then, a bittersweet smile, and pulls his hand from my cheek. "All right. Fair enough."

He scoots his chair closer to mine, scraping it over the gravel. Our shoulders touch as we dip our heads together and debate the menu options. When Sue takes our order, though, we find there are no options. It's mango salad, grilled snapper, and coconut rum cake for dinner.

She sets the plates in front of us, filling the table with food. The snapper is charred and flaky, and I refuse to think about the fish market or the fact this snapper may be the one I gutted. Instead I take in the scent of ripe mango, charcoal, and lime. Sue sets two glasses in front of us filled with rum, simple syrup, and freshly squeezed lime.

"Bon appétit," she says, smiling at me with motherly approval. "I expect you to clean your plates, or there's no dessert for you."

I hold back a laugh.

"Yes, ma'am," Aaron says, laughter in his eyes.

She bustles back into the restaurant. There's the splashing of water, the clatter of dishes, and then, over the sound, the soft tones of Sue humming a tuneless melody.

After a moment of contemplation, hunger gets the better of me and I decide to dive in. I stick a forkful of the snapper in my mouth. It's flaky, delicate, and sweet. There's a mild nutty flavor that blends perfectly with the mango chili sauce Sue prepared. The snapper is pink and firm and delicious.

Aaron glances at me when I give a soft, appreciative moan. He holds still, watching me with a quick hunger.

"Good?" he finally asks, his voice rough.

I nod, swallowing a bite of mango. "Better than good."

He watches me take another bite, a fire growing in his eyes. I think about leaning forward and kissing him, tasting the soft flavor of mango and lime on his lips.

"Tell me," he says. "Last night we pretended you didn't know me. Tonight, tell me something about you that I don't know. Pretend we've never met."

"Like a first date?"

He nods, his gaze steady.

The sky is dark now. A cool evening breeze shifts over me, dragging strands of hair across my neck and bare shoulders. I can almost hear the waves, rising and falling, building, maybe, to a storm.

Inside Sue hums. Outside the crickets sing.

I think about what to tell Aaron. Something about me that he doesn't know.

But there's so much he doesn't know. So much I could tell him.

"I don't want to stop with one thing," I say. "So I'll tell you it all. If you want to know?"

The side of his mouth kicks up in a smile. "Of course I do."

I take a drink, the sugary lime tart and sweet. "All right. The first thing you should know is I love being a mom. I love it more than anything in the world."

He tilts his head, his eyes drinking me in. "You do?"

I forgot. Here, according to Robert, I never wanted to be a mom.

But I nod. "I never knew I would. But it's a love so big, so overwhelming. I was given this person to protect and love. I'm in awe of it every day."

"I know exactly what you mean," he says, watching me with a funny expression.

I lean forward, a glow lighting between us. "I didn't think I could do it. But I had help. I had my family."

Daniel.

"Maranda." He nods. "She helped us a lot after Amy was born."

I look up at the stars then back to him.

I want Aaron to know me. Not the me he thinks I am, but me.

"There's one thing you don't know about me."

He tilts his head. The candlelight bounces off his sun-kissed skin. "Yeah?"

"I love time." I smile, reaching out and tapping the wristwatch he's wearing. "I love watches, clocks, timepieces. Everything about them. I love the history, the science, the mechanics, and the art. I love how a watch can be self-winding, as if there's a little heart inside that keeps beating on its own. I love how for thousands of years humans have been fascinated by the sun casting its shadow on a dial, or the trickle of grains through an hourglass, or . . ."—I smile at him—"the closing of flowers on a clock tree. I love time. I love watchmaking. I love everything about it."

"You do?" he asks, looking at me as if he's never seen me before.

"Yes. A hundred times yes. If you could see the Abry Headquarters in Geneva. The production facilities, the museum, the collection. If you could see the hundreds of intricate steps it takes to create a single wristwatch . . ." I glance at him, swept away by my love of Abry.

A bittersweet ache lodges in my chest. I wish I could take his hand, pull him out of this dream, and show him everything I love. I'd take him on a tour of Abry. I'd show him our heirlooms—pieces that are plain or beautiful, worth little or worth a lot. I'd take him to the production facility and I'd let him see the McCormick, the watch I named for him. I'd show him the Flower Clock and I'd ask if he'd like to stay to see the seasons change.

"You'd like it," I say, my voice thick, my throat aching. "If you like watches, you'd like to see it."

"You've always loved watches?" he asks, his forehead wrinkling. "I didn't know you'd heard of Abry. I've always wanted one." He lifts a shoulder in a half-shrug as if that dream is beyond him.

And maybe it is. Just like I can't bring books to Amy, I can't bring a watch to Aaron.

But I could describe Abry to him. I could make him feel as if he's walking the halls, glancing over a master watchmaker's shoulder, holding the cool metal links of a perfectly ticking Chronomaster in his hand.

A warmth bubbles inside me. "I'll give one to you," I say, and when he lifts his eyebrows I amend, "Pretend. I'll describe it all. Pretend it's real. I know a lot about Abry watches."

"You do?"

"I do. I've been learning about them for a long time." I reach over and take his hand. "Close your eyes. I'll make it so real you'll be able to feel the warm metal of the watch around your wrist. I'll make it so you can hear the ticking of the second hand. Then you'll have an Abry."

He smiles at me then. A delighted look. He closes his eyes and grips my hand.

So I begin. "Abry is in the country, outside Geneva. In the summer, when you look out the windows, the field below is a sea of sunshine-yellow flax and the mountains are indigo-blue, hugged by the dusty olive of the evergreens. It's different than here. Even in the summer there's a softness to the sun and a quiet breeze blowing off the mountains. Two siblings own Abry, a brother and a sister. They love it so much they swore they'd do anything to make sure it survived for the next generation. And they have. They've kept so busy, given so much of themselves, that they've put all their dreams into the watches they create."

As I describe the love that goes into each watch, all the lost arts and the intricate steps, the handenameling and the hand-setting, a mellow richness flows around us. I lean into Aaron, settle into his side, and rest my head against his heart.

I build for him a dream.

And when I finish, having described the watch I'd make just for him, he opens his eyes and stares down at me.

"Thank you," he says, the low rumble of his voice stroking over me. "That was beautiful. I'd like to see it someday."

I press my hand to the heat of him. "I'd like you to too."

He brushes a kiss over my head and wraps his arms around me. "But if I don't, it feels like I already have."

My chest pinches and I look up at him, the world feeling wobbly and unreal.

The jasmine scent shifts to lavender, and from the kitchen there's an insistent beeping.

Aaron drags a finger across my mouth. "I'm falling for you," he whispers, his voice ragged. "I didn't know I could fall so hard."

"Aaron." I reach up, touching the pads of my fingers to his lips.

The beeping grows louder, more insistent.

He grasps my hand. "This falling—it could wreck me. Tell me you feel it too. Please tell me you—"

Bright light flashes and I'm wrenched from the garden, out of Aaron's arms, back into my bedroom in Geneva.

I blink into the morning sunlight at my ringing alarm clock. The pocket watch is heavy and warm in my hand, the second hand frozen in time.

I'm still floating, trying to fall back into reality.

Tell me you feel it, he'd asked.

And I'd left him.

I don't know what will happen now. I imagine if I don't land back in the same moment that the Becca in the dream will leave him. She won't tell him she feels the same. She'll run.

She'll leave him in the garden. Alone.

He said he's falling, that it could wreck him.

In the dream I would've told him I feel the same.

But here in Geneva? In the light of my bedroom, the lavender-scented sheets crumpled around me and a day of work and Mila's camp ahead? It's reality. It's real life.

In the harsh line of morning light falling across the bed, I wonder, if I fall, will it wreck me too?

But then I shake my head.

It can't.

It's just a dream.

A dream to help me live my life.

That's all.

And if Aaron is left alone in the garden? It's not any different than him being left behind when I close the watch back in its wooden box.

When time stops, so does the dream.

With that dispiriting thought, I place the gold watch in its antique box and close the lid.

33

ALL DAY, FROM THE MINUTE I CLIMB OUT OF BED TO RUSH Mila to camp and then on to a full day at work, I'm consumed by thoughts of Aaron. Of the island.

I make excuses to slip out of meetings and check on the progress of the McCormick wristwatch. I stand outside production, mooning like a little girl with her first crush. When Daniel brings takeout into my office for lunch—fish—I smile so wide that he asks if I'm feeling okay.

I startle the woman at the coffee shop when I laugh at a bit of the latte catching on my upper lip, just like Amy. I smile at three white-haired women knitting and chatting while waiting for a bus.

I turn to give double-takes to tall men with black hair and wide shoulders. None of them are Aaron, but somehow I keep seeing him. The tall man on the street corner has the same color eyes as him. The business man jogging toward the taxi has his jet-black hair. The studious man with glasses has his laugh. I see evidence of him everywhere.

He's invaded my world.

Even when he's not real, not here, I still feel him next to me.

But it isn't just him. It's the island and all the people there too.

Walking past the guard desk at the front door of Production, I see Frederic has a baby shop pulled up on his computer screen. I stop, struck by the white slatted cot with blue cotton sheets and a matching rocking chair. Frederic flushes and clicks it closed.

But I only lean close and say, "Can I see the crib, please?"

And so I scroll through, reading about the cot and rocker and picturing Junie rocking her baby to sleep. How will she get a cot? A rocking chair? Nappies? A pram? Is there some way I might be able to help her?

I leave Frederic, distracted, and then get caught up in the blue of the mountains reflecting the sky—the same exact blue of the sea flashing over the seashore.

I'm caught off-guard by the perfume of the orchids on someone's desk, drifting subtly with tropical smells.

The heat of the sun falling through my office window onto my shoulders. The scratch of pen across paper. The rub of the silk lining of my wool skirt. All of it brings me back to the island. Back to Aaron. To the moment when his thumb brushed over my lips and he rasped, "Tell me you feel it too."

I feel it.

Even here I feel it.

Which is why, by the time I'm tucking Mila into bed, I've decided I won't be dreaming tonight.

It's taking over my life. It's becoming too real.

"Mummy," Mila says, her nose and eyes peeking out from beneath her pink duvet. She's buried in stuffies—bears, rabbits, kittens, and dogs.

"Yes?" I drop a kiss to her freckled nose.

"Did you see my painting? The one of my poem?" She looks at me with expectant eyes. "I tacked it to my board."

"I was wondering where it got off to," I say as I wander across her room to peer at her cork art board.

Mila's room is down the hallway from mine, and when I was little it was my bedroom. She decorated it two years ago to match her own personality. There are frosting-pink walls, yards of lace, and twinkle lights mixed with framed concept art of Abry watches, advert posters from decades ago, black-and-white photographs of our old headquarters—a pure mix of fanciful and practical that perfectly suits her.

I stop in front of her art board and scan the marker drawings and watercolors to find the poem painting she created at camp today.

"It's at the top," she says, peeking out from her duvet.

I smile at her and then turn back to the board. At the top edge is the painting.

I still, my breath caught in my throat.

Mila painted the water. It isn't the water of Lake Geneva though. It's the turquoise water you'd find rushing over the hot white sand of a tropical island. There are pink seashells, bright yellow and red flowers, and palm trees swaying in the wind. A yellow shovel and a red bucket rest in the sand.

The poem is written in Mila's childlike cursive.

My heart jerks in my chest, thudding against the walls.

It feels as if Aaron will walk past one of the trees if I just wait one more moment, Sean in his arms, and they'll sit down in the sand and build a sandcastle. Amy will perch on a hammock in the shade and read Robert Louis Stevenson.

Because this is his poem, isn't it?

Yet Aaron and Sean and Amy are there too.

Mila painted it so vividly, so beautifully, that I can smell the salt, feel the prickle of heat.

And I know that I can't not dream. I can't not go back.

My dream may be crashing over my real life like a storm wave crashing over the beach, but I can't turn away.

I have to tell Amy another poem, don't I?

I have to help Maranda at the fish market.

I want to help Junie find a cot for her baby.

I have to go back and tell Aaron that I do. I do feel the same.

You can't close a chapter before it's over. You can't stop a dream before it's finished.

We're not done yet.

"Don't you like it?" Mila asks, worry pinching her voice.

I turn to her, my vision hazy. "No, I love it. It's a beautiful painting. A beautiful poem."

She nods then and snuggles down into her pillow, her eyelids dragging low.

I stride back to her, kneel at her bedside, and drop a kiss to her cool forehead. "Sleep tight."

She yawns. "M'kay."

At that I switch off her bedside lamp and close her door with a quiet snick.

Then, in my bedroom, I climb into bed with a book of poetry and a pocket watch. I memorize another poem and then I fall into sleep, hoping I'm in time to say—

Yes. I feel the same.

34

The noise is deafening. I bolt upright in bed, clammy sweat dripping between my breasts, my heart thundering.

The black is absolute. Not even the silver-gray of moonlight breaches the darkness. I feel around the bed, kicking the sweat-soaked sheets aside, and reach for the lamp. I turn the switch. Nothing. The room remains dark.

The air is humid, sticky-damp, and stagnant. I wipe my hand across the perspiration on my forehead and breathe in the stuffiness of a house hunched down and locked tight.

"Aaron?"

My voice is drowned out by the roar of outside. It sounds as if I'm standing in a tunnel and I'm seconds from being mowed down by a charging train. Rain thunders against the tiles of the roof and the wind slams against the cottage walls, howling and raging.

So this is the storm.

I resist the urge to cover my ears. Instead I inch to the edge of the bed and toe my foot toward the floor. I'm surprised to find cool stone tile. The cottage has wood floors, smooth and glossy.

I'm not in the cottage then. And Aaron isn't here.

I stand and inch my way across the floor, my hands stretched out in front of me, until I hit a wall. I slide along the cool plaster until my fingers catch on a ridge of wooden molding.

My breath is loud and nervous. I grasp the metal doorknob and swing open the door.

The soft glow of yellow light spills across me and I breathe out a sigh of relief. I let my eyes adjust. The light is weak. It's filtered down a long hallway.

I was right. I've never been in this house before. The walls are coral, the trim is white. The tile floors are beige and cracks run through them. The walls are crooked and the ceiling is low. There are two closed doors across from me, and at the end of the hallway there's a kitchen with coral cabinets and a round table. A hurricane lamp glows on the kitchen table.

I don't see anyone.

But just when I believe I'm alone in this house, I hear him.

It's a sharp, unhappy cry. The type of whimper that makes every parent bolt upright from a dead sleep and rush into their baby's bedroom.

I hurry down the hallway toward the sound of Sean's cries.

When I step into the kitchen the lamplight spills over me. I turn toward the sound of his ragged cry and stop at the threshold.

Aaron's there.

He's holding Sean in his arms, rocking him, running his hand over his back, pacing the length of the small tile-floored living room.

Aaron's back is to me, his head tucked next to Sean's. He's in a T-shirt, jeans, his feet bare and his black hair rumpled.

Sean's head rests on Aaron's shoulder. His cheeks are red and wet from tears, his eyes swollen. He tosses his head back and forth and lets out a heart-wrenching whimper. His ragged bunny hangs from his arms.

The wind continues to howl, raging against the house, yanking at the metal shutters closed over the windows. The house moans and Sean whimpers again.

Then above the noise I hear Aaron.

He's singing a quiet, low melody that I can barely make out. It's a whispered, hushed song. "Don't cry, baby, don't cry, little one, your dad is here, he'll make it all right."

Sean clutches Aaron's shirt and buries his face in his shoulder. Then Aaron turns. When he sees me standing in the threshold he stops. His hand stills on Sean's back.

Something flashes in his eyes. As quick as lightning. Impossible to decipher.

"Hey," he says.

At his word Sean twists in his arms. When he catches sight of me he bends toward me, holds out his chubby arms, and cries, "Mamamama," as if he's telling me all about how scared he is, how terrible the noise is, how much he needs comfort. And once he says it, his lower lip wobbles and he says, "Mama."

I hurry forward, taking him in my arms. He cuddles into me, burying his face in my long cotton T-shirt. His cheeks are damp and his tears wet my T-shirt. I wrap my arms around him and take his weight.

"It's okay," I whisper, rocking him. "You're okay."

Aaron watches me, his face clear of emotion. Something prickles in the air between us—something electric and storm-like.

I want to ask him where we are, what happened, but instead I rub slow circles over Sean's back and rock him as I pace the small living room.

It doesn't take long for me to realize where we are. The furniture is overstuffed floral rattan. There's a weathered wooden coffee table with a collection of conch shells and sea glass in a bowl. Near the window is a tall bookshelf. The bookshelf is key. On it are two dozen framed photographs. Most of them are of Aaron—from baby to teen—with his parents, with friends, with his Grandma Essie. A few are of Aaron with Amy as a baby. The rest are of a man and a woman who look like Aaron. He has his mom's eyes, his dad's height.

It looks like for the storm we've moved inland to his parents' house. It makes sense. The cottage is so close to the beach it would be dangerous if there was a storm surge.

As I turn I glance at him. He's watching me, the quiet from the last time back in place.

"When did he wake?" I ask.

Aaron looks at the clock hanging on the wall near the kitchen table. "Eleven."

It's three now. Aaron's been up with him for four hours. "You should've come for me."

It's always better to have someone to share the load.

He frowns. "I did. You told me to let you sleep. Said you were dreaming."

Is that what I said?

I shake my head. "I'm sorry. You should get some sleep. I'll stay with him."

Aaron rubs a hand down his face and smothers a yawn. "I'll make you a coffee. Room temp, instant, but a coffee all the same."

"Make two," I tell him.

He flickers a smile at me as he crosses to the tiny kitchen.

Sean grows heavy, and soon he feels as heavy as Mila when she was five and too tired to walk any further. She'd always beg to be carried and I'd hoist her in my arms, gasping at how big she'd grown.

His head has lolled to rest against my chest, his mouth hangs open, and his eyelashes flutter on the edge of sleep. His body is soft and boneless against me. Slowly I pace the room, swaying him in my arms, whispering, "Shhh shhh shhh," until finally his fingers loosen from my T-shirt and his hand falls free. His head drops forward and he lets out a little sleep whimper.

"He's asleep," I whisper.

Aaron looks up from the mugs he's stirring packets of instant coffee into. When he sees Sean's eyes are closed, his limbs relaxed, his shoulders drop and he lets out a sigh of relief.

"He's always been scared of the noise."

"Did Amy wake up too?"

He smiles. "No. You know Amy. She thinks it's an adventure, and then when she's tired of the noise she rolls over and sleeps like the dead."

That does sound like Amy.

A raging gust slams against the house, beating with renewed vigor. I look toward the walls, worried.

"This house has stood for a hundred years. Through a Cat 5, countless 3s, innumerable 1s. Don't worry, Becca. A little storm isn't going to blow it down."

I glance back at him. "This is a little storm?"

He gives me a tilted smile and picks up the mugs. "You never did like hurricane season. You're like Sean that way." He sets the mugs on the wooden coffee table. "I'll make him a bed out here. Hold on."

He pulls two thin coral cotton blankets from the couch and piles them on the floor in a little nest. My arms are aching enough that I gladly lean down and carefully roll Sean onto the blankets. His eyelashes flutter and he tenses for a moment, so I set my hand on his chest and murmur, "Shhh, shhh," until he relaxes back into sleep.

"I can stay out here. Sleep on the couch next to him," I offer, glancing again at Aaron.

He has purple lines under his eyes, tired hollows in his cheeks. His hair stands up from where he thrust his fingers through it and stubble lines his jaw. He looks as if he could fall asleep standing up.

But instead of taking me up on my offer, he sits on the couch and rests his elbows on his thighs. He leans forward then and stares at the mugs of coffee.

So I sit next to him and reach for a cup. I take a hesitant sip. It's exactly as I thought it would be—bitter and dark, cold—but since Aaron added about three tablespoons of sugar it's also delicious in a middle-of-the-night stormy drink sort of way.

"Thank you," I say, cupping my hands around the mug. I scoot closer to him until my bare thigh rests against his and my arm brushes the warmth of his.

My T-shirt inches up my thigh. Aaron looks down

at my leg pressed to his. Then he looks back at the table and reaches for his cup of coffee.

He takes a long drink and then, looking down at his hands balancing the cup on his knees, he asks, "Where did you go?"

I glance quickly at him. Does he mean where did I go since I last dreamed? As in, Geneva? Or . . . ?

"What do you mean?"

He looks at me then, and his eyes are as storm-filled as the night outside. Thunder rumbles and the house shudders. Lightning flashes. The light leaks through the hurricane shutters and streaks across his face.

He looks into me. I swear. He isn't looking at Becca —the woman everyone sees. He's looking at me. Fiona.

"Two days ago I asked you if you felt what I felt—"

"Two days?" My hands shake. I set the mug back on the coffee table. Some of the coffee spills on my hands.

"You made it clear I'm not . . ." He looks up at the ceiling, then back to me. "And I couldn't disagree, because I didn't feel it anymore either. We were friends again. Parents. What we've always been. What we agreed to. That feeling was gone. But now here it is again. You walk in the room and all I want to do is kiss you. All I want is to love you. Tell me I'm wrong."

The wind rises with his words and the house groans. I grip the hem of my T-shirt. Hold it tight.

"I can't," I whisper, my words barely heard above the storm.

He nods as if he knew that was how I'd answer all along. "Then it's a dream," he says. "You're just a dream."

Maybe so. Maybe that's what reality is when you're inside a dream.

When you're awake your dreams aren't real. When you're dreaming your life isn't real.

He glances over at me then, the yellow light of the hurricane lamp glowing softly over the room. "Fi?" he asks, his voice hopeful.

Slowly I nod, my cheeks heating. "Yes."

His lips curve into a slow, sad smile. "If I kiss you now, will it hurt much tomorrow when you don't want me?"

He isn't asking me. It's a question for the storm and the dark of the night, but I answer anyway.

"I'll want you."

"Will you?"

It's like he's asking if I'm going to put him away, stop the watch, lock it in its box, and never open it again.

"Yes," I say, moving closer, pressing against the warm line of him. "I wanted to tell you. The other night in the garden. I wanted to tell you I feel it too. I'm falling too."

He searches my face, catching every glimmer and nuance of expression.

"You're falling, but . . ." He trails off and waits for me to finish the sentence. He knew there was a "but" there, a hesitation.

"I'm a little scared," I say, "of what happens when the music ends."

"When the blackbirds stop singing?" he asks.

I swallow down the tight lump in my throat and nod. My stomach tilts and dips.

He reaches forward and runs a finger soothingly across my cheek. "Don't be scared. I'll be there too. When it ends."

He looks solemnly into my eyes when he makes this

promise. I reach up and hold my hand over his, then I link our fingers together.

"Tell me something else about you," he says. "Something I don't know."

I catch the light glinting off his jet-black hair and it reminds me, "I love to sail at night." I used to with my dad and Daniel in the Greek isles. "There are so many stars when you're out in the middle of the ocean. You've never seen so many. It's like the sky is painted with diamonds. When you lie on your back and stare at the sky you nearly burst from the wonder, the awe. You feel so small and so big at the same time. I love it." I glance at him. There's a glint in his eyes. "Someday we could go out together."

"Yeah?"

My heart gives one hollow thump. "Yeah."

"What else?" he asks, tucking me into his side. He leans back against the couch cushion and I settle into him.

I rest my head against his chest and his fingers tangle in the ends of my hair. "I have a brother."

"I know that." I can hear the smile in Aaron's voice.

"Maybe. But you don't know that I think he's one of the best human beings on the planet. He'd do anything for me. And I'd do anything for him. When I was a kid I'd save my allowance and buy him marzipan because I knew he loved it. And even though I never liked the beach, I always took him because he'd beg—" I smile up at Aaron. "You'd like him."

"I already do like him. We grew up together."

"He'd like you too," I say.

"Well, if Miami hasn't changed him then he still does."

And Max. Would Max like Aaron?

I don't know. I think at first Max would be wary of him. Max is wary of everyone when he first meets them. I was the rare exception. It takes months, sometimes years, to earn his trust. But once you have it he's loyal to the end. I think if Max met Aaron in the real world, at a gala or a business function, he would respect him, and that respect would turn to like.

My chest pinches at the thought, a bittersweet tug. Aaron at a gala? In my world? The real world? There isn't even the slimmest possibility of that ever happening.

"One more thing," I tell Aaron, leaning into his warmth. I breathe in the scent of coffee and cool pounding rain.

"What's that?"

"I love coffee in a rainstorm."

He smiles at me, the edges of his eyes crinkling.

"Now you tell me something," I say.

He thinks for a moment, his eyes searching. Then his fingers curl in mine and he says, "Just being near you . . . it feels like all my rough edges are smoothed out. You make me feel like I can—"

"Fly?"

"Get in the water again."

I push off his chest and sit up. "You'd swim again?"

His jaw tightens and he gets a faraway look in his eyes, as if he's considering the hundreds of kilometers he'd swim alone. Through currents, through shark-infested waters, through jellyfish stings and storms. "Before, when I thought about it, I could only see me, alone. If I lost myself again I'd be on my own. Now I see you there too."

Me.

He means me, me.

Not the Becca who loves Robert. Who wants to leave the island. Who married Aaron as a friend to be a parent to their baby.

He means me.

He's willing to dive into the water again. Face his fears.

Because he sees me there.

Am I willing to do that too?

To dive fully into love?

"I'll be there," I tell him. "If you need me, I'll come in after you."

He smiles at that, thinking I can't swim. He'd be surprised.

"I didn't mean you being on the boat. I meant in my life."

I smile at him. "I know. Will you kiss me now?"

The rain is still lashing against the roof. The wind shudders over the house.

He pulls me to him and I straddle his lap. My T-shirt rides up and I feel the heat of him thick against me.

I sink against him. Then he takes my mouth in a soft, slow kiss, gentle and seeking, the opposite of the raging storm. I dig my hands through his hair, pull his mouth against mine.

I taste coffee and shared confidences, longing and dreams, and in the silence after the kiss, in that quiet moment, I lean into him, my heart beating in time with the rain, and I find one more thing.

In the stillness, in the quiet, I find his love.

35

The days leading up to Friday are spent in juxtaposition. In Geneva I spend long days in the office reviewing our second-quarter numbers, forecasting sales in our new push into emerging markets, and monitoring the progress of production on our new watch. Mila and I picnic on the lake shore, and Daniel joins us on a bike ride in the country. The days are long, summer-rich, with the sun hanging in the sky until late, urging me to stay awake and enjoy the light a little longer.

But I want to sleep. As soon as Mila is tucked into bed I rush to my bedroom, pull the watch from its box, and drop into bed. And into sleep.

On the island the days are filled with cleanup. The howling wind and the driving rain slowly drizzled to a stop until light peeked through the hurricane shutters and singing birds let us know it was safe to venture outside.

When I first stepped out of Aaron's childhood home I didn't know where I'd be. It turned out the house was on the far side of Charlestown, far enough from shore, elevated enough, that no waves or storm surge would reach it. Everyone on island had decamped from the shore, vacated low-lying flood-prone areas, and moved inland to stay with relatives or friends.

I was stunned at the aftermath. There was plenty of damage for something Aaron called "just a little storm." The first day I blinked into the bright light. The sun, since it had been covered by heavy, violent storm clouds for two days, seemed to shine with renewed vigor. It hit every flooded street, every puddle, every water-slicked roof, and reflected with bright white light.

There was plenty of flooding. All the sandy gravel road was washed out and a little river of brown water rushed down the "runway" to the sea. All the low-lying grassy gardens were filled with wind-blown green pools. The storm had uprooted mango trees, flattened banana groves, and ripped metal gutters and roof shingles from homes and then sprinkled them on the muddy ground. The soil squelched under my feet, cool water seeped into my shoes, and the scent of mangrove and wet, loamy tropical soil hung heavy in the air.

The wind was still brisk although not violent. It tugged at my hair and whipped my dress against my legs. The waves of the sea crashed taller than a person, roaring over the beach and then receding to be swallowed by deeper waters. Aaron claimed the sea would calm in a day or two, and it did.

In the days after, the island put itself back to rights. The island birds, right away, started singing again, chasing bugs and hopping between trees. Even the chickens emerged from wherever they'd weathered the storm. They pranced around, pecking at the muddy soil, unruffled by the wind and rain.

So for days we worked together. For one single moment Aaron was surprised when I offered to help climb up on Essie's roof to nail down new shingles. But after that he didn't blink when I helped him fix Maranda's gutter and then dry out Sue's, which had six inches of standing water in the kitchen.

We worked as a team, Aaron and I, while Junie stayed with Amy and Sean at the cottage. As the crisp breeze chased away the last of the storm clouds and the sun dried out the flooded streets and gardens, Aaron and I worked under the shining sun.

He told me stories when I asked, about what swim he liked best—South Eleuthera to Nassau, Bahamas— about how he could swim for forty hours—he enters a place in himself where there's only focus, him and the water; he envisions it ahead of time, he's already swam it, he's already seen it happen in his mind, and then he swims—about how he'd swim again—with me there— about his favorite book— "Robinson Crusoe," (where did I think Amy got the tattered, dog-eared copy?)— about his favorite food—Essie's banana bread—about his favorite place—the cove on the northside of the island. Would he take me there? Yes, he would.

While we put the island back together we drew closer and closer, until on Thursday, when I was mud-covered and messy from hauling downed banana trees from the back garden, Aaron put his hand to my wrist, tugged me to him, and held my face as he kissed me.

The electricity had been crackling between us for days. So much so that even if I closed my eyes I'd still be able to point to the exact spot Aaron stood. I was aware of his every movement, his every breath, even the quiet scrape of his cotton shirt over his skin.

So after days of talking and working and not ever touching or kissing, I wasn't surprised when Aaron tugged me against him and said, "Fi."

My pants were mud-slicked and wet. My white T-shirt was muddy and molded over my breasts. My cheeks were red and my face was sweat-slicked. Aaron took one look at me, and the heat that had been growing between us like the heat building in the noonday sun exploded. I dropped the banana leaves. The branches rushed to the grass and the sweet fragrance of leaves and fruit fanned around us.

He didn't wait for me to say yes. Instead he took my mouth as if he'd been starved for days and I was the answer to his prayers. His calloused fingers stroked the sweat and mud on my face. I gripped his T-shirt, working my hands over the planes of his chest and the hard width of his shoulders. He dragged his mouth over mine, a prayer on his lips.

"Yes," I whispered.

And then his hands were on my shirt, tugging the mud-soaked fabric free. His hands went to my abdomen, spanned my hips, dragged over my thighs. I pressed against him, taking his mouth and his heat.

Until . . . he stopped. His hands stilled. He rested his forehead against mine and opened his eyes. I stared into his brown eyes and he stared back. His breath came out in a shuddering exhale. And then he gave one last hard kiss and walked away.

I was left in the back garden, dizzy and aching. And then I was gone. Back to Geneva.

And now it's Friday. Tonight I have my date with Max. And then I'll dream.

36

Max knows me well. And so, when he pulls into the chateau drive on Friday in his red AC Cobra, wearing his "casual Max" gear of jeans and a leather jacket, he takes one look at me and says, "Fi, you missed me."

He says it with a sideways smile—one full of dry humor and self-deprecation.

Because when he steps out of his car, I'm standing on the weathered stone steps of the chateau, bathed in the gentle evening sun, wearing a short burgundy-red dress. And when he pulls up I realize I haven't worn a red dress—of any shade—since I was shot. And, even more, after dreaming of Aaron I completely forgot I was ever shot. The ache in my abdomen is gone. The nightmares are gone. The pinched worry that was lodged in my chest is gone. Even the drumming in my mind—*Christmas Eve, Christmas Eve*—it's gone.

And that fact stuns me so much that my hands shake, my skin goes clammy, and I draw in a shuddering breath. A tightness grips my throat, and suddenly I'm plunged back into the moment where I was lying beneath Max, warm blood gushing from me, my limbs numb and cold, with the woman's voice echoing, "Christmas Eve, tell them it's Christmas Eve!"

So, Max being Max, he smiles at me and says the first thing that comes to mind. "Fi, you missed me."

"I did," I say, realizing it's true. "Of course I missed you."

He's my best friend. He's who I always go to when I need someone to talk to. While Daniel is the extrovert to my introvert, Max is the person I can always count on to give another perspective. While we see the same world, it's as if we're viewing it from two different facets of the same diamond. Our angles are different. I appreciate that about him. I've always relied on it. Like he relies on me.

Now he looks down at me, taking in the color leaching from my cheeks and my trembling lips, and pulls me into a tight, comforting hug. I go readily, breathing in the warm leather of his coat and the French milled soap he prefers.

"I'd forgotten being shot," I say into the soft leather of his jacket, "until I looked down at my dress. I forgot. I can't believe I forgot."

He rubs a hand over my back in a slow circle, quiet and soothing. He holds me tight until I stop shaking, and then I bury my face against the warmth of his chest.

"If it makes you feel better," he says, his hand moving gently over my back, "I forgot to pay the parking meter this morning. I got a citation."

I tilt my head up and smile at him, warmth

spreading through me, replacing the chill and the shaking. "It doesn't make me feel better."

"Hmm." He thinks for a moment, looking up at the sky, his winged eyebrows rising. "I forgot my new assistant's name. Again. So she poured spoiled milk in my coffee. I watched her. How's that?"

I narrow my eyes. "A little better. What's her name?"

His lips press together and he shakes his head. "I can't remember."

I laugh. "Still no. What else?"

"Hmm." He considers for another moment, the cool breeze off the lake rustling his glossy black hair. "In Paris a woman asked me to watch her French Bulldog while she went into a café. She was flirting—"

"Of course."

"—and I forgot the dog was there. She'd tied it to my café chair. So I started to walk away and the dog sprinted after me, the metal chair dragging behind its leash. It knocked over two café tables, a flower stand, and the easel of an artist painting in watercolors before I caught it. The dog was painted in vermillion and cerulean and chartreuse. It was grotesque. The woman was not impressed. Needless to say, my excuse 'I forgot it was there' was not appreciated."

My eyes widen. "Oh."

Max nods. Smiles. Then he reaches up and pulls a finger down my cheek. "Better?"

I let out a long sigh, releasing all the worry and fear that suddenly rose to the surface and knotted in my chest. "Yes. Better."

He smiles and then pulls his arms from me and steps back. The warmth he was offering lingers as the cool lake breeze licks over me. Behind me the chateau rises, formidable and imposing, a stone castle that's remained for centuries and has withstood much more than a single gunshot. The history of my family behind me and Max in front of me makes my shoulders rise.

He takes me in and nods. "Good."

I look Max over. He's had a long week. His trips to Paris are always long—full days and full nights, working all hours. He looks as if he could sleep for a week. But instead of heading home after his trip he came to me.

"I think," Max says, studying my expression, "we should skip the romantic dinner I had planned. Throw out the champagne, fire the serenading violinists, and burn the roses, and instead we should just . . . see where the evening takes us."

My mouth twitches, and at the light in Max's eyes I grin at him. "Serenading violinists?"

"Mm-hmm. All the way from the Rue de Romance."

I laugh and take his arm. There's a light breeze dancing over my cheeks, the wood thrushes are singing in the deepening forest shade, and the lake glitters diamond-blue in the evening light. Max's arm is steady and warm beneath mine.

Is this what my dreams are leading me to? Giving Max a chance? Opening my heart to him?

I take a cautious peek at him as we stride across the drive to his car. He's the same Max. Sharp nose, high cheekbones, austere and closed-off until he slams you with his dry observations and hidden humor.

I imagine he'd be easy to love. If I could let myself.

Is that what I've been waiting for? Permission to love Max?

Is that what my dreams are teaching me? That I have permission to love? To be loved?

The thought makes me wonder.

Have I ever really given myself permission to be loved—to truly be loved by someone else?

My heart pinches as I remember Aaron gripping me to him, his mouth hot against mine, as he asked between urgent kisses, "Will it hurt much tomorrow when you don't want me?"

Max opens my door and I slide onto the soft caramel leather, and the cool interior of his car. When he closes his door and starts the engine he turns to me, the space tight and intimate, and says over the purr of the engine, "Ready?"

I smile and nod. "Yes. Let's see where the night leads."

~

The night leads to a tiny medieval village on the shores of the lake, about an hour outside Geneva. Max follows the summer-leafy road winding around the lake, his car rumbling soothingly, the leather warm on my legs and his voice filling the intimate space with stories of Paris—the tight-fisted dealer with his golden monocle, the haughty broker with her two misbehaving diamond-collared toy poodles, the doe-eyed greedy daughter with her nasal accent and trust fund of Australian opal mines—until I'm laughing and out of breath from the caricatures he paints.

Then, as the setting sun sprays lacy, tree-filtered light through the car window and Max reaches over and squeezes my hand, I see it.

The village is like a painting. Or a dream. The sunlight lies golden over the old stone houses and steepled stone churches, the cobblestone streets and the old stone arched gate painted deep plum in the sweeping dusk.

"There," I say, pointing to the narrow turn-off leading down to the shore of the lake. "I want to go there."

And so Max turns down the cobbled street and parks just outside the thirty-foot-tall medieval gate leading into the village. He opens my door and then takes my arm.

I'm drunk on laughter and the fear I'm falling in love with a dream and I'll never be able to undo it. I lean into Max and breathe in the cool evening air.

"Have you ever been here?" he asks, his eyes questing over my flushed cheeks.

"No." I shake my head.

We pass under the shadow of the gate's archway and into a narrow stone walkway that jig-jogs us into the village. There are people outside, walking the street carrying groceries, sweeping their front stoops, chatting with neighbors. It's a busy close-of-day feel, and no one pays us any mind.

"It reminds me a bit of Canterbury," I say. "My mum would take overnights sometimes. We'd sit in the cathedral at sunset or visit Greyfriars. But I'd get antsy and run off to explore the cobbled alleys. I was always tempted by the flowers hanging from the walls."

I smile at the vast displays of ivy, pink climbing roses, and wisteria trailing over the gray stone homes. The street is flush with pinks and whites and soft lilac purples, and the soft floral scent teases around us, as soft as the evening breeze.

The village is tiny, cozy, with winding streets only wide enough for two bicycles—certainly no cars. The houses are small, stone, with painted wooden shutters and hanging flower boxes. It sounds as if an entire forest of songbirds has perched on the rooftops. They're singing to the falling sun.

"Let's take this one," I say, pointing down a narrow alley with purple clematis climbing the walls.

"All right," Max gives me a smile as we plunge into the shadow of the alleyway. There's a shop at the end, a small boulangerie with the enticing scent of fresh-baked bread, golden and warm.

Max makes a happy noise and then stops to buy two crusty baguettes wrapped in waxy brown paper. He holds them in the crook of his arm, and by unspoken agreement we follow the cobblestones winding down toward the grassy lawn at the edge of lake. On the way Max buys a spread of brie, a carton of just-picked jewel-bright strawberries, and a bottle of Gamay—a red wine from a local vineyard.

We settle in the cool grass at the edge of the lake. It falls in a soft mound toward the glistening blue water. Small waves ripple against the shore and lap against the stone walls. There's a short wooden dock parallel to the stone wall, where three small white fishing boats knock against the wood. They're not as big as Aldon's boat, but then again, they're on a lake, not the sea.

I cross my legs. The grass mats beneath me and tickles my bare skin. The sun is arching toward the water and sending the final soft yellow rays over the grass. In the water a family of mallards swims close. The green on the male flashes and the brown female speeds past him. Behind her, three fuzzy ducklings paddle to keep up.

"I think they expect dinner," Max says, lifting an eyebrow.

I smile and breathe in the golden scent of the baguette. I pinch off a crusty bit, crumble it in my hands, and toss it into the water. The mother ruffles her neck feathers, quacks in appreciation, and guides her babies to the treat.

Max follows, tossing small handfuls of breadcrumbs to the ducks. We watch as the sun reflects gold on the water and the bread sends ripples circling about the ducks. Here on the grass the air is cool, the wind is soft, and the floral scent of the town has faded to a soft, forgotten murmur.

There are still the singing birds, the quack of the ducks, and a child's call every now and then, but otherwise the evening is quiet.

Finally, with a quarter of his baguette shared with the ducks, Max turns to me, and says, "Something's weighing on you. Is it tonight? Is it this?"

I look into his eyes, at the concern there, and the question. Then, across the lawn, the songbirds stop singing. Their night song drops into silence. And there in the moment of pure quiet, my heart flips over and I'm tugged, literally tugged, away from the moment and back to Aaron when he said, "After."

I shake my head, pull myself back to Max, and say, "It isn't you. It's not this."

He watches me, the shadows falling over his black hair. He leans back then, settling in the grass, and gives me a searching look. "Is everything all right then? Can I help? Is it work? Mila?"

I shake my head and look down at the blades of grass bending beneath me. After a moment Max reaches over and touches the back of my hand.

"Fiona?"

I look up then, a smile on my lips. "It's something . . . strange. It's . . . You'll think it's strange."

He lifts his eyebrows. "You lit my dead parents' liquor on fire in a birdbath. Nothing you do can shock me."

My smile grows at his statement. "That's fair."

He opens the brie, sets the strawberries in front of us, and then takes a corkscrew from his pocket and opens the bottle of wine.

"You came prepared."

"I'm always prepared, for anything."

I nod. It's true. Max's childhood made him dislike surprises and taught him to be prepared for any inevitability so that surprises couldn't knock him out.

I reach forward and pick a glossy strawberry from the top of the pile. I grasp the leafy top and then pull the fruit free. It's sun-warmed, sweet and tart, and the flavor reminds me of the sweet, earthy mango at Sue's, of the sun shining down on me as Aaron took my hand and pulled me to him and took my mouth. Cherry-bright and sweetly tart.

"I've been dreaming," I say, licking the strawberry juice from my fingers.

"Of what? Goals? Plans?" Max spreads a bit of baguette through the soft, herby brie.

"No." I smile. "I mean I've been dreaming. I've been having vivid dreams. As if . . ." I wrinkle my forehead and stare out over the lake, the sun diving toward the water. "As if they're real. And the people there are real." I look over at Max and ask, "Have you ever had a dream like that?"

"I don't remember my dreams."

"Ever?"

He shakes his head and takes a long swallow of the wine, drinking from the bottle. "I used to. I'd have nightmares as a kid. Finally, I told myself, 'You have to dream, but you don't have to remember them.' And after that I never remembered another one."

I take the bottle of red wine from him and take a long swig. The cool red sweeps over my mouth, tasting of wild cherry and red currant. It's uncomplicated and sweet. I hand Max the wine bottle and smile.

"Well, I have the opposite situation. I'm dreaming about an island every night, and it feels real. And there's a man there." I look over at Max and my cheeks burn under his gaze.

I take another bit of baguette and throw it into the water. The ducks, though, have left, and it sits on top of the water, until it finally sinks.

"And?" Max asks finally, after the bread has disappeared beneath the surface.

I shrug. "I'm falling for him." I look over at Max, my skin prickling. "It sounds mad, I know. But I'm falling for a man in my dreams. I see him everywhere. In everything."

I don't want to look at Max. I'm almost scared to. But this is Max and I tell him everything. And he's never judged me—not for anything. And I want his perspective.

"What do you think?" I ask, reaching for the bottle of wine.

I hold the cool neck of the bottle in my grip as Max considers my question. He isn't laughing. He isn't teasing. He's taking it seriously.

Finally, he tilts his head, and my heart picks up speed because he's come to a conclusion. "I think," he says slowly, "that sometimes we dream what we wish we had in life. Or we dream what we're afraid of in life. Dreaming something lets us live it without actually having to live it. If you can convince yourself you've fallen in love in a dream, then you won't have to fall in love in real life. Perhaps you're trying to protect yourself. Or perhaps you're denying yourself what you really want."

I consider his words. Let them settle over me. My mum said the watch would let me live my dreams, that I'd see what I wanted most. Max says we dream what we wish we had. Or what we're afraid of.

Maybe they're both right. What I'm most afraid of is also what I want the most.

"It feels real though," I tell Max. "It feels . . ." I touch my hand to my heart, settling my palm over the soft chiffon of my red dress. "I feel it, right here."

He smiles then and his brown eyes grow dark. "Like the wind?" he asks with an ironic twist to his lips.

A surprised smile flashes across my mouth. He's referring to when I asked how he knew he loved me and he said it was like the wind. He knew it was real even though he couldn't see it.

"Yes," I admit. "It feels just like the wind."

"Hmm." His eyes flicker over the water. The boats thunk against the dock, and across the lake a gull lets out a lone call, sailing on the wind toward land. "Which is it, do you think? Do you want love, or are you afraid of it?"

When Max looks at me, I feel as if his question is stripping me bare.

"Both," I admit.

He nods.

"Are you upset?" I ask.

He shakes his head and looks over at me. "Not at all. If you can fall for a dream, you can fall for me."

I nudge my shoulder against his. "Arrogant."

"Practical."

"Persistent."

"Loyal."

"Idiot."

"Friend."

"Friend," I agree.

Then we eat the rest of the baguettes smeared in herby brie, devour the pile of sweetly ripe strawberries, and take greedy sips of wine straight from the bottle, passing it back and forth.

As the sun slips like a golden coin beneath the indigo waters I smile at Max, tipsy and warm.

I'm full and happy, and my head is muzzily sweet. The first star winks bright as we sit under the purple sky.

Max glances over at me. I perch against his shoulder, leaning close.

"I'd like to kiss you," Max says, his mouth close to mine.

This feels like a dream. The sky is expansive, the mountains are shrouded in night, the stars are winking to life. Behind us a centuries-old medieval village falls asleep.

"May I, Fi?" he asks, a soft question in his voice.

My heart gallops and my stomach clenches nervously.

I think of Aaron. Of the way he looks at me. Of the way he holds me. Of the way he asks if it'll hurt when I don't want him anymore. Of the way he tells me he's falling.

He's a dream.

This isn't a dream.

This is me.

And this is Max.

"Yes," I whisper.

And then Max leans forward, careful, slow. His hand rests against my cheek and then he brushes his lips over mine. There's strawberry on his mouth, the soft cherry of wine, the sharpness of fresh-baked bread.

His mouth is warm. His lips are soft. And as he runs his mouth over mine my heart breaks, just a little.

Because while it's nice, his lips caressing mine, his hand stroking through my hair—while it's all perfectly nice, it's not . . . it doesn't feel as if the world has stopped spinning on its axis. It doesn't feel as if time has stood still just so I can press my mouth to his.

He pulls back then, opening his eyes, his hand still on my cheek.

He gives a smile and then says, "Well, they didn't make it to the moon on the first trip either. It took . . . how many tries?"

"It was Apollo 11," I whisper.

"Ah. So another ten tries."

"You didn't feel a spark?"

"I'm not looking for a spark. I just realized you are."

"Mm-hmm," I nod and Max pulls his hand back. "Why aren't you?"

He shrugs, settles back again, and pulls me to his side. I rest against his warmth. "Sparks are overrated. Fire and passion are overrated. I don't want the kind of love that makes you crazy or makes you feel like you'll die if you can't be together. I don't want to be so consumed by love that I'm crazed with it. By all accounts, that's what my parents had before my brother and I came along. I don't want that. Who would want that? I don't."

I lean my head against his shoulder. "You might someday. You might regret not finding it."

"No." He shakes his head. "The way I love you, it's like sipping from a bottle of wine holding hands under a purple sky." He tips his chin toward the sky. "It isn't sparks or flames. It's the cool breeze of lying under the stars. With my friend. With the person I trust. That's what's important to me. But if you want sparks, I'll try to give you sparks."

I study Max's face—the firm line of his jaw, his hawkish, determined look.

"It's not something you can force," I say, thinking back to how the second Aaron touches me sparks light up. They're just there. They just are.

"Maybe. Maybe they don't even exist."

"They do in my dream."

He laughs. "Well, that's why it's a dream. Dreams and movies, the land of sparks."

"You think you should try again? Another ten times? I have to be honest, I didn't feel anything."

"Right," he says, taking it in stride, "I know. Neither did I."

"Well!"

He smiles over at me. "It was a bit like kissing a friend, not a lover."

"I am a friend."

"But if you want sparks, well, the space program—what did it cost them to get to the moon? Twenty-five billion? I'm not that wealthy, but I am quite rich."

"Quite rich" doesn't cover it. Max's fortune puts Abry to shame.

"I'll spend mountains of money, I'll take the time, and I'll find a way to give you sparks. That way, when I propose, you'll say yes."

I think about this. "If you propose and I love you as more than a friend, and there are sparks, I'll say yes."

He grins then—a happy, contented smile that spreads over his familiar face—and reaches out to me, inviting me to smile back.

"I don't know why you want to marry someone like me. I think I'm falling for a dream man."

"Yes," Max says. "But when you realize he isn't real, then you'll settle for me. I'm perfectly fine being your second choice."

I laugh and shove him, and then he gathers me in his arms and we end up laughing and rolling to the grass and lying on our backs staring up at the starry night sky.

And if I realize that while we lie there the hours are passing and the night is ticking away, well . . . it only hurts a little bit.

37

It's after midnight by the time I settle under the whispering sheets and warmth of my lavender-scented duvet. I thanked Annemarie for watching Mila, peeked in Mila's room, found her sleeping soundly, and then dropped a kiss on her head.

Now I'm clutching the cool gold watch in my hand, its ticking loud in the quiet stillness of my bedroom. Outside the wavy lines of my bedroom window the stars are bright and glowing. My eyelids flutter, my eyes are heavy, and I'm warm and relaxed.

Max didn't kiss me good night. Instead he took my hand and asked me to consider the benefits of a calm, balmy kind of love. Then, with a wry smile, he added, "With sparks."

I agreed to go with him to an evening outdoor concert next weekend, and then with a wink he told me it'd be in Paris.

I smile, settling into the darkness, and let my eyes

drift closed. Maybe Max is right. Maybe turbulent, flaming, sparking love is only found in dreams. And maybe, as he suspects, that kind of love always comes to an abrupt end.

I don't know. But I suspect I'll find out.

The watch sounds, reverberating through the stillness—

Tick,

Tick,

Tick,

—and I fall into the inviting, wide-open warmth of my dreams.

∼

"Mom! Wake up! Mom!"

I blink, bleary-eyed into the bright, sun-studded light of the island. Amy perches on the bed above me, grasping my shoulders and shaking.

"What? Who?" I shake my head and clear away the cobwebs of Geneva.

Amy grins down at me. Her cheeks are still baby-fat round and her hair bounces around her as she springs up and down on the bed.

"What do you mean, what?" she asks, jostling the bed. The tiny room isn't big enough for her vibrant morning exuberance.

I sit up and blink at her. "You want banana pancakes?"

"Please, no," she says, pretending to cross herself. "You turned me off those for life."

I climb out of bed, step onto the warm, worn wood,

and take three steps to the plastic clothesline. I pull off a sea-blue dress with tassels and ruffles.

"You won't need that. It's Saturday!"

I look back at Amy. "Sorry?"

"You forgot." She grins.

"I forgot," I agree. Or, in reality, I had no idea in the first place. Hopefully, the other Becca, the dream Becca who wreaks havoc when I'm not around, hasn't gotten me into a terrible fix.

"Dad's teaching you to swim today!" She says this with so much relish and zeal that I can only blink in confusion.

"Sorry?"

She pulls open the dresser and grabs a cherry-red bikini. She thrusts it at me. "You. Dad. The beach. Swimming lessons!"

"Why are you excited about this?"

Amy shrugs and turns to the side, hiding her expression. She pushes aside dresses and swim coverups, looking for something, and says, "Because last night you said all I ever do is read, that I'm a bookworm —like that's a bad thing—and I should expand myself and try new things. And I said, I'd try new things if you try new things, like swimming. And so I agreed to take Sean and go make baskets with Grandma—a new thing —as long as you go and learn to swim."

She pushes her curls back from her face and grins at me, completely satisfied with the arrangement. Even so, I don't especially like how my chest pinched when she mentioned that I said "all you ever do is read." She had a breezy, unaffected voice covering something that sounded an awful lot like hurt.

Amy's confident. She's one of the most confident fourteen-year-olds I've ever met. But even so, if your mum doesn't approve of you, it hurts. If you're confident, you might hide it better, but it still hurts.

"Amy," I say, and she turns and thrusts a white swim cover-up at me.

"You're going to finally have swim lessons. Dad's a terror as a swim coach. All us kids hated swim lessons, he's like a drill sergeant." She puts on a deep voice, "Tread for three minutes. Tread! No touching! This is an important life skill! Tread!"

"Amy."

She looks at me then, her eyebrows pulling down. "What?"

I take the bikini and the cover-up. "It's all right if you love to read. It's all right if that's how you want to spend your time. It's okay to just be you. To do whatever brings you joy. You shouldn't ever let anyone take your joy from you. Not even me."

Her cheeks turn pink and she looks to the side, out the window toward the bleached sky. "I know." She looks back at me then, a glint in her eyes. "'To go wrong in one's own way is better than to go right in someone else's.' That's Dostoevsky."

"Ah. It's never too early for Dostoevsky," I say, smiling at the tilt of her chin.

Then I stand up, my T-shirt falling over my thighs, take a step forward, and wrap Amy in my arms.

She stands in my hug, her shoulders hunched, and then she sighs and hugs me back.

"Love you, Mom," she says.

I squeeze her tight, looking over her shoulder at the

tiny room with the cracked plaster and the wedding photo on the wall. My heart flips in my chest as I hold her and say, "I love you too."

At that she pulls away and gives me her brassy grin. "You better go. Dad's already at the cove."

38

The cove is on the northside of the island, and long ago someone decided to call it Camelot because it's so beautiful, so unreal, that it seems to be made of dreams. Which, I suppose, it is. This is where beach weddings, family photos, picnics, and proposals happen. And where swim lessons happen.

Aaron stands on the soft white sand. It's as fine as powdered sugar, still cool even in the morning sun, and it sifts softly beneath my bare feet.

Aaron's back is to me. He's looking out over the sea, and the wind whips at his black hair and tugs at his navy shirt and swim shorts. His back is broad, his shoulders stiff, and the rising sun falls over his bronze skin and the lines of black tattoos on his biceps.

He looks lonely. Or perhaps he just looks very, very alone. As if he's wishing he were out in the ocean, swimming for hours and hours until he found who he was looking for. The line of his shoulders speaks of longing and wishes yet to unfold.

I step over the powder-soft sand and breathe in the scent of salt water, warming sand, and bright green sea grape leaves covered in morning dew. A blackbird sings in the stretching branches of an old ironwood tree shading a wooden picnic table. I set the picnic basket—made by Maranda—on the table. It's full of water jugs, sliced banana bread, mangos, and bananas. The sweet scent of it floats up to me as I consider Aaron.

He knows I'm here. When I set the picnic basket down he stiffens at the noise. But he doesn't turn. Instead he continues to look out over the sea.

It is beautiful here. It's a horseshoe-shaped beach with the finest sand I've ever felt. The ironwood trees dapple the ground with shade and the sea grapes tint the air with a sweet, earthy smell. A long, wide stretch of coral limestone circles into the sea, forming a large C-shaped pool. Farther out the reef breaks the waves. But here, at the cove, the circle of coral limestone protects the beach. The limestone extends about thirty feet into the water and wraps around twenty feet more, so that the water inside the cove is mirror-smooth.

It's a clear turquoise-blue, and from the beach I can see through the water, all the way to the sandy bottom. There are fish—canary-yellow, iridescent blue, orange and white—all flashing around the limestone and into small mounds of blue-green coral.

The sun has barely topped the water. It's still peeking over the sea into the new day. Even so, it kisses me on the cheeks with a bit of golden warmth. So I pat the picnic basket and stride across the sand. My white cotton cover-up flutters against my thighs, and the string of my bikini pulls at my neck.

I stop next to Aaron, and when I do, he looks down and gives me a tight smile.

I wonder.

Last night I hurt Amy.

Maybe last night I hurt Aaron too.

"Are you ready?" he asks, his voice absent of the familiar warmth.

"Aaron?" I reach out to put my hand on his forearm.

He looks at me then, a quick glance, his eyes widening almost imperceptibly. "Not McCormick?"

Ah. So I did. The dream Becca said something last night to hurt him.

"No. Are you all right?" I ask, touching the warmth of his forearm with the pads of my fingers.

He lets out a breath at my touch and I think he's going to touch me, say "Fi," kiss me. But then he closes his eyes and shakes his head. "I can't keep doing this."

"What?" My heart picks up speed at the gravelly hurt in his voice.

He opens his eyes and looks down at me. There's a raging storm in the depths of them. "This. This tug-of-war. This back-and-forth. I can't keep doing it. Last night you kissed him. This morning you're here."

Kissed him?

Kissed Max?

How does he know? Can he somehow see my world? Or is it my subconscious dragging Max into this world?

"He's my friend," I admit, my mouth dry. "He's been my friend for a long time. He doesn't have anything to do with us."

McCormick stiffens. "I think he has everything to do with us."

There's so much hurt rolling off him, so much confusion and pain in his eyes, that I take a step back.

And before I can think, I say, "This isn't real—"

"You think I don't know that? Do you think I haven't known that for fifteen years? This may not be real, but our life is real. This island. Our family. Our kids. Our life—it's real. If you don't want it, you only have to tell me. All you have to say is 'I don't want this.' I'm not holding you here. I love you, but I'm not holding you here. I married you, loving you, knowing this wasn't real. You—"

He cuts himself off, turning his face to the sea.

I stare at him, stunned at the lines around his mouth. At the bleak light in his eyes. He stares at the limestone rocks, craggy in the water. At the edge of the rock there's a lone ironwood, stunted and bowed from the wind but still growing, its roots clinging to the rocks.

Some might think the rock is stronger. But truly, the lone ironwood will work its roots into the stone and crack it open.

I think once, I might have believed my heart was like stone. I didn't want love. I couldn't accept love. But something as small as an ironwood tree, something as insignificant as a wildflower, can start to grow, to bloom, and then the rock will crack open and let in sunshine and light.

I step close to Aaron, slowly reaching over and taking his hand. I thread my fingers with his. He takes a shuddering breath but doesn't pull away.

The warmth of him rolls over me like the sun rising and rolling over the water. I stare out at the sea and let the soothing tide wash away the hurt, the fear—everything I've been scared of.

Finally, I say, "I'm here now. With you."

Aaron turns and looks down at me. The breeze blows, tugging at my cover-up and licking over my skin.

"You're not the same Becca as last night?"

I shake my head, gripping his hand. "I'm confused about a lot of things. For a long time I never let anyone love me. I'm trying to learn how. I came here thinking you were the one to help me. Remember what you said? You'd stay to help someone you love."

I see it then. Why there's a curling of fear still lodged in my chest. Why a prickle of sweat lines my brow. I'm scared he'll leave me. That even in a dream I'll be left behind.

"I need you," I whisper, my throat aching and raw. "From the start. I need you to help me. I kissed him last night because I love him as a friend, because he means a lot to me. But I kiss you because—"

His stares down at me, his eyes glowing, molten-hot in the sunrise. "Because why?"

I take a tight, aching breath and admit, "Because if I don't, I'll regret it for the rest of my life. Because when I'm near you I feel sparks and flames, and"—I throw out my hand—"you consume me. I think about you all the time. I want you all the time. Even knowing I can't have you. I want you. I want you so badly. And I'm terrified, absolutely terrified, that—"

I cut myself off.

Aaron's cheeks have tinted red. His gaze scrapes over me, looking into my heart. He steps forward, bringing the scent of sunshine and sea with him. "Terrified of what?"

I shake my head.

"I told you my truths. You tell me yours. Terrified of what?"

I swallow, clench my hands, and then leap into the turbulent waters. "I'm terrified that I love you. That I love you desperately, deeply, and that I can never have you. None of this is real and I can never have you."

Aaron cracks then. That's all I can describe it as. The tension, the stiffness lining his shoulders, the protection he'd wrapped around himself. It cracks, breaking away.

He grips me then, picking me up in one swoop. The air rushes around me and my stomach tilts. I gasp and grip his shoulders. Wrap my legs around his middle.

"Fi?" he asks, looking down at me.

My heart pounds, crashing against my ribs. "Yes."

His mouth hardens. "Why does that damn word make me want you so much? Why does that damn word confuse me, tie me up, make me question everything I know?"

"It's not a damn word. It's me," I say, touching my finger to the dark stubble on his jaw.

"So you're the one tying me up, confusing me, making me question everything." It's not a question, it's a statement.

He strides across the sand, following the sunlight toward the cool crystal waters.

"Where are you going?" I ask, looking at the determined glint in his eye.

"Into the water, where I can think."

"You think best in the water?"

"It'll cool me off."

Then the water is splashing around his ankles, and

the sandy slope edges down. I cling to Aaron, the hard planes of his abdomen pressed to my breasts. I clutch his shoulders as he strides further into the sea, the tropical fish darting around him, diving into the crags of the limestone and the protective embrace of the coral.

"Why do you need cooling off?" I ask, as the seawater licks at my thighs, then drenches my cotton cover-up. The water is soft, cool, as light as a cloud. It strokes over my skin and laps against me in gentle waves, until it's up to my shoulders, and I'm nearly submerged.

I press myself tighter to Aaron, wrapping around his heat. Letting the gentle current rock us together.

His eyes flare at the movement of my hips against his.

"Because," he says, his voice rough, "I want to drop you to the sand, strip off this dress, that red bikini, and make love to you all morning long. I wouldn't care who came along. I wouldn't care if the world was ending. That's how much I want you. I'd make love while this whole island was sinking into the sea and I wouldn't give a damn. When you say those things, when you look at me like that, I want to make love to you like it's the first time. That's why I need cooling off." He bites out the last, his cheeks flushed, fingers curling into my thighs.

I realize something that I didn't before. If I make love with Aaron, if we make love, I'll never, ever love anyone else. Even if it's a dream, even if it isn't real, he'll entwine himself so firmly around my heart that it'll crack open and let him in. Not just let him in but invite him in and build a home for him, where he'll stay for the rest of my life. A deep, desperate love, residing in my heart. Not just in my dreams but everywhere.

"You want to make love?" I ask, my heart pounding against his chest.

"No," he says, watching my mouth. "I'm trying not to."

"Why?"

"Because I know you'll regret it. When we make love, I want to know you'll never regret it."

"I wouldn't," I say, but we both know that's not true.

He shakes his head, a sad smile at the corners of his lips. The soft current flows around us, tugging at my cover-up and the cotton of his shirt.

"Aaron?"

"Yeah?"

I raise my hand to his cheek, watch a rainbow of waterdrops fall back to the sea. I set my fingers to his mouth. "I may be scared, but I won't ever regret loving you. I'm sorry if I leave. If I hurt you."

"Then don't leave," he says. "Stay in the water with me."

I watch his mouth pressing against my fingertips. I wish I could, but, "I can't. You don't understand, but it's just a dream."

"Then stay in the dream with me. I'll dream a dream of you, and you can dream a dream of me, and that's where we'll meet."

"All right," I whisper, my throat aching, the sun reflecting off the bright blue sea. "You'll stay here? You won't leave?"

"I'll stay," he promises.

A wave rolls over us and I rock against him. Aaron closes his eyes as I move over him, my legs wrapped tight around him. The coolness of the water is gone, replaced by a soft blue warmth. I'm floating, weightless, in Aaron's arms.

Sparks—the sparks of dreams—travel up my legs, over my thighs, and pool like air bubbles floating through the water to settle effervescent wherever Aaron and I touch. I feel suddenly as if I'm a star, floating in the sea of the sky.

"Will you kiss me?" I ask, and something in my voice makes Aaron's eyes turn a darker shade.

"Is this the last time?"

"I hope not."

"And what do I do when you don't feel this anymore?"

I shake my head. I don't know. What does he do when I'm not here? When the watch stops ticking and I put it away.

"Wait for me to come back to you."

"I'd rather let you go," he says.

I wonder if that's permission. If he's telling me I can keep seeing Max, keep trying to find that spark. But then I can't think about that anymore because Aaron takes his hand and brushes it over my cheek.

Then he feathers his thumb over my mouth and I taste the salt of the sea on him. He pulls my bottom lip down, touches the warmth of my lips and tongue, and slowly I drag my teeth over him.

He makes a noise, a quiet, low noise, at the back of his throat. Then I grip his shoulders and lean forward, and I take his mouth.

I close my eyes so I can feel all of him. The bittersweet taste of the sea, the longing of dreams, the yearning for the sun right before it rises. He's still under my mouth, as quiet as the smooth surface of the water. But then, at the touch of my tongue to his lips, he curses, clutches my thighs, and pulls me close.

"I want you," he says, rocking against me. His mouth drags over mine, pulling at me, spinning me down, deeper underwater. "I need you."

"Yes," I say, as the hardness of him hits me in exactly the right spot. He grips my thigh with one hand, his fingers clutching my hip. His other hand presses into the curve of my back, rocking me closer, driving me so that I ride over him.

His mouth moves over mine, taking my kisses, my breath, my small, desperate noises. Over the sea, the wind tugs at us and the current rocks us closer. Aaron moves me over him, holding me tight and close—so close I can feel the wanting need of his heart beating against mine. My breasts scrape against his chest, the fabric of the bikini and his shirt abrading over my sensitive skin.

He drives me closer, rocking his hips into mine, and I curse the clothing we're wearing. I curse the grip of the sea and the distance of dreams.

"Love me," Aaron says, taking my mouth, breathing against me. "Love me."

I send my hand to his face, taking his words in a kiss.

"Love me like I love you right now." He rocks against me again, the water flowing around us, between us.

Sparks dance over me, coalescing and catching fire, until heat rolls over me and through me.

"Don't go," he says. "Stay and I'll love you like this for the rest of our lives."

At that he slips a hand between us, touching the space where we meet. He brushes his hand over my bikini, the fabric scraping over me. And that friction, that promise, sends a rush, a wave of sensation, rolling through me. I cry out, arch against him, throw my head back, and ride the turbulent wave of his love.

He strums me, strokes me, so that I stay high, riding him, until my body is tingling and flying and he's kissing my jaw, my cheeks, the edges of my lips, and then my mouth.

He catches my whispered, broken "Love you. I love you."

"I love you," I breathe.

And I realize as I float back into him, cradled by the ocean and his arms, that I was wrong. I didn't need to make love with Aaron to fall desperately, irrevocably in love with him.

I'm already there.

I'm already gone.

I'm in love with a dream, with a man who isn't real, and there isn't any coming back from it.

39

I THANK HEAVEN AND ALL THE STARS ABOVE WHEN THE next night I land back at the cove in the same moment I left. I didn't want any more misunderstandings. I didn't want any more hurt on Aaron's face.

He's smiling at me—his soft, happy smile. We're sitting in the brindled shade of the ironwood in the cool, soft sand. I stripped out of my cover-up and now lie in my red bikini with sand sticking to my damp skin and the lacy sun dappling over me.

Aaron has a mango in his hand. He's cutting off chunks, the juice running over his fingers. The scent of ripe mango floats over the sweet perfume of the sea grapes. Far off there's the murmur of the waves crashing against the reef. Nearby, a small, iridescent white butterfly flutters near the cluster of sea grapes hidden in the glossy green leaves.

"When I kiss you," Aaron says, smiling at me over the mango, "I always think you smell like a butterfly."

"What?" I smile at him and dig my heels into the cool sand. "Butterflies don't have a smell."

"Yes, they do," he says, handing me a slice of mango.

I take the cool fruit and place it in my mouth. It's soft and sweet and so ripe it melts as soon as it hits my lips.

Aaron's eyes darken at the noise of appreciation I make. "They do. Every day butterflies visit hundreds of flowers. Over their lifetime they land on millions of blooms, dancing in the pollen, drinking the nectar. I think butterflies smell like the perfume of a million flowers dusted on their wings. Like you."

I stare at him, shocked. "Amy is definitely your daughter. You're both poets."

He grins at that, his black hair still wet from when he dunked under the water.

Waterdrops drip down his shoulders and sluice down his chest. He's stripped, leaving only his swim shorts on, slung low over his hips. His bronze skin is golden under the shade, broken by the tattoos rippling over his muscled abdomen and shoulders. Looking closer at the tattoos, they're locations—all his swims, all the seas and oceans and crossings, waves and whirls and water.

His body is marked by the sea, just like his heart.

He hands me another slice of mango, smiling at me gently. I take it, brushing my fingers against his, and then bite into the soft fruit. Aaron watches as I lick the juice from my fingers.

"Do I always smell like butterflies?" I ask him, growing warm at the heat in his eyes.

"No," he says, "just when I kiss you. When I say 'Fi.'"

My heart tumbles, knocks around my chest, and then kicks back to its normal rhythm.

I pick up the jug of water and take a long, cool drink. It tastes of minerals and rain and sun. Cistern water. Island water. I drop it back to the sand and wipe the back of my hand across my lips.

My shoulders are pink and tingling from the sun. Aaron spent an hour with me in the sea teaching me to swim. Even though I told him I already knew how, he had me tread water, float on my back, swim underwater to collect sea shells. And then, as I swam out to sea to a spot so deep I couldn't touch the sand, he stayed with me, and when I stopped, he kept his hands spread around my naked middle, at the bare line of my stomach where my bikini ended. For a moment I was so scalded by his hands on me I forgot to tread water. I dunked under and Aaron pulled me back up.

"Tread," he said, and he sounded so much like Amy's imitation of him that I laughed.

And then he kissed me, which made me dunk under again. And so he pulled me up, swam with me back to shore, and kissed me more.

Above us a blackbird perches in the ironwood, eyeing the plate of banana bread. I smile at the bird, at the bleached blue of the sky, and at the still, sea-blue cove. The tide is rising, rolling over the sand, the ebb and flow reaching the dappled shade of the trees.

I scoot across the sand, the grains scraping over my skin, and lean against Aaron. He widens his legs and pulls me against the warmth of his chest. He wraps his arms around me, and as I settle into him he drops his chin to my head.

"I've been thinking," I say.

"About what?"

"I want to build Junie a crib. For her baby."

"Yeah?" There's a soft, pleased note in his voice.

"Yes. I made plans. I think we have everything we need. All the wood. The paint." I tilt my head up, looking at his soft lips. "Will you help me?"

"Of course."

I grin. "Good. I also thought, next time you order supplies from the mail plane, we should order books for Amy. I'd like her bedroom to be filled with books. Bookshelves teeming with them. Yesterday I made a list—"

"Yesterday?"

I blink. Yesterday in Geneva I made a list. I went to the bookshop in Carouge and asked the owner for a long list of recommendations. But there was no yesterday on the island. There was today when we were kissing, and then there was today again, with us under this tree.

I shake my head. "I made a list. Do you think we could get them for her?"

"When she asked you to pick up books in New York you said she already had enough to read. Did you change your mind?"

"She deserves to be happy."

Aaron rubs his thumb over my cheek and gives a happy rumble. "What else? I can see there's more."

"I want to get Odie a comfy chair for when he's on crossing guard duty. And I think Maranda and Essie and Dee could sell their baskets. We could send them to the big island. There's an entire market for baskets like that. People would pay hundreds for just one."

Well, that is if there are people outside this island. But it wouldn't hurt to try.

"Why are you looking at me like that?" I ask, shifting in his arms to look at him.

His mouth is firm and his long eyelashes drift low. There's surprise hidden in his eyes. "You care."

"Of course I care."

He thinks about this for a moment.

"And what," he finally asks, tracing his finger in a slow circle over my arm, "are your plans for me?"

I think about how he said he felt like he could swim again. How with me here, he could swim knowing I'd be there in the water with him.

"You said you might swim again."

He nods, his eyes suddenly solemn. The shadow of the ironwood leaves, rustling in the sun, drifts over us.

I scoot closer, the sand scraping my thighs, and Aaron's arms tighten around me.

"I've been thinking about it," he says. "If I swim again, each location, I'd swim for a local charity. Each swim, I'd raise money for a cause. That way it wouldn't be about the thrill or setting records. I'm past that. This time it'd be about helping others." He peers down at me, his eyes clouded. "What do you think?"

I press into his sun-warmed chest, feeling his solid heartbeat and his strength. The sea lies only a few meters away, lapping over the shore. Above a gull soars along the coastline, his shadow flicking over the sand, before he veers away.

The breeze shifts the sand, pulling my wet hair across my cheek. Aaron takes the loose strands and tucks them behind my ear, his fingers brushing over my skin. A trace of heat follows the path of his hand.

"I think," I tell him, "you're a good man. I think I'd love to see you do it."

I wish he could do it with me. I'd bring him to Geneva, ask him to swim the lake, the city perched on its edges, the mountains rising in the distance. Daniel would love it. He'd ask Aaron to model our watches, construct an entire PR campaign around him. He'd gift the entire crew Abry watches and make us the official sponsor.

I'm grinning, swept away by the thought. Aaron looks down at me, his gaze curious.

"What?" he asks, his voice a soft rumble.

"I want to be there to see it. That's all. And someday, maybe you could swim Lake Geneva. You could go to Geneva and tour Abry. I'd like that. If you went to Abry and got your watch."

He makes a soft noise of assent, and then pulls me against his chest.

I rest against him, breathing in the scent of mango warming in the sun and the salt drying on our skin. In the soft, gentle quiet, Aaron brushes a kiss over my head.

"All right," he says, "we'll plan on it. Someday we'll go to Switzerland. We'll swim in Lake Geneva and get ourselves an Abry."

"Good," I tell him, my throat thick.

Then he leans back in the sand, a powder-soft bed. And I lie on top of him, my cheek pressed to his heart. He strokes my back, a gentle, soothing rhythm as I stare out at the turquoise sea.

40

August arrives with the suddenness of a summer rainstorm. I'm caught unaware and surprised.

In the two weeks since the beach I've existed in a haze of summer heat, with morning swims in the cove, cool kisses in the shade, and pink cheeks burned by the sun as Aaron drags his hand through my salt-kissed hair and we dream up futures: double-decker bus rides in London before a Channel swim; the swim around Manhattan so Amy can finally see New York; a trip to South Africa to swim False Bay—futures that don't exist.

I launch into the dream, though, with the fervent wholeheartedness of a child instinctively knowing summer is ending. The last days are here. So I play, I run, I abandon myself to experiencing everything the long, hot days have to offer.

In the real world, Mila and I take evening trips to the beach, splashing in the cold lake water and eating picnic baskets full of tart red grapes, sweet nectarines, and pungent summer cheeses spread on crispy baguettes. Daniel joins us on weekends, diving deep in the water with Mila or joining us on long, rambling bike rides through the countryside. In the last two weeks we fit in a full summer of memories.

Max joins us for a train trip winding along the lake, where we hop off at a lakeside village and climb the slope to a cobblestone-studded town. There's a tiny vineyard planted by monks hundreds of years ago where we drink sweet young wine and grape juice and gorge ourselves on cheese and olives. In Paris Max holds my hand at an outdoor symphony. In Gruyères we play tourists. At Chamonix we soar to untold heights in cable cars and then stand at the pinnacle of the world, and my chest expands at the wide blue ocean of the glacier fields and valleys below.

In Geneva, at August's close, Mila will start school. Cool winds will blow down the mountains and spread autumn colors across the valley. Our halcyon days will come to an end. School, work, busyness, all leading to the tumbling of leaves from the trees, the cold edge of winter, and then our Christmas Eve Gala.

But even before autumn and winter have arrived, there's an ending. And a small voice inside me, the one that tells me the truths—in my dreams, if not in life—whispers that everything is coming to a close.

That whisper has been there since I said the words "I love you."

It's as if the moment I uttered them, the watch I grip in my hand during sleep has been ticking down. It's that mechanical movement where the second hand slows, slows, then finally shudders to a stop.

I feel it.

So I dive into my dreams. I cling to them.

Whether it's my subconscious or the watch, every night that I return I land back in the moment with Aaron. I wake in the morning and I leave when I fall exhausted into bed, curled into Aaron's side.

So I've had two weeks of summer bliss.

I glance over at Aaron now. His hand is tangled in mine, his thumb stroking over my skin. He smiles at me, the corner of his mouth lifting. The breeze rustles his hair and the shouts and laughter of our neighbors bounces around the back garden at Sue's.

"Do you think she likes it?" I ask him, nodding toward Junie.

"Yes," Aaron says, his brown eyes warm. His look makes a flush rise over my cheeks. "I think so."

He smiles at the pink rushing over my face. Junie and Jordi are exclaiming over the crib we built them. We threw a surprise baby shower. There are dozens of people here, everyone bringing baby clothes, cloth nappies and pins, bottles and bibs. Amy even made the baby a book of poems, handwritten and illustrated, with a poem for every letter of the alphabet. I wish I could take it with me back to Geneva. I'd share it with Mila and then with anyone else who asked.

"This is how you make a crib," Junie says pointedly, rubbing her hand over the smooth white slats.

"Babe," Jordi says, sensing the tears lurking at the corners of her eyes.

"And look at the yellow onesie. Look at the sun hat."

"Babe, it's all right."

"Maranda gave me a rocker." Junie's voice wobbles and she wipes the back of her hand across her cheeks.

Jordi shifts uncomfortably, twisting his hands. "Aww, babe, don't cry."

Junie hiccups, scowls at her husband, then punches him in the arm. "Don't tell me not to cry! My ankles are swollen. My back hurts. It's hot and I'm the size of a hippopotamus. I have a rocker now. I have a crib! I can cry if I want."

Jordi looks around the back garden, frantically searching for help. No one is paying enough attention to give him any.

Pink and blue bunting hangs from the eaves and crisscrosses between the branches of the flowering trees. The late-afternoon sun slants low enough that shadows fall across the garden. There are grills glowing bright with coal, with fish charring and strips of mango blackening. There are long wooden tables full of crab dips, mango salsas, spicy pepper and olive tapenades, grilled sweet potatoes, and rum cakes and coconut pies.

Above it all, the Beach Boys (Jordi's favorite band) play on the old speakers, sending out sun-bright music.

Maranda, Dee and Essie camp out at a table, eating pie and arguing about how they'll set up their basket business. Amy dances with Sean under the white pom-pom flowers of a shade tree. Robert, Aldon, and Chris man the grills. Odie plays solitaire while eating a massive piece of coconut pie. There's more. Kids running after the chickens. The rooster and his hens somehow knew there'd be a party today. Families I recognize from the anniversary party and the search for Amy, new faces too. Sue's back garden is full, and none of them are going to help Jordi.

Junie wipes at her face, tears tracking down her cheeks.

When Jordi sees no one is paying him and Junie any mind, he sighs and says, "Babe. If you're gonna cry, do it right here." Then he holds open his arms.

Junie gives a little hiccup and then buries herself against Jordi. He folds his arms around her and rubs her back.

"It's a crib!"

"I know, babe."

"We're having a baby!"

"Yeah, we are," Jordi says, and a wide smile grows on his face as he rubs his hands over Junie's back and stares at the crib.

"They like it." I look at Aaron and he nods.

He brushes a hand over the pink on my cheeks. He knows why they're flushed. When he measured the wood, when he screwed the slats—really, when he did anything—I was mesmerized by the line of his shoulders, the strength of his forearms, the steadiness of his hands, and I couldn't help but touch him and kiss him and put my mouth on him.

So the crib ended up taking at least five times as long to build as it should have. I have a bruise on my back from lying on a scattering of wood, kissing in the grass. I scrubbed for fifteen minutes one day to get all the white paint off my skin from when we became a little too enthusiastic stroking on paint. Making the crib was literally a labor of love.

Across the garden Robert's eyes narrow as he follows Aaron's hand drifting over my cheek. He and I haven't spoken since he warned me about playing games. But there's a building tension in the looks he sends me, and I can't help but remember him saying we'd be leaving come Christmas.

A chill washes over me, leaching the flush from my face. I turn from Robert, putting my back to him.

Aaron's watching me, curiosity in his gaze. "You all right?"

I nod, stepping closer. Aaron tucks me under his arm and pulls me into his side. I fit there. Perfectly. His salt-and-sun scent wraps around me. I press my hand to his chest, to the warmth of him and the beating of his heart.

The sun slips lower, nearing the close of the day. The warm breeze of summer blows over my cheeks and tangles my cotton dress around my legs. I take it all in. The feel of Aaron's arms, comforting and solid. The beach music singing of waves and summer. The grill smoke charring the air, the perfume of the garden. Amy waving from under the shade tree, grinning as she tickles Sean's nose with a palm leaf.

"I wish today could last forever," I say, thinking about how this morning we were wrapped around each other in the soft salt water of the cove, and we touched and kissed, and I whispered, "I love you," as I threw my head back, and he kissed me and said, "Say it again."

"Maybe it does," he says, looking down at me tucked into his side. "Who knows, maybe every moment lasts forever. What is that poem Amy loves? 'To see a World in a Grain of Sand...'"

"'And a Heaven in a Wild Flower.'"

He smiles. "'Hold Infinity in the palm of your hand.'"

"'And Eternity in an hour,'" I finish.

He holds me close, wrapping me tight against him. "Maybe this is our eternity. And even after we're gone we'll still have this moment."

I nod, my cheek rubbing against his chest. "Maybe so."

He strokes a hand over my back and places a kiss on my forehead, butterfly-soft.

I look out over the party, at the daylight leaking away, and I feel the ticking of time deep in my chest.

Tick.

Tick.

Tick.

It's stuttering to a stop.

So I fling myself into the moment, grasping the end of summer, clutching it to my heart. I hold Aaron's hand tightly and say, "I love you."

It feels like the last time. Like I'm a leaf set free and floating on the wind, and when I fall the ground I land on will be back in Geneva, far, far away from here.

"I love you too," he says. "Fi. I love you too."

And that is the end of the dream.

41

Max studies me from across the soft glow of candlelight. The candle's yellow flickering lands on the white tablecloth, the china, and the glistening silverware. The light casts over him, highlighting the sharp line of his cheekbones and the wry twist of his lips. His black hair is combed back, his jaw clean-shaven. He's in a dark suit and a white collared shirt, and he's absently twisting the gold signet ring on his finger. He's working through a problem. And he's nervous.

We're at a restaurant in Old Town, a low stone-walled, stone-floored space with burgundy velvet cushions, gold trim, and lead-paned windows. The restaurant has been here for centuries and has always served food that delights the senses—fresh-baked zopf, our sweet braided bread, local cheeses melted in white wine, glossy new potatoes slick with fresh butter and thyme, wildflower honey and plump figs, mountain berries and peppery rocket.

The scents of the kitchen tease and promise pleasure, and the gentle hum of conversation and dining is muted by the ancient stone and sumptuous velvet. The candlelight bathes our table in intimacy.

If there were ever a place for sparks, this would be it.

My stomach clenches as I take a slow sip of wine—a Bordeaux. It's dry and cerebral, a thinking wine rather than a sensual wine. It's full-bodied and hints of autumn rains sprinkling over wet gravel and black raspberry thorns pricking your fingers as you pluck the fruit free. The prickly, savory flavor dries my mouth and leaves me wishing for a cool sip of water from an island cistern.

"I thought the candlelight might work," Max says, his voice as dry as the wine. A smile tugs at the corner of his lips.

"I do love it here," I say, rubbing my finger over the soft weave of the tablecloth.

"I was aiming for sparks, but I think I got a guttering candle." He gestures to the small votive flame flickering in the glass.

I shake my head. I've been distracted all day, the gnawing end-of feel worrying at the edge of every interaction. Even Daniel noticed. He brought me an extra cup of coffee after my morning meeting and told me I looked like I could use a good night's sleep, but in lieu of rest I should have an espresso. And Mila, when she climbed from the car for her last day of camp, ran back and gave me a tight hug, saying, "Don't worry, Mummy, I don't mind that camp's over. There's next year too."

Max picks up his fork and spears a thin medallion

of steak. He contemplates the wine sauce and then drops his fork without eating and looks back up at me.

"I'm involved in a new project, working with a designer."

I lift my eyebrows. Max has that light in his eyes he gets when he's chasing a new design line or a new acquisition, or even a new idea to explore.

"Tell me about it."

"It's a ring," he says, studying me carefully. He pulls a piece of paper from his suit coat interior pocket—the one that rests against his heart. The white paper is folded into a small square.

He hands it to me.

The paper's still warm from resting against his chest. I open it up and it crinkles in my hands as I smooth it out.

On the page is the design for a ring. It has a double band made of lustrous yellow gold, and it cradles a large ruby ringed by diamonds. The ruby is the exact shade of my Bordeaux flickering in the candlelight.

It's an engagement ring. A beautiful engagement ring that speaks of love and friendship and hope. A flickering hope.

"What do you think of it?" Max asks. "Just in case."

"In case of sparks?" I look up from the paper crinkling in my hand.

He nods. "Although I might give it to you even if there aren't sparks. It could be your Christmas present."

I fold the paper back into its many-creased square. "What? I thought you were getting me a bread maker for Christmas. You swore you would after the last loaf I burned turned into an inedible brick."

I smile at him and he lifts a shoulder. "I like bread

that I can chew. It's a failing of mine. If you keep making me eat your baking, I'll keep threatening to buy you cooking tools."

I laugh and he grins at me then, taking the paper back and slipping it into his suit pocket. His shoulders relax and he finally takes a bite of his dinner.

"Not bad," he says, chewing the steak.

I'm having the salmon. I shouldn't have, though, because it tastes nothing like the grilled fish I ate last night. It's a poor imitation of a freshly caught fish grilled on charcoal and sprinkled with lime juice.

"Mila starts school on Monday?" Max asks.

I push my fork through the butter pooling around the tiny round potatoes. "She does. She's ecstatic."

"Summer's over," he muses. "As a kid I loved the end of summer. It meant I'd get to leave for school and not come home until Christmas. It was my favorite time of year, that goodbye."

I think about Daniel. At age twelve my dad sent him to boarding school too. He was shuttled off to England, and I was left at sixteen without my little brother for the first time since he was two. My dad didn't think I needed boarding school. Instead I was kept in Geneva at an international school, close to home. I hated the end of summer after Daniel turned twelve. It meant our days of roaming mountain meadows, sprinting around the flower clock, and spending hours at the beach (him in the lake and me on the swing) were over. Our childhood was over.

Two years later I was at university. Then Daniel was at Oxford. And we didn't see each other except for when my dad took us sailing. And then Dad was dead and I was pregnant and Abry was failing.

But all that ending, it made space for something new.

"Do you still love the end of summer?" I ask.

The rumble of conversation shifts and quiets as a waiter carries a white frosted cake from the back, glowing with birthday candles. A couple on the opposite side of the restaurant beams as he sets the cake in front of them.

Max turns back to me. "Yes. Old habits."

It's true. Even if he doesn't want to be, Max is still gripped by the harsh lines of his childhood. Some wounds settle deep inside you, and it takes untold, unknown events to set them free.

"I've been thinking about autumn. About sailing on the lake and watching the red and orange leaves reflect in the water. We could drive out to a vineyard or walk the city at night. This winter we could take the train to Lucerne and walk along the lake. The Christmas market will have vin chaud. You're always greedy for it in the cold." He smiles at me then, the promise of future happiness in his eyes.

Suddenly I know why my dream has felt like it's ending. Because a choice has to be made. I can either stay in my dream, living a life that isn't real. Or I can take what I've learned there—that I can love, that I can be loved—and I can accept it in my life.

When I was little and my mum moved us from house to cottage to floor to tent, I cried every time. And she said, exasperated, "Moonbeam, you have to let go of the old to let in the new."

I didn't agree. I wanted to cling to the old. To hang on and never let go.

I didn't want to move, to change, to leave.

And then, eventually, I didn't want to love.

But now, I suppose, my mum, in this one thing, was right.

I have to say goodbye so that I can say hello.

It isn't fair to Max to stay in this dream world. It isn't fair to me. And even if he doesn't know it, it isn't fair to Aaron either.

He's helped me love again, and now I need to let it in.

"How does that sound?" Max asks, an eyebrow raised in question. "You look sad at the prospect of vin chaud at Christmas."

I shake my head. "I'm not sad," I say, lying to myself since I'm awake and able to. Then I reach over and take his hand. I grip Max's fingers. "It sounds wonderful. I'd like to sail with you. I'd like to see the fall colors reflect in the lake. I'd like to walk the city at night. I'd like to spend Christmas with you."

After dinner, in the August breeze, the indigo light falling around us and the hush of the city quietly settling down for the night, I take Max's hands and press a quick, whisper-soft kiss to his lips.

"Thank you," I say.

"For what?" He looks down at me, a bemused smile on his face.

"For letting me love you all these years."

He pulls me to him, the wool of his suit scratching my cheek. I breathe in his leather scent and take in his rangy strength.

"We're quite a pair," he says.

And then we stand there. Me in his arms, the sky tinting from indigo to deep plum, swallows swooping down between spires and rooflines, their wings fluttering in the night.

As the first star lights overhead, as a church bell tolls the hour, I say hello to Max, and I say goodbye to my dreams.

Goodbye to McCormick.

42

I hold the weight of the gold pocket watch in my hand with the knowledge this will be the last time I feel its ticking against my palm.

The moon is high, its light bleeding through the window and slashing across my bed. I settle under my duvet. The thick stone walls of the chateau are already absorbing the late-August chill. Lavender rises around me as I sink into my pillow and close my eyes.

My chest aches, a heavy weight settling there. I'm about to say goodbye.

Outside, the wind gusts and the long branch of our old chestnut tree knocks against the walls with a loud, cracking thud—

Thud.

I jerk upright. Blink.

Shake my head.

Thud!

Robert smacks his fist to the kitchen table. "Say something! For crying out loud, say *something*!"

I'm disoriented and dizzy, and it takes a moment for the ringing in my ears to settle and for me to land back on the island.

I'm sitting at the little round table in the small kitchen of the cottage. The kitchen light is bright, sending a harsh glow over the room. Outside the sky is a faded bruise, blue-and-black. In the kitchen a crackling electricity rides the air as if lightning is about to strike—or it already has.

The air is humid, the heat thick, and the prickly current rides over my skin.

Aaron stands across from me, his jaw hard, dark eyes fathomless. I search his face, and when I do, my stomach drops and my chest clenches. He's in pain and he's hiding it. He looks just like he did when we were on the beach and he said to me in a broken whisper, "I thought I'd lost her."

There's a well of emotion buried deep and contained only by his will.

He's in shorts, a navy T-shirt. His thick black hair is messy, and on the kitchen counter is a stack of books. It looks like he was in the middle of unloading a cardboard box full of them. And when I see the titles, I understand they're the books I asked him to find for Amy.

He did it. He did it as a surprise.

And on the counter there's something else.

A travel book.

For Switzerland. And on top of it there's a small gray velvet box with gold lettering. I know exactly what's in it. I picked out those boxes almost a decade ago when Daniel and I rebranded our packaging.

Aaron's bought me an Abry.

The mail plane must've come while I was awake. And in the delivery, Aaron carried his heart.

The kitchen is quiet except for Robert's harsh breathing and the ticking of the clock hanging on the kitchen wall.

Robert stands next to me. He's as perfectly put together as the day I first saw him. Linen pants, a buttoned shirt, short copper hair, and perfectly symmetrical features. Before, he hid his intelligence with a purposeful look of naivety, but now the naivety is gone.

"Aaron. We just told you we're leaving the day after Christmas. That Becca is moving in with me until then. That she's leaving you." He thrusts a hand at the pile of suitcases I missed, stacked in the living room. "You have nothing to say? Call me an asshole. Hit me. Do something so I can leave holding my head high."

Aaron shakes his head. And I remember what he told me when I asked him what he'd do if someone he trusted betrayed him. He said he'd hold his anger, he'd hold his rage, because he wouldn't want to live to regret his actions or his words.

"Robbie," Aaron finally says, and Robert flinches as if he's been hit. "Robbie, what are you doing?"

Robert flinches again and then looks away, his jaw clenching. "Becca and I are going to New York. I love her. I'm sorry. I didn't mean to hurt you. You're the best friend I ever had, and I know that makes this worse, but I can't help it. I've never been as *good* as you. I've never wanted to be. I broke when Scott and Jay died. I broke when I saw you not able to go on. Becca understands, because coming back here broke her too. We're leaving together. I didn't want this, but I can't stop it. I'm too weak to stop it. Like I said, I'm not as strong as you. I'm sorry."

He lifts his shoulders then steps across a discarded toy truck and a sippy cup on the floor to grasp the handle of a suitcase.

"Becca?" Robert asks. "Ready?"

I'm struck by the moment I've landed in, by the discarding of a life. I knew it was goodbye, and this dream, it acquiesced and placed me in the moment where I let go.

I can't say to Aaron that I'm leaving, going back to my real life in Geneva, but I can do what the dream Becca wants. What this dream has been leading toward since I arrived. I can say goodbye tonight and never come back.

It's the end. Not in the way I wanted, with a soft closing of the watch's case, sliding it back into its antique box to collect dust and memories. No—it's a painful, rip-the-bandage-off, game-over type of ending. But perhaps that's the only ending this dream can have.

Robert's waiting in the half-light of the living room, the suitcases in his hands. Aaron's face is turned away, and when I follow his gaze I see that he's looking at the travel book with the snow-capped Alps on the cover.

"Can I talk to Aaron alone?" I ask quietly, and when I do, Aaron's shoulders stiffen and he jerks his gaze back to me.

His eyes widen as he scans my face, looking for something, and when he finds it he takes a small step forward.

"Really?" Robert asks.

I nod, watching Aaron. "I'll meet you at your place. I won't be long."

After a moment of strained, tense silence, Robert nods.

"Fine."

And then there's the sound of his footsteps and the door as he closes it behind him.

After he's gone I expect the electricity riding in the air to sputter out. But instead it builds, pulling and arching between Aaron and me. It's so pronounced it feels like if I reached out and touched Aaron, a flash of electricity would snap between us with a bright blue-white spark.

The current grows and grows, the tension rising. I scoot my wooden chair back and stand, letting the folds of my white dress fall over my thighs. The cottage is quiet and the kitchen window is open, letting in the crashing waves of the ocean and the rich perfume of a humid night. I don't know where Amy or Sean are, but I do know that Aaron and I are the only ones here.

I step around the table, my dress whispering around my legs, the damp heat of the evening clinging to my skin.

As I move closer, the iron will that Aaron holds himself still with breaks. His mouth trembles and he presses his lips together, and once I'm within reach, he whispers, "Becca. Don't. Don't do this."

My shoulders fall and I reach out, putting my fingers to his heart. When I do he stiffens, looks down at my hand, and then lets out a long exhale.

"I'm sorry. I have to. I have to go."

He looks at me when I say this, his eyes swimming with emotion. "You don't. I don't understand what's happened. If you'd asked this a year, six months ago, I would've stepped aside. I would've understood. We weren't ever what you wanted. What you needed. But then we had this summer. We . . ." He closes his eyes, taking a painful swallow. "Fi?" he asks, a broken whisper.

When he opens his eyes again I nod. "Yes."

Tension crackles off him, a storm growing inside. "I hate that word. I hate it and I love it. The first time you said it I wanted you. And then I loved you. And some days it's gone and some days it's here. But when I say 'Fi' and you say 'yes,' don't you think . . . doesn't it feel like the hand of fate? Like we can't help but love each other?"

He lifts a hand to my cheek, spreading his fingers in my hair. "I've known you my whole life and I've loved you for fifteen years. But this, what I feel right now, it's a hurricane compared to a sprinkle. It's a tsunami compared to a ripple. Don't—" He looks down at me, his jaw shaded as he tilts his head, his eyes hungrily scanning my features. "Don't go. Stay. Stay with me. Stay as this Becca, the one I love—the one who loves me. Stay with me."

"I can't." I close my eyes, knowing I dreamed this moment because it's time to go.

Aaron rubs his finger over my bottom lip, spanning his fingers over my cheeks. "You made me fall in love. You made me dream again. Why would you do that if you were always planning on leaving?"

I stare up at him, transfixed by his question, by the sensation of his fingers running over my lip and the sparks lighting over my skin.

I reach up, take his hand, and press his fingers to my mouth. Then I pull his hand back, resting my fingers over the beating of his pulse.

Maybe Aaron isn't real. Maybe he isn't alive. But that doesn't mean he can't feel, he can't love, and he can't hurt. Or, I suppose, it doesn't mean that I can't feel and love and hurt for him.

I need to explain so that when I close the watch case in the morning, tuck it away forever, I won't regret leaving him.

"You," I say, my throat tight and raw, "are the only man I've ever wanted to give up everything for. When my mum asked me what I dreamed of, I couldn't answer, but the first moment I saw you, I knew in my heart that what I've always dreamed of is you. I was afraid for years of being left. It's the worst pain being left by someone you love. I was so afraid of it that I never loved. Not even my best friend could find his way into my heart."

"But you've always had me," Aaron says, reaching to rest his hand over mine, the thudding of his heart steady beneath my palm.

I shake my head. "I haven't. I've only had you this summer. And I didn't really have you. I knew from the start that none of this was real—"

"It is."

"That it would have to end."

"It doesn't."

"That dreams don't become reality."

"But they can."

"I'm sorry," I say, tilting my chin up, wishing I could take him in my arms, kiss him, love him so hard and so much that I could pull him and Amy and Sean from this dream and right back to Geneva.

"I wanted to tell you, thank you. After tonight I won't see you again."

"Becca—"

"No. I'm Fi. I won't see you. So I wanted to tell you, thank you. You let me love you, and you made it so I could accept your love. I've never had that before. You made my life infinitely better, and even if you never get to see it, know that I'll be grateful to you for the rest of my life. For the rest of forever. I won't ever forget what you've done for me."

"Fi," he says, shaking his head. Then he pulls me against him and wraps his arms around me. The warmth of him surrounds me, the sea and the salt and the need. "You're talking like you're leaving tomorrow. Like you'll never see me again. I have until Christmas to convince you to stay with me."

I shake my head, burying my face against his chest, trying to memorize the feeling of him holding me. "No. I won't be here. I'll be gone."

"You mean you won't be Fi anymore. You'll go back to the Becca you've always been?"

"Yes," I whisper, acknowledging the truth of what will happen when I stop coming back.

Except perhaps when I stop dreaming this entire world will end. Although I don't want to think like that. I'd prefer to think this island and all the people here will keep on living even without me.

"Why?" Aaron asks, his hands running down the sides of my ribs, curving over my back. "Why?"

I shake my head, molding myself to him. "Because. I can't stay on this island."

His hands pause, lying still on the curve of my spine. "No matter which Becca you are then, you can't stay here."

"No."

"And if I leave with you? If me and Amy and Sean—if we all leave with you? What if we all leave? We could go to Geneva like you wanted. We could go to all the places we talked about."

I close my eyes, wishing that what he's asking could come true. "I can't," I tell him. "I'm sorry. I can't."

There isn't any way to explain it. Only that I can't.

I look up at him then and I see all the pain there, the hurt, the raw vulnerability. I see a mirror of myself when I was left by someone I love.

My mum said she had to leave me and I told her I understood. She said I was the one thing in her entire life she regretted leaving behind. And now here I am, and I find that the leaving feels just as horrible as the being left.

Aaron studies my expression, and at the change in me his eyes shutter. He hides his vulnerability and tucks away his hurt. And he says, "I told you if someone I loved betrayed me, I wouldn't say something I'd regret out of anger. That I'd hold my words." A muscle in his jaw ticks, and then he looks down at me and says, "But I didn't realize I'd have to say something or risk regret."

His hand cups my cheek. The tension tightens and snaps between us, as loud as the waves crashing over the beach.

I nod, licking my lips as his eyes linger on my mouth, his gaze as firm as a touch. "Tell me."

"I won't beg anymore," he says. "I won't crawl after you. But you promised me that you'd come into the water after me if I needed you. Now I'll give you that promise too. If you ever need me, if you ever find yourself awake at night wanting me, I'll be here. I'll be here loving you."

My heart thuds hollowly in my chest. "You said you'd let me go."

"I lied. I'll be here, my hand held out to you. All you have to do is take it."

"I love you," I say, knowing I'll regret it if I don't.

Then stay, his eyes say. But he nods and then asks, "Can I kiss you?"

The words sound like goodbye.

And his kiss, it tastes like goodbye. It tastes like an ocean wave crashing over me and washing away everything that came before—everything but him—and then he's gone too.

And when I walk out the door of the cottage, I walk back into my life in Geneva.

43

THE AUTUMN FADES IN A SMUDGE OF GRAY, BLOWING crisp leaves and bare, lonely branches toward the white forgetfulness of winter.

September. October. November.

December arrives on the coattails of a cold wind sweeping down the mountains.

Geneva is a dream at Christmastime. It always has been. The Christmas markets sparkle with lights, tinkle with reindeer bells, and smell of fresh gingerbread and roasting chestnuts. We ice-skate under the stars, Mila gripping her mittened hand in mine. Max is there too, his wool-coated arm threaded with mine. We spend long nights in front of crackling fires, Max, Mila, and I, sharing a plate of raclette, the melted cheese savory and comforting. Lazy weekends in bookstores, a cup of hot chocolate. Daniel and Mila ahead on the ski slope, racing down the white expanse.

Four months of living. Four months where the only dreams I have are nightmares—they came back. The woman with the gun, whispering urgently, "Christmas Eve, Christmas Eve."

Yet during the days I've kept busy. Daniel and I took a trip to New York in October. And if I sat on the steps of the New York Public Library—just sat for an hour beneath the shadow of the library lions—well, no one knew the reason why but me. If I left a little note with a poem—*"Hope"*—on a slip of paper at the base of the steps for a girl who isn't alive, well, that's okay, isn't it? And if I leaned over the cold metal railing in Battery Park to stare out over the rippling gray water—well, lots of people look at the water, don't they?

In November Max asked Mila and me on a three-day holiday to the Canary Islands. We lounged on the sunbaked seashore, hiked into the mountains, and ate fresh oranges, the juice sticky and sweet. And while the bright sun rained down on the white bleached houses rising from the cliffsides, I held Max and Mila's hands and didn't think about white sand beaches or kissing in another turquoise sea or the smell of salt and the feel of powder-soft sand on my feet.

In December, Daniel and I reaffirmed that yes, we were hosting the Abry Christmas Eve Gala. There wasn't any reason, not even a gunshot wound, to cancel our annual celebration.

Life goes on. It does.

I loved—love—Aaron. He was the tide that washed over me and opened me to all the good that love can bring. He loved me, and I loved him.

There are some things we hide from ourselves. For our whole lives we'll keep certain truths hidden and buried deep inside. Those truths come out in dreams.

And now I've seen my dreams, I can't ever hide from myself again.

I love Aaron. And letting him go felt like losing a limb. There's a phenomenon where people still feel pain, still have sensation, where an arm or a leg used to be. It's as if the missing limb is still there—and it hurts.

I have the ghost of Aaron, the ghost of his love. I still feel it, as real as if it's there, yet unseen and untouchable—and it hurts.

Some days I take the gold pocket watch from its antique wooden case. I pull it from the whisper-soft velvet and hold its heavy weight in the palm of my hand. I stare into the blue-wave enamel and try to conjure my dreams. I try to pull them into real life. But it never works. Aaron doesn't appear. And I promised myself I wouldn't dream anymore.

I'd live.

I'd love.

Isn't that what he'd want me to do if he knew?

So I close the watch back in its wooden box, let the lid settle with a quiet snick, and lock the golden clasp, closing it tight.

Now, it's December 22—the winter solstice, as my mum would say.

Outside my office window the winter sky is a bright cerulean blue and the sun sparkles in diamond light over the first dusting of snow.

The sky reminds me of how I felt this summer. I thought of them as halcyon days, idyllic and peaceful, but really, this is the halcyon day, isn't it? Because long ago, on the winter solstice, a mythical bird, the halcyon, built an island nest at sea and calmed the wind and waves.

I smile at the thought and lean my elbows on my desk. I look out over the purple and blue snowcapped mountains and wonder if the island was built by the halcyon.

On my desk I have a pile of end-of-year reports, budgets to approve, and my Christmas letter to all our employees with our Christmas bonuses to send out. It's late-afternoon, and at the end of the day Abry will close for the holidays.

A mug of piping-hot coffee sits on my desk, sending up a curl of aromatic steam. The soft reach of the winter sun falls across my office and adds a soft warmth to the empty room. I've always liked the modern cleanliness and clutter-free atmosphere, but now it feels cold and barren.

I tug my red cashmere sweater close and clasp my hands around the hot mug of coffee.

No matter. Soon I'll head home and Mila will want to decorate Christmas cookies. Max asked to see me tonight to give me an early Christmas gift. I just have to finish the last of my work.

There's a soft knock at my office door. I look up to find Daniel smiling at me.

"Fi, everyone else has left already. Why are you still here?"

I grin back at him. "Everyone else but you."

He shrugs and strides into my office. He's in a navy suit and he needs a shave. He's been working long, late hours for the past two weeks so he can take the holiday off to spend time with Mila and me. We've both been working like mad so we can have a few days for family. I've been pulling more 6 a.m. till midnight workdays than I should. After tucking Mila in I've been going back to my computer to work. It's a habit I returned to once the nightmares started again.

"Well, one of us has to keep this company afloat," Daniel says, straight-faced, his eyes mirth-filled.

"You've been working too much. You can't be bothered to shave. I'm fairly certain this is the suit you wore yesterday. I thought you made a bet with me that you'd find someone to love."

He tugs at his shirtsleeves and frowns. "Is it?"

"No," I say.

He scoffs and pushes his hand through his sandy-brown hair. He looks so much like our dad that sometimes it shocks me. Sometimes it knocks me off-kilter. Like now. When he frowns at me, he looks just like Dad preparing to give me a lecture at age ten on not running down the hallways of Abry like a hooligan, because someday I was going to be working here.

"I've been working on it," Daniel says. "I went sailing last month with a few—"

"Stop right there. No." I hold up my hand and Daniel grins at me, fully himself again.

He steps forward, and it's then that I notice he has a box in his hand. It's the plush gray velvet we package our watches in. When you open the velvet container, with its scripted gold lettering, you find a smaller white leather box. And inside the white leather, resting on satin, is an Abry watch.

The small velvet box is just like the one Aaron had on the Swiss travel book the last night I saw him. There's a hollow thump in my chest at the thought.

"What's that?" I ask, pointing to the box.

Daniel puts on a smug look—a little-brother look

that tells me he's happy to know something I don't. "I wondered if you knew. Apparently not."

"Knew what?"

"I'm glad I get to be the first to show you."

He steps across the wood floor of my office and slides the velvet box across the glossy white surface of my desk. The velvet whispers a smooth whooshing as he passes it to me.

A tingle of awareness, a frisson of a sea-salt breeze blowing the strands of my hair, a spark of electricity, crackles in the air around me.

"What is it?"

"Open it." Daniel nods to the box then rocks back on his heels, an expectant smile on his face.

I take a deep breath, and instead of coffee I smell the memory of humid, loamy tropical forests and sea-salt waves cresting on white sand.

The gray velvet box sits in front of me, right in the middle of my desk. Even though it's only four inches tall and four inches wide, the amount of energy pulsing around it makes it feel as if it's as large as the room.

Slowly I reach forward and lift the velvet lid. It slides open with a smooth snap, and I let out a shallow, tight breath. I pull free the smaller white leather box. It's cool in my hands, pebbled and soft.

My throat is tight, my mouth dry, and a slow tattoo starts in my chest. I lift the lid, and when I do, I let out a long, pained exhale.

I forgot.

Or maybe I didn't forget, I just didn't want to think about it.

"Beautiful, isn't it?" Daniel asks, a smile in his voice.

"Dad'd be proud. We already have record orders for a limited edition. You did good, Fi. You did good."

I nod, unable to speak.

I don't look at Daniel. Instead I stare into the face of the watch.

It's my watch.

McCormick's watch.

The one I dreamed up after our date to the top of the island.

The enamel on the face is the exact shade of the sea as it breaks over the reef and spills over the shore. It's turquoise and cerulean, it's indigo and sea-green, and it's opal-white with waves that fall onto moonlit sand. Not truly. Not really. But that's what it looks like. Peering into the dial, at the blue, at the diamonds glittering in the face, at the soft gold case, the smooth pearl and emerald bracelet, at the ticking of the watch in my hand, I'm transported to the island.

I'm pulled back to the hilltop. I'm lying in Aaron's arms under the soft shade of the whistling pine, the breeze whispering through the boughs, the needles crinkling beneath us, letting up piney scents, Aaron's heart beating against my cheek as he holds me tight and we look out over the island.

"Why are you crying?" Daniel asks, stepping forward and putting his hand on my arm. "Fi?"

I shake my head. Hold the watch in my hands. "I'm not." And at Daniel's disbelief, because there are truly tears trailing down my cheeks, I say, "It's only, I'd forgotten how beautiful it was."

He nods. "It is, isn't it? The McCormick."

I glance up at my brother then, standing next to me, his hand resting on my forearm, comforting me.

"I'm still not sold on the name though."

I smile at him. "Tough. I like the name."

"What does it mean?"

I think about it for a moment, then I say, "Some say it means an almost, a never-was, a dream that didn't happen, but I say it means an always, a dream that still goes on."

Daniel lifts an eyebrow. "That's poetic, Fi."

"You know me."

"You don't like poetry."

"I do now. People change."

He smiles at that and steps back, seeing that I'm no longer in dire need of comforting. "I have to head out. I'll see you tomorrow? Mila wants to ski and I want to drink hot chocolate, so." He shrugs, a happy gleam in his eyes.

"See you tomorrow."

Daniel leaves. I'm left at Abry, in an empty winter-hushed building, with sunlight fading and snow falling outside.

Instead of closing the watch back in its box, I open the clasp and I put it on my wrist.

44

The sitting room at the chateau still smells of the popcorn Mila, Max, and I strung on a long thread while we watched "Drei Haselnüsse für Aschenbrödel"—Mila's favorite Christmas movie. We watch it every year, just in case we're tempted to forget there's magic at Christmastime. When the movie was over we draped yards of popcorn garland over our little tilting family tree set in the corner of the sitting room.

Now Mila's tucked in bed, full of ham-and-cheese crepes, Christmas pudding, Brun de Bâle—crumbly chocolate hazelnut cut-outs (beloved by Max)—and Miroir—delicate vanilla cut-out hearts filled with strawberry jam (beloved by Mila).

Outside silver moonlight falls over the hushed quiet of snow falling over bare-limbed trees and watchful pines. The night is black, quiet. The only noise is the pop and crackle of the logs burning in the stone fireplace.

The little fire glows red and orange and gold as it

sparks, cheerful and hopeful, in opposition to the cold night and the icy flowers drawn in frost on the tall, lead-paned windows.

I breathe in the smoky popcorn scent and smile over at Max. We're settled on the thick handwoven rug in front of the fire. I lean against his side, and the gentle heat of the low-burning orange flames curls over us.

He's in a hunter-green cashmere sweater and dark jeans. The green brings out the gold flecks in his brown eyes, and the fire casts a golden glow over his blue-black hair. In the four months we've spent dating we've kissed—occasionally—we've held hands—often—and we've laughed—always.

Max is still my best friend. And by the way he's been twisting his ring, by the solemn gravity in his eyes, and by the way he wraps his arm around me and pulls me close, I know.

He takes a long breath and then exhales, his chest expanding, the softness of his sweater rubbing against my bare arm. I'm in jeans and a silver silk camisole. I took off my sweater hours ago, when the fire warmed the room so much that I felt like I was back on the island.

Now it's died down to a low golden heat, but I won't put my sweater back on.

Max draws his hand down my arm, stroking my skin slowly, absently, as he stares at the fire.

"I have your Christmas present," he finally says, his voice deep and controlled.

"I know," I say, and when I do he looks down at me, his eyebrows lifting in that supercilious expression my mum said she'd recognize anywhere. "You said so earlier," I tell him with a smile.

His expression clears and he nods. "That's right."

My chest tightens, and the watch still nestled around my wrist grows heavy and pulsing. I look down at it, at the face of my dreams.

Max reaches into his jeans pocket and pulls an object free. His hand closes around it.

"I thought I might take you to Paris, ask you at the Eiffel Tower. Or take you sailing and ask you at sunset. But"—he shrugs, a small smile tugging at the corner of his mouth—"I'm me and you're you, and it felt right to ask you like this."

He leans forward, his warmth curling around me, as comfortable as the fire. He opens his hand and the glow of the flames reflects and glimmers on a large red ruby surrounded by diamonds, cradled by a double ring of yellow gold.

"Marry me, Fiona," he says then, his expression questioning, hopeful.

He holds the ring between us and an overwhelming love wends its way through my chest. The ruby gleams in the firelight and it reminds me of Max's love. The first time we met, the unselfish support he gave me when I was a new mom, the years of summer picnics in the country, the business advice exchanged, the dry wit and the comforting shoulder, the time I pulled him from the brink, and the days he carried me across a cliff. I love him so much.

But I don't love him in the right way. I still don't.

Perhaps yesterday I would've said yes. I would've said yes right away.

Yes.

I could see myself spending my life with Max and being perfectly, acceptably content. Happy.

But I know too that I have to be honest with myself.

You can love someone wholly, completely, and it doesn't mean that they're the one for you. You can love someone and they can still be the wrong someone.

I didn't want to acknowledge that.

Or maybe it's that the weight of the watch on my wrist is reminding me I haven't truly let go. That I still love a dream so much I've not let myself love real life.

"It's a no, isn't it?" Max asks, searching my expression.

"I love you," I tell him, "but not, I think, in the right way."

"Is there a right way to love?"

I let out a breath. "I don't know."

"Still no sparks?"

I lean into him, breathing in the smoky wood, the piney scent of the Christmas tree, the popcorn and chocolate and hazelnut sweets. Outside the snow falls heavier, flickering in the moonlight in fat, slow-falling flakes.

"What happens to us if I say yes?"

He tugs me close, the fabric of the rug scraping against my jeans, the cashmere of his sweater soft and warm.

"Then we get married and I move out of my dismal family home and join you and Mila in your delightfully drafty chateau. And you bake terribly burned bread and brick-hard porridge, and I bring home takeout. You'll make watches and I'll make jewelry, and sometimes we'll make things together. We'll continue on as we are, except we'll have agreed to do it for life. I'll be here for you and you'll be here for me. And, if you like, we'll have children. Or we'll decide that we're happy just the three of us." He still holds the ring between us, and it glints with the promise of his words.

I'm hot now, and cold, and my chest aches, and that phantom limb, the ghost of my dreams, it hurts.

"And what happens to us if I say no?"

Max's hand curls and he nearly closes his fingers around the ring. The firelight plays over the angled lines of his face, the sharp cheekbones, the straight nose, his high, dark eyebrows. He's austere, hawklike Max—the one determined to succeed in whatever he sets his mind to.

"Then we'll be friends. We'll always be friends, Fi. It's the price you pay for saving a degenerate like me."

"You're not a degenerate."

He smiles. "Anymore."

I touch his hand, my fingers light against the dry warmth of his skin. He opens his palm, the ring there between us.

"Will anything change?"

"Everything and nothing," he says, his face tilted toward mine, the smoky scent of the fire drifting between us. "Whichever you choose. Everything and nothing."

I nod. "I need to think about it."

He takes my hand then, turns my palm up, and brushes his thumb over the soft, sensitive spot in the middle of my hand. "Here."

He places the ring in my palm. It's warm and solid.

"I haven't said yes."

"It's a gift either way. I made it for you. It reminds me . . . do you remember the night you came to my place, burned up all that liquor?"

"This ring reminds you of that fire?"

"No," he says. "It reminds me of your heart."

I close my fingers around the ring. The diamonds and the cut of the ruby prick my skin. "My heart?"

"You think you can't love, but I've never met someone who loves so much." He smiles then and says, "I'm honored to be your friend. I'd be honored to be more."

I hug him then. I wrap my arms around him, my right hand clenching the ring he made for me. After a moment he tugs me close and I lay my head against his shoulder.

"I hope you say yes," he murmurs into my hair, his hand feathering over my back.

I should say yes.

I could say yes.

Only.

The watch wrapped around my wrist calls to me. It whispers . . . *You still love him.*

I'm still in love with Aaron.

Which means before I can answer Max, I need to know why.

Why did Adolphus Abry's watch show me a man, a dream, that I could never have but also could never let go?

45

My mum picks up her phone on the second ring. "Hullo?"

Her voice is muffled by the throbbing beat of a dozen drums. Ah. She's at a drum circle.

I walk to the window of my bedroom and peer through the frosted pane at the half-moon waxing over the snow.

"Mum—"

"Moonbeam! Happy winter solstice!" Her voice has that high, chipper beat I recognize from weeks-long spiritual retreats and fireside chats outside camper vans.

"Right, happy solstice," I say, speaking loudly to be heard over the bang and thunk and beating of at least twenty people banging drums.

I should've expected my mum would be at a party, but once Max left for the night, after pressing the ruby and diamond ring firmly into my hand and saying,

"Think about it. Take as long as you need," I felt the urgent need to call my mum.

I pace across the length of my bedroom, the soft wool rug whispering under my feet. There's a draft spilling through the window, a cold winter chill that no amount of modernizing can fix. This is a centuries-old chateau. Drafts are part and parcel. Still, once I left the warmth of the sitting room I threw on a wool sweater over my camisole.

"Mum," I say loudly, hoping I don't wake Mila, "I have to ask you about the watch."

"What watch?" she asks. Then, "Just a moment, Felicia. I'm speaking with my daughter. What watch? You have a lot of watches."

I'm back at the window, my reflection wavy in the glass. My pale face is superimposed over the dark night sky, the smudges of trees coated in snow, and the wide, dark expanse of the lake, flat and fathomless. I press my palm to the glass and the cold seeps into my skin.

"I mean the watch you gave me on summer solstice. Adolphus Abry's watch."

The white frost, hoary and spidery, begins to melt and the glass around my hand clears to black.

"Oh, the watch I stole from dear old Leopold?"

"Yes. That watch. I was wondering, did Uncle Leopold tell you what happened after you dreamed? Did he say what you were supposed to do?"

"Well . . ." My mum trails off, and for a moment the only noise is the throbbing beat of the drums, rising and crescendoing.

My hand is nearly numb from the cold, so I pull it from the glass. My handprint, surrounded by frost, remains behind.

"He only said that it let you live your dreams. So, I suppose you're supposed to live them."

I let out a sigh and my breath fills in the handprint, leaving a fog over the window glass.

"He didn't say anything more?"

"What happened? Moonbeam—"

"Fiona."

"Fiona. You don't sound as if you're happy. You don't sound as if you're living your dreams. I thought this watch would help you find yourself. It's why I took it."

I shake my head, the weight of the pearl bracelet heavy around my wrist. "Max proposed."

I don't know why I tell my mum. We don't have heart-to-hearts. We don't have chats where she gives worldly advice or even loving advice. I haven't shared anything with her in decades.

"The hoover salesman?" she asks.

"Mum."

"Fine. I hope you turned him down."

"Why?" I clutch the phone, knowing precisely why.

"Because he isn't right for you."

"I love him."

"Of course you do. But that doesn't mean he's the man you should spend your life with. Or even a few years with. I'm still learning about life, but there's one thing I know. You have to trust yourself. You can only live a true life if you trust yourself. What is your heart telling you?"

I look down at the floor, breathing in the cool stone and the scent of lavender that always lingers in my room. I look toward my nightstand, where I still keep the antique box and the gold pocket watch.

"It's telling me to dream."

"All right. Then do that." She says it as if it's simple. It's not.

I think perhaps Uncle Leopold knows that too. After all, he left Abry, Geneva, all of this behind, because life and love weren't simple.

"Do you have Uncle Leopold's phone number by any chance?" I ask.

The clouds have parted and the moon throws its silver light across the garden, where a winter hare sprints across the snow, leaving only its tracks behind. Overhead the shadow of a hawk falls over its path. I watch, my breath held, until the rabbit dives beneath a snowy mound at the base of the chestnut tree.

"I do," my mum says. "I'll send it to you."

"Now, please," I say, my heart still beating fast at the rabbit's flight.

In the background the drums pick up speed. "Sent. Done. I'm off then."

"Thank you—"

"Ta-ta," my mum says, and then she's gone.

So, before I can think about doubt or delay, or waiting for the morning, I ring Uncle Leopold.

~

Uncle Leopold, from what I can tell, is ninety-nine years old and the younger brother of my great-grandfather. That he still lives on his own and has a phone he answers at ten o'clock at night is quite incredible.

I've moved down to the study. I don't want to wake Mila if I have to shout to be heard. I lean against the old walnut desk. I'm surrounded by bookshelves, full to the brim with old horology hardbacks, encyclopedias, handwritten Abry records from two centuries of meticulous bookkeeping, old adverts, proposals, and hand-drawn designs of our watches. It's an archive of Abry history. It has the familiar, comforting smell of the beeswax used to polish the walnut desk, and of old parchment.

The walls are insulated with walnut paneling and the rug is thick. The brown leather chair is cracked and comfy. I perch on the edge of the armrest, my back straight.

"You used the watch? You dreamed?" Uncle Leopold asks. His voice is creaky and rough, like an old rocking chair squeaking under a heavy weight.

I woke him up from a dead sleep, but he didn't seem too terribly upset once I told him who I was. For a man who left the family, he was surprisingly cheery to be phoned by an Abry.

"Yes. I'm sorry my mum took it—"

"Sorry? Sorry? I practically had to dangle the thing in front of her. I nattered on and on about it. I nearly shouted 'Take the darned thing, give it to your daughter!' I thought I might have to brain her with the fire iron and drop it in her handbag. Lucky me, when I refilled the tea she slipped it in her pocket."

"You wanted my mum to take it?" I ask, astonished.

"It *belongs* to the family. I don't have a use for it anymore. I failed it. I hoped that you would do better."

I shake my head and stand, walking to the bookshelf. The books line the wall from floor to ceiling and I run my hand over them. I imagine if Amy were here, she'd curl up in the leather chair by the window. In the afternoon the sun always falls through the glass and settles over the chair like a golden blanket on your lap.

She'd love it here.

Except.

"How could I do better? What is there to do better with?"

"By dreaming!"

I frown. "Yes. I know. I dreamed. It felt real. Just like you, I found love. But . . . it's a problem."

He coughs, a phlegmy, chest-rattling noise. "What do you mean, it's a problem?"

"I can't forget him. The man I fell in love with. I learned my lesson. I found what I desired. I haven't used the watch for four months so I could live and find love in the real world. I get that a love like his is my heart's desire. But I can't forget him."

"What did you say?" Leopold asks, his creaky voice sharp.

I frown and pace across the study, dragging my hand over the edge of the walnut desk. The computer monitor glows a soft, ghostly blue.

"I said I can't forget my dreams. I can't forget or let go of the man I met there."

"Why would you?"

I frown, a line creasing my brow. "Because he isn't real."

The stillness of the room presses down on me.

"What?"

"He isn't real."

My lungs are tight, my breath short. There's something wrong here. Something I'm not understanding.

"He's real," Uncle Leopold says. "What do you mean, he isn't real?"

A prickle starts at the back of my neck and climbs, heat flushing over my skin. "I mean I dreamed. It was all just a dream. He's just a dream."

"My word. Is that what your mother told you? I told her the watch let you dream your heart's desire. I told her it let you see what is true. What is *real*."

He says "real" with a hard conviction.

My heart slows and there's a shrill ringing in my ears. "You're saying the place I dreamed, the people, they're all alive?"

"I'm saying they're real. I'm saying that I dreamed my Annalise and I couldn't get to her in time. I lost her." He says this bitterly, viciously. "And you let four months pass? You, who had the watch, let time pass? He's waiting for you! Just like she was waiting for me!"

The room tilts and my skin goes cold. The smell of parchment and old stone wraps around me, keeping me in the here and now. I stumble, catching myself on the leather chair.

It's what Aaron said. That he'd be on the island, holding out his hand, waiting for me to take it.

"He's real?"

"What else could he be? Couldn't you feel it?"

The heat of the island, the sea-salt breeze, the taste of Aaron's lips as I lay on a soft sand beach. It was all real.

My legs fold and I fall into the chair, the leather cold beneath me. I take a breath, trying to breathe around the tight constriction in my chest.

I shake my head. "But I wasn't myself in the dream.

I was someone else. Everyone thought I was someone else."

"And I was a Polish officer in the army. Annalise was a nurse. What does it matter who they see? You're you. He's him. My word, you had it all wrong. You aren't supposed to learn a lesson. You aren't supposed to dream and then forget. You're supposed to *find* him. The watch shows you your desire so you can grasp it."

"Find him," I repeat.

Aaron's alive. Aaron's real. Amy is real. Sean. Maranda. All of them are real. And Aaron's waiting for me. He might not know it, but he is. He's waiting for *me*.

"I have to go," I say.

"I'll say," Uncle Leopold says. "Go find him."

And then he hangs up.

I drop my phone. It clatters to the walnut desk. My hand shakes as I reach out and unlock the computer.

The room is still, the snowy night quiet and hushed. The chateau, the world, feels as if it's holding its breath.

The ocean-blue enamel of my watch glistens in the study light as I type in four words.

Aaron McCormick Marathon Swimmer.

And there, on the glowing computer screen, is the biography of the man I love.

46

He's real.

Aaron McCormick is real.

His smile peeks out at me from the humming light of the computer screen. He's under a sun-filled sky, water dripping down his shoulders, his hair wet, brown eyes alight. He's in swim trunks, his chest bare and streaked with tattoos and hard lines of muscle. His shoulders are wide and solid and he's standing on a large white catamaran, his legs spread wide, a grin on his face as if he just conquered the sea.

And he did.

The caption of the photo reads "Aaron McCormick, age 18, World Record Holder, after completing the South Eleuthera to Nassau, Bahamas route for the second time."

I stare at the shining light in his eyes. He's young in the photograph—as young as he was in his wedding photo. And he has that same carefree, easy, life-is-fine-life-is-wonderful expression. This is before the Gulf

Stream swim. Before Scott and Jay died. Before Becca. The sea shines behind him, diamonds glittering on a great blue expanse.

The wind tosses the boat high, the white sail snaps behind him, and he looks as if he's about to take a step forward. A gust of wind tousles his black hair. His cheeks are pink from the wind and the exhilaration of completing a forty-hour swim, and I expect him to lift his hand out to me and say, "Fi."

My chest cracks and my heart tumbles about as if it's rocking on the waves in the photograph, tossed about by the sea.

It's him. He's alive.

All this time he's been here, waiting for me on the island.

I read the first article pulled up on the screen.

I scan the words lightning-quick, consuming every spare piece of information. It tells of the swims I already knew about—the channel, Barbados, Ibiza to Mallorca—they're all there, more, and it has a quote from Aaron when asked how he accomplishes feats most people would never dream of.

He says, "I love being in the water. I love it. You can do almost anything if you love it enough."

The article ends with the sentence "McCormick prepares to swim the Gulf Stream next month."

My hand shakes and the quiet of the study presses down on me. It's as if the rows of books, the tomes on horology, the timepiece diagrams on parchment, all of them, are still holding their breath, afraid of the exhale.

Outside the tall, lead-paned windows, the snow has stopped falling and the night has entered a watchful quiet. The moon strides over the cold with its silver light, and the bare branches of the trees reach and bend in the snow-filled gusts. I shiver and pull my sweater closer, the air in the study dry and cold.

"He's alive," I say, and when I do, my heart leaps. My voice echoes off the wood paneling, filling the still air. "He's *alive*."

I select the next article, and the next. They're all of the same theme: from age fourteen to eighteen Aaron swam the world—just as he said. I drink in the photographs, the details of his life.

There's a picture of him grinning, his arm slung around a young, happier Robert, standing next to two boys—twins—with black curly hair, brown eyes, and Dee's smile.

There's another photo, all of them happy and relaxed on the metal benches of a large, rusty fishing boat. Aaron and one of the twins have their arms flung about each other. The gold of the setting sun streaks across their laughing faces, and the caption reads "Aaron McCormick, Crew, False Bay, South Africa, stories of white sharks."

There are more. I drink them in greedily, thirstily, reading every article from the top of the page and moving down through the years of his life, when he was still swimming.

And maybe he will again. He said he would, didn't he? He said he'd swim, knowing I was there.

I lean forward, the warm leather of the chair slick against my thighs. The chair creaks beneath me as I shift, scanning the screen. The computer hums, kicking soft, hot air into the cold.

There's an article about his home—Saint Eligius, nicknamed Frying Pan Island—a tiny, remote island in the Caribbean, northeast of Brazil, sister island of Saint Noyon, the larger of the two.

It's *real*. It's a real place.

I smile at this in amazement, that a place like the island is *real*.

I could fly there. I could fly to London, then to Nassau, and hire a small propeller plane to land on the sandy runway along the beach. Odie would hold out his crossing guard sign, stopping all pedestrian traffic as the plane circled the runway and then bumped to a stop on the sand.

I could be there by Christmas.

My breath comes in short bursts and a prickle tingles up and along my spine. Mila and I could be on the beach by tomorrow, Christmas Eve at the latest. We could spend Christmas Eve on the island. Would Daniel mind? Would he host the Abry Gala on his own if I told him I had to fly across the world to meet the man I love?

And Max? What will he say? I called Leopold because of him. I learned Aaron is real because of his proposal.

And what will Aaron say when I arrive? A tall, auburn-haired, hazel-eyed woman named Fi? Will he know me? Recognize me?

My stomach flips as I flick down the computer page, my body electric, skin buzzing, mind urging me to do, go, fly.

To find Aaron. Right now. To go. This very moment.

The quiet of the study crackles with suppressed, breath-held energy.

And then something catches my eye. An article I missed before, buried at the bottom of the page.

The last article on the screen.

The very last article.

Buried, shrouded, and hidden beneath all the records and accolades and life.

A chill creeps over me, down my arms, over my limbs, until even the center of me is numb.

I stare at the words, unable to make sense of them. But then they coalesce, the black letters coming together in an irrevocable sentence that cannot be undone. Can't be unread.

He's alive, I'd said.

He's real.

He's alive.

I touch the warm glow of the computer, feeling the vibration of my fingertips against the screen, trying to wipe away the words.

They stay.

And the breath that the world was holding—the breath I didn't realize I was holding—it tears out of me in a pained, jagged exhale as I read—

Aaron James McCormick, 33, World Record Holding Marathon Swimmer, Dead.

Dead and gone.

47

I clutch the gold pocket watch in my hand. The metal sides dig painfully into my skin. I wind the watch, my breath tight as the gold second hand springs to life. The ticking lurches forward, jarring the timepiece out of its hibernation.

Four months.

I left Aaron for four months.

And now he's gone.

It's worse than that though. Worse than I ever could have imagined.

A numbness seeps through me, as if I've been left out in the ice and the snow and the cold has traveled into my bones and settled deep in my marrow.

I remember the night my dad died. Daniel called, and as soon as he spoke the words a wave of shock struck me and jarred me out of myself. The pain was too much. It was so much that I couldn't feel it at all. It's like when you touch a hot pan and you can't decide whether it's burning hot or icy cold. For days I was numb. Just a walking, talking human with blood pumping in my veins, a heart beating in my chest, and no way to let myself cry. No way to let myself fall apart.

The numbness held me like the deepest grip of winter.

The same happened when Joel told me he was married.

And the same happened when my mum left me, just dropped me on my dad's front steps, and didn't look back.

I know this numbness, this shockwave of despair, so deep that your mind can't accept it. I've felt it before.

But I can't accept the despair. Because if I do he'll be gone—they'll be gone. Everything. Even me.

I huddle in the center of my bed, my bedroom as dark as a tomb, the moonlight shrouded by a veil of black clouds. I breathe in the faded scent of lavender, as worn as dried flowers forgotten and crumbled into dust.

"Please," I whisper. "Please."

Before, when I fell asleep, I went to him. I don't know how. I don't know why. But I always went to him, even though it should never have been possible.

Please.

He said he'd be there, holding out his hand to me. He promised.

I didn't know that when I left, I'd left him alone treading water, when I'd promised to always come for him.

I didn't know.

There's a black wave rushing toward me, a tsunami of thought and emotion I can't think about. I can't feel. I won't.

The images on the computer screen. The photographs. The words. They blur together in a tidal wave threatening to crash over me and drown me.

I push it away.

I'll dream tonight.

I'll go to Aaron.

And in my dreams he'll be there.

They all will be.

I fall back into the deep folds of my mattress. letting the weight of the duvet settle over me. The cold, dark air falls silent. I pray for heat. I pray for humidity. I pray for a sea-salt breeze. I close my eyes and I pray, *Please, please, please—*

48

"Please."

I jar forward, my hands hitting the hot sand and the scuffing of spiky green grass. The sun reaches down and smacks my back in sharp streaks of heat.

I draw in a ragged, grateful breath, half-sob, half-joy.

The bright, sea-washed light assaults me, and I blink into the hot sun.

A scurry of gulls flies overhead, cawing and quarreling, white dots against the sun-bleached sky. The wind wraps around me and tugs at my blonde hair and my black cotton dress. I'm Becca then. Although now I know Becca is real. Maybe I lived her life, or maybe I lived her dreams. I don't know.

I only know that I'm kneeling in the coarse sand, the salt-soaked wind whipping around me, and the waves are crashing, harsh and wild, at my back.

My heart pounds at the crashing of sea against shore, and there's a salty, bitter taste on my lips. My throat aches even when I pull in another gasp of humid air, and my eyes burn.

The humidity presses over me and sweat runs down my back. Close by, a stand of whistling pine—casuarinas—twists in the wind. The scantest line of shade flickers beneath their boughs. I'm on a beach. One with rough-limbed pines, gulls sailing the wind, and the sharp scent of old pine and salt.

It's not a beach I remember.

When I stand, a ghost crab scuttles across a long ribbon of olive-green seaweed and disappears into the sand.

I turn, scanning the rugged shoreline and the whistling pines, bent and weeping.

It's all wrong.

I'm on the island, I know I am, but it's all wrong.

I can see the line of the reef with its white-capped waves breaking and the water edging to turquoise, but the reef is further out now, by a few hundred meters at least. There's the mangroves to the south, a thick line of them, with their tube-like red roots reaching into the saltwater, but at least half of the mangroves are gone.

The hill that Aaron and I biked? The one that was a fifteen-minute ride from the cottage? Far from the beach? I trail my eyes over the rise, following the sandy path to the top of the hill, sitting on the water's edge.

A mosquito buzzes then lands on my sweat-covered forearm. I slap it and then step under the line of trees, the pine needles crunching under my feet. A picnic table, a gray, worn, splintered thing, sits hobbled and lonely under the trees.

A lone blackbird watches as I walk further from the ocean, toward the tall granite marker. The bird isn't singing. It's perched on the stone, its feathers glossy black, its head cocked.

When I reach the stone, the blackbird flutters away in a spray of wings and wind.

I don't want to look.

I don't want to see.

I know what I'll find.

I'm too late.

I step forward, pressing my fingers to the pink-and-gray granite. The stone is warm, almost hot, in the sun. It's unyielding. Unfeeling.

It's a memorial. A granite marker. The kind placed in cemeteries or at battle sites, or where people want to remember or perhaps never forget.

"You came back."

I turn at the deep, craggy voice.

My heart jolts, kicks, and then settles. It's Odie. Or a version of Odie I've never seen. His long, black pants are wrinkled, his white shirt salt-stained, and his face creased and worn with wrinkles that weren't there the last time I saw him.

The tears, the fear, the shock, the wild rage that's been pressing on me since I read the article, and then the next, and the next, claws and fights to be freed.

I want to fall to my knees and weep at his feet. Instead I nod.

"I'm back."

He gives a sharp nod. Looks at my hand pressed to the granite. The name my fingers trace.

"Hard to think it's been two years," he says, studying the memorial.

My throat tightens and I nod.

"Will you come back every Christmas? Pay your respects? It gets lonely, me being the only one left."

"Why do you stay?" I ask, thinking about the emptiness of the island, the loneliness of living in a place where you're the only person left.

He shrugs then looks out over the sea. The shadows of the whistling pines fall in bars across his face. "I figure I should've died here too. I might as well stay."

I look back to the gray stone then. To the marker that tells me in harsh, stone-cut lines, what happened on Saint Eligius. There's the date, Christmas Eve, two years ago.

The words—"In memory of the residents of Saint Eligius who died on December 24"—and a list.

That's all.

A list of names.

As if names written on a stone can tell the world how much they have loved, how much you have loved them. As if words on a stone can describe a life.

The names are all there.

Amy Marie McCormick.

Sean Alexander McCormick.

Aaron James McCormick.

I wonder. Did he try to save them? Did he struggle to free them from the water? Or was it sudden? A flash. A raging sea. Gone so quickly he didn't know he was losing them.

Those names, set together in stone, they don't tell anyone how much he loved them. They don't tell how Amy loved poetry, how she dreamed of the New York Public Library and of flying into literary worlds. They don't tell how Aaron sang to Sean during storms. How much he loved his kids. They don't tell about how he loved the sea. He loved it even when it took him and everyone he loved.

There's Junie Avery Finch.

Jordi Finch.

And under their names—

Adelle June Finch.

They had their baby. A girl.

The list goes on. Cold, unfeeling type. All of them. Maranda. Essie. Dee.

Robert Stanton.

Gone.

Sixty-four names.

Just words in a stone.

"I wish," Odie says, watching my fingers trace over the names, watching me press my hand to the unyielding stone, "I hadn't listened to McCormick. He told me, 'Go find Becca, she's on the hill, make sure she's okay.' He went back to get the kids. To help. I wish I'd said, 'You go get Becca. You take the kids up the hill.' Then I'd be on there"—he points to the stone—"and he'd be right here."

Sweat trickles down my back, the heat punishing.

"He knew something was wrong?" I ask, my voice as dry as a husk, hollow and ghostlike.

"Course he did," Odie says. "We felt the earthquake, didn't we? The airport crumbled like mud. Essie's roof collapsed. He was sprinting back toward the cottage. Toward the damned sea. Grabbed me, pushed me toward the hill. Then I got there, and you and Robert were running down, and Robert said, 'Stay here, I'll help Aaron,' and then—" His eyes cloud. "We stayed. We watched as half the island got swallowed, didn't we? And us two, how come we survived? How come we were the only ones who got to live?"

I stare at the stone, at the names there.

They've been gone for two years.

When I started dreaming, they were already dead.

I was living their past, when in my time they'd already died.

When Amy said she'd die on the island and no one would care—she was already gone.

When McCormick said he'd be here, holding out his hand waiting for me—he'd already left.

When I said they weren't alive, that they didn't exist—I was half-wrong and half-right.

Two years ago a 7.8 earthquake hit off the coast of Brazil. I remember it because our leather supplier was badly affected. We sent aid: potable water, medical supplies, sat phones, and more.

Six months ago, Daniel and I sat in a meeting and I turned away from the reporter on the television screen recounting the effects of the earthquake. I didn't want to see someone else's suffering when I was already hurting so much. I didn't know I was turning away from Aaron. The reporter stood in front of what looked like a decimated fishing village. I wouldn't have recognized it. I hadn't yet dreamed it.

But now I know where she was.

Charlestown, at the very edge of the town. The photographs online showed only three buildings survived. None of them were occupied.

The rest?

They didn't crumble in the earthquake.

They didn't collapse.

There was no tsunami.

No.

Instead there was an aftershock.

It struck off the coast of the island.

And then the soft, sandy soil that composed half the island's geology—it fell into the sea.

It's happened in history. Entire islands swallowed by the ocean. It happened a few hundred years ago in the Caribbean. An entire city was consumed by the water in seconds.

An earthquake hits and then the vibration in the sand causes liquefaction.

And suddenly, something that was solid—sand—becomes liquid.

Or at least it acts like a liquid.

And so, on Christmas Eve two years ago, all the people on the island were buried in the sea. It happened in seconds. The ground was solid and then it wasn't, and the homes, the boats, the people, they fell into the deep, deep sea.

Robert once said other people die, but not McCormick.

He was wrong. Not even Aaron could survive this.

And he couldn't save anyone else either.

"Why did I come here?" I ask, the sun beating down on me, the hollow note of the gulls' calls echoing in the wind.

"Don't know," Odie says. Then he clasps my arm, his callouses rough. "Don't stay out too long. The mosquitos are bad this year."

He turns to go, to walk back along the rough, newly carved shoreline, toward the last skeletal remnants of Charlestown.

"Odie?"

He pauses. When he looks back I begin to shake, my hands vibrating with all the waves of emotion I'm not letting out.

"Yeah?"

"Why would I love someone if all along they knew they were going to leave? Why would I love someone when it turns out they were already gone?"

He looks at me then, his eyes shaded, his figure weathered and worn by the wind and salt of the island. I don't know if he loved anyone. I don't know anything about him, except that he sat on the road with his stop sign and played solitaire in the shade of a tree. How stupid, to know so little about someone when they're the only person who has known who you loved, who maybe loved who you loved too.

"Why?" he asks.

He considers the cold granite, immovable, casting its shadow over me. He considers the wind bending the trees. He considers my hand, shaking against the stone.

"I suppose," he says, "you just couldn't help it. Mostly, we know loving means losing. But we still do it 'cause we just can't help it."

I take my hand from the granite, clenching my fingers in a tight ball. "I thought this time I couldn't lose. I thought I couldn't be left. But he was already gone before it even began."

He rubs a hand down his grizzled face. "You talking 'bout Robert?"

"No."

"McCormick then." He nods.

"I wonder if I can save him. If I can save them all."

Odie shakes his head. Then he points at the sun

sinking into the dark, depthless sea. "Don't stay out too long."

"I won't."

And then, as the sun sinks beneath the surface and the ocean and the dark swallow the world, I sit under the whistling pines, and I listen to the wind blowing through the branches, I breathe in the salt and the stars, and I feel the scratch of the sand over my legs, and I think about loving and leaving and losing and then loving again, because that's what we do.

I fall asleep, my cheek pressed into the cool sand, the ocean breeze stroking over me, the crash of the water a lullaby. In my dreams, inside this dream, I hear Aaron's voice—

If you ever need me, if you ever find yourself awake at night wanting me, I'll be here. I'll be here loving you.

"You said you'd let me go."

I lied. I'll be here, my hand held out to you. All you have to do is take it.

I hold out my hand.

He isn't there.

49

I wrench out of the dream and back into Geneva with jarring finality. For long minutes I pant in the middle of my bed, my head spinning, heart pounding. The dry, cold air of my bedroom and the icy draft from the frosted window tug at me and yank me back to the here and now.

I'm in Geneva.

It's winter.

I'm alone.

There's a hollow ache, a deep hole in my chest where memories echo. I press my hand to my warm flannel pajamas and settle my palm over my heart. I feel the steady rhythm, and for a moment I'm surprised my heart's still beating. But it is. I'm here, still living. Still breathing.

If someone were to ask me, "Fi, what's wrong?" what could I say? The man I'm desperately in love with is real and he died two years ago. His whole family and all the people I loved died with him. And I only just found out he existed at all. I only just found out they're gone.

I had four more months with him and I willingly turned away and set him aside. I foolishly thought I had all the time in the world. That if I wanted, I could someday pick up the watch and dream of him again, just for a night or an hour. I thought he would be there forever. An eternity in a single moment. Being an expert in time, I should've realized, the only thing in life we can be sure of is that time moves on, and if you don't reach out and hold onto what you love, then its time may have passed forever.

Aaron said the tears of regret are worse than the tears of sorrow. I regret leaving him. I regret not realizing he was real sooner. I regret not learning about Christmas Eve sooner.

I shiver at the icy temperature. At my regrets. Outside my window the sky is a brilliant, bright winter-blue—the cloudless kind only seen on days when the temperature is below freezing. It's the sort of winter day where the second you step into the ice-coated snow your nose pinches, your cheeks burn, and your fingers lose all feeling. It's exactly the type of day where Mila and I stay inside, cuddle under a soft wool blanket by the fire, and drink hot cocoa while watching a Christmas movie.

That's not what we'll be doing today.

It's the day before Christmas Eve.

There's the gala to prepare for.

And there's . . . my dreams.

I throw the duvet off my legs, ignore the memory of

lavender spritzed on the sheets, and instead jump down to the cold wood floor. I clutch the warm case of the pocket watch, not willing to let it go.

The second hand has stopped. All movement has stopped.

But does that mean the watch has stopped for good?

That everyone is truly gone?

This June, when I first dreamed of Aaron, it was June on the island. Two years ago exactly. We flowed parallel, our realities. My mountain-strawberry June for their ripe-mango June. My gentle, lake-breeze July for their humid, salt-scented July. My winery and last-days-of-summer August for their beach-bonfires-and-sunlit-coves August.

We ran parallel for months.

Last night it was December 23 on the island—of this year.

Somehow I hit the wrong time.

I need to go back two years.

When I dream tonight, I need to dream December 24, two years ago.

If Aaron is real, if all the people are real, if the island is real, then if I dream them, I can save them.

The only question is, am I dreaming reality, or am I dreaming a memory of reality? Is it a shadow, or is it the real thing?

I don't know.

I only know that tonight, when midnight passes and Christmas Eve arrives, I have the chance to go back two years, to hours before the disaster.

If only the watch will take me there.

Let me dream again.
I can save them.
At least I can try.

50

The day passes in a whirlwind of preparations and snowfall. While a hard, drumming insistence pumps through my veins—*dream, dream, dream of him*—the snow falls in great soft flakes, coating the world in swathes of sparkling, dreamy white.

Mila races from one end of the chateau to the other, running through the ballroom while Daniel supervises the setup.

This year, he asked Mila what she wanted to see at the gala. She told him glitter. And so the driveway is lined with hand-carved ice sculptures—snowflakes, reindeer, elves, and a sleigh—all set to glitter in candlelight and the headlights of chauffeured cars arriving in the dark.

The ballroom is looped and frosted and painted in golds and silvers and sparkling lights. Stepping into the room is like spinning into the shining heart of an ice cave, with the midnight sun sparkling in diamond rays across the glittering ice.

It's beautiful, and it makes my heart ache.

The chateau is filled with the Christmassy scent of freshly cut evergreens, warm gingerbread, and mulled cider spiced with cinnamon and cloves. The stone hallways echo with the bustle and busy of dozens of people hurrying about, creating a winter wonderland.

Every year it's the same, the ordinary transformed into the extraordinary within hours. It always holds a hint of magic, but this year I'm pulled too far away to notice. My heart isn't in Geneva, it's on a tiny island thousands of miles away.

Every few hours I slip away, wind the watch, close my eyes, and try to dream. But I'm wound too tight, my muscles and tendons so alert that I feel as if I'm stretched low at the racetrack waiting for the gunshot.

Daniel asks over a lunch of savory thyme-and-rosemary barley soup and fresh-baked bread, "All right, Fi?"

Mila glances at me, a slice of bread suspended halfway to her mouth as she waits for my answer. She doesn't know what's wrong, but she can sense the ache and the storm whirling inside me.

Earlier, on one of her racing sprints through the ballroom, a glitter ribbon trailing behind her, she'd stopped, flung her arms around me, and said, "Don't worry, Mummy. This Christmas Eve, Uncle Daniel hired security. He told me so. The lady can't get you."

I hugged her tight and told her, "I'm not worried. You don't need to be worried either."

Daniel's eyes cloud after he asks if I'm all right, maybe concerned I'm regretting this Christmas Eve Gala and remembering the gunshot.

That isn't what I'm worried about. The thought

hasn't crossed my mind. Instead I'm praying for the hours to pass so I can fall into bed, exhausted and ready to dream.

So I grip my hand under the table, nails digging into my palm, and promise him, "I will be. Tomorrow."

And now it's late. The chateau is sleepy and quiet. The cacophony of footsteps and laughter and all the noise of the Christmas setup has faded. The bustle is long gone, hidden like green grass under a heavy blanket of snow.

There's a muted hush, a quiet lull, settling over the night. The sky is velvety black and the moon watches the night with a soft, gentle glow. My bedroom is illuminated by the faintest silver light—it falls in soft threads across the gold satin of my duvet.

I lean back onto the soft folds of my mattress and the cool satin sheets whisper beneath me. My heart has taken on a throbbing, pulsing ache that ticks with the same rhythm of the pocket watch. There's a strange, muffled quality to my bedroom, so that the only noises I can hear are the ticking of the watch and the beating of my heart.

I hold the watch up to the light of the moon. The gold is cool in my hand, the round edges slowly warming in my palm. The enamel blue waves, painted on the face, glisten in the moonlight and then start to flow with a strange, rippling motion.

The gold second hand sweeps over the blue and the iridescent enamel swirls and spins. The cold prickle of the room tugs at my cheeks and an icy draft scrapes against my skin. I sink further under the weight of my duvet and breathe in the cold, lavender-tinged night air. Then, as I breathe out, my eyelids grow heavy. The watch grows warm in my palm, heavy too. I drop my hand to my bed and my eyelids flutter shut.

I fall then.

It isn't a tumbling spin.

It's not a jarring descent.

Instead I drift through a velvet darkness like a snowflake slowly feathering down to earth.

I land, set down gently in the world of my dream.

The island's heat and the vibrant sun don't welcome me.

Instead, when blink, I find myself standing in the snow. My cold white breath hangs in the air in front of me. My nose is numb. My cheeks are icy cold. My fingers and toes tingle from the snow and the ice. The air smells of freshly fallen snow, winter, and cold.

It's night. Black and dark.

I lift my chin, letting my eyes follow the trail of candles lining a winter snow-covered drive. And I find the chateau, my home, glistening, lit like an angel on the top of a Christmas tree.

51

It's terribly easy to enter a house uninvited. Especially when that house is your own.

I slip in the door near the kitchen, hidden by crates of wine and stacked boxes full of ornaments and unused garlands. The smells of mulled wine, melted chocolate, savory tarts, and Christmas spiced treats hits me with the strength of a crackling-hot kitchen. I avoid the hustle of the kitchen. There are banging pots, shouts, and hurried orders coming from that direction. Instead I slip down a side hall, hugging corners and shadows.

I walk quickly, with purpose, just in case someone sees me and asks why I'm here. My nose and cheeks are starting to thaw and there's a painful tingling in my fingers as blood rushes in at the newfound warmth.

Down the hallway, reverberating through the stone walls and muffled by the thick old rugs, is the sound of an orchestra. They're playing a Christmas waltz. I remember the song. I danced it with Max.

It's Christmas Eve.

Mila is tucked in bed upstairs, dreaming Christmas dreams.

Daniel is—

I duck around the corner, my heart racing.

Daniel is kissing a blonde in the study. I remember him leading her out of the ballroom, his hand at the crook of her back.

I lean against the stone wall and take a deep breath, willing my heart to slow.

I hear the woman's laughter, Daniel's murmured response.

The golden light from the wall sconce spills over the stone floor and hits the shadows at my feet. I clutch my hands. They're still icy cold and prickling from the rush of warm air.

The waltz is picking up speed. Right about now, Max is telling me he wants more. He's telling me he loves me.

There's a weight in the pocket of my parka. It hits against my leg when I walk. Right now, it's pressing into my thigh. I know what it is. I know without having to be told.

But all the same, I reach into the slick pocket of the long black parka and close my hand around the cold metal of the gun.

My breath is short, my lungs painfully tight.

When my fingers slide over the gun I shiver from the cold.

How did Becca know me? Did she dream when I dreamed? Or is it that Dee or Essie or Maranda told her who I claimed to be that first day I was there? Fiona Abry, British and Swiss citizen. It wouldn't have been hard for her to find me. Or perhaps Aaron asked her about Fi; Robert asked her about her inconsistent behavior; someone told her about me saying my real name, acting strange.

I don't know. I can't say.

I only know that she's here, on the first anniversary of Aaron's death, with a gun.

There's a woman's tinkling laugh from the study, the soft murmur of Daniel's voice.

I push away from the wall and hurry down the hallway. As I move down the shadowed hall, I push my blonde hair back and bring up the fur-lined black hood, pulling it tight around my face. I hide my features, burying myself in anonymity.

I remember the bulky black of the coat, the way the shadows of the hood hid the woman's face. No one knew who she was. No one could make out her features.

I turn right, away from the sitting room, down another stone hallway, toward the ballroom. My heart beats faster and a cold prickle travels down my spine.

As I near the ballroom the music grows louder and I can make out the individual instruments. The arpeggio of the violin, the sweeping crest of the cello, the slow, mournful sigh of the bass. The clatter of champagne glasses, china clinking, and the high laughter of a hundred guests urges me toward the ballroom.

The noise surrounds me and I take on a floating feeling, as if I'm tied to a string and I'm being pulled forward, whether I want to go or not.

At the entry to the chateau there's a gathering of

guests donning furs and wool coats. The clock over the old walnut entry table reads 11:47 p.m.

"Madame?" someone calls.

I ignore them and turn toward the ballroom.

I step into the bright lights. The music swirls around me. It's beautiful. It truly is.

The Christmas trees line the room, decorated for all the countries where our watches are sold. The scents of fir and cinnamon and allspice swirl through the air. The life-size gingerbread house is coated in glistening frosting. It's whimsical and sweet, and the giant Abry timepiece, the spun sugar Chronomachen, is ticking down the seconds until Christmas day.

There are dozens of guests still dancing. The colors are bright. The mood is high. There's Mellisande and Arne. Phillipe too. Vincent. Jean. There's a tuxedo-clad waiter carrying a silver tray of champagne flutes.

From the ceiling hundreds of hanging snowflakes twirl and swirl, glittering overhead.

I step further into the ballroom, weaving through the crowd. I'm a black shadow moving through the red and green, gold and silver.

My mouth is dry, my heart pounding in an irregular rhythm as a cold sweat drips down the back of my neck.

I stop.

Across the ballroom the spun sugar Chronomachen reads 11:48 p.m.

The minute I was shot.

And there I am.

It's strange to look across a crowded ballroom at myself. I look different than I imagined. I'm taller, fairer, my hair more fiery auburn than I knew. My deep red dress flairs around me as Max spins me in the waltz. The me from a year ago tilts her head, an urgent line between her brows. Telling Max, "I love you, I always have—"

But not in the way he wants.

He turns me then, blocking my face from view. He dips his head toward me, the line of his back tight as he asks, "Can you know for certain that I can't make you happy?"

I take a slow step forward, dodging a waiter, a dancing couple.

It's strange to find myself here. This is the day it all began. I just didn't realize it until now.

I was shot and then...

Then my mum had the strongest premonition, an irresistible urge, to visit my Uncle Leopold.

Then my Uncle Leopold dangled the watch in front of my mum, making certain she took it.

And then my mum gave me the watch.

And I dreamed.

If I walk away now, if I turn around and stride out the door of the chateau into the cold, bitter night, I'll never be shot. My mum won't visit Uncle Leopold. She won't steal the watch. And I won't dream. I'll never meet Aaron, and I'll never have the chance to go back and save him.

My chance to save the island hangs in this moment.

All I have to do is aim the gun across a crowded ballroom and pull the trigger.

It won't be hard. My Dad used to take me to shoot clay pigeons. I can aim. I can shoot.

Besides, I'm still not certain if this dream is a shadow of reality or reality itself.

Maybe if I shoot I'm merely replaying something that already happened.

But then again, maybe not.

I can't know.

I can only know that if I don't shoot, I might never meet Aaron.

So.

With my limbs heavy, heart pounding, and the blood in my veins throbbing with an urgent rhythm, I pull the gun from the pocket of the parka.

A woman screams. High-pitched and terrified.

The waiter drops the silver tray and all the champagne flutes slide through the air. The golden liquid sprays free, and then the flutes hit the floor and explode in a glass shower.

The orchestra fumbles, cellos slide to silence, and violins screech to a halt. A cymbal ricochets and quiets.

Across the room Max turns toward me. Sees the gun. He clutches the other me, trying to push her behind his back, shield me from myself.

I blink as Mellisande and Arne dive to the side.

My skin runs cold as Phillipe stumbles and slams to the floor.

I falter and feel a thick, halting heartbeat knock against my ribs as Jean's glass of champagne slips from his fingers and shatters.

I stand there in front of myself. My dress is vibrant and blood-red.

My hand shakes and then steadies.

I've always wondered why I was shot.

I've always wondered why the woman seemed to know me.

Why she seemed to want me to understand.

Now I know.

The nightmares that haunted me for months? It was me, warning myself.

There's a sharp screaming, and then I say urgently, desperately, trying to make myself understand, "It's Christmas Eve. Remember, it's Christmas Eve."

Perhaps this time I'll understand. In the months I'm with Aaron, on the island, I'll remember this moment and I'll look up the news. I'll look up Aaron, I'll realize he's real, and I'll tell them what happens on Christmas Eve.

"Tell them it's Christmas Eve," I beg myself.

And then I aim.

And I pull the trigger of the gun.

∼

I sprint through the maze of hallways in the chateau. My breath comes in frantic, panicked bursts. Screams and shouts chase me and a sharp, black panic tugs at the edges of my vision.

My footsteps echo over the stone as I run down a dark back hall. The battery acid of fear coats my mouth and the gun bangs against my thigh with every jarring step.

The darkness of the hall tightens around me as I run deeper into the old stone hall. It leads to the cellars, down, down, deep into the centuries-old storage rooms. I hit the thick wooden door at the end of the hall, not bothering with a light. Instead I grasp the iron handle and yank the door open.

The musty wooden cask and dusty air whooshes

out with a heaving sigh. I dive into the dark, tugging the door shut behind me. When it closes, all the sounds of the gala, the shouts and the cries, are cut off like the quick slice of a knife.

I grasp the old wooden rail and sprint down the uneven stone steps. They were carved hundreds of years ago and are weathered and worn. I could run down these steps blindfolded I've walked them so often, from age six to now. And so I keep the lights off and descend into the dark.

I don't want anyone to see the glow of a light from under the cellar door. I don't want anyone to come looking for me.

I sprinted from the ballroom. And in the shock no one stopped me.

I didn't wait to see Max dive over the me of last year. I didn't wait to make sure he pressed his hands to my bleeding abdomen. I didn't wait to hear him tell me not to be afraid. I know he did. I know he kept me safe until Dr. Gaertner pushed him aside and the ambulance arrived.

I had to run. I had to get away.

I have something I have to do.

I wind through the labyrinth of the cellar until I've made it to the center of the caverns underneath the chateau. There, with my heart pounding and the musty, stagnant air heavy and watchful, I pull the chain overhead and turn on the light.

I blink at the buzzing, electric glow and wait for the blue-white sparks to settle. I'm in the storage room where my Dad kept his favorite wines. It's cold, the walls are carved from the gray stone under the chateau, and the room stays a chilly autumn temperature year-round. There's water leaking from the stone, bleeding to the floor in a slow *drip, drip, drip.*

The walls are lined with dark wooden wine crates, stacked six feet high. There are hundreds of bottles. They're covered in cobwebs and dust, and through the dust the bottles sparkle a dull summer-green in the harsh light. The dust tickles my nose and I sniff at the damp, musty scent. There's a trace of vinegary wine from a bottle that's turned.

I sneeze and then flinch at the scattering of claws on the floor and a quick squeak.

Rats then.

I wait for a moment, but the cellar is quiet and still. There's no noise leaking in from upstairs. No one is at the door.

Still, I have to hurry.

I stride to the center of the room, where a large wooden wine barrel is turned upright. There's a rusty corkscrew there, a dusty wineglass my dad would use to taste the bottles he opened. He'd come down here when he wanted a break from the world. Next to the glass is a small notebook and a three-inch-long pencil. Its lead is dull, the eraser gone. In the notebook is my dad's neat, precise handwriting. He left notes on all his bottles—the chateau, the year, his impressions.

My heart gives a sharp pang, and then I tear an empty page from the back of the notebook. And I quickly scrawl a note to myself.

I grip the short pencil in my hand and write:

It's real. You can change what happens. Save them.

Then I fold the note, take the gun, and thrust them

both into the lowest wine crate, behind a bottle of my dad's favorite wine.

If it's there when I wake, then I'll know I was really here.

I plunge the cellar into darkness and—

Wake up.

52

I open my eyes to the blackness of my bedroom. I gasp and clutch at my pajamas. Then I press my hand to my abdomen. The star-shaped scar, flat and ridged, is still there. It pulses beneath my hand.

The watch lies on the bed next to me, the time stopped. It's midnight. Christmas Eve.

I still have time.

I can dream again.

I can try again.

But first—

I grab the watch, fling the duvet back, and then sprint across the cold floor.

I fly down the darkened hallway, down the stairs, down the shadowed back hallway, until I'm at the wooden cellar door.

I yank it open and the same musty, stagnant cellar scent heaves over me. I flick on the lights and the buzzing yellow glow illuminates the winding stone steps and the narrow stone walls that lead down.

The wet chill of the old stone cellar coats me as I run down the uneven steps.

I grasp the cold wooden handrail and then run across the stones. The cold seeps into my bare feet.

My hurried steps echo across the stone and I hear the responding echo of scurried claws rushing to dive into a shadowed corner.

There's the dripping of leaking water, the mineral, dusty scent, the muffled quiet of an underground cavern cellar disturbed by my flight.

The chill sinks into my bones as I sprint through the cellar. Dust kicks up after me.

Until I'm there.

I tug the old chain and the blue-white light buzzes. It washes the storage room in harsh light. I set the gold pocket watch on top of the upright wine barrel.

And then I drop to my knees. I hit the stone with a hard crack and thrust aside the dusty wine bottle. The cobwebs stick to my hand as I reach into the crate.

I hit the wooden sides, brush aside sticky webs and dust, and then my hand hits a damp, cold, folded piece of paper. The cold metal of a gun.

My heart leaps, clattering into my throat.

I tug them out.

The cold of the hard stone digs into my knees, and I shiver at the chill abrading my skin.

My hand shakes as I wipe the cobwebs from the black handgun. I set it aside, dropping it to the stone floor.

The buzzing of the overhead light is loud, and the musty, vinegary scent of the cellar chokes and taunts.

The paper is wet from the damp air. I unfold the note, careful not to tear the paper.

My stomach clenches. My breath catches in my throat.

The words on the paper are stark. Real. Written one year ago.

By me.

It's real. What I dream is *real*. I can change what happens.

I focus on the last words I wrote.

I grip the note in my hand.

Save them.

Save them.

I jump up, grab the pocket watch, and sprint back to my room.

To dream.

One more time.

53

I clutch the wrinkled, damp note in one hand. My words are scrawled in faded pencil and the sheet of paper scratches the palm of my hand. I clasp the gold pocket watch in my other hand. Its rounded edges press into my cool skin and the ticking of the watch reverberates through me.

It's 12:30 a.m. Christmas Eve.

The day is just beginning.

Two years ago Aaron died, and everyone he loved died with him.

Except Becca. Except me.

I don't know why I dreamed the current year or why I was sent to last year. I only pray that this time I'm sent back two years. To the Christmas Eve when everyone was lost.

I've studied the photographs, the maps, and the news reports. I know exactly where the island fell into the sea. I know which beaches were gobbled, which forests were consumed, which buildings were spared. I know the exact jigsaw of where the island fell apart and dropped into the sea. And I know the exact time it happened.

11:48 a.m.

There were so many clues. If only I'd looked for them.

But I'm here, my eyes closed, the dark blanketing me. The weight of the watch heavy in my hand. The weight of the words in the note just as heavy.

I take a deep breath, full of the cold winter air and the stillness of the night, and I let the ticking of the watch rock me asleep.

As I fall, winding down with the slow heartbeat of the watch, I feel the slow ebb and flow of a gentle tide.

I think of Aaron. Of his arms around me. Of his hands sliding over my salty, sand-covered skin. I think of him whispering my name, "Fi." And then the light in his eyes, right before he kissed me.

For years I believed I didn't want my dreams to come true.

But that was before I had dreams that were worth fighting for.

It was before Christmas Eve, before the gunshot, before Max proposed, before Buttercup gave me the watch, and before I dreamed.

Now, as the watch echoes the beat of my heart, I have one single prayer.

One prayer that crashes against the shore of my heart, beating out a single desperate plea.

Dream.

Dream.

Dream.

Let me dream of him.

One more time.

I wake up to heat, to humidity, to the rumble of an earthquake.

54

I trip and slam to my knees. The ground bucks beneath me. I grasp at the sharp blades of grass and the hot sand as the earth shakes and rolls.

The whistling pines shudder and sway, and their needles hiss in the jittering. My knees sink further into the burning sand and I grip the rumbling soil. The heat presses down, stinging my back, and I take in a gulping breath of the humid, pine-thick air.

I'm here.

I'm *here*.

The day is blue-sky bright and the white-hot sun is at its peak. Long stripes of shade fall across me and dance with the shaking of the earth. A flock of blackbirds launches from the pine boughs and flaps wildly into the sky. They caw in outrage at the shaking, rumbling ground.

My stomach slides as I try to catch myself. I clasp a root sticking out of the sand and a dark red beetle skitters across my hand. I'm dizzy and disoriented, and I clasp the pine root as the world shakes.

I've never been in an earthquake. The earth tosses beneath you, rumbling and rolling like a sailboat on a rocky sea. It's as if some monster has awakened far beneath the earth's surface and it's stretching and rolling, and the world above is its casualty.

The heat pricks at me. I'm sweating and flushed. My stomach rolls and slides again. And then the world shudders to stillness.

There's a quiet, stunned, breath-held silence.

I stare at the ground, watching it to make certain it isn't about to rise up and shake again.

But no.

It doesn't.

It won't.

This is the first earthquake. The aftershock? When Charlestown falls into the sea?

That's coming in exactly forty-two minutes.

I'm on the hill far above town. Right now, according to Odie, Aaron is sprinting back toward the cottages.

"Becca?" Robert grabs my arm, pulls me up, and clasps me in a tight hug. "Are you all right?"

He pushes back, rapidly scanning me. My knees are scraped and covered in sand. I'm dizzy and flushed.

"Was that an earthquake?" Robert asks, looking back toward town.

His face is pale. His copper hair stands straight in the wind. He looks the same as ever. Linen pants, blue button-down shirt, lean and handsome, and . . . in less than an hour he'll be dead.

Unless.

"Listen to me." I step forward, grabbing his shirt,

"Listen. It was an earthquake. An aftershock is coming. Everyone in Charlestown will die. Half the island is going to slide into the sea. We have to run. We have to get everyone to the hill."

"What?" His head jerks back and he shakes away from me. "What are you talking about?"

"Robert. We have to run. Now!"

And then I sprint from the glade at the top of the hill where Aaron and I picnicked in the shade.

I don't wait to see if Robert will follow. In seconds he's running next to me. I kick off my flip-flops and sprint down the sand-and-gravel road. The rocks stab my feet and the heat scorches my skin. It doesn't matter. I'm dragging in lungfuls of humid air and my heart bangs in my chest as I fly down the hill back toward Charlestown.

"Becca, what are you talking about—?" Robert heaves, sprinting next to me. "The island—"

I shake my head, gasping, "Promise. Promise you'll get everyone back to the hill. Everyone in town. Promise."

I glance at him. He gives a sharp nod, his jaw tight.

Then in the distance there's Odie, jogging up the base of the hill. His figure is gangly and tall, a dark silhouette in the noonday sun.

"Becca," he shouts as we sprint downhill. "McCormick told me to check on you. He's helping at the shore. Essie's roof caved in."

Robert grips my arm as we're running. He slows, pulling me to a stop next to Odie. My lungs burn and I drag in hot-air breaths as the sun beats down.

Robert glances at me, taking in my sweat-soaked sundress, and the sweat dripping down my forehead.

My eyes sting from the sweat and the sun and my chest burns. My legs ache and my feet are pulsing with pain. They're scratched and bloody.

It doesn't matter.

"You stay here," Robert says worriedly. "Stay with Odie. I'll help Aaron."

"No," I say, yanking my hand free. "No one stays. Go to town. Get everyone on the hill. We have less than thirty minutes. Odie, get everyone on the hill. The island is going to cave into the sea. Go. Now."

I wait, and when they only stare at me, I shout, "Go!"

Odie must see something in my eyes. Or maybe he sees a memory of a future where it's only the two of us standing on this island and he's wishing he hadn't climbed that hill with me. Because when I shout, "Go!" he turns around and runs back toward town.

"Go," I tell Robert, and he takes one look at me and then nods.

"Where will you be?" he asks, gripping my hand.

"I have to save Aaron. Amy and Sean. The rest of them."

He nods, squeezing my hand. "Becca. If you can't save them, save yourself."

I shake my head. Then I tug my hand free and sprint toward the beach.

∼

I fly. I've never run so fast in my life.

I don't know if it's adrenaline or it's something that can only happen in a dream, but after I leave Robert I stop feeling the pain in my legs and burning in my lungs. I feel as if I've left my body, and instead of running, I'm flying toward the beach.

I cut across the sun-bleached grassy hill, tear down the sandy path, and sprint past the low-lying mangroves. They'll be gone soon. A flurry of white egrets flies above, their wings stark against the pale blue sky.

Over the pounding of my pulse I hear the crash and roar of the sea. The humid, loamy, tropical-perfumed air I've been gasping in lungfuls switches to a clean, salty breeze. Then I crest the final sun-splashed rise, and there's the indigo-blue sea.

And the row of cheerful cottages.

They're the same. Little wooden houses in shades of coral, sea-foam blue, goldenrod, and salmon-pink, all of them perched under the shade of palm trees blowing in the wind.

And every one of them is about to be lost.

There's Essie's. Half the roof has collapsed. My heart stutters at the sight.

She's outside, storming around in front of the porch, the chickens flapping about around her. Maranda and Dee are there as well.

Amy's on the front porch of our cottage. Sean's in her arms.

"Mom!" she shouts.

And I almost stumble from the leap in my heart at that one word. I sprint to her, drag in a great lungful of hot air, and say, "Another earthquake is coming. This half of the island is going to fall into the sea. Tell everyone. Knock on all the cottages. And then meet me here. We have to get to the hill. Do you understand? We have twenty minutes."

"Mom. What?" She stares at me, her expression thunderstruck. I have a memory—one where she shouted, "Dad, Mom's acting crazy!"

"Amy! Please!"

Her mouth trembles. She turns her face away, toward the ruin of Essie's cottage. "You're talking to me now? What, one earthquake and suddenly you care again?" She looks back at me, and in her arms Sean reaches out his chubby arms and says, "Mama."

"You don't even like me," Amy says. "Why would you care if we all fell into the sea?"

There's nothing I can say. Nothing I can do to convince her I care, that I do love her, truly, as much as I've loved anyone. I can't fix the heartbreak of a mom discarding her daughter. I don't know if I can make her trust me, but I have to get her to act. To run.

"I love you," I say.

She shakes her head, looking away.

"'To love someone means to see them as God intended them,'" I tell her.

"Don't quote Dostoevsky to me."

I will. I'll quote him to her for the rest of her life. But first she has to live.

"I see you and I love you. Now, listen to me. This island is going to fall. Everyone will die. Run. Knock on the doors. Tell everyone to run to the hill. Meet me back here in five minutes. Okay?"

Sean reaches for me again, a whimpered, "Mama."

I step forward then, into the shade of the porch, up the wooden steps, and press a quick kiss to his pink, flushed cheek. Then I grasp Amy and say, "'Don't fail me.'"

"Another Dostoevsky! Fine."

Then she pushes away and runs down the wooden steps, into the sandy, prickly grass lawn. Sean's in her arms, and she hurries under the shade of the clock tree.

If I could read it I'd know the petals are turning, bleeding to burgundy, counting down the seconds.

Then I look back toward Essie's cottage.

I suck in a sharp breath.

Aaron strides toward me. His gaze is focused and intent. His features are firm, his expression hard. Amy runs past him, toward Essie and Maranda and Dee.

He keeps his gaze on me. My heart clatters in my chest as I take him in.

He's alive. He's here. For this moment he's still here.

His black hair blows in the wind. His eyes are dark, his expression searching. His tattoos wind over his arms. He's solid and strong. As he strides toward me he notes the blood, the sand, the cuts, and he when he looks into my eyes he starts to run.

I let out a sound, half-sob, half-need, and run down the steps and fly across the grass. I hit him under the shade of the clock tree. The burgundy flowers are open above us, sending down a spicy perfume. I leap at him and cling to him. I clasp him.

The breath whooshes from his lungs and he catches me, holding me to him.

"Becca?"

His voice. It rolls over me and I shake my head. "No, it's me."

He stiffens then. His breath catches and he looks down into my eyes. I grasp the cotton of his T-shirt, wrapping my legs around his middle.

"Fi?"

I nod, and then he takes my face and kisses me.

The kiss is the turbulent storming of a raging ocean. In his kiss I taste four months of want and need and pent-up longing. For me it's the salty tears of the ocean, the knowledge he's gone, and the prayer that I can save him.

He kisses me as if he'll never let me go.

But he will. I won't ever meet him in real life, as me, unless I save him.

"You came back," he breathes, kissing the edges of my lips, feathering his hands over my face.

Then I shake my head. "No. Aaron."

He pauses, looking into my eyes.

"I'm not Becca."

He doesn't understand.

"I'm Fi," I say. "That's my name. I dream that I'm here, and in my dreams I come to you. But I live in Geneva, two years in the future."

"What?" He pulls back from me, scanning my face.

I tense in his arms, and my pulse pounds, *Hurry, hurry, hurry.*

"Another earthquake is coming. An aftershock." I glance at the clock tree. "In twenty minutes. This half of the island is swallowed by the sea. In my time you're dead. You, Amy, Sean. Everyone—"

"What are you talking about—?"

"I came back. I'm here to save you. Please. You trust me?"

His arms circle my hips, holding me against him. I feel the strong beat of his heart. He weighs my expression, his eyes searching. He's teetering between belief and disbelief while the island waits on the edge of disaster.

I reach up, pressing my hand to the heat of his cheek.

Hurry.

"Please. I promised to come into the water after you, and you promised to keep holding out your hand. Please."

"What you're saying ... it doesn't ... ."

My heart beats, a desperate ticking, counting down until the island is swallowed.

"If we go to the hill and nothing happens, then fine, we wasted an hour. If we go to the hill and there's another earthquake, then you live. You live and you can come find me, in Geneva, in the future, where I'm loving you."

The waves crash against the shore, the chickens crow, and down the beach I hear Amy pounding on a cottage door. The thick heat of the island pulses between us.

"Please," I whisper.

And then Aaron nods. "Okay. Yes."

He sets me down, and then we run.

∼

With three minutes to spare, the last of us climb the slope of the whistling pine hill. The shade falls over us and everyone watches and waits. Some are unsure. Some look toward the sea. Everyone is talking about what they were doing when the earthquake struck.

We stand in the flickering shade of the tall pines. The sappy evergreen scent is strong in the noon heat. I hold Aaron's hand. Sean's in my arms.

Aaron runs his thumb over the back of my hand,

and every few seconds he looks down, just to make sure I'm still me.

Robert is with Junie and Jordi, their baby girl between them. Robert has a cooler full of bottled water he's set to hand out to the older people who are exhausted from the run.

I scan the crowd, count the people, *sixty-one, sixty-two, sixty-three, sixty-four.*

I stop.

Sixty-four, including me.

But there are sixty-five people on the island. One more with Junie's baby.

Then my heart slams against my chest. "Amy!"

She's not here.

I glance around the hill, checking every face, every figure. "Amy's not here."

Aaron drops my hand. "She was. She helped Robert with the water."

We run to him, and the heat and the weight of time presses down on me. "Where's Amy?"

Robert shakes his head, running his hand through his sweat-soaked hair. "She said she had to find Dost something, Dost—"

"She went back for a book. She went back to the cottage." My stomach plummets and I turn, scanning the grass at the bottom of the hill and the long, empty sandy path.

Sean grips my neck, his wet cheek pressed against my shoulder. He cried nearly the entire run up the hill. "Mimi," he says, sniffing into my shoulder.

Mimi is his name for his sister. It's what he calls her when he wants a cuddle or to be picked up.

"When did she leave?" Aaron asks. The lines of his

shoulders tense and his entire body vibrates with a suppressed tension. He scans the empty horizon.

"Five minutes ago," Robert says, his mouth drawn, eyes worried. "I didn't know she was leaving. I didn't think—"

"I'm going after her," Aaron says.

Robert grabs Aaron's forearm. "If Becca's right and you go back for her, you die."

"Then I die," Aaron says. He shrugs out of Robert's grasp.

Then Aaron turns to me. He doesn't say anything, he just looks in my eyes.

And for a single moment, a second that lasts an eternity, he tells me everything in a glance.

I love you.

I wanted more time with you.

I would've found you in Geneva.

I'm sorry.

And then he sprints down the hill.

∼

I wait at the line of demarcation, where I know the rocks will fall, the sand will cave, and the island will end.

For one second, two, time slips like water down a drain.

The seconds tick past slowly, a stuttering heartbeat.

Robert stands next to me, not speaking, just watching the green fade into the blue of the sky. Waiting for Aaron to reappear.

The islanders stand behind us, casting worried glances toward the sea.

The heat presses on me, relentless and absolute. I squint into the light, my lungs aching, my heart breaking. This will be the last time I dream, I know.

I have a feeling that once this day is done the watch will stop ticking for me. Just like it stopped for Leopold. He failed his love. I pray I haven't failed mine.

"It'll be all right," Robert says, his voice gravelly and tight. "Like I said, other people may die, but not the great Aaron McCormick."

"He can die though," I say. "He can. But he wouldn't be able to live with himself if he didn't go after Amy. He couldn't live with himself if he didn't try."

"I know," Robert says bitterly.

"Would you?"

"Go after her? No. Live? Yes."

I nod, clutching Sean tighter to my chest. A drop of sweat travels down my spine. The loamy tropical scents press down on me. The sun reaches its zenith.

I look down at Robert's watch.

11:47 a.m.

There's a rumble. A scraping.

A jarring tremble shudders through the island.

It's here.

My stomach drops and my skin runs cold. I lift my chin, clutch Sean to my chest, and keep my eyes on the horizon.

I'll keep watching. I keep watching until there's nothing more to see.

The ground shakes and someone behind us screams. It's a short shriek, quickly cut off.

My arms shake as Sean twists in my arms, whimpering at the rumbling and shaking of the ground.

"You were right," Robert says in disbelief. He glances at me, but I keep my eyes on the rise. "He's gone then. They won't make it."

The jarring rumble grows, and Robert grabs my arm, holding me steady.

It's 11:48 a.m.

And the world is about to fall.

He's not there.

He didn't make it.

That granite monument will still have two names etched in stone.

I lift my chin, reaching out to him with everything in me. "Please," I whisper. "Hurry. Please."

And then they're there. They peak over the rise.

Aaron sprinting. Amy next to him.

The ground shakes again, a jarring roll, and they both stumble.

They're fifty feet away. Another shudder jolts the island.

Forty feet. Another rolling jerk.

Thirty feet. Amy trips, slamming to her knees.

Aaron catches her arm and yanks her to her feet. Another crack, and then a giant, crashing roar sounds.

Twenty feet.

Sean lets out a piercing wail.

The ground shakes, shifts, spills sideways.

Ten feet.

Aaron clasps Amy's hand. Sprints for the safety of the hill.

Then the ground disappears. The sand, the soil—all of it collapses in onto itself. The sea floods over the earth. It consumes. It devours. Where there were mangroves, palm trees, grass, and sand, there's only the roar and rushing of water.

Aaron's eyes widen.

Amy cries out.

Five feet away.

Three.

Aaron shoves Amy forward just as the ground sinks beneath them.

Amy rolls to the ground, hitting solid rock. The water reaches up and grasps Aaron. He catches my eye, holding my gaze for one split second.

He's going down. There's no way he'll survive the flood coming, or the suction of an entire island collapsing. And so I do what I promised.

I thrust Sean into Amy's arms and then I leap toward the water. Aaron reaches out to me, the maelstrom pulling at him. I clasp his hand. It's slick with water. The sea pulls him under. I fall to the ground, slam against rock, and hold onto his hand. I grasp his wrist. He comes up again, choking on air.

The water is too strong.

It yanks him under and I'm dragged across the gravel. The ground cuts into me as I'm catapulted toward the churning water.

I can't hold on. Aaron's hand is slick. My grip is failing.

Another rumble, a giant tremor hits, and then the water reaches up and grabs me.

The water is cold and deathlike. It grips me, and I cling to Aaron as the waves threaten to bury me.

And then, just as Aaron and I are about to be consumed, lost in the turbulent sea, Robert grabs my ankle and yanks me back to dry ground. The gravel batters me as I cough and suck in great breaths of air.

Robert grips my leg, yanks, and shouts, "Pull, dammit!"

I cling to Aaron's wrist. I hang on with everything I have.

"Pull!"

I hold onto Aaron. Robert holds me. And behind Robert, Amy holds him. And little by little, we pull free of the grip of the sea.

I collapse to the rocky ground.

Aaron falls free of the sea. He crashes to the solid ground next to me. He coughs up seawater and yanks in gasping breaths. He's soaked, his eyes clouded.

I crawl to him, my wet skin scraping over the gravel and sandy soil. There's roaring and heat and the pressure of sixty-three people shouting at once.

Aaron rolls onto his back and stares up at the blue sky. The earth has settled; the shaking has stopped. His shirt is drenched and I can see the tattoos of the sea through the white fabric. His clothes soak the earth around him.

When I reach him I brace my hands on his chest. The warmth of him scalds me through the cold wet of his T-shirt.

He looks up at me, his eyes brown and warm. He focuses on me, a small smile playing at the corner of his mouth.

He's alive.

He's *alive*.

"Fi?"

I smile down at him, my heart squeezing out a warm, slow rhythm.

"I love you," I whisper, my throat raw and aching.

His eyes crinkle at the edges, his smile widening. "Amy?"

"She's okay."

He reaches up, touching a hand to my cheek. And then he gives me a new smile. One I haven't catalogued because I've never seen it before. It makes my heart sing.

"You came after me," he says.

"I told you I would."

He brushes his fingers over my skin. Touches my lips, a gentle kiss. Overhead the sun blazes bright. Beyond us the island is broken, ravaged, and gone.

But the people—they're still here.

He's still here.

"You're leaving again?" he asks, watching my expression.

I shake my head, my chest aching, "Come to me. Find me in Geneva. Come on Christmas Eve two years from now. I'll be waiting for you. My name is Fi—"

"Fi?" he says, his hands reaching for me.

But then there's another rumble. A tremor that rips through me. Spins and tosses and tears me apart. It tears me out of Aaron's arms.

And I'm tumbling through the dark. I'm falling out of my dream.

And as I fall, I feel myself unraveling.

I feel my memories unraveling.

I know this feeling.

It's the feeling of waking up.

It's what happens every day when the sun shines over you and you open your eyes. You forget what you dreamed. You forget everything you experienced, everything you knew in the dream world.

Sometimes you'll remember a flash.

Sometimes you'll remember a feeling.

But mostly, you forget everything.

You forget your dreams.

You don't take them with you into real life.

In a split-second I understand. I saved them. My dreaming is done. The time on the watch has ended, and like any dream finished in the depths of sleep, I'll forget everything and everyone that I dreamed about.

If Uncle Leopold had succeeded he would've forgotten his Annalise. It was only because he failed and never finished dreaming that he kept his unfulfilled dreams.

So as I fall into the darkness of sleep, I send out a final desperate cry. "I love you. Find me!"

And then I fall.

And the flow and ebb of a sleep-filled tide washes over me, and it washes away my dreams. It washes away —I cling desperately—I hold onto fragments—a beach cottage—a turquoise cove—a mouth pressed to mine on a moonlit beach—I struggle—I fight—*remember*—a grove of whistling pines—a hand pressed to my cheek —*remember*—a song in the dark—an endless sea—*him* —*remember*—*him*—I love him—I love—I love?—I—

∽

I blink awake.

My head throbs and my mouth is sand-dry.

The winter light speckles across my face. The warm sheets rustle under me as I kick the duvet back, letting in a puff of cold morning air. I yawn, the winter light weak. Through the thick stone walls there's the sound of a gentle wind, and the high, cheerful singing of birds foraging for winter berries.

I stretch and let out a low moan, staring blearily at the wavy blue ripples of my bedroom window. The soft morning light shining through almost looks like waves in a gentle sea. I can almost feel the current of them flowing over my skin. I turn my head away, back into my pillow, and breathe in the soft floral scent.

Time to wake up.

My muscles are sore and my hand cramped. I must've tossed and turned all night long.

I unfold my stiff fingers and stare at the old pocket watch in my hand.

"What?"

It's the watch my mum gave me, Adolphus Abry's, the one that doesn't work. The gold is dull in the weak sunlight and the hands are still.

I shake my head. Drop the watch to the wood of the nightstand. It hits with a thunk and then clatters to stillness.

"Not sure why I slept with you," I tell the watch.

When I shift to the edge of my bed, something crinkles beneath me and scratches my leg. I reach under the sheets and pull out an old wrinkled piece of paper.

I can barely make out the faded writing. It's a short note, scratched out in pencil, almost illegible.

It's real? Save them?

What?

Was I sleep-walking last night?

I scrub my hand over my face and try to clear away the cobwebs in my mind.

I had a dream.

A strange dream tugs at the corner of my mind. I stare at the wavy ripples of my bedroom window. The sky is a dull blue-gray and clouds hang low in the sky. The cold, drafty air wraps around me. I shiver and rub my hands over my arms.

There's something—

Something I need to remember.

I watch the ripples of the old glass while the cold of the bedroom wraps around me. There's something about the waves that's tugging at me.

But then the door bangs open and jars me out of the swirling eddy. Mila charges into the bedroom, her nightgown flying around her, an exuberant light in her eyes.

"Mummy! It's Christmas Eve!" She jumps onto the bed and throws herself into my arms.

I laugh. "It is!"

She grins at me then scrambles upright and bounces up and down on the mattress. Her red hair flies in the air with each leap, and she sings, "It's Christmas Eve!"

"Happy Christmas Eve." I smile up at her and rub my chest. There's an ache there. A heavy, hollow ache.

I don't know.

I don't understand why I'm so glad it's Christmas Eve, but also so desperately sad.

I don't know why it feels like I've lost something infinitely dear. I don't know why it feels like I've lost a love I've never had.

55

I spin around the ballroom. The world is a glittering wonderland, and as I whirl in the warmth of Max's arms the gold and silver sparkles and shines. I'm dizzy with the glitter of snowflakes and ice crystals and diamonds lighting silver Christmas trees.

Max holds me close, his hand settled in the curve of my spine. The pressure, the heat of his hand through the silky waterfall of my gold dress, keeps me anchored in the moment.

I lean my head against his shoulder and breathe him in. The warm leather and spiced shaving soap, the sophistication and humor. He's in a tuxedo, and the black brings out the dark loneliness that still lurks in him. I can see it there. He's like his family's estate—a giant, cavernous home, stately and magnificent, but empty. It echoes with the footsteps of ghosts and the breeze of forgotten laughter.

Someday someone will step inside, throw on the

lights, and burn away all the dust and all the ghosts. They'll fill his home and his life with love.

But that person, it's not me.

I press my hands into the warmth of his wool tuxedo and close my eyes as we slow to a quiet, rocking dance. We're near the ice sculpture garden at the edge of the ballroom. There are snowflakes, Christmas trees, presents, and ice trains. And there's a giant, twelve-foot-circumference pocket watch carved from ice. The glitter-coated silver hands tick the minutes away. It's nearly midnight.

"Happy Christmas Eve," Max says, his cheek brushing the top of my head. His chest rumbles as he speaks, and I press my face to his shoulder, closing my eyes against the brightness of the ballroom.

"Happy Christmas Eve," I whisper, my throat thick with emotion.

Around us the ballroom glistens with lights and sounds. Everyone kept to the theme and wore black tuxedoes or ballgowns of silver and gold and white. Sequins and diamanté and diamonds abound. The lights catch the sparkles and shoot prisms around the room.

The world is alight with glitter and gold.

The orchestra plays a sweet, lilting song—one that reminds me of sitting at a frost-covered window watching the snow fall over a great, lonely field, where there are no birds, no people, no trees, nothing but snow, covering the memories of summer.

"I was wondering," Max begins, tilting his head and speaking in a low, quiet voice, "if you had an answer." He looks around the ballroom, at the dreamland around us. The sparkling scent of champagne and white-chocolate-dipped gingerbread swirls past.

I look up at him then. At the depths of his brown eyes, at the hawkish line of his jaw, and the softness of his mouth as he stares down at me. His hand rubs a slow circle over the curve of my back.

He holds me close.

And it's strange, because even though he's holding me, I feel alone.

How is it that you can be in the arms of someone you love, yet feel so lonely?

I hold onto him—the friendship I rely on, the love we share—and I reach up and brush a hand across his face. "I'm sorry. I can't."

His eyes flicker. A shadow passes through them and I see a door closing, a choice, a life not taken. He tilts his head close, steering us further toward the quiet edge of the ballroom, where the glitter and prisms fade.

He smiles down at me. "I thought that might be your answer."

"I wish it weren't," I tell him. "But I wouldn't make you happy. Not really. And I love you too much to confine you to a life you'd regret."

"Fiona," he says, stroking his hand down the silk of my dress. "I'm not waiting for happiness."

"Someday you will be. That's my wish for you. That you'll find your happiness. I'll be so glad when you do. I'll be the happiest person in the world for you."

He shakes his head. "What about your happiness?"

I glance across the ballroom. Daniel's there, dancing with a French actress. He's laughing and I imagine dreaming about spending tomorrow with us eating Christmas dinner and playing in the snow. Mila's upstairs, tucked in and asleep, watched over by Annemarie, dreaming, I'm sure, of presents and stockings and chocolate sauce poured over waffles.

I look back up at Max, my best friend. "I'm happy. It's Christmas Eve. I try always to be happy on Christmas Eve."

At that Max gives a rueful smile. "So. Friends."

I nod, holding him tight. "Friends."

"I won't ask again, but . . ." He looks over the room, at the shimmering light. "Was it the man from your dreams? I never managed to light you up like he did."

I stare at Max, a slow tug pulling at me, a hollow note in my chest. I shake my head. "What man?"

He smiles down at me, a lock of black hair falling over his forehead. "The one that gave you sparks. I tried for months to give you what one dream did."

I search through my memory, trying to recall the dream he's talking about. I remember us sitting under a purple sky, drinking wine, toasting sparks and dreams, but I don't remember what my dreams were about.

If I concentrate on it too long, there's an ache almost too great to bear. So I let it slide away, receding like the tide.

"No," I tell him. "I don't remember my dreams. I don't remember sparks. They'd be nice, though, I think."

Max touches my cheek. "Tell me when you find them. I'll be happy for you."

"Good. We can grow old being happy for each other."

The music ends then, a slow sighing, a gentle snowflake falling to the muted silence of deep white snow.

There's the quiet sigh, the silence just after the music ends.

I pause. Hold still in the quiet.

There's something there. Something hovering at the edges of my mind ever since I woke up. It's as if I heard the most beautiful song in the world. As if I was surrounded by a melody that swept me up, wrapped me in its warmth, and filled my heart with love. It's as if I once heard the greatest beauty, saw the most beautiful love, but now it's gone—and I don't remember the music. I don't remember the song or the sight. I only have a memory of a lost feeling. A distant echo of something I once heard. The harder I try to capture it, the further it slips away. And so I can only feel the pang of a loss so great my heart aches—for something—something beautiful. . . It aches for a song I can't remember, but know I loved.

It's like a dream, isn't it?

In dreams, we experience everything we're afraid to in real life. In dreams we can fly, we can defeat dragons, we can go back in time, we can see our loved ones who are dead and gone, we can talk to a crowd while naked on a stage, and we can even fall in love.

But then we forget our dreams and we're left only with a feeling.

I glance over at the ice clock.

11:48 p.m.

I stare at the face of the clock and at the swirl of silvers and golds reflected in the ice. I'm struck by the moment.

Then the minute hand shifts, stutters forward, and the time passes.

I look up at Max, gently gripping the smooth wool

of his tuxedo. "Do you ever feel," I ask, "as if you've lost something, but you don't know what?"

He smiles down at me. "All the time."

Then the music starts again. The last song of the night, before midnight strikes and Christmas arrives.

Max steps back, out of our dancing embrace, and I can see in the way he holds himself and the way he looks at me that we're friends again—only friends.

Then he takes my arm and we walk back into the ocean of dancing, glittering people celebrating the light of the season and the passing of time.

56

THE YEAR ENDS AND THE NEW YEAR IS WHISPERED INTO being.

Mila and I light a New Year candle at midnight and watch it flicker and flame as it carries our wishes and our hopes into quiet dreams.

Mila wishes for a winter vacation—somewhere warm where she can swim. She wishes to make new friends and to keep the old. She wishes to see her grandma again, and she wishes to be able to grow up soon so she can make watches, just like me.

I tell her she shouldn't hurry to grow up, that time will take care of it without her wishing. And then I wish to remember what it is that's making my heart ache and my chest feel as if there's a piece of me . . . missing. To find it.

The flame gutters. The candle burns out.

And then the New Year has arrived.

We put away Christmas. We wrap in paper the glass ornaments, we close cardboard boxes full of garlands and colorful lights. We sweep up the dried Christmas tree needles scattered on the floor. The gingerbread, the roasting chestnuts, the spices of cinnamon and clove and the vin chaud—all of it is set aside. The Christmas markets are disassembled like toy wooden buildings, folded up and boxed away. It's all gone, and it won't return until next year.

A snowy, blustery wind rushes down the snow-covered mountains and sweeps through Geneva.

The freezing winter wind carries away the warm glow of Christmas lights, the evergreen-scented wreaths and garlands, and replaces it with the chill and frost of January.

The mountains surrounding the city are white-capped. The cold bites your fingers and nose and the sun shines on a frozen, wintry world.

Sometimes when the sun catches and dances on the white snowdrifts, I think it looks like the sun lighting on powdery golden sand.

Sometimes when I pass a bookstore on a cold, gray day, I look at the warm lights inside and the rows of books waiting to be read, and I think it looks like it might be the happiest place in the world.

And sometimes when I'm at my desk, lost in thought, I absently run my finger over my lips, and at the sensation I sit straight, feeling as if I've woken from a dream. I look around, certain someone should be there with me.

But most of the time I keep busy.

Work—Mila—school—homework—work again—sleep—no dreams—Mila—work—and—

It's mid-January, but it feels as if years have passed between Christmas Eve and now.

I rub my forehead, massaging the spot between my eyebrows, and close my eyes. At the edge of my desk a mug of hot coffee steams, sending out a warm, sugar-scented fragrance.

The low hum of the heating vent fills the space and a gentle, warm draft blows over me. I lean back in my leather chair and roll my shoulders. The sun shines through the window, the afternoon light falling on the blue satin of my dress. The light catches the pearls and the gold of the watch I'm wearing. The one I designed last summer—the McCormick.

I've been wearing it every day. I love it with an unreasonable passion.

Outside my office, there are the sounds of a busy Monday. Impromptu meetings in the hallway, the whir of printers and answered phones, the hurried click-click of heels, and the "How was your weekend?" of colleagues who have worked together for years.

I've spent the morning locked in meetings and international conference calls. Daniel and I are headed to New York in the spring, and we're already planning the trip. Mila and Annemarie will come; Mila will love touring the city, and I'll love sharing it with her.

But before then I have the first quarter's projections, the supply chain issue out of Asia, the increased export tariffs on our enamel powder, the twenty percent increase in the cost of our raw materials, the canton's tax proposal, and—well, I'll get to it all.

But for just a moment I'll close my eyes, let the sun fall across my face, and listen to the soft ticking of my watch.

"Fi?"

I open my eyes.

Daniel's at my office door.

I smile at him. "You caught me dreaming."

"Did I? Sorry to interrupt." He flashes a quick grin and strides into my office.

He wore a navy-blue suit today, but he's discarded his jacket, and the sleeves of his white dress shirt are rolled up. His blue tie is loose and his hair is ruffled from where he's been running his hands through it. Usually, this means he's been in a meeting he's found interesting and fun enough to let loose and be himself.

"You've met someone amazing," I joke, sitting straight in my chair, "and you're leaving early to have a lunch date."

He raises his eyebrows. "Not even close."

At the look on his face I lean forward. A tingle of electricity pulls at me. "What is it?"

He rolls his shoulders and looks to the side. I know Daniel as well as I know myself. He doesn't want to tell me.

"What? Daniel?"

When he looks back he frowns, his forehead wrinkling. "You know the watch you designed?" He nods to my wrist.

My hand automatically reaches for the pearl and emerald bracelet and I close my fingers over the ticking blue watch face. "Yes?"

"Well..." He takes in a deep breath. "Why did you call it the McCormick?"

My heart stumbles and then starts again. The warm air from the vent pulls at a loose strand of hair that tickles my neck. I shake my head. "I don't know."

Daniel nods. "Right. That's what I thought. But, look... Fi."

"What?" I ask, my body coiling tighter, tension winding taut in my chest.

"After Christmas, when we officially released the watch, we were contacted by a man named Aaron McCormick."

I stare at Daniel. He's waiting for something, I just don't know what. The pain in my chest pulses and I stand, pushing my chair back.

"Fi?"

"I don't know him," I say, shaking my head. "I've never heard of him. What does he want?"

I smooth my satin dress down, brushing the soft fabric until it falls to mid-thigh. The watch is heavy and warm on my wrist as I brush the wrinkles away.

"That's the thing." Daniel smiles then. "I hadn't heard of him either. He's a marathon swimmer. He holds a few world records. He retired, but two years ago he started swimming again. Fi, he's brilliant." Daniel grins at me, and I immediately know why he looks as if he's been enjoying himself.

"You've met him?"

Daniel nods. "He swims for charity. He just finished swimming a hundred miles nonstop, unassisted, between the Bahamas and Juno Beach, Florida. Everything he raised went to local disaster relief. The man's incredible."

"He sounds all right," I say, pressing a hand to my chest.

Daniel's eyes light. "Yeah. He's all right. I have it all planned, Fi. We're going to sponsor him and his crew. Outfit them with Abrys. He's in Geneva. He said he wanted to meet the person who designed the watch with his name. We'll do media campaigns. Donate to the charities he swims for. He said his family likes Geneva—he might stay for a bit. I told him when it warmed up he could swim the lake."

A warm, rushing wave falls over me and there's a buzzing in my ears.

"What do you think?"

I swallow. There's a strange quality to the moment. The sun is still shining, the snow is still sparkling in the field outside my window, and the mountains are still there. Outside my door there's the murmur of conversation and the sound of the printer running. Yet everything feels as if it's changing.

"I think it sounds good," I say, looking past Daniel, toward the hall.

"Did you want to meet him?" Daniel asks. He gives me his protective-little-brother look. "I held off. He contacted us back at Christmas, but you were down, and we had the holidays and family—"

"I'm not down," I deny.

Daniel gives me a disbelieving look. "And then he contacted us again. And I figured, well, I'll meet him. I think it's a good opportunity. He asked to see you, to meet you, but if you aren't interested I'll fob him off—"

"No, I'll meet him. It's fine."

"How about now?" Daniel flashes a smile. "He's down the hall in the executive conference room."

I give Daniel such a stunned look that he laughs.

"Or not. You don't have to see him."

A tremor passes through me. I send my hand through my hair and stare at my open door, at the hallway that leads to the conference room.

"It's okay," I say.

There's a jarring laugh that echoes down the hall, and I shake out of the strange, otherworldly feeling.

"All right," Daniel says, nodding toward the door to my office.

I walk with him down the hall, nodding at the people we pass. The white of the walls and the blond wood blend into a blur as Daniel tells me more about Aaron.

He's from a small island in the Caribbean. He's been breaking records since he was a kid. He's a dad, and his two kids travel with him when he completes a swim.

I take it all in, building a picture in my mind of Aaron McCormick. I imagine he's bulky, wide-shouldered, like most swimmers. Short. Shaved hair, I'm sure. I picture him older since he'd retired once before. Sun-weathered. A stoic man. Although he's probably friendly since he swims for charity, but, honestly, you can never be sure. He's clearly business and PR-savvy since he's here, meeting with Daniel.

And then we're at the executive conference room.

It's the showpiece conference room where we take important visitors and hold our annual meetings. It's where the chairs are soft brown leather, the long table is glossy mahogany, a crystal chandelier hangs over the table, and a wide glass window looks out over the mountains. There's a hushed, beautiful elegance to the room.

Daniel opens the wooden door and the cool air and bright sunlight greets me.

And the picture I built of Aaron McCormick disappears the minute I lay eyes on him.

He's at the conference table, sitting in one of the leather chairs, his hands crossed, head tilted down.

But when the door clicks open and whooshes over the wood floor he looks up.

I stop in the entry, arrested by the look on his face.

He's not at all what I imagined.

There's a magnetic force that swirls around him—a pull that has me taking another step forward. A spark lights on my skin, then another, until my whole body is lit from within.

Aaron searches my face, his gaze seeking, wanting, questioning. The force of his attention strokes over me. He stares into my eyes and I feel as if I've plunged off dry land and fallen into a deep, turbulent sea.

I drag in a cool breath of air, breathing in the lemon wax used on the mahogany table, the leather of the chairs, the coffee set out on the table. And then a more subtle scent—one of the sea. But that's not actually there. It's more like the memory of it.

Aaron stands then, pushing back his leather chair. It scrapes against the hardwood. As he unfolds I see he's taller than I realized. Six feet at least. His shoulders are wide and athletic. He's in jeans and a dark blue sweater, and I smile, because I can't imagine him in a suit, and I'm glad he didn't wear one. His hair is a thick, glossy black, longer, almost down to his collar.

And his face. He has a beautiful face. Not the kind of beauty in magazines or movies, but the gentle kind of beauty that comes from laughing and smiling and living a kind life.

I smile then, and his gaze roves over me, as if he's drinking me in after years without water. I tingle and spark at the weight of his gaze.

"Aaron?" Daniel says, stepping forward into the conference room. "This is my sister, Fiona Abry, CEO of Abry Watch Company. She designed the piece you admire. Fiona, this is Aaron McCormick."

Aaron's waiting for something. Some cue from me, some acknowledgment. I can see it in the way he stands, the way he looks at me. As if with one word he'll step forward and take me in his arms.

Kiss me.

But why? Why would he? I don't know him.

A line forms between his brows as he watches me. He steps around the table, striding toward me. As he moves closer the air tugs and pulls between us.

He holds out his hand.

I stare at it. At his hand held out to me.

I'm jarred into action. "Nice to meet you, Mr. McCormick," I say, placing my hand in his.

His hand is warm and his clasp firm. Sparks light and travel up my arm, all the way to my heart.

His brow wrinkles at my formal words and the impersonal grip of my hand.

"You don't know me?" he asks.

His voice is rolling, with a lilting accent that reminds me of sunny afternoons listening to waves rolling over a sandy beach.

I pull my hand free. Step back. "No, of course not. We've never met."

He blinks then. One blink. And all the coursing waves, the heat, the scorch and want in his gaze is pulled back, reeled in, and put away.

I'm struck by the loss of it.

"You admire the watch my sister designed," Daniel

says, unaware of the world spinning and the sparks flying.

"Yes," I say, my throat dry and my voice raw. "It's here."

I hold out my wrist to show Aaron the watch. He studies it for a moment, his head tilted down, heat pouring off him and pooling in my belly.

He nods then, his hands clasped behind his back. "It's beautiful."

"Thank you," I say.

"You didn't name it for anyone?" he asks, studying me, his expression carefully neutral.

"No. No one. I'm sorry for the mistake. But"—I shrug, smiling at him even though it hurts—"at least you're here and now Daniel will have fun kitting out your crew."

"Ah." Aaron nods. "Right. Well." He glances at Daniel, smiles. "My kids are at the bookstore near our hotel. I should be off." He turns back to me. "It was nice meeting you."

I nod. "Yes. You too."

Daniel takes his hand then, giving a firm shake. "Thanks for stopping by. Do you need a driver to take you to...?"

"Carouge," he says. "Amy, my daughter, found a bookshop she loves."

He smiles then and I'm tugged toward him at the tight beating in my chest.

"I'll call a driver for you," Daniel says.

"No need—I have a car." Aaron strides back to the table, grabbing a leather bag and a gray wool coat.

He pauses and looks to me, and I know he's about to say goodbye. There's a terrible emptiness in my chest at the thought of it, so I hurriedly say, "Let me walk you out."

His brown eyes search mine and then he nods.

He's quiet as we walk down the halls toward the front entrance. As we leave the back halls the wood transitions to marble, and the white walls gain rich wood paneling.

I move close to Aaron as we squeeze past a group of people chatting. And once we're past I stay close. My hand brushes against his; our arms touch. I can feel the whisper of the wool coat he's wearing and the heat of him.

I take a quick glance at his features as we stride into the lobby.

The space was built to impress. It's six stories tall, with marble and glass and a giant, ten-foot-tall timepiece on the wall. The front windows rise high above us and capture all the light the winter sun affords.

We pause at the front entrance, the glass doors holding the chill at bay. Aaron's in his wool coat, his bag slung over his shoulder. But me, I'm in a short-sleeve satin dress, my jacket still slung over the back of my office chair.

"I'll walk you out," I say.

He shakes his head. "You don't have to."

"I want to."

I lead him out then, and when I push open the doors the freezing chill hits my bare arms and legs. The wind tugs at my hair. The auburn strands blow around my shoulders and face and I sweep it back.

The stairs and sidewalk have been shoveled and de-iced and the parking lot is clear. Mounds of white snow line the edges of the lot, and the trees surrounding us are weighed down with heavy white powder. The air is brisk, snow-filled, and winter scented.

I shiver at the cold wind dragging across me.

"Here," Aaron says, holding his coat out.

I shrug it on gratefully and then, when the warmth of him seeps into me, I breathe in his soft, sea-like smell.

"It must have been a shock to see a watch with your name," I tell him as we walk across the parking lot.

He glances down at me, the sun playing over his skin. "It wasn't, actually."

And when I give him a startled glance he says, "It looks just like the island I was born on. It reminded me of home. I thought maybe you'd been there."

I shake my head, and he nods as if he expected that answer.

Then he stops in front of his car, an SUV, perfect for winter in the mountains.

I begin to pull off his coat and the chill brushes over me. He shakes his head. "No. It's all right. Keep it. You can give it back to me next time."

Next time?

I nod and pull the coat tighter around me.

"Goodbye then," I say, the cold wind tugging at me. "Nice meeting you."

"Goodbye," he says, searching my face. I wait for him to say something more, but he doesn't.

So I nod and then turn. The wintry sun shines over my face. The cold light hits my eyes and they burn with tears from the cold and the wind. I wait for a moment longer, and when Aaron doesn't say anything I begin to walk into the wind and the quick gust of blowing snow.

The cold bites my cheeks and I blink against the wintry air. I duck my head, waiting to hear the sound of Aaron's car pulling away.

Then there's the fast beat of his footsteps. He's running.

I stop. Turn.

My heart pounds when I see him there, standing in front of me.

He draws in a deep breath, his dark eyes intent, and my hand shakes from the near irresistible urge to reach up and set my hand on his face.

He looks down at me as if he can't decide whether or not he should kiss me. There's a yearning, an ache, that mirrors the sound in my heart.

"I forgot," he says.

A warmth pulses between us, chasing away the icy cold.

I look up at him and fight the urge to lean into him and let myself be wrapped in the arms of a man I've never met.

"I forgot to ask," he says.

His warmth calls me closer. "What?"

He reaches out, holding his hand an inch away from my face, the heat of him calling me.

"Fi?"

An earthquake rumbles in my mind. I shake my head at the roaring, at the world shaking.

"Fi?"

I'm plunged into a wild, turbulent sea. The waves consume me and I'm spinning.

And suddenly lights are shooting at me, images hitting me at light speed, snapshots of memories and pictures of dreams.

—What does Fi mean? It's a code word. Why? It's so you know I'm me.—

—*"Hope" is the thing with feathers—That perches in the soul*—

— You want me to kiss you? Yes. Right now? Yes.—

— *Hold Infinity in the palm of your hand. And Eternity in an hour.*—

— If you ever need me, if you ever find yourself awake at night wanting me, I'll be here. I'll be here loving you.—

— Come to me. Find me in Geneva. Come on Christmas Eve two years from now. I'll be waiting for you. My name is Fi—

"Fi?" Aaron asks.

He holds me up, his hands gripping my arms, keeping me upright. The world snaps, pulls, shudders, and then, as suddenly as an island falling into the sea, as quickly as diving into the depths of the sea, I remember.

I remember.

I lift a shaking hand, brush it across Aaron's warm cheek, let out the breath I've been holding since Christmas Eve, and whisper, "Yes."

The snow begins to fall in earnest, and Aaron McCormick, the man I love, kisses me.

57

Aaron holds me in his arms, whispering my name, and then his mouth crashes over mine and I cling to him as a wave of love washes over me. I forgot. How could I forget this?

Aaron runs his hands over me as if he's desperate to touch every inch, as if he has to hold me to make certain I'm real. I lift my hands to his face, feel the heat of the stubble at his jaw, and run my hands through his hair—longer now than before.

He makes a low sound in the back of his throat and takes my mouth, kissing me with the passion of years of waiting for this single moment. His mouth is warm, his lips the seeking softness I remember. Snowflakes light on my skin and melt in pinpricks against my heat.

The aching hole in my chest, the echo of a song forgotten, is filled with the sound of my name on Aaron's lips, the feel of his hands brushing over my face, and the light of sparks dancing over me and settling in a sun-bright glow in my heart.

He settles his mouth on mine, and in the touch of his lips and the whisper of my name I taste the yearning and the love he's kept these past two years.

I fold into him then, pressing my chest against the warmth of him, and he pulls me closer, wrapping his warmth around me. I'm spinning like the snowflakes whirling around us. My cheeks sting from the cold and our kiss tastes like the salt of the ocean. A tear pools at the corner of my lips and Aaron kisses it away.

"It's okay," he whispers. "Fi, it's okay. I found you. I came to Geneva."

I look at him then, pressing my hand to the warmth of his cheek. "I forgot you. I forgot my dreams."

He nods, settles his hand to the crook of my spine, and holds me close. "I couldn't find you. Geneva is a big city to find one woman named Fi." He smiles down at me, his eyes warming. "Until you made that watch."

I wrap my arms around him and hold him close. "Aaron."

I feel his lips curve into a smile against my forehead as he traces kisses over me. "So, you're Fi."

"I'm Fi," I say.

A gust of wind rushes past, blowing snow in a whirlwind around us. I shiver, and Aaron pulls me closer. I rest my cheek against the beating of his heart. He was gone. Yet now he's here.

I've remembered my dreams, everything that happened in the past. But now, standing in the falling snow, wrapped in Aaron's warm arms, I remember another dream.

A dream where I'm loved. Where I love. Where every day I accept love and give love. Where I give my heart, where I dive in to the ocean of love, and I'm not afraid.

Aaron strokes his finger across my lips, a warm light in his eyes. "You're real. I found you."

"Do you remember when you said it felt like the hand of fate pulling us together?"

He nods.

"I think you were right."

He smiles then and says, "Fi, I want to know everything. I want to hear everything. I want to know you. I want to love you in this life. Will you let me? Will you take my hand?"

My heart opens. It opens as wide as the great blue sea. "Yes."

58

I lie down on my bed, the gold pocket watch nestled in the palm of my hand. It's heavy and warm, and the blue enamel swirls with the enchantment of dreams.

The warm noonday light shines across me in ripples and waves. The gold satin duvet pools beneath me as I settle deeper into the soft folds. Aaron takes me in, his gaze traveling over the naked line of my shoulders.

The chateau is quiet, buried in snow and a sleepy winter light. Outside, a winter bird sings and another calls back. Inside there's the sound of the duvet whispering beneath me and Aaron dragging in a shaky breath.

The sheets rustle as he shifts closer. My bedroom is filled with warmth, an electric, tingly energy. An expectant pull that rushes between us.

"This is the watch?" Aaron asks, his voice scraping over me. "That let you dream?"

"This is it," I say, holding it out to him.

On the drive here I told him about the watch, about how I thought he wasn't real, about how I learned of his death and how I was able to save him. I told him how I forgot him until he came to me and said my name.

He held my hand as he drove along the winter-blue lake, the snowdrifts lining the edges of the curving road.

I asked him, "How are you so calm about all this?"

And he said, "I've had two years to accept it. The first few weeks I was shocked. The next two years I just wanted you."

"Did Becca remember me?" I ask, wondering what she thought of it all.

He shook his head. "No. She didn't. She left for New York with Robert the day after Christmas."

"And Amy? Sean?"

"Amy wants to meet you."

"She figured it out?"

He grinned at me, the snow-covered trees flashing past. "She's too smart not to. Dostoevsky? Becca would never have pulled out those quotes."

Becca left. She and Robert married last year. She didn't want to exercise her parental rights. She hasn't seen the kids in more than a year. It's something I know a bit about—something I can relate to.

Amy is at the bookshop with Sean. Maranda came too. She wanted an international adventure. Later today they'll all come to the chateau and have dinner with me and Mila.

Aaron slowly takes the watch. He turns it in the light and the gold glints in the sun shining through the window.

"You dreamed me first." He sets the watch on the nightstand. "But Fi, I've been dreaming of you for the past two years."

I smile at him. "Even though you didn't know what I looked like?"

"I knew your heart."

"Did you always recognize me when I was there? When I wasn't me?"

He reaches out, stroking his hand over my cheek, down my jaw, to the edge of my mouth. "You were always you. Looking back, I knew each time I was with you. How could I not? And today, when you walked into the room and I saw you—soft hazel eyes, fiery auburn hair, intelligent and generous, your kind smile, the warmth of your touch—you were my Fi."

"It's not hard for you to believe?" I ask, thinking he didn't have a childhood like mine, where I was prepared to accept there are more things unexplained in the universe than explained, and to accept the things we don't understand.

"I believe in love," he says. "I think just about anything is possible with love."

"You love me?"

He smiles, leans forward, and pushes me back to the bed. I fall beneath him and he straddles his hips over mine. "I love you," he says. "Fiona Abry. Fi."

Instead of saying yes, I whisper, "I love you."

Then we're lips and mouths and hands. I pull off my dress, the satin scraping over my skin. Aaron slides my bra free, catches my nipples in his mouth, and presses a kiss to each freckle, each fairy kiss. He slides his hands over my skin, caressing the curve of my hips, stroking the softness of my abdomen. His jeans whisper over my skin, abrading me like the sand of the beach. He rocks against me. His mouth is hot, his movement a gentle wave.

I reach for his jeans, tugging them free. I pull off his shirt. Then I run my hands over the smooth muscle of his abdomen and the dark ink of his tattoos. I roll my hands over his shoulders and arch up to him.

I tug his boxers down and he springs free. He closes his eyes and draws in a shaky breath as I move against him.

I reach around him, holding him over me. He's as hot as the sun, as welcome as the warmth of the sea sliding over me.

He takes his mouth to mine, kissing me with all his love. "I love you."

I reach up and pull him closer. Taste the sweetness of his mouth, the promise of a life well-lived and well-loved, a future of dreams.

I wrap myself around him, and then he pauses, keeping himself still at the heat of me.

"Fi?" he asks—a question, a proposal.

I smile up at him. "Yes," I say, and then he kisses me and slowly, gently, plunges into me.

My breath catches as I stretch around him, taking him in. His heart pounds against my chest as he stills over me. I clutch his back, the heat of him searing me.

He looks down at me, a fierce, wild-love expression on his face—the same one he wore when he promised to love me, to wait for me, to find me. I drag in a breath, overwhelmed by the feel of him.

"Please," I say, tilting my hips, "love me."

And then he does. He loves me with the same passion I dreamed of. He loves me unreservedly and wholeheartedly. He doesn't hold any of himself back. So when I cry out and my heart shatters and then mends, all in the same moment, I know—

He gives a ragged cry, whispers my name, kisses me. I know—

This love. It's a forever kind of love.

Aaron pulls me onto him. His sweat and heat slick over me. His heart beats wildly as he rubs his hand over the curve of my back.

"I'm going to spend my life with you," he says, his voice a low rumble. "I thought I'd let you know."

I smile, burying my face against his chest. "After knowing me in real life for a few hours?"

He drops a kiss on my head. "Fi. It's fate. I've already dreamed it."

With that I close my eyes and fall asleep in his arms.

EPILOGUE

WE MARRY A MONTH LATER.

The wedding is on the beach, a new shoreline on Saint Eligius. Aaron and I stand beneath a wooden gazebo. The turquoise sea crashes against the reef, sending a cool sea breeze over us. Vanilla-and-jasmine-scented tropical flowers hang from the trellis.

The sun shines over the sandy beach and falls in golden dappled light through the twining flowers. The lace of my wedding dress blows in the wind as I clasp Aaron's hands.

Mila is our flower girl. She spread a path of fuchsia, coral, and sun-yellow petals collected from gardens around the island. She loves Amy, who is a worldly sixteen. And she loves Sean, her new brother, who, now that he's four, can't stop talking. He's memorized all of Amy's poems and loves to regale everyone with stories of his outdoor adventures.

Amy, my maid of honor, stands next to us under the

gazebo. When we finally met, the first thing she said was, "Fi, I have a quote for you."

"Isn't it too early for quotes?" I asked.

"It's never too early for Dostoevsky." And then she said, "'We sometimes encounter people, even perfect strangers, who begin to interest us at first sight, somehow suddenly, all at once, before a word has been spoken.'" She smiled then and said, "That's how I feel about you. I think we were always meant to be friends."

I agreed. Later, at the bookshop, I asked, "Now that you've left the island, do you feel as if you've lived?"

"Oh yes. I've lived. But I have so much more living to do." She smiled then, a pile of books in her arms, her little brother clasping her waist.

And so Mila and Amy and Sean have new friends and a bigger family.

At the edge of the gazebo, Daniel smiles at me. He's unbearably happy for me, believing he's the reason I opened myself to love, and that if it wasn't for him, I would never have met Aaron.

I don't mind letting him think that. I only want him to find someone. He deserves happiness too.

Outside the gazebo, in the shade of a stand of whispering pines, the islanders—our friends and family—watch the ceremony. There's Dee, Essie, Maranda, Junie and Jordi and their little girl. Sue and Odie. More. And at the edge of the gathering, standing in the shadows, is Max.

He's happy for me. Incredibly happy. But I get the feeling he's also wondering what will become of him now I've found love.

I don't know. I only know I'll always be his friend.

The breeze whistles past and Aaron grips my

hands. It's that moment, the one he told me he dreamed about, where I look into his eyes and say, "I do."

He smiles at me, the edges of his eyes crinkling, his lips turning up, the light of a thousand I-love-yous in his eyes.

I once told myself Aaron didn't change my life right away. That I didn't fall in love with him at first sight.

But now that I'm standing under this gazebo marrying him, I think this was always meant to be, and I've always loved him. I loved him, had a space in my heart for him, even before I met him.

And so I fall into the love in his eyes and say, "I do."

And then, even though it wasn't the word "Fi," Aaron still pulls me into his arms and kisses me.

I decide then and there that this is a life that dreams are made of.

THE END

Read the next book in the series: *Wished*.

When Anna Benoit wishes she's married to the magnetic owner of the chateau she cleans, she lands in an upside-down world where she's Max Barone's wife.

Find *Wished* and more at: www.sarahready.com.

JOIN SARAH READY'S NEWSLETTER

Want more *Fated*? Get an exclusive bonus epilogue! When you join the Sarah Ready Newsletter you get access to sneak peaks, insider updates, exclusive bonus scenes and more.

Join today for an exclusive *Fated* epilogue: www.sarahready.com/newsletter

ABOUT THE AUTHOR

Multi award-winning author Sarah Ready writes women's fiction, contemporary romance and romantic comedy. Her books have been described as "euphoric", "heartwarming" and "laugh out loud".

Sarah writes stand-alone romances, including *Josh and Gemma Make a Baby*, *Josh and Gemma the Second Time Around*, *French Holiday*, *The Space Between*, and series romcoms including *Ghosted*, *Switched*, *Fated*, *Wished,* and romcoms in the Soul Mates in Romeo series, all of which can be found at her website: www.sarahready.com.

You can learn more and find upcoming titles at: www.sarahready.com.

Stay up to date, get exclusive epilogues and bonus content. Join Sarah's newsletter at www.sarahready.com/newsletter.

ALSO BY SARAH READY

Stand Alone Romances:

The Fall in Love Checklist

Hero Ever After

Once Upon an Island

French Holiday

The Space Between

The Ghosted Series:

Ghosted

Switched

Fated

Wished

Josh and Gemma:

Josh and Gemma Make a Baby

Josh and Gemma the Second Time Around

Soul Mates in Romeo Romance Series:

Chasing Romeo

Love Not at First Sight

Romance by the Book

Love, Artifacts, and You

Married by Sunday

My Better Life

Scrooging Christmas

Dear Christmas

Stand Alone Novella:

Love Letters

Find these books and more by Sarah Ready at:

www.sarahready.com/romance-books